THE
WRAITH
QUEEN

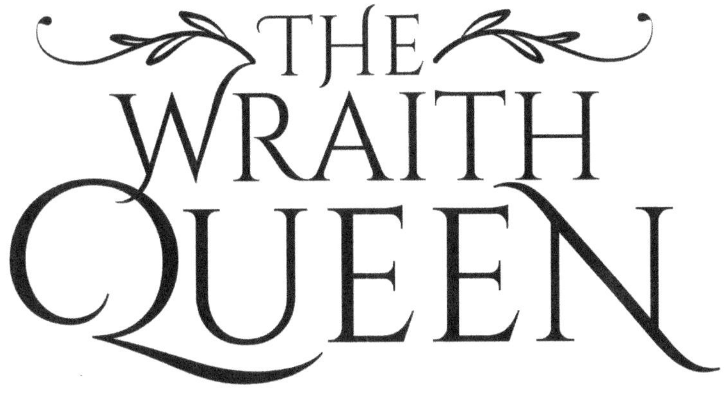

THE WRAITH QUEEN

SARA RAZTRESEN

Paperback ISBN: 979-8-9864876-6-3
Digital ISBN: 979-8-9864876-7-0

Cover & Interior Design by Sara Raztresen
Map Design by Cody James King

No AI was used in the creation of this work, either in writing or in design. All design elements are sourced from Shutterstock and Canva artists, or acquired from contracted artists like Cody.

Published by Sara Raztresen under Sveta Lisica Imprint
Rhode Island, 2024

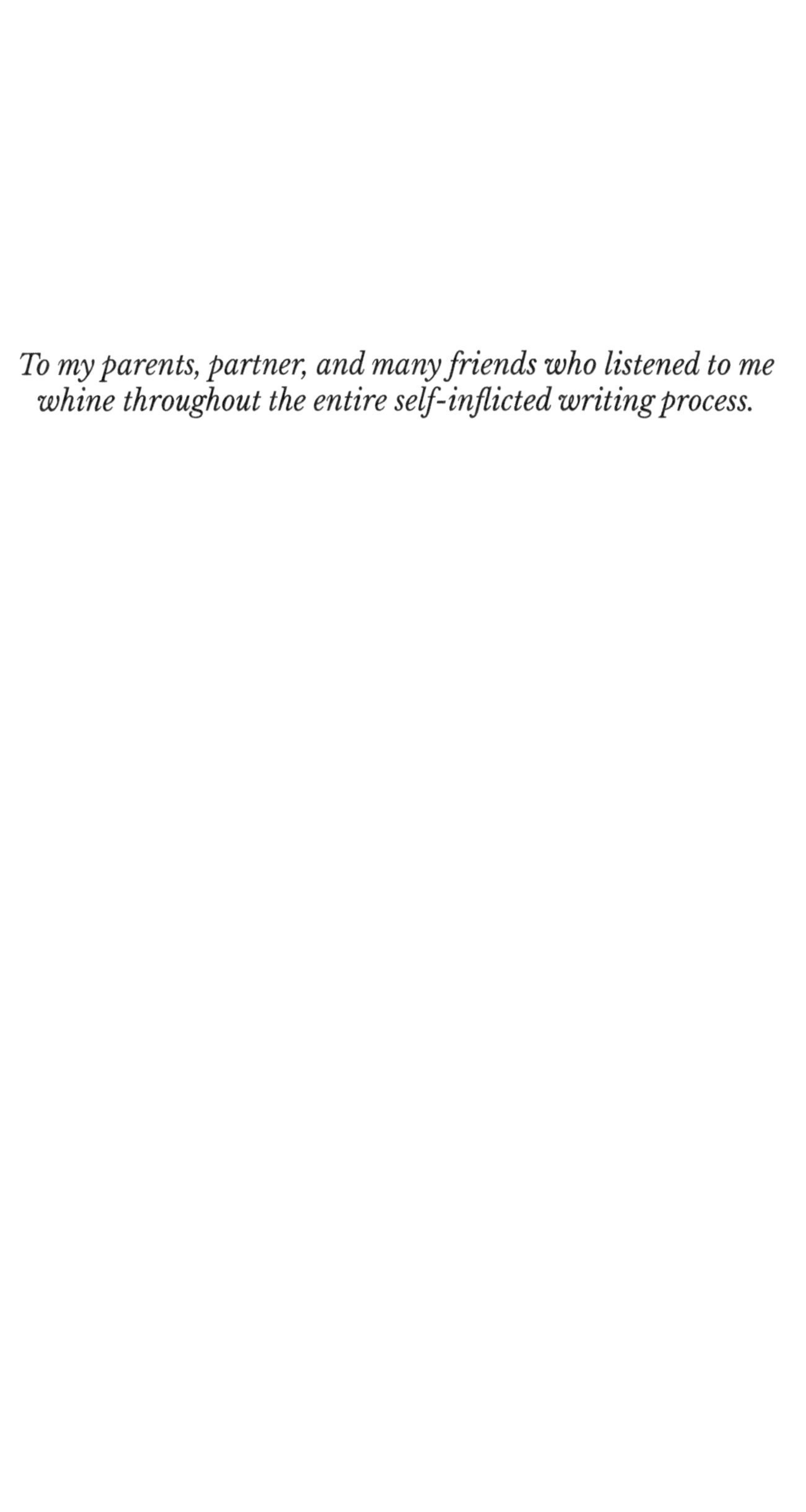

To my parents, partner, and many friends who listened to me whine throughout the entire self-inflicted writing process.

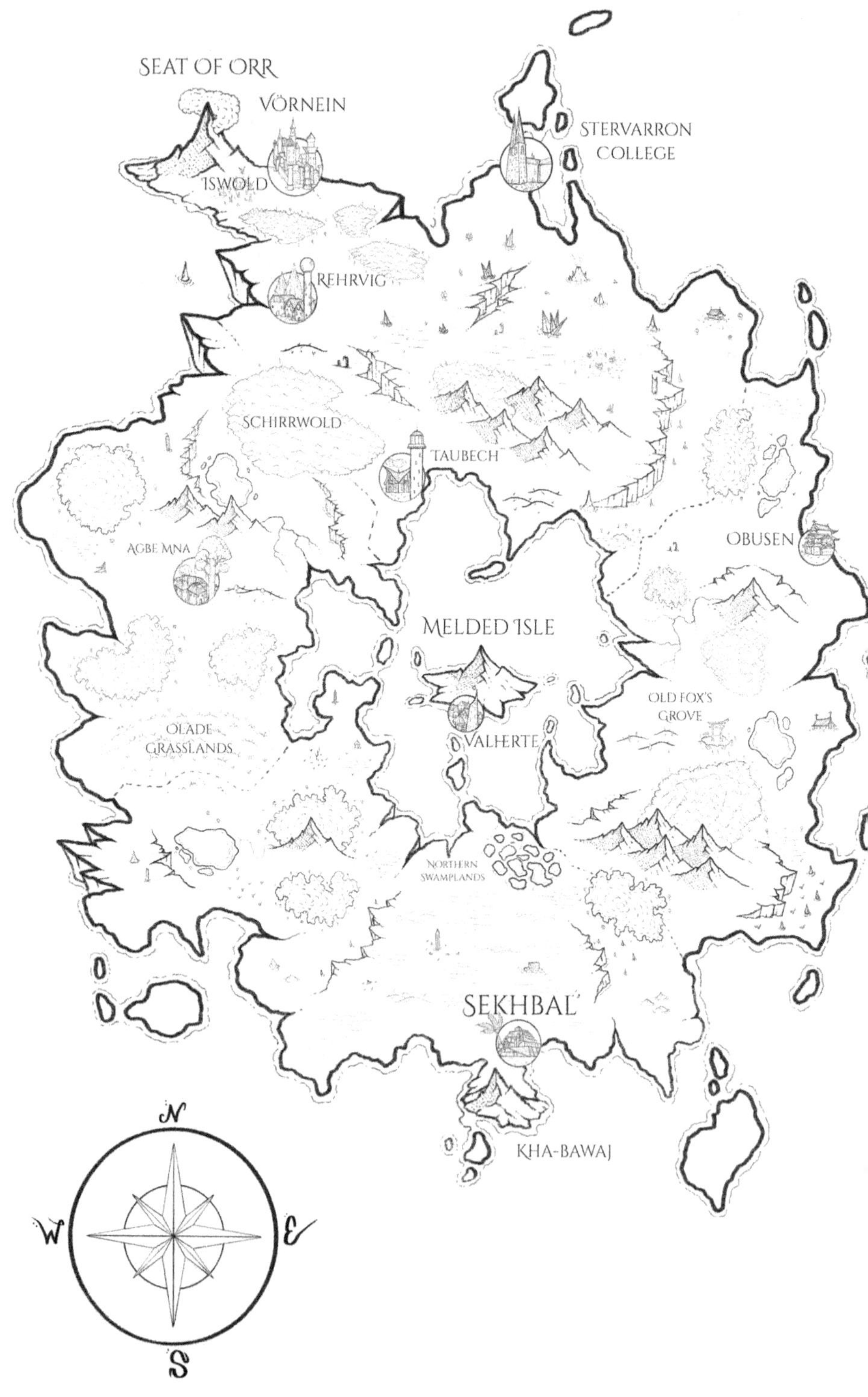

SEAT OF ORR
VÖRNEIN
ISWOLD
STERVARRON COLLEGE
REHRVIG
SCHIRRWOLD
TAUBECH
AGBE MNA
OBUSEN
MELDED ISLE
OLD FOX'S GROVE
OLADE GRASSLANDS
VALHERTE
NORTHERN SWAMPLANDS
SEKHBAL'
KHA-BAWAJ
N
W
E
S

PRONUNCIATION GUIDE
Book 2

AVELINE RACHFEMD: *Ay-veh-leen Rakh-femd*

JÄDRICH FEMMEL: *Yay-drikh Fem-ul*

RISTEF GÜRRENSIG: *Rih-stef Goo-ren-seegh*

PRISCHINA KLASSECH: *Prih-shee-na Kla-ssekh*

CLARA RONTERWEIS: *Clah-rah Ron-teh-vice*

HELEN VORRÜND: *He-len For-roond*

CERVORA: *Tser-vor-ah*

FENG SOURAM: *Fung Soo-ram*

NHALE BA: *Na-leh Bah*

GANARESH TI-VAOUR: *Ga-na-resh Tee-Va-Oor*

SEKHRAN: *Sek-rahn*

UNSEELECH: *Oon-see-lekh*

VÖRNEIN: *Foern-eyn*

KHA-BAWAJ: *Kah Ba-Wazh*

ÇELVEDRARI: *Chel-veh-drah-ree*

KVIRAEG: *Kvee-rayg*

WEIHARTEN: *Vy-harten*

IT STUNG THE FLESH TO BREATHE AIR SO COLD.
Efir rubbed his cracked hands together. By time he'd reached the border between Autumn and Winter, he'd already begun to feel the bitter cold in his bones. Every step after that seemed to pierce his bones with frost, and he cursed the Ismären for building their great stone wall five miles inland from where their territory officially started.

Though what need do walking ice sculptures have for land? Or access to the lake?

He cupped his hands to his mouth and huffed a warm breath over his skin. The wind whistled from atop that wall; it whipped past his ears and scraped the whiskers he'd neglected to shave from his upper lip and chin. Shaving wasn't feasible, not in a place so cold that he didn't dare put water to his skin without a fire going. But it'd be a while longer before he could light one. Even as the pieces of the few Ismar wall guards that discovered him lay scattered around his feet, he knew it wouldn't be long before more came and discovered that this post was unmanned.

Efir sighed, then got to his knees and began swiping all the pieces off the other side of the border. The armor they wore, those big black pieces, also seemed to be made of ice, but those didn't crack when Efir swung his dolabra—not when he swung the pickaxe side, not when he swung the small mace point at the handle. It was unimaginably tough, and it unsettled him, that the ice they wore could be sturdier than the ice they walked in.

He dusted the last few shards of ice off the top of the wall, then went back to warming his chapped hands. He'd mostly caught his breath by then, and he'd head north in a moment—but right then, he was content only to raise his eyes and look. It'd been a century since anyone from Summer saw these white-crusted lands, or the pine trees that sprouted up through the snow like black arrowheads. And the sky—gods, that dead, dreary sky. The light of Drakash was diffused in a miserable wash of gray tones, as if a painter filled their palette with nothing but the colors of stone and shadow. However, for all these eerie sights, it was the *sound* of Winter that made Efir's skin crawl: the sound of silence.

It was kind of silence that roared from somewhere deep in the distance, somewhere unknowable, and it made Efir wonder. When he'd whipped his dolabra into the heads of those ice-folk, something came out of them. Some little orbs of light. They buzzed around him like angry Spring bees before flying north, disappearing into the frozen mists. What made an Ismar what he was? Those orbs in their heads? What were they? And was this roaring silence like a calling bell for them?

Well, Efir got up and stretched his aching knees, *it won't matter soon enough.*

Once the Glass Witch was back in Summer, there would be no need to wonder what made an Ismar a man. Only how quickly one could be made a puddle.

Salt. Gods of sun and shadow, if only Aveline had just a *pinch* of salt. But the absence of such a luxury was only a fleeting thought as the fat of the rabbit—*cooked* rabbit—slicked her lips and dripped down her chin. The crackle of the shoddy little firepit she'd made was nearly impossible to tell apart from the crack of bone as she broke a couple and sucked the marrow from inside. Given she couldn't have brought her babies, her *Unseelechs,* near the terror of the fire, the sounds of her fireside meal were the only sounds in the great, dark forest behind the castle of the Winter King.

My soon-to-be husband.

The thought sat on her mind like early morning mist as she gnawed on the rubbery ends of a leg joint. Her cheeks were flush with the heat of the fire, as if she, too, were cooking alongside the rabbit on that make-shift spit. In that moment, though, it may as well have been the warm flush of too much good aniseed liquor. She huffed a laugh onto the near-stripped bone in her mouth. Of all the glory she could've won from ensnaring the King of Winter and making him her trophy, she never thought something as simple as an apparently *illegal* fire in a snowy clearing and a warm, fresh meal would be worth so much.

That King would break his own law for me? Her quiet laughter shook her shoulders. *How sweet.*

Still, it was only a scrawny Winter rabbit—the most she could catch out here in the deep woods, where the flame she cooked on and the little animals she tore between her teeth could stay secret—and so it was gone far too soon. Its white pelt laid in the snow, only somewhat marred with blood, and Aveline tossed the bones back into the fire, listening to them pop and snap. She curled tighter into herself. Her rabbit fur cloak soaked up the heat as she sat by the fire, and for the first time in weeks, she felt she might get *too* warm—a feeling she was sure she'd never feel again. Yet how heavenly it was. How much she missed it, even though she nearly suffocated not long ago in the hot, dry air of Summer. How she could've spent another hundred years in that clearing, full of food and wrapped in warmth.

"Are you finished there?"

And yet, no matter how comfortable it was by that fire, Aveline hadn't been able to let her shoulders fully relax. The low, rumbling voice that slipped between the trees only made them tighten up that much further, to the point that the muscles between her shoulders and her neck began to ache.

"Another few moments," Aveline whispered as she inched her feet closer to the fire. The crackle of twig and bone in those dancing flames nearly drowned her out.

That low voice didn't respond, but she could feel them: two heavy eyes weighing down on her back. When she closed her own eyes, even the flickering dance of the fire against her eyelids didn't erase the memory of them: those clear, pale blue, utterly inhuman eyes, the blue diamonds passed down from King to King in Winter since the era of Cervora, the doe-like goddess of this frozen land. By the pictures and statues Aveline saw all throughout the castle and its many history books, that "goddess" was hardly different from the little shrapnel of animal instinct that yipped and whined in the back of Aveline's mind. It was that thing within her—that woman with her own face, her antlers and her doe haunches, but with eyes black as death—that haunted Aveline's dreams for so long. It kept Aveline from willingly ending her life on the peaks of Kha-Bawaj in Summer, and it writhed and bucked against Aveline's skin whenever she so much as tried to speak the magical language of the Ismären, as if the words alone were poisonous.

What a nuisance.

Before Aveline came to Winter, that thing would only force Aveline to her feet so that she might scamper and forage and fight wherever there was danger about. As far as Aveline knew, that doe-woman was just a figment of her imagination: a makeshift companion in the otherwise dead silence on Kha-Bawaj. Aveline might've thought she'd distilled the very spirit of her flesh into its own being just to give the soul of her mind something to bounce ideas off and play pretend with as she withered on that mountain. And even if it began to take a life of its own over time, even if it grew more vivid than any of Aveline's other dreams, it'd never done more than complain and howl in Aveline's own voice when it came time to try and learn more complex magic. No matter what that intricate *helzuring* magic could do, this piece of Aveline's animal instinct forbade her from carving a single rune and uttering a single syllable.

And that'd been that, for the most part. The senseless, ignorant piece of Aveline's being didn't care to do much besides fill her with fear and scatter her rationale with a prey's intuition: the need to *bolt* from any perceived danger. In the wilds of the mountain peaks, such intuition had been useful. However, it seemed this spirit of the flesh couldn't tell mountain rock from city stone; it couldn't tell a mountain lion's tracking gaze from the King of Winter's empty stare. Worse, a few days after Aveline accepted Jädrich's proposal, whenever she closed her eyes to sleep at night, she saw a gleam in the darkness behind her eyelids: the black, endless depths of two doe eyes, wide and fearful.

Get out, those eyes said. *Get away. He'll eat us.*

Not *me,* like that fearful instinct once said, but *us,* as if it were becoming its own person and squatting in Aveline's skull. Aveline smiled as she soaked up the heat on her cheeks. Her mountain-born madness was growing, it seemed; no longer did it feel that she was only talking to herself. Moreover, it seemed this doe-eyed thing inherited her *rational* fear of Jädrich and his people—a fear Aveline cultivated since learning they sustained their magic off silvery venison and blood not so different from her own flesh. But she didn't care to look too deeply at that doe-woman, or listen too closely, lest she let her madness ruin all the spoils she'd won for herself in that ridiculous bridal competition.

I'm safe now. It was this mantra she repeated in her waking hours, willing both herself and her fearful instinct to understand it. *They won't eat their goddess a second time.*

Yes, because that was what Aveline was all of a sudden: not a half-breed mutt out to kill a King at the expense of her own life, all for a shy hope at revenge for her heartbroken, dead mother, but a goddess that could order a hundred Kings to kill themselves in honor of her, who could exalt her mother directly into the heavenly palaces of gods proper.

A sudden gust of howling, icy wind ripped past her and sapped every scrap of heat from her bones; it stole the life from the fire and snuffed it out, and it made the trees creak and moan in complaint as it disappeared into their branches. With the fire gone, the grove became so much darker, and the chill of Winter hooked into her flesh all over again, biting worse than if she'd never sat by any fire at all. Aveline shivered as heavy steps crunched on snow and pine needles.

"Come," Jädrich said, and his icy hand landed on her tensed shoulder. It squeezed her, coaxing her to relax, and his freezing thumb brushed her bare neck. His touch leeched the tension right out of her body and made it go slack in an instant. "We've been gone long enough. You have much to prepare before you announce yourself to your people."

Aveline leaned towards his hand sighed. Her victory over starvation and a lonely death was only one battle in what her body told her would be a long war. Piercing hunger, she could survive. Even sneaking about a castle, looking to ruin its keeper, she could survive. But the thought of letting her antlers rise from her head and fur sprout on her legs in front of so many people made her stomach twist in knots. So long as she kept her wings hidden, she knew no one would doubt Jädrich's claims that she was the reborn Cervora—and yet something about putting on such a show took away any sense of safety she thought she'd earned by ensnaring Jädrich.

They won't eat me. Repeat it often enough, and it'd be true. *They won't even touch me.*

The Ismären hadn't taken a bite of her before, after all, as she'd played the role of a mysterious, half-wild wraith-woman trying her hand at queenship. They wouldn't dare now, either, with her antlers taller than any crown could ever be—so long as she perfectly performed a role no one ever taught her how to play.

Aveline sucked in a breath that threatened to freeze her lungs solid. The sting helped rid her mind of the thought, but with the fire out, she didn't dare close her eyes, because she knew what would gaze back at her in that deep darkness. Instead, she took a handful of snow and rubbed it on her face and hands, removing all the traces of her meal that she could. Then she swallowed a mouthful to melt in her belly. Granted, as a half-Winter creature, she was colder than most; it would take a while for snow to become water. But it would satisfy her body nonetheless.

As she stood and brushed the snow from her near cloak-like black dress, Jädrich's hand slipped off her shoulder. He came around to face her, though he kept a careful distance from the dead fire pit, as if the very spirit of the fire would suddenly burst back to life and lick at the ice of his hands and face. Like her, he came dressed so simply: no crown graced his head, no jewels decorated his neck, and no icy boots caught the faint Winter morning light on each of his steps. Only a fur cloak more masterfully made than her own and a pair of slacks and a plain shirt covered him. Jädrich's long silver hair was tied behind his head, though the sleigh ride down to the woods caused a few strands to fly free and drift around his sharply carved face. Whether dressed as a King or as a common man, however, his eyes remained as piercing and brutal as they'd ever been, and his lips held no hint of a smile. Had Aveline not seen him smile before, she would've believed that how his face was carved made it impossible for him to do so.

Though he likely looked the way he did because the work they were about to do together was no smiling matter. They were once again going to the underbelly of the castle to decide which half-melted women should live and which should die. It'd become something of a morning ritual after just over a week of the grim task: find something to eat, then find any women worth re-freezing. But what else was there to do? There were still dozens, even *hundreds* of women who, thanks to the velvet they were wrapped in, didn't die of melt so easily. Whereas men would simply turn to water, their souls flying free from their heads and returning to the Seat of Orr, that great Winter mountain, the women became dilapidated sacks of water with souls trapped in velvet as their bodies gradually melted.

Worse, even those with only a spot of melt would one day be undone. *Innernfröscherl,* as the Ismären called it, was nothing short of a curse: degenerative, deadly, and even able to be passed on from ice parent to little ice child. There was no cure for it no matter how hard Jädrich looked—until, that is, he learned of the frost she could pour from her lips in the the same way the desert Yasilanri could bathe a town in golden flame and cleanse it of all traces of life. It was one of the greatest things that guaranteed Aveline's safety in Winter. No other Ismar could break the curse of her Yasilan mother's god, Drakash Ra-Kedaar, who reigned eternally as the glorious sun in the Summer sky.

That alone makes me god in these lands, she thought. Jädrich gave her hair one gentle stroke. He studied her as if trying to find the traces of rabbit still on her lips— flesh that prey animals like deer did not eat. *That's more than enough to guarantee I'll be kept safe.*

She made the mistake of blinking, and something in the darkness glimmered like two doe eyes in the moonlight. Her own voice answered as that gaze pierced her.

For now.

"We should go," Jädrich said. "The women are waiting for us."

Then he ran his thumb over her cheek, a sweet gesture, before opening his arm to her. When his fingers brushed her face, however, it sent a chill skittering down her spine. So smooth, so *cold,* the body of an Ismar. No matter how much she told herself that these were, in fact, people made of ice, it seemed she always forgot until she touched her husband—because how could creatures that walked and talked like men be anything other than flesh?

How could ice, of all things, touch her and hold her and lie with her the way Jädrich promised he would the night that their marriage contract was finally signed?

Aveline tucked herself into Jädrich's side, nestling herself under the crook of his outstretched arm and under his own cloak. Two sets of fur cloaks out in that frigid air kept her so comfortable that she regretted to leave the place. But off they went in silence, back to the sleigh where the castle's *Unseelechs*—tame, timid creatures, unlike the wild things Aveline befriended—sat ready to drag them back. The creatures stared at them with eyes dead of shine, with heads bald and smooth, and with the puppet-like pieces of their bodies only barely held together with the faintest line of silver magic. They were so still, too. So quiet as they huddled under the icy sheets of their wings and waited for the sound of a cracking whip to spur them back towards the castle.

As she settled into the sleigh, and Jädrich took up that black sleigh whip—as they lurched onward through the snow and started their ride back to the castle—Aveline couldn't help but pity the miserable things. She knew what they could be, and how ferocious and mighty they were when they filled themselves on the venison that the Ismären enjoyed. It was still strange to think that those white deer were, allegedly, the same beasts their own god once was before her wish for more caused her to take on a form like Aveline's, only without the wings of a dragon.

Maybe that's all she needed. Aveline braced her legs against the sleigh walls. *A set of wings to escape on.*

Her own voice answered her, as if her head were empty enough for thoughts to warp when echoing back: *or a set of teeth and talons to crush ice back into snow.*

Aveline blinked the thought away. She snaked her arms around one of Jädrich's. She kissed his shoulder and let one hand trail down his forearm. These times, where she and Jädrich were still so far from the castle, were the only times she felt bold enough to touch Jädrich like this—where no one could see, and where no morbid work they did together made it feel wrong to do so. But Jädrich rarely responded to her touch while they were out in the woods. He stayed stiff as ever, an ice sculpture with no apparent feeling as she slipped her hand from his arm to the leg it rested on.

Jädrich glanced her way, a sparkle shimmering in his eye. "Easy, now."

"What?" The sleigh jostled over a bump in the snow and made her hand slip further down his leg. "You've done more than this to me already. Have I no right to do a little of the same?"

"That was inappropriate of me to do before our marriage," Jädrich said without missing a beat. But by the way he glanced at her again, longer this time, with yet more sparkling magic lighting his eyes, Aveline knew there was more to his mind than his near lifeless body let on. "We should avoid tempting each other further."

"But temptation is exactly what the bards sing about." She inched her fingers further towards his inseam. "Didn't you want to understand? What all the fuss is about in their songs?"

"I'm sure you'll help me understand after we sign our contract. Be patient."

Aveline wondered if her ice-doll simply had an iron will, or if his steely cold words were a sign that he was close to losing his grip on himself. With Jädrich, it was impossible to tell. But she let her hands return to his arm anyway, opting to rest her chin on his shoulder and stare at his profile. Such a sharp jaw. Such a strong nose. Such intense eyes, shadowed by so straight a brow. Yes, her ice-doll was very pretty, and she wanted to put him in a glass case like she heard the wealthy Summer girls did in their desert highland homes. Wanted to trap him there and stare at him every day, her prize. Instead, she studied him, and she peppered another few kisses along his shoulder.

"That contract better be done soon," she muttered. Her voice almost disappeared under the sound of the sleigh skating over the snow. She lifted one of Jädrich's arms so she could lay in his lap and look up at him, and she trailed a finger over the buttons of his shirt. "I've been patient enough, I think."

After all, it'd already been two days since the bridal competition would've officially ended. Already, Aveline had been living this life with the Winter King for the better part of a week—taking care of his people, playing goddess for a small audience, otherwise lazing about in the castle gardens with nothing else to do and no one else to talk to—and yet she had none of the spoils to show for it yet. She might've started to wonder if Jädrich intended to marry her at all, if such a thought wouldn't send that doe-woman in her head yipping into a fearful frenzy.

Jädrich's arm rested on her ribs, though the cloaks cushioned her bones from his ice. He didn't look away from the sleigh's path, but he did shake his head, and his lips quirked into one of those rare smiles.

"The doe is not the hunter, nor should she speak like one."

He's hunting us.

Aveline tried to ignore the twist in her stomach. "I think I could be both, though."

"No, no. Remember: you are a doe, Aveline, not a bear or a bobcat. Your people need to see a doe. They need to *hear*," he stressed, and his eyebrow shot up as he glanced down, "a doe. Life on the Seat of Orr has stolen the meekness from you; it needs to be restored if your people are to understand and appreciate what you are."

She fell silent. Every time he said the word *doe*, the skin near her shoulder blades twitched. It was as if her wings had a mind of their own and begged to rip free just to spite him. But she clenched her teeth together instead and tilted her chin up, lengthening her neck so as not to let the little dragon-glands inside snap with puffs of fresh frost. The pain that shot through her jaw both stilled her body and caged whatever other words might've hissed from her mouth. Her lips stayed still for the rest of the ride to the castle, but that didn't mean her mind was quiet.

I asked for this. There was no way to justify the way her stomach soured or the way her jaw ached. She'd had many days already to come to terms with what she'd traded in return for some semblance of safety. She was well aware of the sacrifices she'd made, and the things she'd failed to do, all to prioritize her survival over other things she thought mattered. She was painfully aware of the emptiness around her neck—the silence, the *absence* of her mother's bell, which she'd tucked in the jewelry box she'd been given and promised only to wear when she could reconcile her love for her mother and her wish for her mother's killer. *I chose this.*

Though she did try, every day, to reconcile it in her mind. After all, would her mother really have wanted her only daughter to try and destroy the King of Winter, knowing that would've likely meant her death? Would that bright and bold Yasilan want Aveline to waste her life on petty ambitions of honor and vengeance, when those had always been the domains of pride-blind, glory-driven men? Once, Aveline thought that wish for vengeance was what spurred her to keep living in the first place, if only temporarily—because what else did she have to live for, with her only family in the world gone?—and yet, with the way her own body rejected the idea of danger altogether, and the way she found something that felt like shelter under the mantel of the Winter King, it became clear what was really driving her forward: a second chance. An escape from the burning lands of Summer, and a refuge from the sharp and hungry gaze of Summer's ruler, the great Sekhran Ganaresh Ti-Vaour, that sent her on this deadly mission to begin with.

Was he serious about taking me for a wife? That one ridiculous letter he'd had Erik deliver to her a couple weeks prior certainly suggested it. *Me, a half-breed with only a set of wings to even prove I have any Yasilan blood at all?*

Likely not. Maybe the Sekhran thought that if he promised her such a thing, she'd eventually come to want the life he dangled in front of her during her brief stay in his palace, what with all the gold and good food and soft summer nights. Maybe he thought she was lying when she said she didn't want him and didn't care for his riches. Maybe that letter was just to spur her on in her mission with false hopes and empty promises, himself hoping she'd be dead and never come claim her prize from him. Whatever the Sekhran had going through his head, though, Aveline didn't want to chance his being serious. Not at all. She would never have a moment's peace seated beside the heir of the Summer sun himself, with Drakash forever burning her under his great golden eye.

I'm sorry, mother. Aveline rubbed the empty spot where her mother's bell would've rested on her chest. Even if her mother would've wanted her to do what was best for her above all, the thought came anyway. *I couldn't melt this man.*

But she could do other things. As goddess, in fact, she could do many things—including have her cake and eat it, too. After all, it wasn't Jädrich that was the problem, only the issue of the seasons not moving. She could

make him move them again, she was sure. If not immediately, then soon enough. Then Sekhran Ganaresh
would have no way of getting to her ever again, *and* no
reason to come and try, given he'd still get what he really wanted: an end to the century-long Summer. All the
while, Aveline could see the entire Ringlands, cloaked
in the comfort of Winter's chill and tucked at the side
of a Lord of Seasons. Then she'd be able to see Autumn,
finally. The one country she hadn't ever been to.

Hmm. A nasty bump on the path had the sleigh lifting
off the ground for a moment, and her stomach flipped
as if she were descending from a short flight. She held
on tighter as the sled sped along the snow. *I wonder what
Autumn is like.*

But that was a thought for another time. The castle
came closer and closer, looming over them like a
mountain in its own right, and Aveline spent the rest
of the ride steeling herself for another few miserable
hours of playing god with the soon-to-be-dead.

RISTEF COULDN'T HAVE STRUGGLED AGAINST THE MAGIC coiled around his wrists if he wanted to; he was too stiff. He'd spent most of his magic trying to slow the carriages down as their party of guards and the King's advisor, Lady Clara Ronterweis, headed back to the castle. Mostly, as they crossed the West Lakefields, he'd tried to lock the wheels up a little bit or create little bumps in the snow and ice that would force the drivers to restabilize. Lady Ronterweis forbade Ristef from driving the carriages himself, and perhaps he should've figured. He was, after all, Aveline's guard for the duration of the King's bridal contest, save for the last week—and he hadn't made such a good reputation for himself, following her as closely as he did. But what else could he have done with a woman like her?

A woman that he discovered was not just an Ismar,

but their dead goddess Cervora returned, made of flesh and bone, hooves and antlers?

The carriage rode so smoothly across one large lake that Ristef might've thought they weren't moving at all, but as he strained his near-magicless body to look out the carriage window, he saw the trees far off in the distance still whizzing by. He tapped his teeth to his lip. What more could he have done to help? What could he do to prevent Lady Ronterweis from putting those slanderous letters in the hands of the King?

All he could do was hope that King Jädrich wouldn't fall victim those letters. The letters they'd found in the house of her father, the late Lord Berlund Rachfemd—they suggested blasphemous and terrible things about Aveline, and Ristef refused to believe them. He refused to believe Aveline was the bastard daughter of a Yasilan whore.

The sky was a blur of grey. The wind occasionally whistled outside. As Ristef tried to rise enough to see more of the outside, the guard beside him—a large, broad-chested Ismar named Ehrwig, whose head was like a thick block, and whose eyes were a strange banded green, malachite—put a hand on Ristef's shoulder and pushed him back into his seat. One of those eyes was out, and in the empty socket, the open needle hole glimmered with the silver light of the guard's soul. That pinprick of light bore into Ristef; he was searching for any hint of magic that Ristef might've been using, leaving no option to continue trying to sabotage the journey back home. Ristef had been careless enough the first time, slowing the wheels once too many times without realizing someone started watching him, and so they'd drained him of what other magic he had left.

"Don't worry about it, Gürennsig," the guard said, his large teeth like pieces of thick stone in his awful smile, "you'll get back to the castle soon enough."

Around the guard's head was a halo of muddy yellow, a tainted joy. The stones of Ristef's eyes, blue lace agate, let him see the radiance of people's emotions; their souls shined with bright colors the way light reflected off pure diamonds or clear glass. Ristef sat down and hunched his head, tapping teeth to lip and trying, desperately, to think of what to do.

The King can't see those letters.

But Lady Ronterweis was determined to show them to the King. It took only two days for the walls of the capital to come back in sight, *two* days, when it was a journey that should've taken three days at a normal pace, a good *six* days if Ristef hadn't been caught meddling. That would've been long enough to miss the end of the competition and therefore the writing of the marriage contract by an entire *week*, if Ristef had it his way. But she hadn't once let them rest; she'd used up seven guards' worth of magic, to the point that they could hardly stand without the ice of their bodies squeaking in complaint. It seemed she intended to drain all twelve men she brought with her, if it meant the carriage wheels could keep turning fast enough for her.

That's why Ristef was so surprised to feel the carriage slowing down at one point. At the pace they were making, Ristef figured they'd be in the city by nightfall, or maybe early the next morning, and then back at the castle not long after that. Whatever they were stopping for, Ristef couldn't guess—until this other guard gave another one of his stony grins. In the night, his one malachite eye looked like a storm cloud crackling with silver lightning; Ristef didn't need blue lace agate to see his morbid excitement. Ristef shrank under his gaze, and that only seemed to thrill the guard even more, even though he stayed silent.

Once the carriage came to a stop, the crunch of

footsteps hurried up a moment later. The carriage door
flew open, and there stood Lady Ronterweis, her face
set hard and her head haloed with grey-blue determination. Her face, however, reminded him of Aveline's
Unseelechs: wide eyed, yet otherwise blank of expression,
as if Ristef was the next wriggling creature she'd rip to
pieces and consume.

"Get out," Lady Ronterweis snapped at Ehrwig. "Get
to the front."

He flashed one more wicked grin at Ristef before
climbing out, and the King's advisor hopped in to take
his place. After she nodded to that guard, and he shut
the carriage door, Lady Ronterweis spawned a little
orb of magical light with the swish of her finger and sat
back. She studied Ristef, and it was hard not to shrink
further under that wide-eyed stare. The onyx made it
worse. With those dark spots for eyes that looked more
like holes, especially as her orb of light floated more behind her, it was as if there was no soul inside her head.

"Alright, Gürrensig," she started, folding her hands
in her lap, "if you want to keep yourself from being
crushed when we return, you best get talking."

Ristef didn't so much as twitch. He knew what she
wanted him to say. He would never say it—not even if
she crushed him to snow right there in that carriage.
The King wouldn't entertain Lady Ronterweis's nonsense if he knew who Aveline really was, and he could
only hope Aveline told him by time they got back. No
matter what nonsense Lady Ronterweis came to the
King with, those antlers and hooves, if he saw them first,
would make it so no lies could ever poison him against
her. Or so he hoped. He hated to admit it, but even his
own mind wandered to blasphemous places.

What if she is *half-dragon? And that's why she looks the
way she does?*

Lady Ronterweis's voice was sharp. "How long have you known Rachfemd is flesh?"

Ristef stayed silent. The carriage lurched forward again, and the sky outside began whipping past them once more. Ristef wondered if the advisor intended to stay with him the entire last night to the city, and the thought made his soul deflate in his head.

"Gürrensig," her voice took a note of warning, her brow arched high, "I know you know. You wouldn't have wanted to slow our carriages or downplay those letters if you didn't. Unless," her lips quirked into a wicked smirk, "you simply feel too strongly for one of the King's suitors? And couldn't bring yourself to believe such a thing? Is that why you're so quiet?"

Damned if he answered, damned if he didn't. Ristef knew how Lady Ronterweis played this game. He'd watched many a castle interrogation, and his only solace was that Lady Ronterweis didn't have any of the tools she normally liked to use: the ice picks, the stone mallets, the flint and steel that even executioners feared to use. Any of that would force him to speak eventually. Even without them, though, his silence would implicate him one way or another—but at least if he didn't answer, she'd never have clear confirmation as to which accusation was the truth.

Lady Ronterweis tipped her chin up, but those pure black eyes made it so Ristef couldn't tell where she was looking. The ceiling of the carriage? Or was she looking down her nose at him? It didn't matter one way or another, but he would've liked to think about anything else than this line of questioning.

"Did you lay with her?"

Smoke and ashes.

Staying silent for this one would kill him and ruin Aveline, and that advisor knew it, by how her smirk became a full serpent's smile. Her emotions betrayed nothing, though; her face was only a mask. Did she know that Ristef could see them? Her emotions? Was that blue-grey halo around her head a mask just like her carefully crafted expressions? Whatever the case, Ristef opened his mouth and ignored the sharp sting that flashed in its corners.

"No."

"But you touched her." Relentless, this advisor. She cocked her head, still smiling. "You can't deny that, can you? Half the guards here have already confirmed it: you held her arm and walked her around. What did she feel like? Ice? Or flesh?"

Stay silent. Ristef squeezed his lips together until they squeaked. Any question that wouldn't catch him or Aveline in some nonsense, he wouldn't answer. He also wondered what the point of asking at all was, given Lady Ronterweis could've told all kinds of lies about Ristef and Aveline if she wanted to. She must've had a runestone on her, recording the sounds of the carriage; she wanted something else to go with those letters when she presented her findings to the King. *Silent.*

Lady Ronterweis blinked, her smile slipping. "Gürrensig," she said, and her voice made his soul shudder. She said his name as innocently as a child, even as she reached into her pocket and pulled out a tiny, yet vicious ice hammer. The thin handle fit her small hand perfectly. "I'd really like you to start talking."

He closed his eyes for just a moment to steady himself. When he opened them, he kept just as still and silent as he had before. That ice hammer was so small, nothing like the ones she usually used on her victims. Surely she couldn't do much with it—especially in this little carriage. Though it wasn't like he could defend himself from whatever she'd do, with no magic and no mobility. Whatever happened, he would bear it for Aveline's sake.

Lady Ronterweis stared. After it became clear Ristef wouldn't speak, she nodded. And as she stood in the carriage, gripping that ice hammer, through her halo of blue-grey came the tiniest crackle of dingy yellow excitement.

Karina's empty eye socket made the cold all that much more acute. The chilly air pooled inside the hole in her face; it sank deep into her skin the way water sank into the earth after a deep rain. Such cold was a fact of her life for the past several decades she'd spent hiding in her family's old Winter home, and yet the ache that sprouted at her brow still made it difficult to focus. Those dull, ebbing aches that lasted for hours were the kind of pain she hated most; a thousand cuts along her body wouldn't irk her as much. Yet those aches were also the kinds of pain she knew best.

In her lap was the chunk of pyrite she used for an eye. The piece of pyrite seemed to gleam at Karina specifically, as if begging to return to its place in her head. Often, however, she found that the stone made the cold more concentrated against her skin, what with the Winter air practically freezing it into her face. Karina took it out where she could, and while it didn't gleam, didn't glow, it *did* reflect the starlight just enough to fake a sparkle. Fool's gold, it was called, as it tricked greedy and inexperienced people into believing they'd be rich for their discovery.

Its gift was useful for a merchant's daughter. With it, she could see the currents of people's greed and hope, the direction of their lusts and dreams, and so she spent many a day with her father, an Akerijin merchant who taught her how to speak without speaking while he tempted customers of all nations with his only slightly

overpriced goods. Back then, she hated every minute
of her work with her father. However, after sitting alone
in her empty Winter home for so long, Karina couldn't
help but look back on those times with a nostalgia
that made her heart sore. So many hours spent under
the merchant stall, looking through a peephole at a
customer and charting the golden hues of their hope
and desire, poking at her father's leg in a code they'd
developed together. So many hours spent alone under
her roof, wishing she could speak just one word to him
again.

She held her pyrite eye in a silk cloth from her father's homeland, that Autumn world of pointed red
leaves and babbling brooks, flute-song on the crisp wind
and scrolls full of calligraphy laid out to dry. Her father
taught her the script of the Autumn people, and how to
let each glyph become its own art as their ink-soaked
brushes glided across the paper, but so many years
alone in Winter made her hands forget the order of
the brush strokes. The fact that she could still read any
of the Akerijin language was solely thanks to the books
and maps and other such things her father kept in their
modest few bookshelves, nestled alongside her Ismar
mother's favorite romances and folktales.

Yet for the second time in one year, she'd been
pulled from that home full of frozen ghosts. It wasn't
easy to untangle where her bitterness over this ended
and where her gratitude began. All she knew was that it
made her mouth taste foul.

Karina sat in the forest on the outskirts of Vörnein,
in the last patches of woods. Just a few feet away was the
road that led from the country into the city; the first
few stones of the city roads were just beginning to pep-
per the frozen dirt path. Only another half an hour or
so, and she'd be in the thick of it again: surrounded by
people and shops and quaint little houses that her child

self always wanted to see. When her father went to sell his goods in the grand market festivals that Empress Feng Souram hosted in Winter's capital, she'd been stuck by his side, unable to explore. Even if she didn't dare fuss under the market table while her father peddled his wares, her little heart ached to see the glimpses of the city, as if the buildings and the people were tugging her heart on a fishhook. To think that there'd be no more festivals, where all the Ringland peoples sold their most beautiful and unique trinkets, was something her younger self would've never thought possible.

She sighed and blinked those memories away. As far as Karina knew, there was no one out there but her that morning, but that wasn't certain. Nothing ever was. After another moment of looking at her pyrite eye, she wrapped it in that silk and tucked it into her bag, where she had another eye waiting: a piece of onyx. The same kind every other woman of Winter had. Karina sucked in a breath, bracing herself, and then popped the frozen stone into her socket. She jolted as the cold thing touched her skin. When the little silver spike on the other side nestled into a tender part of her socket, she shuddered. Even after so many decades of living with these fake eyes, it was the cold she never got used to.

But at least she could see from this side of her face again. Karina blinked, letting the eye settle into her flesh, and looked around. There were no splotches of red, no signs of danger. No hint of anyone or anything that might disturb her. Karina drank up the air in the last deep breath she'd likely be able to take, and then she pulled out the gauzy wraps and head covers from her bag. It made her cringe, knowing she'd look like an injured holy maiden from the monasteries—how she hated those women, with their long faces and dead stares, as if everyone who stepped foot in a cathedral were some filthy vermin that had snuck in through the cracks in the walls—but there was nothing to be done. It wasn't as if the Winter folk would accept her pointed ears or her one fleshling eye.

And they'd chop off her silver tail like a trophy if she ever so much as moved it under her long, loose skirts. Just to be safe, that, too, would have to be gently tied to her leg, and she'd have to walk in a way that wouldn't tug too hard on her tailbone.

I hate this country.

Or, at least, she hated what it'd become. Karina got up and began the last trek of her journey into the city. Even if the Ismären's most charitable reaction in the past was confusion, seeing a mixed-blood child dressed in fine silks, she'd at least been able to walk the streets freely. After the wall went up, though, they expected her kind to hide in the other countries: to live in places that their non-Winter relatives hailed from, yet that they often didn't know as home any more than the frosts of Winter. Worse, people like Karina were told to *just go to the Melded Isle,* as if she had any idea what that strange island even held.

All her life, she'd heard nothing but stories about it, nothing but rumors and whispers and fanciful tales that didn't seem real. In fact, she would've thought the island itself didn't exist, had she not seen other mixed-bloods like herself who had the mark of that Melded Isle tattooed on their necks: a single line of four loops, with a five-pointed star in the space between them all. Each loop had a different colored dot inked in the middle of them: gold and silver, bronze and copper. Solstices and equinoxes. All looped around that one star in the middle.

Maybe one day, you'll have that mark on your neck. As Karina walked, wishing she could ride on the comfort of her illusory clouds instead of walk on the hard soles of her shoes, she found herself haunted by her father's half-smile and the crow's feet around his golden eyes. *And you'll tell me what goods there are to trade in that land out there on the lake.*

Karina shook her head. Always the opportunities on his mind, that merchant. Always the trade, the travel. But Karina wasn't here to peddle goods; she was here to maintain connections and bridge communication. How her father would've sulked, knowing his daughter went more the route of diplomat than merchant. But then, she was something of a smuggler where that half-Summer orphan was concerned—and her sponsor, Erik, wanted her smuggled again. If anything in the message he sent shooting through her chimney was true, and if anything Karina heard loitering outside the inns from the last town were accurate, then for all their sakes, that was the only option. Who would've guessed that the half-wild thing would've actually tried to *marry* the King rather than kill him? That she would use those antlers and hooves to masquerade as a god?

Not that Karina wouldn't, had she the chance. She just didn't think the wild woman cared to act out such a plot—or had the mental fortitude to do so.

It didn't take long for the city and its stone walls to come into view, and not long after that to reach its entrance. After a miserable half hour walking over frozen stone, and after being heckled by a couple guards at the gate about where she was coming from and why, Karina finally stepped over the threshold of the city and gave herself a moment to pause. As much as she hated the costume she wore, at least it got her past security without having to offer a bribe.

Where the endless expanse of fields and forests outside gave her a feeling of being far too exposed, though, it was this gate, which led into three directions of snow-dusted, cobblestone roads, that suddenly made her feel like a rat in a maze. The buildings were tall, their dark wooden beams spiderwebbing across otherwise white walls, and the people at ease as they ambled by. The people around the edge of Vörnein were dressed plainly, of course: these were the menial laborers clothed in grey and brown, and the equally dingy-dressed craftsmen who reserved their fine things for customers, not themselves. But the few men and women Karina watched seemed unhurried in their errands, unbothered by the state of the world outside the walls of Winter—whether the walls of the city or the country borders.

Karina trudged on, up a street that grew gradually steeper and more slippery. If not for the way Winter shoes were built, with their rough soles to grip the ground, Karina didn't doubt she'd have ended up on her face at least once or twice. But she found her way towards the center of the city soon enough, to the square where all the city's happenings seemed to flow in and out, like some great heart. There at the square stage was a huge statue of Cervora that seemed to catch all the shadows the muted, cloudy day had to offer in its face. Shadows ducked under its carved brows, laid under its stone antlers, and nestled between and under its full, curved lips. Despite the little smile this statue had, something about its gaze felt as if it were casting a curse on all who stopped to look at it. Never once did Karina—or her father or any other Akerijin—feel safe under the stare of a massacred god.

Directly behind it was the bridge that led to the castle, that huge stone thing full of sharp roofs and flying buttresses and arched windows. Karina briefly wondered what the orphan was doing in there before her gaze shifted to her real destination, up the hill to the right: the bigger houses, city manors reserved for either the lower nobility or those with more money than sense. Their size made them look like libraries or inns

more than houses, and as Karina got up to that neigh-
borhood of wealthy folk, she found that they were gated
like the finer inns and libraries, too. After passing a few
of these near-identical monstrosities, she finally found
the one she was looking for.

A glance around told her no one was there to see
her. No red flashed from her onyx eye, either; no one
with bad intentions was stalking after her, at least.
Karina raised her hand to the door and knocked, and a
moment later, the door handle clicked, the door itself
creaking open. No one was behind it, but by the muffled
voice she heard come from deep within that house, she
knew better than to stand there too long. Karina hurried
inside and locked the door behind her.

"It's a better position, if you think about it." Inside,
Karina could focus better on what Erik was saying. "I
know it *looks* terrible from the outside, but really, it'll
work. Just keep your folks on the ready. We're almost
where we need to be."

To anyone else, Erik might've been talking about
some construction project. But as Karina followed that
voice through the foyer, through the sitting room, and
into the doorway of a small study, she knew exactly
what he was on about. Erik sat in that study and spared
her only a glance as a pale blue shape of a woman
hovered in the air like a ghost: a conjured connection,
supported by the glowing blue runestone on Erik's desk.

"Erik, you must understand how this looks to the
others," came a woman's echoing voice, as if it were embedded in the very walls. "You're reneging on your word
with every moment we spend waiting for our trade. Our
people can't take much more of this. Their bodies are
at their limit; their souls are soured to a point that'll be
difficult to recover from."

That spectral woman didn't so much as twitch; it was
like a doll, sitting there, but the more Karina studied

the thing, the more she placed the speaker on the other side: a tricorn hat with a long feather, a low-cut dress with silver buttons lining its front, sleeves that ended at her forearm before flaring out in great swaths of white lace. This was a noblewoman of the southern cities—Taubech, by that hat. It'd been a port city before the Winter Wall went up, but after, it was a castrated and struggling city with no access to the lake.

"I know. But I swear to you, I did not expect this. Never in a thousand years did I expect this." Erik shook his head and stared off. "All I can do now is beg you to trust me one more time. Give us time to make it to the south, and we'll be able to force the issue. In fact, this is better; we'll be able to properly decide a transfer to another party instead of the original plan. Who knew what would've happened if we'd let the main asset go unclaimed? Leave the details to me. Trust me; you know we have a good chance here."

The phantom woman paused, and then her voice filled the room again. "That asset isn't up to standard according to what we've found out from our people, Erik."

Erik froze, then barked, "How so?"

"The people say that it's offensive to lay eyes on, and that it isn't fit for royalty. I fear trading on it won't win us much favor with the Crown at this rate, with how the people think it sullies anything it sits by."

Erik leaned back in his seat and hid his face in his hands. "Which folk have said this?"

"All. The nobles, the commonfolk—Erik, you know how such information drifts down. It only takes one butler to overhear something before half the taverns are rife with that same something." The echoing voice paused, then started up again. "Do you really think the people will believe you? About this asset?"

Karina didn't understand the specifics. She could only guess that this had something to do with Aveline by virtue of her being called to Erik's home, which was good. Erik shouldn't have been talking about serious things in a way that anyone with an eye or an ear hidden somewhere could've parsed.

"I believe it," Erik said as Karina glanced around the house and conjured what Winter magic she had in her veins. "I've seen it, my friend. I've seen what our asset can do for the people. And I'll be gathering testimony on those it's been tested on, specifically so that we might sow some hope in our folk again."

You mean I'll *be gathering testimony.*

Karina's mouth went bitter. Every time she encountered this man, it seemed he invented some new task for her, dangling her home above her head like a carrot on a stick. "Gathering testimony"—how quaint. As if she were little more than some common courier of rural folks' gossip. She technically didn't have to do another single thing for Erik; they'd already gone past the statutes of their bargain when the orphan failed to kill that King. Karina had done all she was required to do, and yet her hands were tied, because all her bargains and contracts and agreements only mattered if that Lord of Seasons was replaced.

But as Erik talked, Karina swept; she cast her magic into her surroundings and scanned for anything that glowed blue, any signs of runestone bugs or other things left behind that could record what was done or said. And there was one. Right above Karina's head, there was one thing that shined. She looked up, and had it not been for that blue glow, she never would've noticed the little square of what looked like wood. Its grain pattern was only off from the surrounding wood by a hair. Karina didn't look at it too long, in case it was recording a vision as well as the sounds of Erik's speech. Karina had to give Erik credit: he wasn't a complete idiot, even if he was committing such treason against his King and country for idiotic reasons.

My cousin is already married. Karina didn't have the heart to tell him that his precious Madame Seshino couldn't wait around for a dream—especially when it was both Erik's motivation to break down Winter's walls, and the only carrot Karina could dangle in Erik's face in order to secure the rights to her mother's home. *She's given up on you, Erik. On Winter.*

But Karina hadn't given up. And Karina wouldn't. Even if it meant herding wild women and killing Kings, even if it took a *thousand* years, she would walk free in her mother's country again. She would see the market festivals again, as a merchant carrying on her father's trade. She would even find the wares of the Melded Isle and bring them here one day, doing what those secretive, elusive people of the Isle never did for one reason or another.

The spectral woman's voice snatched Karina's dreams from her mind's eye. "Fine. I'll call the others and see what the word is from the people about your *asset*. But Erik, this is your *last* chance. If all goes to ruin, it's your head, your house. You know how the investors are."

Erik's eyes slipped shut. "I know."

"Update me as you're able, then. I expect better news next time you contact me."

Then the image of the woman faded, and the blue runestone on Erik's desk went dead of all its magical sheen. Erik pinched the bridge of his nose, and Karina felt pity that he had no lungs with which to sigh. After a conversation like that, heaving a mighty sigh would've cleansed him of at least some fatigue. Karina wanted to do so just listening in, but she let it loose from her stomach, instead: silent, yet still soothing.

"I see your *investments* are going smoothly," Karina said, and she tipped her head up to that rune on the ceiling as Erik looked her way. He shook his head, his face long.

"That *asset* you brought me caused a mess," he muttered. "A wretched mess."

"Mm, I can see that." Karina wandered into the study, looking around a moment at the books and parchment and fine furniture, before perching on the desk in a way that avoided her siting on her hidden tail. "My condolences. But it seems you have a plan to get what you're due from it, no?"

And finally uphold your end of our deal?

Erik sat back in his seat and considered her carefully. "That I do. Are you willing to help me with it?"

She would've loved to say no. Would've been more than happy to smash that viscount's head in, if for no other reason than to give her frustration an outlet. Decades, *decades*, this ice-man strung her along and let her hope to claim her legal inheritance as a free woman in this country. Yet every time she saw him, he only had more and more work for her—more bad news, never good news. So she kept herself composed and gave Erik the answer he was looking for.

"If I wasn't, I'd still be curled up at home with a book, miles away," she said with a quirk of her brow.

That got him to at least crack a smile. "Fair enough." The smile disappeared as fast as it came, though, and he whispered, "How is your cousin?"

Lovesick little fool. Karina had neither the mind nor the stomach to make up another bundle of lies for Erik; she'd been telling him the contents of nonexistent letters from her cousin for years, and those fairytales had long since begun tasting bitter on her tongue. "I still haven't heard from her," she said instead with a wave of her hand. "Been busy with all this; couldn't get a letter to her or a letter back."

His eyes shuttered in a slow blink. "I see. Well, fine, then. Should we go for a walk in town?"

"In a bit." Karina shook her aching feet, and Erik dropped his gaze to them. "It'd be good to sit and catch up for a moment first."

Erik stared at her feet a moment longer, then nodded. He understood, even if that slight twitch of his lips told her he wasn't happy about it. "Fine."

She'd never seen him so calm. Though, she supposed it was more that he was deflated of all his confidence rather than calm. Poor usurper, all tangled up in his own ambitions. Karina kicked her shoes off and flexed her feet, and while she hated to see her one ally look so drained, she knew she'd hate even more to hear how this Winter noble would want her to go and make an *asset* of the orphan. After all, if he could speak of that wild woman as if she were just a piece on a chess board, then what on earth did he say about Karina when she wasn't in the same room? And what did he think about her when she was?

She could easily guess. Unlike what she could tell of the orphan, Karina knew full well that a mixed-blood was only welcome around the Ringland folk so far as they could be used.

My country, my country. An acrid taste bloomed on her tongue, and an ugly scab on her heart she thought she'd healed began to peel and bleed again. *But not my people.*

"Your Majesty, please," Helen said. She bowed her head as if she weren't Head Priestess of the castle cathedral, but a lowly maid. "Allow me to speak in honor of your best interests."

It was early in the morning, so early that the dawn hadn't broken yet, and it was the third morning from when Helen was supposed to write up the marriage contract for the King and his chosen bride. He'd given her an extension when she told him that she ran out of the enchanted ink to write it with, but it was all a lie, a stall—and Helen prayed endlessly to Cervora that King Jädrich didn't realize it. That contract was due that morning, and Helen, truthfully, hadn't even started writing it, because she knew by Clara's silver-spun message orbs that she was just about to come back to the city. If Helen could stall a little bit longer, even just half a day, then surely, Clara would come with information that would make the King beg Helen *not* to pen that contract at all.

And more than all that, Helen still had the little rune Headmistress Klassech gave her. If Clara found something, and she had this rune, then surely, *surely,* there was something terrible about Lady Rachfemd that both of these women uncovered. It would all come together, and that was why Helen guarded that runestone until Clara's return.

King Jädrich stared at her. He'd already been working in his study when Helen came, accepting requests of judicial hearings, stamping official documents after laws were agreed on, and reviewing reports on the country's borders, and he did it all as if sunrise and sunset were no different to him. The way he stared at Helen, too, made it seem as if her intrusion were yet another task to settle.

"Speak, then."

The sharp, cold quality of his words felt as if they were made of icicle points. Granted, she'd never known him to speak any other way, but as she flexed her hands and felt the velvet slide again and again over her knuckles, Helen pressed her tongue to the roof of her mouth. It clicked in place, and the perfect way it fit always comforted her when something made her soul frizzle and whirr with anxiety, like her King's voice did right then. In fact, her head may as well have been a beehive, with how loud her thoughts buzzed. Still, she managed to soothe herself just enough to stand up straight and, against all odds, look her King in the eye.

"I know that you hope to have the marriage contract today, but I believe we should wait on writing it until we've heard what Lady Ronterweis has to say. Surely she's sent you a message, too? That she's returning today?"

King Jädrich's pencil paused in his hand. He didn't

move, but Helen understood from watching him with many of the guards that he was listening—even if only to give whoever he was speaking to a chance to correct themselves. Knowing that, Helen could've bolted from the study right then. Instead, she focused on the way the study's starlights twinkled off his grand icicle crown. So bright and blue-white were those starlights that they even made his long silver hair reflect that ethereal glow, as if he were not only in control of the starlight's magic, but lord and master over it, born to rule all things with it. Helen's soul went from buzzing to sinking down to the bottom of her head as she realized that the chance to stand alongside this man as both priestess and Queen was taken from her. This man, the greatest among her countrymen, the direct descendant of the legendary Orr, the one who housed the very soul of Winter itself in his body, he was right in front of her and yet so far from her. So far out of her reach.

Yes, he terrified her—but that was only because he was grand and resolute and righteous enough *to* terrify her, in a way no other man ever had.

"Helen," he said, and her name on his lips rattled her senses to pieces. He set down his pencil, folded his hands, and stared at her head on with the only set of such clear, sparkling blue diamond eyes in all the land. "Are you saying you haven't started writing the contract yet?"

"I," her body shook, but her eyes saw no sign of bright red danger blooming in her King, so she managed to squeak, "I have not. Forgive me, Your Majesty, but I have not."

"Even though you surely have enough ink now for it?"

Does he not hear me? "Yes, Your Majesty. It's my—I'm telling you that as Head Priestess of Cervora, it's my belief that we should wait to hear what Lady Ronterweis has to say about that woman before you bind yourself to her."

King Jädrich blinked. Helen's soul began buzzing all over again, this time loud enough in her skull that she worried her King would hear the senseless, raw noise that she spooled her thoughts from. She pressed her lips so tightly together that they squeaked, and she flinched when her King spoke.

"I will see myself bound to my Queen, Helen. I expect that contract written and on my desk for her and I to sign by tomorrow."

Helen's very soul quaked in her head. Never in all her life did she think she'd have to remind so pious and noble a King of what she was about to say—and truthfully, never did she expect to have the courage to say it nonetheless—but if there was one creature she truly feared more than her King, it was her goddess. Her goddess, whose authority superseded her King's. Just admitting that to herself made her soul prickle with anxiety that shot straight down her arms and legs in a mean river of tingles, but as Head Priestess, this was the one time she hoped she ever had to put her foot down against the Crown.

"Your Majesty," she said, and she cursed herself when her voice quaked, "Your Majesty, truly, I regret to inform you that without the full truth and transparency of both parties to be wed, the keepers of the Church of Cervora are not permitted to support any marriage contract. Not even that between a King and his chosen bride. This is per Statute Three of the Ecclesiastic Council of Cervora, implemented by the decree of the Holy Bishops, in the authority of the Succession of the Originals. It is Cervora's own law, illuminated one hundred and fifty-seven years after the founding of her great Church and revealed to the highest authority the

Church has. Please recognize the authority of Cervora's Church as her chosen monarch."

He'll see reason. Helen kept staring into King Jädrich's eyes, even as her soul shrank and shuddered. It might've escaped her head entirely just to get away from those unblinking things—ones that stared at her much the same way she'd seen wolves stare at little forest creatures. All she could do was have faith in her King. *He will.*

Then King Jädrich smiled. His lips pressed themselves thin as their corners quirked up, and his eyes crackled with a spark of magic that, had Helen not been paying attention, she might've missed. She stood as still as a rabbit staring down a fox, and as he sat up straight again, she waited for her King to acknowledge the truth she'd spoken.

"The Church's authority," he said, as if it were a joke. That alone was enough to make Helen's soul shrink into a pebble in her head. His was voice smooth and cold, even as the empty smile stayed plastered on his face. "Helen, you've served Cervora well as Head Priestess for many years, but I tell you now: your services are no longer needed. Pack your things and leave this castle by tomorrow evening. I've kept you from your family long enough."

Helen blinked. Then her hands dropped by her side. It was impossible to have heard what she thought she heard. Impossible. Over a century, she'd been not just any priestess, but Head Priestess. The one who instructed all other priestesses in their final internships in the castle cathedral, the one who kept the standards of priestesses in perfect order and inspected other churches every single year to ensure all met the Bishops' standard of excellence all across the lands. Only a mere step below a Bishop herself, she was the King's own personal connection to Cervora all this time. Over a century, she'd served both Crown and Church.

What did he mean, *return to her hometown?* This was her home. What did he mean, *I've kept you from your family?* Only Cervora could ever truly be called her Mother. What did he mean, *leave?* That her services were no longer needed? Her head might as well have become a crater, with how the words smashed her sense of self in. But before she could begin to understand—before she could think to laugh at what must've been a joke, surely, a joke—King Jädrich stood and made steady strides for the door. He turned the corner and left her there alone, disappearing into the dark hallway.

Her hands hung limp; her head ached as if bludgeoned. As she stared at the doorway, where her King had just been, her faith in that man she could've called *husband* began to wither like a single leaf from beyond the border—all brown and shriveled with the first frost.

The dim light of the Winter day hurt Aveline's eyes. All the soft grey of the clouds was too bright to stare into, yet not bright enough to make her squint. As she stood out there in that northern garden, overlooking the very edge of the world and all the dark, churning ocean beyond the Ringlands, however, she tried to bear that pain. The flowers of the garden and the horn of the Seat of Orr and the black, jagged shapes of the Iswold's trees—they scattered her thoughts. The dark waters of the sea lapped and curled and raged too much. The clouds, pale and plain as they were, created something of a canvas for her to cast her memories onto, so that they might be all the more vivid.

However, she could only soothe the ache in her eyes with long, slow blinks, where she caught the stare of

the doe-woman that haunted her. That little piece of
herself, one forged in twisting hunger and aching bones
and wicked nightmares, seemed to be growing impatient after a week of fruitless staring; Aveline's body
started twitching here and there with the urge to rip her
wings free and fly far away from the castle. As a result,
Aveline kept her body wrapped up tight in her dress
that morning. The openings for her wings were pinned
shut. Yet every time she blinked and saw the glimmer
of those marble-like doe eyes in the darkness, Aveline
knew: it was asking her a question. A sharp, yet wordless
question. Writing it in her bones. Using her blood as its
ink. Wrapping it in her skin for her to unravel when she
was ready to answer it.

Madness. It could've amused her, that ghost she'd conjured up from her own isolation. Could've entertained
her, if not for how it threatened to swallow her like that
churning sea beyond the limits of Winter. *Madness, pure
madness.*

When Aveline stared into those blank clouds, however, there were only flashes of her own mundane
memories—though not of Sekhbal. No, Sekhbal was
obscured behind fresher memories, ones full of the
ways she spent her otherwise peaceful days in the castle.
Pages and pages of scriptures and prophecies about
Cervora, about music and literature and Winter history, all mixed together in her mind's eye; she'd spent
as much time as she could eating up all she could know
about the god she was supposed to be and the people
she was supposed to convince of her façade. There was
no running away from such work. Not anymore. Aveline
chose her new mask, her new role, her new name, and
she intended to make the most of it—to do what she
could for the Ringlands, and for herself, if not for her
dead mother.

"Lady Rachfemd," called a guard. The sudden noise

made her flinch, and the guard's clipped tone sent a shiver down her spine. "Your presence is needed immediately by His Majesty the King."

Why?

They'd already done their work together; what more could Jädrich need her for? The question hovered over her, even as the haze of her memories made her mind sluggish. Rubbing the ache from her eyes, she tried her best not to acknowledge the stare of the doe-woman, or the way it reached through her body and soured her stomach with its wordless fear.

"A moment, please," she called back, and she stared down at the ground to blink the last of the ache away.

At her feet were two of her children, curled up under their icy wings and staring at the one who interrupted her garden cloud-watching. How ready to pounce they were, those precious *Unseelechs;* they'd stuck by her throughout her three weeks in the castle, and they still followed her everywhere she'd let them go. However, while seeing only two *Unseelechs* instead of three poked a hole in her heart every time, it seemed she was becoming more and more like an Ismar every day: it hurt less and less, knowing that one sacrificed itself to keep her safe, as if her heart were scabbing over with icy, armored scales.

When Aveline turned and stepped away, the *Unseelechs* leapt up and scrambled on the frozen dirt to follow her. They bobbed their silver-haired heads like parrots and flicked their ribbon-like tongues. Once, they'd been bald, with barely any light sparkling in their glassy eyes, but right then, they had as much hair on their heads and light in their eyes as any Ismar—all because she'd been feeding them white deer whenever she could. Whenever Jädrich was doing his duties, and the kitchens were left unguarded, Aveline would sneak in and take pieces of the evening's white deer and bring it to her children. It brightened their magic and made them ever more ferocious. With it, she hoped they'd have a better chance of escaping, should anyone ever try to get ahold of them again and crush them, too.

For the time being, feeding these creatures that deer meat was all she could do to make up for letting one of them die. She could only empower them with the magic, the strength, to survive if a situation like that ever happened again. Of course, she couldn't hide the evidence of her work. It shone too brightly in the faces of the *Unseelechs;* it was too obvious by the length of their hair. But no one dared say anything, nor did any security in the kitchens ever increase, even if the faces of servants and guards alike went rigid whenever she brought her children out to accompany her through the castle. With Ristef gone, though, there was no one she trusted to keep her safe more than these creatures that had already risked their lives for her once before.

The most worthy creatures, she thought as she drifted towards the garden entrance. She wasn't entirely sure where the thought came from. She just knew that it was what she believed from the bottom of her heart. *The most worthy, the most holy things, my babies.*

Aveline didn't have time to think any other thoughts as the *Unseelechs* clustered around her on their wolf-like feet, the talon-tips of their winged arms scratching at the ground. They squeaked, gurgled, cooed, and gnashed their dozens of thin, needle-like teeth in what Aveline came to understand as delight after weeks of watching them.

Finally, Aveline lifted her face to look at the guard. He stood there with an expression carved more of stone than ice: his brows were set so hard that they were like the shelf of a cliff. Even with that harsh look, though, this was a pretty ice-doll—one with short hair and purple chalcedony eyes that she was sure she'd seen before, probably with one of the bridal contestants. As for which one, she couldn't remember, but he was a tall man with broad shoulders and a straight, strong nose, his jaw sharp and his gaze resolute. She didn't like that determined edge in his eyes, but she liked it more than the guard that followed her around before: some *Franzel*, with his raking gaze and too-well-kept hair always managing to make a curtain that hid some angle of his face.

"What exactly does the King need me for?"

The guard hardly let her finish her sentence. "An audience has been called with Lady Clara Ronterweis and your cousin, Lord Erik Rachfemd."

Aveline stopped in her tracks and went stiff as the dead. That saggy-faced runt being back meant that Ristef would be back, too, but if that were the case, why wasn't it him that came to greet and escort her? Her dear friend, where was he? And Erik—what reason did he have to bother with her anymore? Unless he wanted to take this ruse of being her cousin seriously and grab the power of the King in any way he could. He never struck her as one that cared about snatching the throne, only about moving the seasons, though—or at least, that was what Aveline could see. He never did tell her his reasons for why he wanted that so badly.

The only way to find out what was going on was to see whatever circus was waiting for her, though, and so Aveline marched up to that guard while signaling her *Unseelechs*. A quick circle with her pointer finger told them to flank her and stay a pace or two back, so she could walk without tripping over them, and good creatures they were, they fell behind her immediately.

Aveline tipped her chin up. "You are?"

"Dieven Bertrisch, Your Majesty," he said with a polite half-bow, one hand at the breast of his black ice armor as if pledging himself to her. "Come with me, please.

Though," he stood up straight again and stared at the *Unseelechs*, "I don't know if His Majesty the King expects you to bring your—"

"They go where I go," she said as she brushed past him. Her hands folded in front of her, and her spine stayed stiff and straight as a post. Compared to the scrabbling, jerky movements of her *Unseelechs*, she must've looked even stiffer as she stared the guard down. "That will never change."

Where is Ristef?

Dieven gave one curt nod, then motioned for Aveline to begin walking out of the garden and down the hall. He walked beside her, never once stepping a toe in front of her as if her new status made some kind of invisible barrier in front of him, and he was careful not to bump into the gurgling *Unseelechs* as they scampered after their keeper. All the way through the twisting, starlight-washed halls, past the rest of the guest chambers and the map room, past Jädrich's study and the library, they were silent. Without their footsteps and the scratching of the *Unseelech's* talons scraping along the stone, there would've been no sound at all—as if this place were one great tomb.

Eventually, they came to a set of hallways Aveline didn't recognize. Dieven had to unlock a small, unassuming door at the end of an empty hallway for them to access it, and Aveline wondered if she hadn't pestered Ristef to open it once or twice, though there wasn't anything in the corridor that she remembered seeing. There wasn't anything interesting *worth* remembering; it was just stone and this one door.

The corridors that the door opened into, however, were wide set, more so than the rest of the castle, as if they were coming near the throne room—but that room was towards the center of the castle, and this was tucked away in the east of it. At least, Aveline thought it was the east. Navigating the castle's twists and turns left her disoriented every time she'd gone wandering around with Ristef. She would focus more on the art on the walls and the busts and moonflowers on their pedestals while he showed her around—things that could maybe help her remember where she'd been and where she could hide one day, should she need to.

They turned the corner, and Aveline stopped short when she saw the massive wooden doors with three guards watching over it. They didn't so much as twitch, even as Aveline came around the corner with her two *Unseelechs* clawing after her and chittering their strange beast language. Two huge, black metal rings hung from the reddish brown wood, and there were black strips and bolts holding the planks together. The door tapered at the top, creating a shape like a pointed cathedral window, and the bricks around it were old, chipped and worn away. Whatever this place was, it was a part of the castle built long ago, before fire was completely banished from the land—because that was the rough texture of iron.

"Everyone is inside, my lady," Dieven said.

He'd been in her blind spot for so long that when she heard his clipped voice, she jumped. Her *Unseelechs* scrambled around her feet, hissing and clicking at the guard the way they did when a rabbit leapt out while they hunted in the woods. Dieven glanced at them, his face frozen stiff, and he went to pull one side of the doors open.

Aveline slipped past him with her *Unseelechs* in tow. As the doors shut behind her, the *Unseelechs* quickly ran around her, then sat up on their haunches and spread their wings wide, as if to shield her from everyone in that room. Aveline tore her gaze away from her children and took note of the room, hoping to avoid direct eye contact with anyone there for a moment longer.

There was a huge window that let through the shreds of late morning light, and massive black lanterns that looked like cages for the silver orbs of starlight glowing within. A long console table of some rich red wood, similar to the door, held books and a silver vase of twigs with red berries frozen to them like beads of blood. A plush carpet of purple and green threads covered the floor underneath that table, and on the other side from the window were loveseats of rich maroon velvet and wood, as well as small end tables and bookshelves stuffed with old, tattered books. Above them all was a black chandelier full of starlights, and in the back of the room was a stone fireplace, blackened with soot that was never cleaned—a fireplace long since dead, its gray stone cold as any ice. On each side of the chimney were the four banners of the seasons: the orange and gold of Summer, the red and bronze of Autumn, the green and pink of Spring, the blue and silver of Winter.

Except three of those banners were tattered and torn, their symbols destroyed and their edges dirty and soiled. Only Winter's banner, with the deer skull and the snowflake, stood proud and untouched among the four. It sat all the way to the left, towards the window, where it could catch any stray shreds of sunlight and sparkle brighter than the rest. Though Aveline couldn't help but feel it didn't matter how much it shined. It wasn't much of a competition in the first place, given the state of ruin all the other banners were in.

But to look at those banners, Aveline had to look past the statuesque, magic-frosted figure of her husband, past the gleaming icicles of his crown and the glimmering silver of his coat buttons. So finally, Aveline had no choice but to look at him head on—and from there, begin her count of the figures she'd been trying, and failing, to fully block out.

There was Jädrich at the head of the table, hands

folded in front of him. His stare was as sharp as broken glass. He sat tall and straight, his long hair loose and draping down past his shoulders like a thick, shining curtain of silk threads. And the family jewel around his neck, the Femmel diamond, seemed not only to catch light, but absorb it, shining from deep within its center. Aveline wouldn't have been surprised to learn there was something magical in it, with how it sparkled. What light was it even catching to shine like that in this dingy place?

To his right was Clara, standing at attention with her good arm tucked behind her back. Her melted one hung there, a watery sack threatening to rip her arm's velvet clean off, and despite her face being a picture of graceful, if saggy indifference, her black eyes were just as dark, deep, and severe as the ones Aveline saw in her mind's eye. Beside her was the priestess, who, despite being the same height as Clara, looked like a child with the way she hunched and wrung her hands. And unlike Clara's sharp, focused stare, the priestess kept shifting around, glancing between Clara and Aveline and Jädrich like some twitchy bird.

Then on the other side of the table was Erik, his hair as manicured as ever; it cut straight across his brow line and brushed the stiff shoulder pads on his rich blue cloak, silver embroidery catching the light so greedily that it was like the coat itself were desperate to outshine Jädrich's crown. Unlike the other two in the room, his brows were pinched enough to crease the ice between them, and his lips were bent in a hard frown. No doubt, if he could, he'd give her an earful—but at least he was sitting in his chair as a free man, no shackles on his wrists. Whatever he was there for, it seemed no one found out about what Erik was really up to, dragging Aveline across the continent to drop into his King's lap.

Beside him, though, stood someone Aveline didn't

recognize. She wore head wrappings as if she'd suffered some injury, the cloth wrapping around her hair, ears, neck, and half her face. Her one eye was black like Clara's, yet completely devoid of shine, as if it was just an empty hole rather than any gemstone. Her face was as milky pale as Aveline's and any of the other Ismären in the room, and yet something about her clothes—cream-colored, shapeless, thick robes, ivory gloves—struck Aveline as odd. No one she'd encountered in Winter dressed like that, not even the priestess and her servant girls. She must've been a servant of Erik's from his home; that was the only thing she could think of.

Why would he take a servant? The castle has plenty.

Maybe to receive the frost Aveline had. No doubt those bandages were to hide any ugliness brought on by the melt. But as Aveline tore her eyes off that woman, she caught the twitch of something in the chair in front of her, opposite from Jädrich. A hand. There on the chair's arm rest was a glassy, transparent hand, covered in tattered brown cloth. It twitched again—a finger, trying to rise and squeaking from the effort—and Aveline slipped by her *Unseelechs* to get a better look at who this guest was.

When she peered past the chair's back, she and her *Unseelechs* both shrank back from the thing. It looked just like one of her babies, all bald and glassy-headed. But that head seemed thinner than her *Unseelechs'*, thin enough that she could see the glow of a soul radiating from inside. The clothes draped on its transparent body were torn at the edges and, in some places, threadbare enough that she could see through them to the sturdily carved body beneath. There were no pieces like her *Unseelechs*, no joints connected like a puppet's were. Nor was there any thin string of magic running to connect arm to shoulder, neck to torso. The thing—man?—also didn't turn to look at her. In fact, it seemed like it was trying to avoid her gaze.

It wasn't until she craned her neck further in front of this "guest" that she saw that familiar shade of banded blue in its eye sockets: two eyes made of blue lace agate.

She jumped like a startled cat. It made her *Unseelechs* panic, flapping and flying and scratching up the table in such a commotion that even the drained Ismar flinched—and squeaked, *cracked,* somewhere by his shoulder. Before the *Unseelechs* settled, Aveline grabbed the man's face, the ice cold enough to bite her palms, and she gently pushed his head up so she might stare even deeper into those familiar, once friendly eyes.

"Ristef?"

She studied him further as her dread prickled over her scalp, and that was when she got a good look at his hands. That finger that twitched and caught her eye was, apparently, his *only* finger—the smallest one, twitching there on his left hand. All the rest, it seemed, had been smashed off, reduced to nothing but jagged nubs of ice. The back of his hands, too, were covered in cracks that looked like spiderwebs: rings and rings of cracks that crawled across his ice and ended in long, jagged fractures. Aveline's breath stuck in her throat. Her heart fluttered so fast that it made her sick, and with a shaking hand, she reached for his sleeve, pulling it back. Up his arm, too, were more of those cracks, where some round thing had clearly punched into his ice. He thankfully hadn't been destroyed, like her one dead *Unseelech,* but was that anything to be thankful for, really? This here wasn't some monster that the Winter people cringed from. He was a *man,* an Ismar, and yet—and yet he'd still been cracked and broken like this?

His mouth opened just a hair, and the fault lines on the sides of his lips crunched and cracked further. Too much, it seemed, and his jaw would disconnect from his head. Aveline all but fell between his legs, one hand at his cheek as if she could stop his ice from breaking, the other grabbing a fistful of whatever pitiful rag of a shirt he'd been forced to wear.

"Aveline," came the tiniest little echo of his voice, though his lips didn't move. The sound was muffled as if it came from behind a thick wall. "I'm fine. Don't worry."

"You call this fine?"

"No, don't talk—"

"You call this *fine?*" Her voice was like flame from her lungs; it crackled and rasped as it ripped from her throat. All this time her guard was gone, she never dreamed he'd come back to her like this. Her eyes stung with tears as her mind whirred, wondering what could've possibly happened that made him end up like this. "You're a wreck. A wreck, Ristef."

"Aveline," came some voice behind her, but she hardly even heard it. She shot up and busied herself trying to rip the buttons free from Ristef's rags, so she could see where else, if anywhere, he'd been broken.

"Who did this?" Even though she couldn't take her eyes off her mangled guard, her question echoed through the room, inviting anyone to answer. Her voice rumbled like a big cat's growl; it was like the voice of her mother when she took her dragon form, low and deep and reminding everyone of her great and power-ful teeth. Ristef stared at her the whole time she loomed over him; his stare anchored her there and kept her from rounding on the people behind her with fury at her lips. Instead, she sucked in a deep, shuddering breath. "Who?"

"Aveline."

A freezing hand clamped on her shoulder and spun her around. Erik stared at her with silver lightning flashing across his eyes, and the sparkle of it wiped her thoughts clean. It was as if she'd been broken from a trance, between the shock of his cold hand and that silver sparkle, and she glanced around the room again, looking past Erik to see that advisor smiling. It was the only thing that changed about her: she still stood straight otherwise, even as the priestess behind her blinked with her mouth wide open. Even that odd woman that came with Erik sat there scowling at Aveline. Jädrich, it seemed, was the only one who hadn't budged—but his stare stayed just as intense as when she'd first walked in.

"Hmm." The advisor's head tilted. "I've never known an Ismarrin to take a breath like that."

Erik squeezed Aveline's shoulder hard enough to make her wince, his eyes full of magic as if he could strike her dead on the spot with that silver lightning, and then he let her go and returned to his seat. His lips were pressed into as fine a line as ice would allow, and the woman beside him stared into her lap. Aveline blinked at that melted advisor, her rage over Ristef hardening into something like coal in her stomach.

"You did this," Aveline said as she tipped her chin up to that advisor, "didn't you?"

Ronterweis's smile only grew. Aveline could've snatched her up right then and dashed what was left of her head's ice on the table—could've ripped that ugly thing's velvet with her teeth and let the water of her jaw spill all over the floor. And she might've, if she'd been within reach of that floppy-faced rat. Might've moved before she could stop herself. But all she could do was sit there and seethe.

Ronterweis didn't answer Aveline. Instead, she turned to Jädrich. "Shall we begin, Your Majesty?"

"Aveline," Ristef whispered, touching her wrist with his one intact finger, "careful."

That touch didn't do much to soothe her, but it kept

Aveline by Ristef's side, at least. When Jädrich nodded, Ronterweis took her hands out from behind her back. Rolled up tight in her fists was a small bundle of flaky papers. She carefully unrolled them and took one part—a smaller stack of yellowed papers—and set them before Jädrich. There was a small black stone, too, that she put on top of them, but it was too small to be a paperweight, and Jädrich slid it off into his hand easily enough as he took the notes. The other papers Ronterweis had were newer, large and white, and she read from them as the priestess sidled closer to her.

"Before I begin," she said as she looked up from her papers, "I understand that His Majesty has dismissed Head Priestess Helen Vorründ from her post. I have her here as another core witness to what I'm about to reveal, and after today's hearing, I do hope for her reinstatement in the castle's cathedral. Now, let me start in the simplest place: the matter of Lady Aveline Rachfemd's mysterious lack of records."

Aveline's anger cooled as if a Winter wind snatched up the last heat from a dying fire. *What is this?*

Lady Ronterweis continued: "At the beginning of the bridal competition, it was my duty as advisor to the King to vet all competitors. I will admit that I failed on two occasions: the first, in regards to Lady dur Dorrelenn, who proved to hold treasonous motives for joining. Luckily, her secrets were discovered after her moving into the castle, and she was quickly done away with. The second occasion, however, was in the case of Lady Rachfemd, whose records were virtually non-existent past what was necessary for competition entry."

Erik shifted, but he only raised his head high and kept silent.

Ronterweis paused as if expecting him to interrupt, but when he didn't, she continued. "Naturally, I found this suspicious, along with the Rachfemd house's claims that she'd gone on a century-long pilgrimage. More-over, I found her behavior strange in the competition's beginnings, which Priestess Vorründ can also speak to."

When Ronterweis nodded, the priestess stepped forward and squared her shoulders—but those quick twitches of her head towards Jädrich told Aveline that she was scared of him. The priestess gathered herself, nodded, then said, "Lady Rachfemd did display strange behavior, yes. She drank the milk of the evergreens while we spoke in the cathedral and didn't speak unless spoken to, and her answers about her pilgrimage were vague and difficult to parse."

"Thank you, Helen." Ronterweis nodded to the priestess, who immediately ducked behind her as if that half-melted thing could protect her from all the other people in that room. With a quick glance around, Ronterweis started again. "Ismären, as you all are aware, do not drink the milk of the evergreens—only the blood of Cervora's kin. This was the first of many oddities, but the consistent lack of records—birth records, pilgrimage records, anything—was of serious concern. So with His Majesty's approval, I began a deeper investigation into the house of Lord Erik Rachfemd and found no hint of this woman's existence."

Erik opened his mouth to speak, but a stern, sharp look from Jädrich was enough to shut him up before he'd uttered a word.

Ronterweis went on with a ghost of a smile still hanging off her ruined lips. "In any other case, the lack of any findings would clear a person of all doubts and suspicion, but in this case, the lack of records *was* a cause for suspicion. So I went further. I obtained a warrant from His Majesty to travel to the West Lakefields, to the late Lord Berlund Rachfemd's estate, where, in fact, we *did* find something." Clara looked towards Aveline and Ristef, her stare lingering as Aveline bristled. "Something that this guard, Ristef Gürrensig, found and tried to downplay. This is what His Majesty now holds: letters that were hidden in the attic of Lord Berlund Rachfemd's home by means of magical camouflage. These letters hold the truth of Lady Rachfemd's identity and origins."

"And what is the 'truth' in these letters?" Erik's hands clasped and hit the table as he leaned forward, though the shuffle of papers in Jädrich's hands made him pause. He gathered himself quickly and snapped, "Or, rather, what I *should* ask is: how do we know that they're authentic? As in, not something *you* planted there, Lady Ronterweis, with no oversight in my late uncle's home?"

Ronterweis paused, her smile soft, as if Erik were a child asking how many stars were in the sky. She tilted her head to the priestess and said, "Show them."

The priestess nodded, the sharp jerk nearly making her fake antlers slip off her head. She caught them in time and pointed to the little rune on the table beside Jädrich's hand. "Um, Your Majesty, may I?" He nodded without looking at her, and she took the piece, then squared her shoulders and continued, her voice wavering. "This is something captured by Headmistress Prischina Klassech. While Lady Ronterweis was away on this mission, I knew in my soul that something was amiss with Lady Rachfemd. I knew it more and more each week, when she did things that threatened the King—like putting a knife of bone to his neck."

"Careful, Aveline," Ristef whispered again. His voice was like the whisper of the dead, and it made Aveline's stomach flip. Her *Unseelechs,* too, crowded her feet and laid themselves on top of them, as if trying to anchor her to the floor; she felt one's tongue lick at her ankle the way a cat might groom its friend. "Keep quiet."

Aveline stilled. The good guard he was, he'd caught the twitch in her before even she knew what she was about to do, or what she wanted to say. She didn't dare glance at Erik, even though she could see his head snap towards her from the corner of his eye. However, as she settled with Ristef's touch, the truth was that Aveline couldn't have spoken if she wanted to. She found herself stuck, confused, as her body rioted with a mix of burning, squeezing rage in her heart and a heavy, stomach-freezing fear. All the little doubts that laid festering in Aveline's mind during the competition came out in full force, wriggling about and eating up her sanity.

Has this been the goal all this time? Was Jädrich waiting to catch me like this? Did he find the things I did execution-worthy after all?

Maybe that was why there hadn't been any contract to sign yet—but surely that wasn't the case. Couldn't have been. He knew about her hooves. Her antlers. Her frost. She was too valuable to him now; he couldn't just toss her away.

Or is that what he wanted me to think?

"I asked Headmistress Klassech to observe Lady Rachfemd, and the day of her dismissal, she gave me this rune and told me to show it when the time was right. I believe that time is now, though I admit that I don't know what's inside. This will be the first time any of us see its contents. With His Majesty's permission, I'll now show what the headmistress observed."

Jädrich nodded and looked up from those notes, laying them flat. He stayed silent, his face blank as if this were some casual meeting about taxes or land disputes or whatever it was that Kings talked about. Her mind went quiet. All the thoughts—*he's going to kill me, but no, he can't, but maybe he'll do worse, but he asked me to be his Queen*—were at war, battling each other until there was nothing left to think. She could only sit and watch, the way a lizard might watch a fox from under the desert brush, as the priestess crushed that rune in her hand and let the magic pour forth.

What did the headmistress catch me doing? It was anyone's guess. *When did she manage to watch me?*

But as the scene swirled up, recreating an image of Aveline's room in shades of white, black, and blue magical sparkles, her shoulders dropped. She didn't realize how tight they'd been until then. Still, of all the things one might've seen Aveline doing during the competition, this was the least of her worries: it was only a vision from after she'd caved into the urge for safety, for refuge, that dressing as a god would give her. After she'd gotten too close to Jädrich and found herself wanting every drop of his Winter cold. After she'd put on those Yasilan silks she'd asked Ristef to bring to her and knew, far too deeply, that a selfish coward like her didn't have any right to count herself among her mother's people. Her body relaxed as she watched it from the point of view of some little creature, some rat or other small thing, and all that rage and fear, all that confusion, evaporated from her heart. What was left, as she watched a phantom shadow of herself sob, was a deep-rooted numbness.

Ronterweis watched the last bits of magical dust settle onto the table, the rune spent, and her eyes slipped shut. Her smile grew, and she turned to Jädrich. "Again, those tears, that breath, those racking sobs—I've never known an Ismarrin to be able to do such things. And Yasilan silks," she murmured. "That's what Lady Rachfemd put on in that rune-stamp. Why else would she do so, unless the contents of those letters were true? Unless she really was the half-Summer bastard Berlund tried to hide all this time?"

All that made Erik shoot to his feet. "Forgive me, Lady Ronterweis, but you want us to believe *what?* That," he glanced at Aveline, "my cousin is a bastard? Of

Summer? How would an Ismar man even manage such a thing with one of those women?"

The way he said *those women* made Aveline's mouth bitter. She didn't have time to dwell on it, though, because Ronterweis shrugged and continued, "I don't need to know how. I see the evidence of it standing right there: breathing and growling like some beast. Even breathing some cloud of stuff, the way we all know dragons do. You saw it. Is there another reason ice would act like flesh, if not the reason in these letters?"

"Yes!"

Everyone paused. Even Jädrich's attention snagged on that outburst. That response came from behind Aveline, from the broken Ristef. Aveline once again crouched to his side, practically hanging off the chair's arm and taking gentle hold of his stubby, fractured hand. She wanted to tell him to be quiet and just wait until all this was done, so maybe he could get some help for his condition, but he'd opened his mouth enough to make the corners of them crack apart, and while his mouth never moved the way it would when a creature spoke, his voice echoed out of his head anyway, like a boom of muffled thunder.

"There is plenty reason, Your Majesty! Don't listen to her. *I* gave Lady Rachfemd those silks! I told you I'd gotten rid of them, but I gave them to her!"

"Ristef," Aveline hissed, "what—?"

"And those letters are *fake!* I tell you, they're *fake!* I believe Lady Ronterweis planted them, because there was nothing we found on the first day of our sweep of Lord Rachfemd's house! She wants to see Lady Rachfemd gone. I could see her conspiracy radiating from her very soul every time I glimpsed her while keeping my duties as Lady Rachfemd's guard: even now, I can see the wicked halo around her head! I can see just how deeply she *hates Lady Rachfemd!*"

Ronterweis blinked rapidly. Ristef's every other
word made her flinch as if she were getting pelted with
pebbles. The priestess, too, took a step back as if pushed
away by the force of his voice. Aveline's heart thudded
in her chest, as if the boom of his voice had injected
new life into it, and the scrape of a chair against stone
was the only thing loud enough to combat it.

"That guard there," Erik said, "is a faithful man. I've
seen him keeping careful watch over my cousin with my
own eyes. I hardly recognize him now, from whatever
abuse Lady Ronterweis put him through, and yet he
still speaks to the defense of my cousin. He knows, Your
Majesty, that this is slander."

A thick silence hung in the air. Jädrich kept leafing
through the letters as all this commotion went about,
as if no one was in the room with him to begin with,
and Aveline's heart sank. Why was he still reading, if he
knew what Aveline was?

Ronterweis's rasping words broke the silence. "How
could I invent these details, then, Lord Rachfemd?"
She tossed one of her papers down. "Did I forge these
census records, too? Did I invent this brothel, in Sekhbal's Garnet District? Did I conjure this *Lamivah,* whose
name is paired with a certain Aveline as of a hundred
and sixty-two years ago?" Ronterweis cast a curse of a
glare on Aveline and, with her lips twisted in a quivering
scowl, she straightened herself. "I've done my part. I've
given my findings. Now we wait for the King's justice
on you and that guard for this blatant harboring of a
mixed-blood, and for trying to foist it on the King's own
family line. The sacred line of Orr, I might remind you."

Aveline's scalp went alight with gooseflesh, to the
point that she thought she could feel every hair stand
up on her head. *You think this is done, don't you?* She rose
from Ristef's side, even as he tried to paw at her arm
with his almost-fingerless hand. Erik, too, glanced at her

with warning flashing in his eyes, as if trying to tell her to stay quiet—or maybe even to flee while she had the chance. But Aveline couldn't. *You think you've won.*

And the advisor might've won. It pierced Aveline like a knife in the lung, to hear her mother's name in that half-melted mouth. To hear her home, the Garnet District, mentioned. Her heart trembled in her chest, tangled in the urge to both run and hide *and* to rip throats out, to shred fine cloth and velvet alike. All she could do to soothe it was draw in a deep breath and let it loose. She looked at Ristef, glassy and bald like her *Unseelechs* before eating the white deer meat, and she wondered if she might not bring him back to the man she knew by giving him some, as well. There was only one source of honey-blood in that room right then—but that was all she needed. Even if her skin crawled with the thought of what she was about to do, and even if it made her mouth go dry as some feral, bone-deep fear leeched into her veins like poison, she fought her every muscle to bring her wrist to her mouth.

"What color should a half-Summer whelp's blood be?" Aveline stared at the greyish veins just under her skin, then glanced at Ronterweis. "Hmm? Tell me. Red, you think?"

Ronterweis blinked. Her voice was low, her words slow and careful. "I would guess so."

With a nod, Aveline snapped her head forward and bit down hard before her fear could stop her. The sting of broken skin made her flinch, and her mouth filled with the same flavor she'd found in any cup at the castle dining room table. Her *Unseelechs* scrambled from their place at her feet, ripping their talons over the carpet; their warning screeches filled the room, and their wing-talons scraped at her skirts. One even clambered up onto the table and stared around as if looking for the thing that injured Aveline, only to finally give up and huddle close when nothing was nearby. It gnashed its teeth in warning as the one still beneath the table wailed like a mother losing its child. It was a sound that went on and on and on, endless, from deep within the creature's ice; it was a sound that made Aveline's muscles twitch and stomach roil as if her body were revolting from some great sin. And the taste of such sweet blood made her shudder, made her heart race to the point that she thought she'd be sick. She pulled her wrist away, and in that bite mark were bubbles of silver blood. She held her wrist out where all could see it.

"What color is this?" Even if it satisfied her to see Ronterweis so small in the face of her *Unseelechs'* fury, staring like a frightened animal, Aveline pressed her. Her voice barely rose over the shrieks of the *Unseelechs*. Only when she clicked and barked a reprimand at them did their screeching cut off and leave a shocked silence behind. "What color?"

"I," Ronterweis shook her head as if breaking free of the spell the *Unseelechs* cast with their shrieking, and when she dared to look at Aveline's wrist, her eyes went almost too wide for her head, "that's not—"

It took all Aveline's effort to turn back to Ristef. Her body denied every degree of movement; her nerves shrieked and her blood burned as drops of silver rolled down her wrist. And when she blinked, those two doe eyes were so deep and dark in her mind's eye, so full of fury. They spoke to her, not in words, but in a heart-sinking, stomach-churning panic.

You said they'd never eat us again!

She did. Aveline did tell herself that. And yet, this didn't count as eating, when she pressed her wrist to Ristef's mouth. No, this didn't count, couldn't. It was just a little blood, after all. Her heart didn't need to flutter so hard. Her lungs didn't need to freeze like they did. Not for just a few drops of blood.

"Drink," she muttered, even as her lips tried to seal themselves shut, and Ristef stared at her much the same way Ronterweis did. He sat there like a statue with Aveline's blood dripping onto his lips and down his chin. "Drink!" Aveline barked again, and only then did his tongue gingerly meet her skin. As much as her body wanted to buck and bolt from the room, as much as her instinct wanted her to flee for the hills, as much as the *Unseelechs'* screaming echoed far away in her mind as if coming from her own soul, she sucked in a deep breath and forced herself still. She watched, morbidly satisfied, as each drop sank into Ristef's lips and face like coconut oil sank into a woman's skin.

"Aveline, Aveline, hey," came Erik's whisper as he crept up to her side.

He pulled her wrist from Ristef's mouth and inspected it himself, then grabbed her head and held it to his chest in a way Aveline never thought he'd do. Only then did it really begin to sink in, as she stood pressed against the viscount: if the letters were true, then she wasn't just playing a role. If whatever Ronterweis found was real, then in some wicked twist of fate, this cold man that dragged her into this mess *was* her cousin. Her last family in all the world.

Did he believe the letters? That his uncle was really her father? Would that change how he looked at her? She didn't know, and every part of her didn't want to care, either. A cold, haughty man like that wasn't the type of person Aveline wanted to call family. Yet some lonely little fragment of her soul made her curl tighter into her apparent cousin's arm. His gentle embrace tugged her away from Ristef, too, guiding her a couple steps to the side.

"Your Majesty," Erik continued, "you saw the silver. And—and now, look. Look at your guard. The magic spreading in his ice."

Aveline twisted her face against Erik's coat until she could look at Ristef again. It was true: his lips were blooming with that frosted color, and it was spreading across his face, as if the ice were filling with white ink. It was slowly spreading further, up to his scalp and down to his jaw, and little strands of hair began sprouting from his head.

"It's true that there are no records of my cousin's existence in this land," Erik said, and how strange it was, that Aveline felt no rumble from his chest like she might if he were flesh; instead, the voice echoed from above her, from his icy head. "It's true that she's no Ismarrin made of ice. It's true that her father was secretive and strange, and that he kept her hidden. But that's because she—"

"Don't you speak another word, Lord Rachfemd," Ronterweis snapped. "Don't even suggest whatever heresy you're about to conjure, or you'll be executed for that, too."

"It's true!" Ristef's voice rang out from his open mouth, and this time, his lips were able to form the words; his voice sounded strong, proper, not like it was echoing over miles and miles of frozen lands. "I saw it with my own eyes, the truth. And now I've tasted it." Ristef's gaze met Aveline's eyes. "This isn't a mixed-blood bastard. This isn't—it cannot be—a *Yasilan*. This is Cervora's Icon. And I would lose every limb if it meant I could keep her safe from you, Ronterweis."

"Show me."

Erik's hold loosened on Aveline, and she turned to see that mousy little priestess step up. Except she wasn't so mousy right then. Suddenly, she was as hyper-focused and wide-eyed as Ronterweis, her hands clasped perfectly in front of her. There was a coldness to her that Aveline hadn't ever seen before, a haunted air hovering around her.

"Show me the image of my Mother, if you're really her," the priestess muttered.

Those fake antlers reached up tall, but crooked, her hair mussed up from the leather band they'd been sewn into, and Aveline would've loved to put her costume to shame. But as she stepped away from Erik, she found herself glancing at Jädrich as if asking permission. It disturbed her: not once had Jädrich said a word about this circus playing out before him.

Jädrich saw her, though. He watched her with that ever-sharp stare, that ever-blank face. It felt like an hour passed, with him studying her the way he did, so cold and void of all expression. Then, finally, he nodded.

A sigh rushed out of Aveline, and her worries rushed out with it. It seemed those worries were for nothing. What was there for Jädrich to say, after all? He already knew what she was, and it didn't seem these letters changed that for him. At least, she wanted to believe so. But those details were *true*; the name of her mother, the Garnet District, all of it. Nobody would've known where to look for that information if not for those letters saying so; no one would've guessed Aveline were half *Yasilanah*, of all things. Even the advisor would've had a hard time fabricating something like that, surely.

Erik let her go, then gave one sharp jerk of his head, as if encouraging her to do something. And Aveline did. She snapped her fingers at that one frozen, confused little *Unseelech* that still crouched on the table. It startled, then scampered back down to huddle with the other one at Ristef's feet. Then Aveline kicked off her shoes and hopped up onto the table.

She padded towards that advisor and priestess and stared down at them with all the severity she could muster. Then she flexed her feet and scalp, popping the bones of her feet into place and sprouting her antlers from the dull points hidden under her hair. She grew taller still, towering over the little women, and she delighted in the way all expression fell from their faces.

"No," Ronterweis whispered. "That's—that can't—!"

Aveline cocked her head. "Is this not enough for you?"

"No! You're—you have Yasilan blood. This is just a part of your transformation! It has to be! I know what you dragonfolk can do; I've seen it myself!" Ronterweis balled up her one good fist, and Aveline had to admit that she was impressed with the advisor's stubbornness in the face of what she imagined was a frightful sight for her and the priestess. In fact, the priestess looked like she might just fall down and never get up, with how limp her arms hung at her side and how slack her jaw went. Ronterweis barked, "This is a farce! Show us the rest of you, mixed-blood! Show us!"

Aveline's back twitched. Were she an idiot, she might've let her wings rip free. Instead, she decided to show another piece of herself that would hopefully shut the advisor up for good.

"You can look at me and still doubt?" Aveline tutted her tongue and bent down to the advisor, who shook with such rage that her chin and melted arm wagged. Then Aveline whispered, "Fine, then. Take my blessing, which you so foolishly call *dragon's breath,* and know that you were wrong. I'll forgive you for being ignorant. But," Aveline's hand whipped out and snatched Ronterweis's chin, smushing it into a lumpy and awkward shape, and she leaned in closer to hiss, "I'll never forgive you for what you did to my guard. You will carry that sin for the rest of your wretched life; your body will be marked to match your shame."

Then she let her throat click, and before Ronterweis could rip herself free, she showered the runt in a wave of frost. Ronterweis's screams mixed with the sound of rapidly freezing ice.

4

FRANZEL HAD NEVER SEEN A MESS HALL SO GRIM. But then, they'd never experienced something so grim, either—never heard something so foul.

The mess hall was a cozy enough place, with the simple stone room lit by a cluster of starlights in the back wall and with five big, round tables to fit the fifty guards the castle had. It was a small number for a castle of this size, but then, more bodies didn't always mean more security. After all, the guards that worked in the castle were trained for the job, rather than just dressed in armor and tossed on some village post. But the small numbers made it impossible not to know almost every guard after years of work in the castle, and so there wasn't a face Franzel didn't recognize as he found his typical seat for his squad's appointed weekly meal.

He had a serving of silvery venison on a stone plate in one hand, a mug of bloodwine in the other, and he caught sight of Dieven at their usual round table, towards the back, where they were less likely to be bothered by people passing by. Except as he sat, Dieven barely tossed him a glance, and Dieven seemed more content to poke at the venison on his plate than eat it. This was the place where Franzel, Dieven, Gunther, Tirschel, Verrick, and rarely, Ristef, would gather for some reprieve from the chaos the bridal competition caused. It was where they could forget for a moment that they went from highly trained, highly specialized protectors of the King to little more than babysitters for rude, bizarre, and exhausting women. It was a place of peace.

That day, however, it seemed chaos followed them all into that mess hall. Something hung in the air that made the couple full tables of guards silent as the Winter night. Dieven, especially, had a frightening crease to his brow; his stare could've cut clean through the table and into the stone floor. Franzel set his plate down hard enough to make Dieven blink out of whatever fugue he was in, and he plopped himself in his chair, his armor scraping against its wooden frame.

"Some day it's been," Franzel said, then took a sip of the bloodwine.

It was thick, sweet, and cold—and as soon as it touched his ice, he felt the electrifying tingle of magic stitching back into his body. That tingle would become needling when he rested later, dragging the magic from his lips, throat, and stomach to the rest of his body and keeping him mobile and strong.

Dieven ran a hand over his short hair, but he didn't say anything.

"Haven't we all been thrown for a loop?" Franzel brought the cup to his lips again, then paused as he thought about it all. "You sure you heard right, Dieven? That your ear-runes were working right?"

Dieven didn't look up. "Yes."

Word traveled quickly around the guard hall. Once a couple other guards told him they had directives to *remove* the holy skull of Cervora from the throne room later that week, Franzel couldn't help but see what others knew about this. And once Dieven told him the things he'd heard through the ear-runes that guards wore to monitor otherwise entirely secret conversations in the King's conference rooms, it made more sense, why the King himself would do something so blasphemous as move Cervora from her display grave. Especially given what the party of guards that had gone to Rehrvig found out, with the old Rachfemd's letters. *That* story didn't take more than half a question before Gunther went and spilled the whole tale, top to bottom.

Even if the guards weren't court women given to gossiping about all manners of ridiculous things, there was no escaping the gravity of the situation. This was a scandal that took the whole troupe of fifty guardsmen by storm. It was so farfetched that even Franzel didn't want to believe it, really—but there was nothing to doubt by the end of that morning. Between all they'd seen that morning—a partially restored Ristef, a harrowed ghost of a priestess, and a completely frozen Ronterweis—no one could try and say that the story wasn't true.

And what a twist of fate it was that such a woman as Rachfemd, that wild thing, was the bastard child of a Summer whore. Franzel still wasn't entirely sure how such a thing was even possible, but the proof had apparently been walking among them all this time; she was flesh enough to bleed. Worse, though, was the story that mixed-blood was trying to peddle—selling herself as Cervora returned, even though it was obvious that her apparently silver blood and *frost breath* were just a lucky boon from her Summer and Winter halves. She had plenty Ismar magic, so it wouldn't make her blood a normal, brutish red color like fleshlings with no magic at all; he knew that from the other half-Winter abominations that once flitted about the capital. And frost breath? What else could that be, but a feature of the dragonfolk in the Summerlands? She looked no different than any normal woman when she left that conference room, according to Dieven, and so she was obviously nothing more than a fraud.

And the King believes her. That was the worst of it all. *The King believes that woman.*

An unspoken question hung over the dining hall. One so heavy and bloated that Franzel thought it'd drag him down to the floor and crush him while he ate. It seemed, as he glanced around, that the question was just as heavy on the heads of the others, too: they stayed low to their venison, their lips wrenched into deep frowns. None of them would ever say that question out loud— not if they didn't want to get fired from their post at best, executed for treason at worst. But that didn't stop it from swirling in their heads anyway.

"Well," Franzel said as he plunked his flagon back on the table, "no point in sitting all grim like that, now, is there, Dieven? Let me finish this up, and we can say hello to our battered friend, maybe."

Dieven blinked and stared at Franzel as he finished his last couple bites of venison. He opened his mouth and paused, looking something like a fish out of the sea, but someone else spoke up from the back of the room.

"No chance. Your *friend* is in the intensive ward; no one's seeing him until he's out."

Franzel cast a look over his shoulder to the unmannered eavesdropper, and he caught the stare of bright malachite eyes. In the corner of the room, like some backwoods highwayman, was Ehrwig Listermann. Franzel could've winced to see the big brute. For someone whose family name stemmed directly from the Faun's

Tongue word for *quiet,* this man always found a way to wrench that big mouth open and say something that was, at best, downright unpleasant.

Franzel tapped Dieven's shoulder as a silent sign to get up and leave. However, Ehrwig didn't even give anyone time to clear out from the dining hall before he stood up and folded his thick arms over his chest. Yes, Franzel could well imagine a highwayman looking the way Ehrwig did; he only needed cheap leather armor instead of the castle guard's fine black pauldrons.

"And if you ask me," Ehrwig said, "that rat got off easy. A castle guard, trying to slow the advisor down and even destroy evidence? If it were me," he glanced around the room of guards with their faces pinned to their plates, then settled his hard gaze on Franzel, "I would've crushed him right out there in the field. Thought Lady Ronterweis would let me for a minute, too."

Dieven shot up from his seat and squared his shoulders. He wasn't much shorter than Ehrwig, but his family certainly hadn't packed as much snow on him as a youth as Ehrwig's had. Strong as Dieven was, he looked slight compared to the barrels of Ehrwig's arms and the tree trunk he called a neck.

Ehrwig looked down his nose at Dieven, but when Dieven said nothing, the big man chuckled. Dieven looked like he *wanted* to say something, of course, but in a rare moment, it seemed the poor man was at a loss. Franzel didn't blame him, but a staredown with a man like Ehrwig wasn't the best time to be looking so conflicted.

After that tense silence went stale, though, Ehrwig looked around the dining hall at the other men that were starting to unstick their eyes from their food. "Can you believe that? The Gürrensig rat tried to protect a—!"

My Mother bled and butchered.

Somehow, it was Franzel that had to step in and plant a friendly, if firm, hand on Ehrwig's shoulder. "Ehrwig, haven't you hashed out enough of these details? Isn't the story getting a little old now? Maybe it's time to leave it be for a while," he said through a tight smile.

Franzel flicked his head aside as if to get his hair out of his face—but Ehrwig caught the way his gaze lingered in the castle corners. Even if it was the guards' job to keep the castle safe, it was the King's job to keep the guards in line—and the runes that recorded every day's worth of patrol teams taking their weekly meal were instrumental in that. Nobody in that room could ever forget that they were being watched as much as they were watching, and nobody, *nobody*, should've been willing to get an entire platoon tossed in Ronterweis's unholy interrogation rooms for something as ridiculous as sour political talk.

Ehrwig's lips curled into a mean smirk, his banded green eyes coming alive with the silvery magic of his undoubtedly crude thoughts, but he drew back and turned around. It looked like he'd head back to his seat in peace, which was something of a relief. Franzel turned to Dieven, who was still staring with a face carved of cold stone, but then Ehrwig's rough voice bounced off the walls once more.

"There's no 'leaving be' a traitor like that busted up doll we dragged back here today, Hervonder, and you know it. No leaving him be unless you wanna end up just like him."

Franzel turned to retort—something about *camaraderie* and *common causes* and how Ehrwig's ash-talk was effectively ruining both of those among their fellows—but then he found himself standing there alone, because Dieven went storming out the dining hall with steps heavy enough to shake the chairs as he passed them.

Without so much as a glance back at that brute he called a comrade, Franzel hurried after Dieven.

Luckily, Dieven hadn't gotten too far down the hallway, but by the hunch of his shoulders, his mind was already ways away. Franzel managed to get in front of him and take a gentle hold of his shoulder—though that didn't mean he'd get to look the man in the eye. Those two pieces of purple chalcedony were anchored to the floor.

"Dieven," Franzel started, "come on, now."

The stony-faced guard shrugged Franzel's hand off his shoulder and brushed past him without a word. At a loss, Franzel could only trail after him and keep trying to pull his partner out of his march of misery.

"It's not a good idea to lose your head over the words of a half-mad thing like Ehrwig," he said, though he kept his voice low. Cervora alone knew where else any recording runes were hidden in that massive castle. "Things are strange now, but—"

"Strange?" Dieven finally wheeled around and shoved a finger in Franzel's chest. "Strange? That's how you're going to describe this mess?"

A quick glance around the hallway confirmed that they were alone, so Franzel drew closer to Dieven and muttered, "What mess? The King has a Queen. More, she has silver blood and can cure the melt. The people don't know about the rest, and they don't need to if these things are true. There's no mess so long as we follow the King's lead and keep *quiet*."

The air went still, and then Dieven pulled away. His eyes were a shock of purple and crackling, angry silver, and his face once again creased with a harsh scowl.

"Heresy," he muttered. "You and Ristef both, you're promoting heresy, to call that Rachfemd woman Cervora's icon."

"I did not say that's what I thought she was," Franzel

snapped back. His voice was hardly more than a hiss. "I'm only saying—"

"That you'll go along with what you *know* is a lie for convenience's sake; yes, I'm aware. I've known you longer than a day." The scowl deepened on Dieven's face to the point that the shadows pooled between his brows like black water. "Just two weeks ago, you were telling me that woman would be a nightmare to have beside the King. Now here you are, willing to—"

"Yes, because that's *politics*," Franzel said with a tight smile. Meanwhile, he didn't doubt his own frustration was crackling across his eyes. Why did these backwater guards from small towns never understand these things? Franzel wasn't even from a particularly wealthy family, and he knew the value of the right words in the right places; why did people like Dieven never grasp the same? "If the King's willing to marry her and tout her around as Cervora's icon, who are we to say otherwise?"

As the seconds passed, the sparkle slowly faded from Dieven's eyes. All that was left were pale, hollow purple stones in his head as he stared at Franzel. The creases in his brow smoothed out. The hard edge of his frown softened. He blinked at Franzel, and then he shook his head and stared at the floor.

"We are children of Cervora," Dieven muttered, "and I just... after these past few weeks, after all this, I just can't turn on a pin like you, Franzel. Not after everything I saw and heard from that conference. I can't just decide to play along and pretend that thing is my Mother. Not some frost-breathing dragon-spawn that makes pets out of monsters like she does. I just," he shook his head, and then he gave Franzel a pointed look and tapped the corner of his purple chalcedony eyes, those spiritually attuned eyes of the pious that made him a favorite of the priestess for a long time, "I can't fathom it, if you understand. I won't fathom it."

Oh, no.

Then he turned away before Franzel could even think of a response and trudged off to his post. Franzel stared after him, then ran his hands through his hair and rested them on his head, as if his hands could be a helmet against the madness of this mess.

So it begins.

If only there were a runespell to turn back time and stop that woman from ever coming to the castle. Winter was not a country of men like Dieven, too honest for their own good—Franzel had plenty of reasons to conclude that growing up in the capital city—but the ones that *were* like Dieven, stoic and stuck hard to their values and their faith, were a liability. Combine that with brutes like Ehrwig that loved controversy, and they had the potential to take whatever good could be grabbed from this situation and ruin it. So what if the Rachfemd woman was a half-dragon? She could be drained of her frost and blood and dumped when her flesh body failed. Surely their King wasn't so stupid as to sign a *real* marriage contract with the thing, anyhow. He must've just been using her. That would be much easier, cleaner, and simpler than creating some uproar against her and ripping Winter clean in two.

Couldn't Dieven understand that? That maybe, the King wasn't so honest as him? That the King had plans, like Franzel would've? Why wouldn't he, with so much to lose, so much to protect, especially after all he'd already done for Winter?

So. It. Begins.

Franzel tapped his fingers to his head. The sound echoed straight to his soul and scattered all these thoughts, until there was nothing but stone and sconces full of starlight to think about. Then he smoothed his hair out and went to join Dieven at his post. He hoped, with heaviness in his ice, that the only thing he would have to keep watch over was the thickness of the silence that would settle between them—to make sure it never broke in the presence of the wrong people.

Your body will be marked to match your shame.
The castle doctor, Horvan dur Veldem, prodded Clara's chin and arm one more time, then threw his hands up. They clacked against his legs as he shook his head.

"It's true. Your melt is gone. I can't find a single spot of wet in there."

Clara stared at herself in the infirmary mirror. In that little space, with heavy white curtains partitioning each empty bed and full-length mirror, it was as if Clara were wrapped up in a box, like a doll, all blocked off from the world and unable to do anything about the mutt masquerading as a goddess.

Witch. Was the King a fool after all? *Dragon.*

But for all her racing thoughts, which hadn't slowed down since that wicked frost hit her face, Clara found her eyes fixed on nothing but herself. Nothing could've torn her away from the woman staring back at her, at the reality of just how wretched she'd become.

The rest of your wretched life.

Bits of that bastard woman's words scraped against her soul, like icy fingertips over rough stone. It'd been years since Clara looked at herself in a mirror like this. *Years.* She simply chopped her hair when it got into her face and left it at that. What reason was there to watch her face erode into a sloppy mess? What need did she have to remind herself more than necessary that she was doomed to die?

The idea that this melt could ever be fixed never crossed her mind. Before that moment in that conference room, after all, there'd never been any proven way to do it in the first place. She stared at her chin—at the dents in it, where that witch grabbed her and mangled her face before freezing it into this grotesque picture.

Marked to match your shame.

"Will it come back?" Clara couldn't fathom it. Didn't trust it. Refused to believe it—refused to believe there was any shame she had to bear like this. "Is this temporary, Doctor?"

The doctor leaned back in his chair, and Clara caught a glimpse of him in the background of her reflection. He, too, was a man who preferred to keep his hair short; in fact, it seemed he preferred no hair altogether, as the only place any grew was in a goatee around his thin lips. His bloodstone eyes were small, set deep into his sockets and overshadowed by his thick brows, and his nose was broad and flat. His body was hidden under a thick white doctor's coat, the fabric robbing him of any shape save for that of his jagged, work-worn hands.

Dr. dur Veldem ran one of those sharp hands over his bare head; the ice made a soft scraping sound. He stared at the wall and shrugged. "I don't know, my lady. I didn't even think such a thing was possible."

There was a static in the air—a stiffness to them both, a sterility in the silence. This was the King's greatest wish: to reverse the melt. It was his second greatest wish to find Cervora. Yet to gaze on Clara's face in that mirror, to see the melt undone and know the antler-headed beast that did it, poisoned the beauty of her King's wishes. This body Clara was left with showed no signs of holiness, and certainly no suggestion of miracle. Nobody could look at her chin and club-like arm and see anything but a curse.

"Is this something you think we should let happen?"

The question came out before Clara could stop it.

She stared at the doctor through the mirror's reflection, watching him pause and skate his gaze her way.

"I'm not sure what you—"

"The Queen-to-be," Clara bit out, "has been 'healing' people. With this frost." The frost Clara *knew* was the breath of a dragon, even if that witch tried to lie through her teeth with those antlers on her head. Or did the fool think Clara never witnessed a dragon spit its flame and venom before? "What she's done to me, she's done to others. As a doctor, is this something you think the Crown should allow without further study?"

As Clara watched that doctor's mouth open and close several times, his gaze darting from Clara to the floor and back again, Clara's soul shrank into a miserable, bitter lump in her head. Of course, others didn't know what she knew about that half-dragon. Not yet. So what could she expect from the man? What could a doctor say to what looked like such an easy cure to the melt?

No self-respecting doctor would've given up the chance to solve one of the greatest problems to plague the Ismären. Clara knew that. Even her own soul found itself tugging and pulling in different directions, knowing that bastard or not, dragon or not, Clara's face was healed—and so too could others' bodies be, if they used that half-dragon right. But no matter the benefits, Clara's mind reeled. How it twisted her soul in knots— how it tore her soul to *pieces*—knowing that witch would use such a blessing to lure the King into her filthy hands. Marriage was no trivial thing, not to even the most common Ismar. Marriage to the King—that *thing,* that beast, married to the *King* for all eternity—

"I do think it," the doctor eventually said, and it scattered Clara's thoughts. She let her eyes slip shut. "We don't know the long-term effects of this frost, true, but for all I've examined of you this afternoon, Lady Ronterweis... you are whole again. Perfectly un-melted. If this is something she can do for the people, if this is a terror she can save us from, then who are we to stop her from doing so?"

Now, don't give the beast that much credit. But Clara had nothing else to say. There was a piece of her that knew: no matter how convinced she was that the Rachfemd woman was a bastard, a fleshling, a rat that had no business attaching herself to the King and sullying the line of Orr... there was a nation of people waiting to be liberated of their fear of that wicked sun and all its melting heat. As advisor to the King, Clara knew that the King was first priority, and that *his* first priority was his people—making them essentially one in the same.

The door to the infirmary opened, and the sound of heavy boots on stone made Clara and the doctor share a wide-eyed glance. She tore her gaze from the mirror just in time to see that very King appear between those partitioning curtains.

Not a hair was out of place from when Clara saw him earlier that day, as if nothing in the world could've upset him and his peace—and for the most part, save for the first time Clara ever met her King in person nearly a century prior, nothing ever had. He stood tall, his white coat rimmed with greyish-white rabbit fur, the Femmel diamond sparkling in the middle of his chest. The icicles of his crown caught every scrap of light the infirmary had to offer and made it seem as if he were crowned in the very stuff of the heavens, and his face— Cervora's velvet, his face. Clara saw it every day, but rarely did she see it like that: with hard eyes gone half-closed and at ease, with the typically flat mask of his expression softened with the smallest hint of a smile.

A smile for her—as if she, in all her disgrace, were something worth his joy.

"I see you're well," he said. His voice washed over her, low and soothing, like a dusting of fresh snow.

King Jädrich's gaze never left Clara's face as he stepped into the small space. Dr. dur Veldem scrambled to attention, but he paused and sat back down when the King offered him a glance. When King Jädrich once again focused on Clara, and his gaze tracked all over the hideous mess that was her chin, the giant frozen club that had become her arm, it took everything Clara had not to shatter in shame. She stood tall, not daring to so much as duck her head, as her King had reprimanded her for that enough over the many years she'd been serving at his side.

"Your melt is fixed?" King Jädrich approached her as if she had the sweet and pious face of a court lady anyway; there was no wrinkle to his nose, no crease to his brow, as there were with so many other people that looked at her. "Completely?"

Clara nodded and motioned to the doctor. "According to Dr. dur Veldem, I am perfectly intact."

A smile broke out on the King's face, a *true* smile. It pulled his lips, it balled his cheeks, it made his eyes twinkle—and Clara could've stood there like a little fool forever, witnessing it.

"Good. Though I see," his smile slipped away like the evening light, and his gaze tracked over every odd curve of her chin, "that there may be some room for a change. It must not be comfortable to have your ice so out of place."

It certainly wasn't. Specifically, Clara's arm felt strange; the huge orb of ice at the end still threw her off balance when she walked, and with it refrozen, when she accidentally hit it on things, it ached with the threat of fractures and breakage. It was a wicked torture, a salvation and a curse all at once—just like that witch wanted.

"It is," Clara said, her voice clipped. Her next words rolled around within her, sharp and stinging as if she'd dumped briars into her head, and it took some effort to get the things out of her mouth. "Though it's what... our *Queen* decided I'm worthy of."

King Jädrich's face smoothed out into the plain, empty expression Clara was used to. He glanced at the doctor, and said, "Excuse us, Dr. dur Veldem. We have matters to discuss."

Without a word, the doctor slipped off his stool and scurried away. King Jädrich looked back at Clara with a gaze so piercing that it could've drilled a hole in her, all while the infirmary door creaked open and softly clicked shut. Once the doctor was gone, the silver mist of King Jädrich's magic wisped off his shoulders and from his hair, and as he lifted his hand to trace a glittering silver rune in the air, one word slipped free.

"*Låseleitum.*"

A silencing runespell. One to seal the sounds of this room from anyone outside. She held his stare, as she'd always done, and waited to see what he was hiding behind that mask—what would need a silencing runespell to say. Did he not like her tone? Did he have something to say about her case against his bride? Did he plan to punish her for her work, for the weeks she spent trying to prove that witch was not what her King thought she was? If so, she would stand and bear it—but what she presented that day were facts, *truth*. She would not recant truth, no matter what title the King wanted Clara to call that half-dragon.

"Don't trouble yourself with the whims of our Queen," King Jädrich said. Clara's brows smoothed out—though she hadn't realized she'd been bracing for the worst. She blinked, confused, as he continued. "She is of a different kind than us. I'll speak to her, and in the meantime, I'll call a Body Sculptor to relieve you of your current state."

But she's more than Queen. Clara forced her lips

straight. *She wants to crown herself goddess. Above you, my King.* How they twitched, though. How her lips begged to stretch into a smile. *Yet you're willing to—*

"In the meantime, are you well enough to continue your work?"

Clara paused. "I—of course. What can I do for you, Your Majesty?"

"In one week's time, I'll be leaving with the Queen to begin our tour around the country. I've already seen to it that the carriages are prepared and the guards to come with us have been chosen."

"What," Clara blinked in surprise, "but you haven't announced anything yet—!"

The King took a seat where the doctor had just been, and he took Clara's good hand. He ran his thumb over her velvet. Both of them were silent as the Winter mornings before he continued.

"This is what I need you to do: draft letters to the lords of Winter. Tell them that I will begin my departure from Vörnein in three weeks' time. Meanwhile, let Vörnein know that the wedding announcement will be at week's end. Let no one know of any plan otherwise, save for the list of guards I'll give you in advance." He sat back, his hand still in hers, and said, "Do not let a single one of them speak on this arrangement."

Clara shook her head. "I don't understand. Why—?"

He squeezed her hand, just enough to make her flinch at the sudden sharp twinge in her ice, and he shook his head. The infirmary's starlights made his crown sparkle.

"Another letter I need you to send," he whispered, and he paused, as if the words were gravel on his tongue, "is to the Sekhran."

What?

"We can't," Clara said. Her whole soul revolted against

the idea. "We—there are no fleshling messengers who can survive the other—"

"You will send it by stone-bird, directly over the lake," King Jädrich continued, as if Clara hadn't spoken at all. "I will instruct you by week's end what to write. You will give it to me to read over and mark with my seal before you send it, just as you will the letters to the Winter lords and the public announcement *today* after you've drafted them. And you will be ready, in one week's time, to send the stone-bird and take over my duties here in the castle until I return. I will be in touch with you as necessary for the duration of the tour, and I expect you to be in touch with me as necessary in kind."

What are you planning? She wanted to ask so desperately, but there was something in the half-lidded eyes, the long face of her King, that gave her pause. Still, a stone-bird? Those magic-animated contraptions hadn't been used in well over a century; the ones that remained were virtually defunct antiques. *What do you mean with this?*

And the Sekhran? What could he possibly want to say to the Sekhran? Unless perhaps he *had* heard Clara's report, and he *did* believe her about the mixed-blood. But then, why was he still pretending, in that silenced room, that the mutt would be his Queen?

"I—yes, Your Majesty, of course." The questions wouldn't form on her tongue, and the mention of the Sekhran all but fell from her head, as if she'd never heard it. She certainly didn't want to hear it. Nor could she quite grasp that King Jädrich was suggesting such a thing. "Is there anything else I can do? Any logistics you'd like me to take care of?" *Any terrible plans to talk you out of?* "Any other tasks I can take on for you—?"

He shook his head. "No. This is my responsibility, Clara," the King muttered. "I will manage this tour with my wife, your Queen, our Mother. All I need you to do is send those letters, an announcement to the public, and the stone-bird. All else, I will do."

A knock came at the door. While the runespell sealed all sounds off from within the room, all sounds without were still muffled only by the door, which was thin enough for the doctor's voice to leak through.

"Your Majesty, please excuse me, but I have a guard injured from training that needs an examination."

King Jädrich stared so deeply at Clara that all she could focus on were the blue diamonds of Orr's royal line. Little shimmers of magic crackled across the blue like wisps of dry snow. He whispered, "Trust me, Clara." Then he lifted his hand, traced a new rune in the air, and muttered, "*Galdum.*" The cancelling runespell.

"Come in," he said, and he rose from the doctor's seat. As the door clicked open, and the sound of footsteps echoed on the tile, King Jädrich once again looked down at her. "You've had a long journey, Clara. You should rest," he said, and he smiled as if he were a father smiling at a well behaved child. "I'll need you to be in proper wits when Lady Rachfemd and I leave to visit the other holds. As my advisor, I trust you to manage things here in my stead."

Then he tore his gaze off Clara and left, just as the doctor and a guard with a mangled shoulder pauldron entered her view. King Jädrich's steps were slow and sure and steady, quieter and quieter as they went farther and farther away. The only sound after that was the murmuring of the doctor to the injured guard. Clara wondered what kind of plot the King had brewing. One he wouldn't tell her, his own advisor, in a silenced room.

It'd been a week since the deer-antlered woman fixed her, and yet Hilde still couldn't believe how *strong* her leg was. After first feeling her toe break off inside her velvet so many years ago, she thought for sure that her whole body would melt and crumble piece by piece, until she was like those other women she'd seen that day in the King's pressing room: dilapidated sacks all half-conscious, their souls waterlogged and nearly dissolving into their ruined bodies. Hilde didn't understand why their families would've waited so long to ship them to the King; it would've been kinder to them to just pop them open with any old farm tool at that point.

Hilde drove one of those farm tools into the ground outside her family's house, far on the outskirts of the capital. It was a pick mattock for breaking up the frozen ground. While native Winter plants *could* dig their roots through frost and even rock, it still helped to give them some more coarse ground to start in. Hilde's family grew a variety of Winter's finest berries—frost berries, winterberries, glass grapes, all of that. They grew them once for the sake of making wines or aromatic jewelry and such for the travelers of other seasons, and now mostly for the rabbits and squirrels and things that pet shops sold to noble families. What anyone needed something strange and furry like a rabbit for, though, was anyone's guess. Not like one could hold the creature long without it freezing to death or without its body heat risking the melt.

That'd been how Hilde got caught, so long ago. While others were ruined by the High Summer, Hilde found herself noticing something amiss with her pinky toe not long after one of her family's sheep finished napping by her side. The residual heat from that stupid beast leaning on her foot for a little while—that was all it took to start the long and agonizing process of losing her leg, and then the whole rest of her body.

Her family begged her not to throw her life away by applying to be pressed in the castle. They demanded she stay and feel piece after piece of her drift away into the waterskin that became her leg. Had she not done that, though, and had she not snuck out to the castle after her application was approved, she never would've met the deer-lady that saved her.

Tell no one what you saw.

The King looked so severe that day, after that woman sprouted antlers and big cloppy hooves. The whole time that was happening, Hilde knew exactly who this deer-woman was—exactly who she was *supposed* to be. But one thing bothered her: how could a deer-woman breathe frost? She'd heard that clicking sound before, and it wasn't a sound that came from anything she considered holy. In fact, she remembered exactly where she'd heard it: years and years ago, decades ago, before the last Tour of Seasons. A few of those clicks came out of the throat of an orange-eyed, golden-haired Yasilan before he breathed the tiniest flame to light his tobacco pipe with. He'd had to stick the pipe in his mouth to light it, after a lot of whining and moaning about not being able to find any matches in this "gods-forsaken country."

But how was Hilde supposed to explain that? The King, he told her not to tell anyone—but what could she even tell? Who would believe her, if she told everyone that a deer woman with a dragon's... *frost* fixed her leg? Dragons didn't even have frost. None of it made sense in her head, never mind out loud. So she told her family that the King had found a way to reverse the melt, like he'd been trying to do ever since the Winter Wall went up. She even showed them that her leg was *frozen,* not simply amputated and replaced with a new leg—a half-fix that never guaranteed the melt wouldn't return somewhere else in the body. Like a fleshling disease, once melted, there was no hope of escaping it, no matter what one did to cut it off or replace their body parts.

What a ruckus that'd caused, though, telling her parents that her leg wasn't just replaced, but healed. It didn't take long for her parents to tell the others in their little village, nor did it take long for the news to reach inside the city, too. She could only hope that the King didn't fault her for telling people he'd found a cure for the inner melt, but surely he didn't think she could just come back to her home with a perfectly healed leg and stay quiet about it—especially when she wasn't supposed to come back at all.

"Hello, there."

Hilde nearly flung her mattock out of her hands when some voice echoed behind her. She spun around to face the stranger, and while the voice might've startled her for a moment, she wasn't surprised to see a woman with a bandage wrapped around her head. All her hair was likely stuck under that wrap, too, if there was any left, and only one black eye looked at her, the other eye covered by her wrappings. Her clothes were thick and near shapeless, as if she wore *layers* of heavy wool cloaks rimmed with furs, and her boots were likewise thick and clunky things. She smiled at Hilde, though not much; it was a smile she'd seen time and time again on the hopeless half-melts that bumbled into her garden looking for answers.

"Hi," Hilde said. She leaned on her mattock like it was a gentleman's cane. "Who are you?"

The woman's smile grew. "My name is Karina. I'm here to see about the woman whose leg was healed."

Hilde poked her healed leg out from under her skirts and tapped her hard calf. "Well, that would be me. I'm afraid I can't tell you anything I haven't already told everyone else in the village, though." Hilde eyed the woman. "There's a form, you know, if you're looking to get to the castle—"

Karina shook her head. "No, no. I'm not here to get myself fixed. I'm here to hear your story." She tilted her head, that one eye pinning Hilde. "The full story. I come from the castle, you see; I'm here to follow up on the refrozen people and share their testimony. Rest assured that anything you tell me will be anonymous."

"Oh," Hilde said with a blink. "I—um, well, alright. In that case, we should probably come inside. I can't talk long, though; no telling when my parents will be back."

Or Martin, for that matter: the boy she'd loved all her life in this hamlet, who never looked at her twice after he found out her foot was melted. But he'd come back to her once she walked back into the village on two stable, strong, fully frozen legs, and that in and of itself was nothing short of a miracle.

Karina nodded. "Just a few questions, and I'll be gone."

Erik could've counted his lucky stars that the servants around the castle were so simple minded—though their loose lips was something of concern. Still, overhearing that the King ordered the removal of Cervora's skull from the throne room, and spreading the rumor around the city, was easy for his half-fox assistant. She had an uncanny way of creating figures that could walk and talk and act just like people, and she sent them out among the unsuspecting Winter people in a way that made Erik wonder. What an odd way she stitched Akerijin theory with Ismar magic: using the latter to fuel the substitutes and puppets within the tradition of the former. Yet as much as such a fusion unnerved Erik, he couldn't deny the benefits of keeping the real half-fox close to watch over the half-Summer fool while puppets went about collecting information and sowing rumors.

But are the rumors enough? The things Isolde said still haunted him. *Is that enough?*

Maybe. According to Karina, half the town was in uproar with such a rumor, the other half in dismay, and all of them were itching to flood the palace looking for answers. It was the perfect recipe to gather a crowd in the town square that would make the bridal competition itself seem like a dull affair. Just the thought made Erik thankful he was already staying in the castle for a while; driving a carriage anywhere in the inner or middle parts of the city on the day of the wedding announcement would be a nightmare, no doubt.

Though three weeks seems like a long time to wai to start the tour. One could only hope the people would stay patient once they discovered the King and Aveline would be on the move.

In the meantime, Erik had other things to do—like ensure his allies stayed within his sight. Enough unexpected things had happened in the last three weeks, and neither Erik nor his allies could take any more surprises in the next three. Thankfully, by virtue of being Aveline's "cousin," Erik had some say in who came along in their tour around the country, and nobody faulted him for including the seamstress of the future Queen in their entourage; after all, she, too, knew of Aveline's flesh *and* had testimony of her healing frost. So there he sat, in the foyer of Aula Verrinson, the little seamstress in charge of weaving fine and regal coverings for the half-breed that maybe *wouldn't* end up torn and tattered by week's end.

It was a quaint place, despite Aula's renown: a sitting area in the front had a few small, round wooden tables, where Aula had moonflowers in pretty ice vases. The walls were lined with benches, all covered in green and blue cushions with Aula's embroidery on them: deer antlers, flowers, swirling silver patterns, bright red berries. A large grandfather clock ticked away in the very back, and across from it all was the counter, where bolts of fabric stuck out of dark cubby holes lining the wall. A door led to Aula's sewing room, where Aveline had been fitted for the past few pieces she'd gotten, and to the side of that, against the wall, was a stairwell that led up to where Aula rested her head for the night. The store counter itself was covered in order sheets, sample buttons for coats, sample furs in a variety of colors, and a small lockbox where Aula kept her more minor payments. Erik thought half the time that it was more a decoy than anything; he knew well enough that the money he'd paid her for the half-breed's dresses wouldn't ever fit in a lockbox that small.

So much money. Erik tapped his teeth to his lip. *For such an animal.*

When he thought about how Aveline looked at him, and how her eyes shined that day in the King's conference room, he bit harder on his lip. It was the softest he'd ever heard her speak that day. The gentlest.

Do you think, maybe, that Berlund really was—?

No. Not for a moment. He would've bitten straight through the ice of his lip then, had the sting of his magic underneath not warned him off it. The fact that the advisor could invent such a wicked tale just to bury the half-breed was abysmal. From what gossip he'd picked up at the ball on the first week, that advisor had been doe-eyeing the King for years, forgetting her place with all that melt in her face and her arm. No doubt she would've dragged any bridal competitor by her hair right down to the dungeons for looking at the King too sharply, just so she could stay relevant to her Lord and master. Erik found it pitiful, to be so content living like an Autumn lapdog, those tiny and miserable pets.

But to go to such lengths to make such a pile of letters? Why? Erik didn't understand that part. Surely one or two and a census record Erik apparently didn't pay enough to purge was enough. *Why so many?*

If, somehow, those letters *weren't* forged, then Erik could've drilled a hole in his own head and let his soul fly home. It would be his luck, that the only family he had left in all the world would be a wildling of Summer, a bastard his uncle sired on a whim in a foreign country.

The door behind the counter opened, and Aula hurried out with an arm full of new dresses. They were in that ugly, looser style, the skirts thick and limp like curtains, the sleeve cuffs swallowed by all the extra fabric that the sleeves had. And the long drop in the neckline, that v-shape, it made everyone with half a lick of sense understand that Aveline was something strange. One

could see the bones of her ribs against her skin with
a neckline so low. The more Erik had to look at such
things, the more he wondered if he could see the influence of Summer silks in them: the tops and skirts, the
loose and flowing things built for arid deserts.

None of that mattered, though. Aveline liked them,
and she wouldn't destroy them, so Erik would buy
them. Or, rather, the King would buy them, because
Aveline had become his responsibility to clothe and
feed.

"And here you are!" Aula, chipper as ever, plopped
the dresses down on the table Erik had been waiting at.
There were three: one an icy, light blue, another black
one with silver embroidery, and one a strange lavender
color with gold embroidery around the waist. It moved
from the waist down, as if the threads were actually a
heavy belt weighed down around the hips, and it trailed
down into the folds of the skirt, little bits of gold peeking out as the light, gauzy fabric rustled in the slightest
bit of wind. "What do you think? Will she like them?"

Erik had to admit: Aula's stitchwork had improved
considerably since Aveline cured her of the melt in her
fingers. But the gold wasn't something he'd asked for.

"What is this?" He pointed to it and then noticed,
underneath that lavender thing, that there were bits of
gold peeking from the black and silver, too. "Gold, on
the Mother of Winter?"

Aula's smile slipped. "Well, I just—I thought she
might like the gold. She is from Su—"

"Ah-ah!" Erik raised a hand, and Aula fell silent. "Quiet. You never know who's listening. But Aula, you know
better than to put gold on someone like my cousin's out
to be."

That made Aula start. "'Out to be'? What do you
mean by—?"

"Enough. The dresses are fine for me, I suppose, but

it's Aveline and the King that'll have to make that final call. That said, Aula," he glanced at her, "should they need alterations, we'll be needing you to come along and make them while those two are on the road. The King is requesting you to come with us when he and his Queen make their rounds through Winter."

Aula blinked. "What? But I can't leave my studio. All my tools are here."

"So take your tools. I'm sure the King will even rent a whole carriage for your most important fabric bolts." Erik stood up straight, and at his full height, he dwarfed the little seamstress to the point that one might've mistaken her for a child. "We need you, Aula. Not only for your skill with dresses, but," he nodded to her hands, "for your testimony. Maybe you've heard the whispers?"

Her face was starting to scrunch, her velvet wrinkling as she pursed her lips. She was thinking too hard about a simple command again, as she always did. But she managed to pull herself out of those thoughts enough to shake her head.

Erik said, "I'm hearing through the network that someone's been stirring up some trouble before Aveline even gets on the road. Someone's been out, preaching heresy—saying not to trust a goddess that can be eaten twice." And Erik could only guess the source of whatever nonsense Karina picked up in her own rumor-spreading. He'd sent exactly the right words to Isolde, for her to sprinkle through her own people as new gossip—and yet what did he expect? There would always be naysayers. There would always be fools, ready to spit on a gift too good for them. Maybe Isolde was right; maybe the souls were too sour, and their campaign against the King all these years worked a touch too well. But if a course could be started, it could be reversed. No doubt enough rumors about Aveline, good and bad, would mix until all the confusion would settle into a raging need to *know* what it was that claimed to be Queen and Mother—and when they saw her, experienced her frost for themselves, then they would certainly know. Erik leaned towards Aula. "Your testimony, Aula—Aveline needs it, before lies poison the people. So come with us. Stay by your savior's side."

Her lips wrenched further, her frozen hands squeaking with how tight she balled them into fists, and she looked around at her studio. "But... but Erik, what about—?"

"What about what?" He saw where her stare went: past him, towards the stairwell. "What about that tomb you have upstairs? It'll be fine, Aula. I have plenty connections here. Trust that your home will stay exactly as it is until you get back."

She deflated so dramatically that it was as if her ice were melting down into a sad little lump under her velvet.

"Aula," Erik said, softer, "this is a house. Not a fleshling graveyard. You don't need to tend to it like one."

That made her flinch. She loosened her hands, only to wring them together, and she cast one more wide-eyed look to those stairs. Her head drooped, and her gaze snagged on the dresses next. Then she shook her head.

"But... the seasons aren't moving. We didn't do anything we were supposed to, Erik. What right do I have to leave when I couldn't do anything to make sure we did what we needed to do?"

Erik tamed the urge to frown. He landed a gentle hand on her shoulder and said, "You don't know what Aveline will do. Stop speaking as if our Queen and Mother abandoned us. Come and speak to her yourself, if you wish, but trust her, will you?"

Trust me. Aula blinked at him. Then, a moment later, the worry began thawing off her face, until finally, her mouth set in a hard line and her eyes sparkled with something strong and resolute. *Trust my plan. We'll get what we want yet.*

"Only for a little while, right?" Aula squared her shoulders. "Just for their run around the country? Right?"

Erik paused, then smiled. "Of course. It might take a couple months or so, but you'll be back before you know it."

Aula's eyes fluttered with rapid blinks, and then she nodded. "You let me know when it's time to go, then, and I'll shut down the shop and come up to join you." But it seemed her resolution wasn't as strong as Erik would hope, because again, she glanced towards the stairwell—towards the place where the poor thing watched her Spring butterfly husband be shattered to pieces by Winter guards after Winter's deep frost claimed him. "Only a couple months, right? I'll only be gone a couple months?"

Erik squeezed her shoulder. "Only a couple months."

Even in the face of the seamstress's worry, it was surprisingly easy for such a lie to roll off his tongue. Surely, after the last part of his plan happened, and Aveline was taken for ransom, the whole lot of them—Erik and all his allies, including one as seemingly innocent as a seamstress—would have a long wait ahead of them to see who would buckle first. The King had his crown, yes, but the oligarchs-to-be, well—they had his people. A good deal of them. What was a King, at the end of the day, without his people? What hope did he have to keep his crown when nobody wanted him to have it?

And Aveline—hapless, naive Aveline. The half-breed would have to be reminded of why she was taken off her miserable mountain and brought to Winter in the first place. She would have to learn that her antlers, hooves, and frost were not the protection she thought they were, but her greatest liability.

Efir knew the journey to Summer's allies in this country would be difficult, but he'd never expected it to be so slow, too. He cursed the snows, cursed the clouds, and especially cursed the people, who he had to be careful of even some miles away from town. Only at night did the ice-people seem to pause their work and turn their lights out, much like true men, and Efir found that strange. For what reason would they need to pause at all? Were they not immortal, fleshless, and full of magic? What should've stopped them from working all day, every day, forever?

Yet as he snuck through the woods one night and came upon a small hamlet, he once again found that this was not the case. He was near where he wanted to be: the port city called Taubech, where some treason-ous little noblewoman might've been able to tell him what happened with the witch. She might've also been able to help him achieve his mission, though in what way, he wasn't sure. As a Summerland assassin, he was content to do all his work alone, and yet his own mother insisted on getting any scrap of help he could from the ice-people.

He waded through easily waist-high snow and thought maybe his mother was wise to suggest it, after all. Even through his layers of thick furs, and even with the heating stones strapped into the middle layers, that snow threatened to liberate him of at least a few fingers and toes. Maybe even a whole leg, if he wasn't careful. He was a young dragon compared to his broth-ers and sisters, born after the Tour of Seasons stopped; all he knew about the Winters his homeland once experienced were from his elders' stories, and they all described them as terrible, miserable times. Yet if any of his countrymen could feel true Winter, and how cruel the frost was in its native lands, they'd likely have to redefine the very meaning of *misery*. How anyone could wish for such bitter cold in Summer was almost unconceivable. Almost.

Wicked as Winter was, so long as the desert spread, and the crops died for lack of water, and the seasonal fruits were all leaf, no flower, there was no choice but to invite this wickedness back into their homes. It became clear very quickly to desert and swampland dragon alike: the temporary death of Winter was necessary to stave off the permanent death wrought by the restless golden dragon god the Yasilanri feared.

Efir crept towards the tree line, where the snow was thinner, until he eventually noticed lights in the distance. Careful to stay out of sight, he slowed his steps and crouched low. After a moment, however, it seemed there were no guards in sight, and only one or two people out on the roads, too. They were distant shapes, skinny things, though the way they hobbled about with their stiff, limping gait made them seem more like wraiths from scary stories his older siblings used to tell him. He should've kept slipping past, and yet he couldn't. Against all his instincts, he drifted closer to the little hamlet, until he risked leaving the cover of trees entirely.

Someone was definitely walking closer, from the other side of town. The closest house was only a few feet away from Efir, the distance no more than a road's width, and it was one of the only ones that still had any light in it. Blue, ghastly, eerie light, of course, no candleflame—it looked to Efir as if Malouçe had lost a piece of her radiant self in that house—and this person was going towards it as if drawn to it. The moon was nowhere in sight that night; it was only the lantern posts full of those eerie lights and this house that gave off anything to see by. Luckily for Efir, seeing in the dark wasn't *as* much of a problem as it was for his desert-blooded siblings, but the blue tint of this unnatural light made his eyes hurt.

Still, the person hobbled on, shuffling over the frozen ground and letting one arm hang limp. As they came closer, Efir thought it might've been a man, what with the dirtied pants and workman's tunic, and it seemed this man was bald, too, bald like the old men of Sekh-bal. Over his shoulder was an axe, from the shape it cut, and it looked like he was trying as hard as possible not to move the hand and arm that held it to him. But then there was a crack, loud and sharp as wood cleanly split, and that arm fell. The hand still held onto the axe, though. It scraped along the ground in a way that made Efir's skin prickle with gooseflesh, as it had been doing so very often during the short time he'd been past Winter's wall.

The door of this still-lit house burst open with a bang, and out came what looked like a woman. Efir couldn't quite tell at first if it was a woman or a child, with how small the Ismar women tended to be, but if the hat-like wrap on her hair and her apron didn't give it away, her voice did.

"Ehrmond! *Vach seidens din za sparlet najunt? Komm!*" The woman barked what sounded like reprimands, though in a language *this* gutteral and snappish, Efir thought he might've mistaken even simple tavern conversation as an argument. It'd been so long since he'd spoken the Winter language, however, that it took him a moment to understand what was being said. *What are you doing out so late? Come!* The words had some strange slant to them, a fierce accent that seemed to make more use of their hard teeth and tongue than their voice.

Efir should've kept moving. He had things to do, after all, important things. Yet he couldn't drag himself away from the tree line as this *Ehrmond* fellow dragged himself closer to his house and his apparent wife. Unlike him, his wife moved like a real person, her skirts billowing as she rushed to him and her arms easily, fluidly reaching for him. She took his axe from him and inspected that cracked arm as she walked alongside him, then shook her head.

"You're going to break yourself," she snapped. "I told you to stop this!"

The man hobbled in silence for a moment, then muttered so miserably that Efir could barely make it out: "We need the money. I told you: we need the money. For Petra."

"Oh," the woman looked around as if seeking help from the very night air, "enough with that! We can make do! We can ration the meat a little better! Petra and I don't need nearly so much as you!" When Ehrmond was silent, she added, "What good is all the extra money if you break your arm off and we need to spend it getting a *Korbeldauer* to fix you?"

A what? Efir never heard that word. It must've had something to do with their ice bodies—maybe a doctor or the like. Strange, that ice-people should ever have need of a doctor.

"I won't break," he muttered. "I'm careful."

"*This* is careful—?"

"Might we not argue about it in the road, Herda?" They came to the door, and Herda stopped her husband from reaching for it. She opened it for him and let him through, then set his axe against the wall outside.

As he passed the threshold, however, Efir caught one last grumble from that woman: "This isn't right. Damn the King. Damn him for abandoning us like this."

"Herda!" A sharp squeak, like ice under serious pressure, nearly masked that man's hiss. "Hush! You never know who listens!"

Indeed, they did not. Though better Efir heard them than some town guard. But Herda fell silent and followed her husband into the house, and then all Efir might've heard of their conversation was muffled by wooden walls and thick windows. He didn't know what ice-people even needed money for if they could make their own clothes and didn't need food—but then, by the looks of that man, they needed *something*. Something, perhaps, like the stuff he'd heard the Winter people used to bring along on the Tour of Seasons.

Dried pieces of their country's divine deer. Pellets of the creatures' blood.

The thought made Efir's throat squeeze. Sinful, these people; they lived forever in the worst sin, one Efir and his people could hardly imagine. It was deicide that started these creatures' existence, and it seemed they made a centuries-old tradition of it—ritualized the continuous culling and consuming the flesh of the very deer they claimed their goddess rose up from. Efir's gooseflesh turned to outright pins and needles along his scalp the more he thought about it, until he had no choice but to push the thoughts from his mind and keep walking.

But if his map and compass were correct, then this was the little hamlet of Venderhein. The old port town he wanted to go to was only a short way west. And as disturbing as that conversation was to overhear, as odd as that man was to watch, it confirmed it all the more for him: he was in a land controlled by the King's enemies. His mother told him about what their Winter spy reported: that their allies within the walls had been poisoning the minds of the people against the King, so that when he fell, the people would be more willing to accept new rulers that would move the seasons once more. It was a sensible plan—if Winter would ever get the chance to dispose of their King in the first place. It was far too late for that, though. Far too late for the rest of the Ringlands to risk trying another plan and sparing these unnatural, unholy ice-people.

Still, as Efir crept on, he didn't let his guard down. His mother impressed that on him before he'd left; she, the Head of Surveillance, had personally tutored him in the ways of Winter from what their spies told them, so that he might know exactly the lands he was stepping into.

No matter how much they come to hate their King, they'll never hate him more than a Yasilan. Her eyes—he'd never seen her eyes so bright green, burning with urgency. *Never let the common people see you. Not even once. Not on the ground, not in the skies. Never, my son.*

Had she spoken to or looked at him any other way, he might've thought it wasn't *so* serious. He was prone to taking risks. But that look in her eye haunted him as he crawled through the snow. Made his heart thud with a deep, black poison he thought he'd long sucked out of his veins—a poison that his mother always told him would keep him safe in small doses.

Be afraid, my son, so you might remember to be cautious. Be afraid of being alone in the world of this enemy, that you might come home to me.

THREE DAYS AFTER THAT WRETCHED MOMENT in the conference room, Helen could put off her leaving no more. She stood by the carriage the King provided her and held her trunk's handle tight enough to make her ice smart. In that trunk were her robes, her jewelry, and her ceremonial headwear—the antlers of one of Cervora's kin that she'd worn for decades, carefully maintaining them so that they always looked as if they were still attached to a living creature. All her life, ever since she was a girl, she'd looked up at those statues of Cervora and felt love crystallize deep in her soul. Her goddess was so beautiful in every book she'd read, in every painting she looked at, in every statue she'd seen: soft and sweet faced, innocent and yet motherly all at once. Forever young. Forever gentle and graceful.

What is that monster? King Jädrich really wanted Helen to believe she'd been looking at her goddess for three weeks without knowing. He wanted her to believe that Cervora, the delicate thing of all their most cherished stories, was actually a bony, wraith-like thing, all sharp nails and strange accent and dark, star-filled eyes. And the evidence Clara brought—of her being half-Yasilanah? Half *Summer*?—it all connected when she spewed up that frost the way a Yasilan dragon might spit fire. There was no denying it. *What is that demon?*

It wasn't Helen's goddess. Not the one she'd devoted her entire life to. No, that thing, that wraith, was nothing short of a curse—though what her people did to earn such a curse, she couldn't guess. She only knew that this was wrong, all wrong. There was no love in her soul as she slid her trunk onto the carriage's back end and strapped it in with the others. In fact, her head felt empty. Dead of thought, dead of feeling.

Dead of faith.

It was empty on top, too, lighter without her antlers reaching up from her head, and it was strange, looking through the curtain of her hair that her headband normally kept out of her face. Her body, too, felt heavy—both because of her dread, and because of the heavier fabric of her civilian dress, the blue and white wool weighing her down. Even if King Jädrich hadn't insisted she leave and return to her home village, she knew she could no longer wear her antlers or her robes or her priestly jewelry after witnessing what she did in that conference room. She knew he'd intended her to be a priest for a smaller crowd, back among her friends and family that hadn't left her little village, but what would she preach about then? And *how* could she ever bring herself to preach it?

If this thing was really what her King saw as Cervora returned, then they were lost as a people. They were doomed. A half-Yasilanah, a whore's daughter, *Cervora?* Helen couldn't bear the thought. Couldn't tolerate it.

She would sooner puke up the idea like a piece of rabbit flesh, full of hot red poison, than accept it. She would sooner melt than bow her head to such disgrace and call it *holy*.

"Are you ready to leave, Lady Vorründ?"

One of the castle attendants came to her side: a common man, face marked with fault lines from years of smiling and laughing and whatever else without enough magic to keep him fluid. Many times had Helen given him his due during the cathedral services, but it seemed he used more magic than the services and castle rations could keep up with while working around the castle. His brows were bushy, his head bald, his mouth rimmed with fine silver hair in a well-maintained goatee, and his citrine eyes reminded her of the sun on those rare clear evenings. He gave her a brief smile, but it didn't reach his eyes. As he scanned her, she thought maybe he was just disturbed to see her dressed so plainly. She would've been, too, if a Queen were decided and the Head Priestess that would've overseen the marriage was told to *leave*.

Helen glanced one last time at the castle. Then she said, "I am."

"Come along, then. We've got a long journey."

"Do you have enough provisions to get us through? Enough meat?"

"That and a skin full of bloodwine, yes. We should be fine."

Helen nodded, comforted. Then she let him lead her to the carriage door, and he helped her up into the empty space. The window shades were open, and so she got to look at the castle for another few moments while her driver got settled onto the carriage. After a moment, the carriage lurched forward, the driver's magic hard at work turning the wheels, and they were off.

As the castle grew smaller and smaller from the

bridge, as it disappeared amidst the cluster of houses and buildings in Vörnein, and as the city gates themselves eventually passed over them, shutting them out of that beautiful place, Helen thought hard. She turned this tragedy over in her mind, again and again, and she also revisited the words of Clara, that poor thing. Just before Clara was taken into the infirmary to be checked over after being washed in that beast's frost, she looked at Helen and gave one simple command: *tell the people. Tell them.*

Helen liked to think she knew Clara well enough to know what it was she wanted the disgraced priestess to tell.

So Helen decided: she would still preach, as was her duty. For her people's sake, she would preach, and she would warn the people of what was coming. Helen would tell them about what she'd seen—the mixed-blood that *must've* lied about being Cervora. She would not let their faith wither like hers, stomped underneath the hooves of that *thing*. Helen's soul squeezed, prickled as if full of needles, as she thought of her misled King. She clasped her hands and prayed to whoever would listen:

May the true Ismären never bow to that woman. May the true Cervora stay alive in their souls' memory, the true Mother. May the King see his mistakes.

"Why can't I see him?" Aveline could've slapped the guard by the door of the intensive care ward. It'd already been a few days since he'd been admitted there, and Aveline thought she'd waited long enough to see him again—yet this guard refused to let her in. At least he had the decency to look contrite, his mouth all twisted up in a frown as he kept his gaze to the floor, but he didn't move the hand that blocked her from taking the door handle. "Why?"

Her *Unseelechs,* too, gurgled and growled at the guard, who somehow managed to pretend they weren't there. He stayed perfectly still and kept his eyes glued to the floor.

"I'm sorry, my lady," he said, "but Mr. Gürrensig isn't well enough for visitors. He has to be restored by a *Korbeldauer*; that takes time with injuries like his."

Aveline blinked. *What is that?* The word sounded strange, and she could only guess by its parts that it meant something like *body-builder*. Perhaps that was the kind of physician that could cure a body as broken as Ristef's. Still, she looked around the otherwise empty, isolated hallway, so far away from anyone else, and wondered who would know if she'd gone in right that moment.

"I won't hurt him," Aveline insisted. "I'll even leave these two with you, if—"

"Ah, no, please," the guard jerked his head to reinforce that sharp *no*, "I'm not so skilled with them as you are, my lady. I doubt I could manage them like you can. And even so, it's not that I think you'll hurt him. It's that he's fragile, and he needs careful attention. And," the guard blinked, then finally looked Aveline in the eye, "if I had to guess, I'd assume he wouldn't want you to see him this way. He wouldn't want you to worry."

That made Aveline pause. What an idiot Ristef would be, to care about such a thing. But then, there was more than that to it, wasn't there? Made of ice or not, poor Ristef was a man—and she'd never known men of any season, any tribe, to want others seeing them weak. Her throat squeezed; she tipped her head up to keep it from cracking with frost. Then she stared at the door as if she could send her thoughts through it.

Ristef, I'm here. Her poor guard, alone in that room. *I'm here.*

It was obvious that this other guard wouldn't let her through no matter what she said, so Ristef would never know—unless he could hear all the commotion through the door. So with nothing left to do, Aveline and her *Unseelechs* slinked their way back to her bedchambers, where she finally allowed herself a little rest.

Except rest did not find her. One would've thought it would. After all, after the advisor debacle, Aveline was blessed to be allowed to miss her morning drudgery with Jädrich for at least a little while. She could simply lounge and eat and rest until it was time to begin a tour around the country, and she savored that quiet time. However, that empty time also gave her plenty of space for the thoughts to flood in and torment her.

How did they find my mother's name so quickly? What else do they know about me? Does Jädrich believe any of it?

Over and over, those thoughts tormented her. Beyond that, there was also the issue of her apparent father, who she'd finally had a name for after all these years. And the issue of her cousin, her *real* cousin, who had not a lowly servant by his side, but the half-fox that got her into Winter in the first place. Aveline only knew after Karina quickly showed Aveline the golden eye hidden under her bandages. After they'd left the conference hall and left Jädrich to deal with a shocked Ronterweis and a couple castle doctors, though, her *cousin* had no familial words for her.

Don't even start, he'd snapped. All she did was look at him. She hadn't even said anything yet. And when she finally *did* say something, he was just as cold. *We are* not *family. Get the idea out of your head.*

But they were. They *were* family, if her father and his father were really brothers. And wasn't he in the same position as her? Left abandoned, alone in the world, after that High Summer, just as she'd been robbed of her mother during the Endless Summer? If they were family, then they were all they had. More, she was going to be the King's wife, his Queen. She was already seen as Cervora's icon, too; he knew about that for a while yet. Even someone as unlettered and unlearned as Aveline could tell that made her *powerful* in this country, more so than a simple viscount. So why weren't they family? Why didn't he want her?

Her chest ached as if someone caved her ribs in with a mace. In that room, with only four walls and a couple gangly little *Unseelechs* to call companions, she found herself feeling exactly as she had on the first couple nights of the bridal contest: alone and unsure. Her *Unseelechs* were curled up at her sides, a rare, quiet moment for them, and their silence only made the room seem smaller, more desolate. She patted the silver hair of one of them, and it twitched and purred, making a little *brrp* sound not unlike a cat's.

"Are you my family?" She cooed in Yasilan, but quietly, as if the walls had ears.

In return, she got a little chitter from her ice-pet, and it nestled closer to her. What family she was, that she let one of them sacrifice itself for her—but then, it didn't seem like they faulted her for it, and it wasn't as though she'd lost all chances to avenge the fallen one, anyhow. In fact, it didn't mean that she even had to avenge it with Jädrich's death to begin with. So she told herself. The idea of killing her prized King-doll was losing its appeal more and more with each passing day.

Moreover, if there was anything her mother taught her, it was not to keep holding onto guilt others had already forgiven her for. It was like carrying around proof of debt even after it'd already been paid—and if one was going to walk around with their debt slip like that still, then that was an open invitation for the cruel and wicked to keep collecting past their due. So Aveline resolved to finally push that thought out of her mind for good, with a deep, heavy sighed.

What's done is done. She stroked one's hair. *What's yet to be done is what matters.*

After a while of swimming in her thoughts, a knock came at the door. Aveline's heart squeezed, and her eyes stung with sudden exhaustion. Of course she could only retreat into herself for rest when the opportunity disappeared. But as her *Unseelechs* jerked their heads up and chittered, Aveline patted them until they quieted down and summoned her voice.

"Yes?"

"The King wishes to see you in his study, my Lady," came Dieven's voice. "Please allow me to escort you there."

Aveline heaved a sigh. No guards had been in that conference room, but she still wondered if the guards stationed outside could hear anything within. Maybe, maybe not. Aveline didn't want to take chances with what they did or didn't know, though, and so she kept her antlers tucked in, her hooves hidden, and her breathing as stable as possible, as she had all the weeks prior. Jädrich agreed to no wedding or grand show on that day she'd refrozen that hapless girl, but he did want to announce the return of Cervora's icon, and that meant keeping her other pieces hidden until it was time to reveal it. Though, if he was calling for her now—when all the dust had settled with the advisor's return and the priestess's leaving—

Is it time? To sign the contract?

A thrill skittered under her skin, one that sent her heart leaping and twisted her stomach. Finally, she'd have some ironclad security. It'd been three days since Jädrich said he'd set the priestess to drafting the contract, and with her gone, it only made sense that that's what Aveline was being called for. Apparently, according to what Erik told her before he'd left for his city home, these contracts were unbreakable once signed, with no room for divorce or changing one's mind or anything. And there was no remarriage, either—even after death. Once Aveline signed this, for better or worse, Jädrich would never be able to wash his hands of her. Even if he killed her, there'd never be a legitimate heir for Winter if she didn't bear one first. The line of Winter Kings would end without Aveline. Jädrich would be the final Lord of Winter. And even with Aveline there, she could make sure he was the last of his family. All it took was a certain medicine, and the hope for their precious *line of Orr* would pour out of her in a wash of blood.

So he can't get rid of me. Not ever. And that was enough for her—until another thought echoed back in her mind. *But one day, we can be rid of him.*

A muscle twitched in her jaw. A patch of gooseflesh trailed down to the base of her neck.

Aveline ignored the echo, and the strange feeling that came with it, and slid off her bed. When her *Unseelechs* tried to follow, she hushed them and motioned for them to stay. They twitched, whined, shook their heads in irritation, but they'd learned not to scramble after her without permission. With a smile, she went and opened her door to Dieven, who looked at her with the same blank and stony face as always. Or, at least, it seemed the same at first—until she saw the little whispers of magic crackling in those purple gems, and the sharp set of his brow.

Run.

Perhaps Aveline was a prey animal. It took everything to master her body then: to keep her smile pinned up, to resist her feet's wish to pivot and push away. Tension coiled in her hips; her muscles twitched as she flexed her toes to stay rooted to the spot. Still, she met the focused stare of that guard, and even as her heart fluttered and sent a flush of panic seeping up her neck, she managed to keep her breath even and hopefully unnoticeable.

Her mouth opened, but it took a moment before the words left her lips. She just managed to offer the guard her arm. "Take me to him, then."

Dieven moved as mechanically as a puppet. He took her arm and moved only when she moved; he matched her stride for stride, and if they hadn't been linked by the arm, Aveline might've forgotten he was there altogether. But no conversation happened with Dieven. The walk was silent, leaving Aveline stewing in her thoughts. The castle halls were empty, too, which only made Aveline's nerves worse. Shadows danced about in the corridors, gently waving with the pulsing glow of blue starlights in their sconces. Aveline walked quickly, if only to get out of that ghoulish silence as soon as possible, and Dieven, damn him, matched her pace easily.

Once at Jädrich's study, Dieven knocked on the door. "Your Majesty, Lady Rachfemd is here to see you."

"Let her in."

Dieven opened the door, and Aveline peered in. There sat Jädrich at his desk, with a massive sheet of paper in front of him. The starlights that hovered around him cast odd shadows off the few books and envelopes and pencils scattered around his desk, but in his hands was a quill—one tipped with silver ink. Aveline stepped inside, shut the door behind her, and peered at that silver bottle beside the paper.

He looked up at her and put the pen back in the bottle, but he stayed silent. Just like in the conference room, his face gave nothing away. Aveline paused. She'd expected a smile, at least, but after a moment, she collected herself and motioned to the paper.

"Is that what I think it is?"

Jädrich glanced at it. "Half of it, yes."

"Half?" Her feet unstuck themselves from their place by the door, and she wandered around his desk. "Didn't the priestess draft it?"

"No. She wouldn't until she heard what Clara had to say." Aveline frowned, hearing Jädrich call the runt by her name. "I dismissed her for it. So now we have to write it."

We! Aveline drifted closer, then half-perched on the arm of his chair. She slid her hand across his broad shoulders and took comfort in the way the satin overlay of his coat glided under her palms. "What still needs to go on it?"

"Your wishes." He glanced at her, and finally, he gave her the barest whisper of a smile. "Our wedding contract is built on what we expect from each other going forward."

Hmm? Aveline cocked her head. Something about the way he said that felt sharp. Pointed. His smile did nothing to soften whatever thorns laced his words, too, and Aveline finally looked at the contract itself—where his signature was already there, in bold, beautiful letters at the bottom, but everything else was written in a script she couldn't read. The Faun's Tongue.

She could make out a few glyphs here and there, but with the many runes she didn't know, it was anyone's guess what the contract said so far. Trying to read it, however, made her head hurt and her throat pinch as if she were soon to be sick, and she gave up on trying to figure it out. This was a mean trick, she knew deep in her bones—and yet why would Jädrich want to trick her? What for? She shook the thoughts away, blamed her unease on that guard that walked her there, and tried to settle against her King-doll.

"What did you write so far?"

"You can't read it?"

Aveline shook her head. "I never was able to master the runes the headmistress tried to show me."

Jädrich's eyes flickered with a snap of magic. He nodded and said, "A shame. It reads," he pointed to the first line of runes, then followed along as he read it to her, "that you agree to be Winter's sovereign Queen and Mother Goddess, fulfilling all duties associated with these positions. You agree to serve your people, the Ismären, tirelessly, never ceasing to do what's best for them. You agree to stay faithful to your husband all the days of your life, preserving his wellbeing, and to produce an heir to Winter within the first decade of our union. And you agree," his hand hovered over the last collection of runes, "to never lie to your husband. To be truthful about anything he may ask you."

A wash of gooseflesh trickled from Aveline's head down half her back, as if she'd been sprinkled by frozen rain. She couldn't sign this. Deep in her bones, she knew: she couldn't sign this. Reason be damned. Security be damned. Her very fingers seemed to revolt against the idea of writing at all. But to refuse signing it would make Jädrich suspicious.

"I," she grasped for something to say as her nerves became like insects writhing under her skin, "why would I lie to you, Jädrich? Is that so necessary to put there? Feels like you're wasting space on the paper."

"We have plenty of paper," he said, his words quick and cutting through her remark like a knife through a leaf. He reached a hand up to cover hers on his shoulder, stroking his frozen thumb over her skin. The little smile widened across his lips, and this time, it did reach his eyes. A smile like that was still a surprise to see coming from an otherwise stoic, lifeless thing like Jädrich, and Aveline wanted to bask in it. Wanted to so badly. "What would you like to add to the contract, Aveline?"

But Aveline didn't break their stare. It felt like if she

turned away even for a moment, she'd find herself with the teeth and claws of a mountain lion in her back, and she did not understand why. Another wave of gooseflesh broke over her as her mind and body wrestled with each other. *He's safe,* she whispered in her own head, to nobody in particular. *We're safe.*

When she blinked, she saw a flash of sharp teeth in her mind's eye and flinched.

She found herself stuttering as Jädrich snaked an arm around her waist, trapping her, "I—um, I need to think for a moment." When Jädrich blinked and let his smile slip, she quickly added, "I expected this to be already written. Didn't think I'd need to give my own terms."

My own terms. It felt like a trap once she'd said it out loud. *My own terms.* Was he waiting to see what she would put down? What she would make him do during their marriage? What if she put down what she really wanted? Would he outright scrap the contract and kill her right there on the spot?

Jädrich nodded. If he was aware of the panic pulsing through her, he didn't show it. "Take your time. Meanwhile, I have some questions for you as Cervora's icon." He took a book from the little stack behind him: one about the prophecies of Cervora, if that fat deer head and the old script on it was any indication. She'd seen him with it before. He flipped it open to a certain bookmarked page, one heavily underlined, smudged, and notated. After tracing his finger down to the third paragraph, he tapped the words and muttered, "Might you tell me what this prophecy means? I felt as if I understood it, but after today, perhaps I don't."

Aveline leaned over to look at the page, but her mind registered no words. It was too busy whirring with ideas, with fears, about what she might add to that half-finished contract—and how she might get out of the trickier pieces Jädrich wrote. What did it mean, *fulfill the duties* of a Queen and Mother Goddess? What would Jädrich ask, if she couldn't lie?

The entire story of Aveline Rachfemd is a lie.

"It says here," Jädrich said after a moment of strained silence, "that our Mother would return to us in a body we can't stomach. That's the exact wording." Aveline never looked up from the book, but she could feel his stare shear through her skin as he continued, "We always thought this meant a body made of ice, or stone, or something else. Something we couldn't eat. But today, I saw your blood feed that guard as well as any bloodwine of your kin. So what does this mean? Surely you know."

Aveline pinched the bridge of her nose in a useless attempt to hold off her brewing headache. *Think. Slow down.* She hunched down to get a closer look at the text, and she read the Ismar words over and over again, but it didn't look like it meant anything different than what Jädrich said. Still—a body they couldn't stomach wouldn't have been one Ristef could've drank from. That much was true. There was only one other way to take an otherwise straightforward statement like this, and Aveline could never come out and say it to Jädrich. She chewed her lip, her mind holding no room for ideas when it was buzzing with other things. So when she had nothing to say, she shut the book.

"Whoever wrote these prophecies," she said, though she barely registered her own words, "took the words too literally."

A body the ice folk can't stomach. Aveline's wings twitched under her dress, begging to come free and stretch wide. *A body the ice folk can't accept.*

Jädrich stared, then nodded. "I see. Well, then, have you decided what you want to include in the contract?"

She wanted to strike all his demands from the record. The idea of the contract compelling her to do anything in any way made her shudder. But maybe she could take some of the vagueness of those commands and use it to her advantage.

Granted the runes really mean what Jädrich says they do.

Her nerves were already as thin as the ice-crust on a puddle, and that thought went and shattered it. Bile rose in her throat and threatened to make her frost-glands snap. What a gamble. Aveline chewed the inside of her cheek and stared at the contract's blank bottom half. Jädrich still held the pen, the ink going dry on the nib, and all she could think was that this was one awful, wretched gamble. But what else was there to do, except march on?

She held her hand out. "Pen, please."

"I can write for you—"

"I didn't get to see what you wrote before you wrote it," Aveline muttered, and her heart quivered in her chest despite how tall she tried to stand, "so give me the pen."

Jädrich's hand stayed still. "You can't write in the Faun's Tongue."

"I don't need to." Before Jädrich could say anything else, she plucked the pen from his hand and slipped from the arm of the chair directly into his lap. The thin fabric of his pants did nothing to soften the harsh cold of his legs against her bottom. She leaned over the paper, careful not to smudge it, and she dipped the pen into the well of silver ink. "Just wait."

Then she wrote. Her body hopefully hid what she was writing, but once it was signed, it would be signed. Jädrich already signed it, too—a stupid move, all things considered. Aveline could've written on that paper that he was to kill himself immediately, or that he was to execute everyone Aveline said without question, or that he was to give his crown away to a man on the street. But no, she knew exactly what she wanted to set in magical ink there, and she was determined to do it before Jädrich caught on.

As she wrote, however, swirling the blocky Ismar script over the paper in a way that felt strange with something so fluid as ink, icy hands slid over her hips. Aveline didn't slow down; she wrote with all the speed and fury she could muster, even as those frozen hands squeezed what little softness she still had. Jädrich's touch drifted up to her waist, squeezing her there, too, and as his fingers brushed under her breasts, his icy lips drifted over the back of her neck. She shivered against him, forcing her to pause her writing so she wouldn't make the word illegible, and Jädrich whispered against her skin.

"What will you make me do, Aveline?"

His voice was as raspy as the Winter winds, and it made her chest squeeze. "You'll know when you try to do or not do any of these things," she muttered, and she wrote her last few words with such urgency that the words started to look like a Summer doctor's scrawl. She blocked Jädrich's view of the paper when she felt Jädrich's chin graze her shoulder, and then she went to sign her name with as much swirl and flourish as Jädrich did. She even intended to add *Cervora's Icon* to her name, like a title, just for good measure.

Don't. Trap. It's a trap.

Aveline's pen hovered over the paper. She couldn't take more than a bird's breath; her lungs squeezed and froze. Her head swam, her stomach roiled, as if her body were trying to wrangle control from her mind.

Do not.

She let her eyes slip shut to steady herself, and there was no mistaking the nature of the blackness behind her eyelids—the shine of the dark doe eye staring back at her.

Do not sign this.

"I have to," Aveline whispered, so low it was barely audible even to herself, because she couldn't push the thought through those massive black eyes. She wrenched her eyes open and stared at the contract, where a drop of ink had already slid off the pen.

Don't—

With enough force to shatter bone, Aveline pushed her pen towards the paper—and a nearly equal force *in* her bones tried to pull her hand back. Still, as she bit her lip hard enough to make it bleed, she wrestled her body into doing what she needed to do. She signed her name, just large enough to be legible: *Aveline Rachfemd.*

Then Aveline threw the pen on the desk and slumped against Jädrich as her mind became a mess of unintelligible, wicked hissing—and a moment later, the whole paper began to glow. All the ink, both the Faun's Tongue and the regular Ismar script, shined so bright that the words became illegible; the paper may as well have been one large shining silver square. It was so bright it nearly blinded Aveline.

Then all the ink lifted off the paper and took the form of several silver chain links. The paper rolled up tight, like a scroll, and the chain link wrapped around it several times, as if that paper were the very fabric of reality, and the promises Jädrich and Aveline made were what held it together. After, those chain links melted into the paper like water into rich earth.

Before she could tilt her head to look at Jädrich, the contract paper fell back on Jädrich's desk, looking like nothing more than a completely mundane scroll. As it fell back open, there were all of Aveline's and Jädrich's vows, written in what looked like old, reddish-black blood. Jädrich reached past her and picked it up, then read it, all with one hand pressing against Aveline's stomach and forcing her against his chest.

Aveline didn't dare move as she waited for him to

speak. The vows she'd put down for him to uphold were dangerous—but then, he'd given her a blank, pre-approved contract to write whatever she wanted. If he was to complain about anything on there, there was only himself to blame. Aveline knew only one thing, and that one thing made her fear shrink down to nothing and instead give way to a mind-numbing excitement.

The contract was signed, and they were both bound to it. Which meant Jädrich couldn't do anything to her, because one of the things she'd written was that Jädrich would keep Aveline safe from all injury, imprisonment, and injustice, so long as his soul remained in his head. Whereas Jädrich hadn't been so specific, Aveline had.

And now he can never hurt me. Some little part of her was satisfied, deeply so, and it purred its contentment through her veins. But it was not the part, apparently, that was making her body tense and tremble. *I'm safe,* she told herself. *Truly safe.*

I'm an idiot, came the echo of her thoughts, as if to spit in her face. *Truly an idiot.*

"I see." He put the contract down and put his lips to her ear, then whispered, "So that was your goal."

Aveline froze. Not so much because of what he'd said, but because of how he'd said it. His hand left her stomach, and his freezing arm wrapped around her, trapping her with a squeeze that almost hurt. *Almost.*

"I have a question for you."

She stayed perfectly still. She didn't so much as blink.

"Once I asked you if I'm seeing all of you. Then you showed me your antlers and your hooves." His other hand came up, trailed his icy cold hand up her sternum, then grabbed her chin with a firmness that made it impossible to move her head. "I'll ask you once more: am I seeing all of you? Or is there more you're not telling me about?"

Aveline froze. A wave of gooseflesh rippled from

her temple down to the base of her spine; her heart flushed with terror. She wanted to play dumb. To ignore him completely. And if he asked again, she wanted to pretend she didn't understand his question in the first place. If she could've, she would've batted her eyelashes and asked him what he'd said. But his one question was actually two—because he'd asked in crisp, lightly accented Yasilan, and she'd understood his question perfectly.

Her breath quickened, her heart thudding in her ears. She felt the yoke of the contract then, as if those magical chains had sunk into her instead of the paper she signed; she felt the icy weight of it pierce her heart like an arrowhead. It seared her with frostbite the more she sat silent, dug deeper into her heart until she thought it might pierce her very soul, and the longer she waited, the more it threatened to steal the life from her. *Her*, of all people—*Aveline*, the Glass Witch, the Winter-faced thing that no cold could freeze, that no frost could bite—she thought she might become little more than a piece of ice herself in that moment.

"Aveline?"

Jädrich's finger trailed up her jaw. Maybe if she held out long enough, he would assume she didn't understand him. But gods, it *killed*. The cold in her heart, it—

"Aveline, is there more to you than even your antlers and your horns? Tell me."

Don't speak to me in my mother's tongue. Aveline's eyes stung with tears as the pain in her chest became sharper, deeper, colder. *Don't. You have no right to it.*

"You're shaking," he whispered, and the Yasilan words that left his lips sounded like the hisses of the dead. "Are you hurting?" Then, softer, "Are you fighting our covenant already?"

No, she wanted to say, *if* she had to say anything at all—but just beginning to form the word made her heart go so rigid and cold that it skipped a beat. And then, to her horror, the frost began seeping into her lungs—threatening to take away her chance to respond at all.

"Yes!"

The word ripped out of her before she could stop it, and immediately, relief warmed her lungs, thawed her heart, flushed her veins. Jädrich stilled beneath her.

"Why?"

"Because!" It was the Ismar language that came to Aveline first, what with how much she'd been speaking it, and that made every word taste like bitter poison. "Because you—because what you ask is—"

"So you have been hiding something from me."

The cold in his voice was sharper than whatever frost infected her a moment before. It didn't match her mother's language at all. Every word he spoke in Yasilan sounded like it came from the mouth of a desert night-demon. Aveline heaved a breath and steadied herself. What he said wasn't a question, and she didn't have to say anything; he could say what he liked, and he could think whatever he wanted of her silence.

"Aveline—"

To her surprise, he let her shoot off his lap and back away a few paces. They stared at each other the way a deer stares at a wolf spotted in the underbrush. Then Aveline caught that book of prophecies from the corner of her eye and lunged to snatch it. All the while, Jädrich sat still as death itself.

"What do you think it means?" Aveline swallowed her panic down and let a shuddering breath loose. "Your 'prophecy.'"

Save this. Who was supposed to hear that prayer? No god would claim a thing like her. *Save us.*

Us, us, us.

Jädrich picked up his chair and turned it to face her.

He crossed one leg over the other, then leaned on his desk as if they were discussing something as simple as a child's riddle. Aveline would've wondered if he was enjoying this, smug as he looked there, but all the while, his eyes crackled with angry flashes of silver magic, like a Winter night's storm.

"I can't imagine," he finally said—still in Yasilan.

He knows.

"Still not very imaginative," she muttered, though something stopped her from responding in Yasilan. It was as if the language was hiding from her, as if she'd disgrace it to speak it with an ice-doll like this. Her skin prickled with dread; her throat squeezed in fear. When her frost glands clicked, her next words left on a cloud of frost. "A shame."

Without another word, she let loose her antlers, her hooves. She looked no different than she did the first time she revealed herself, and she stared at him like that a moment longer before she finally let the last piece of herself loose. She flinched as her wings peeled from her back; the pull of wing membrane from skin stung like a rebuke. They popped and snapped as they stretched out through the open slits of her dress, and they spread wide, brushing Jädrich's desk.

"This is me. All of me. Every bit of me," she whispered. "Your advisor told the truth in that conference room. She discovered things about me that even I didn't know—like the name of the father that never once visited me in my homeland."

Jädrich folded his hands and studied her. His eyes tracked the length of her wingspan.

His silence rattled Aveline enough that she found her words pouring out as quickly and easily as her frost. "I know you hate my people, and you have no love for mixed-bloods either, but my antlers and hooves and frost are *real* and can help your people. We are married now, and I expect you to help my people in kind, no matter what you think of them. I expect you to protect me and understand that I can be your icon of Cervora— that I *am* your Cervora."

She never broke her stare with the King of Winter as she spoke. As he stayed silent and hopefully listened, she licked her lips and sucked in a deep breath of the freezing air. Then she managed to find her mother's tongue—just a few simple words, a phrase that held the double meaning that Ismar speech did not so readily lend itself to.

"But you—can you stomach it?"

Jädrich went so still that Aveline wondered if his soul left him then. The magic in his eyes slowly faded until all that was left was the icy blue of his diamonds. While no expression graced his face, his stare carried a focus so sharp and wicked that they might've tried to shear the wings right off Aveline's back.

Then, finally, he reanimated. He pushed himself off that desk and rose to his feet, slow as an old man with bad bones. Then he took such slow steps towards her that he might've thought Aveline was little more than an animal about to bolt—which wouldn't have been far from the truth, the way Aveline's heart squeezed.

"I don't hate your people," he muttered, once again speaking in his native tongue.

Aveline's anger flared before her sense. She, too, kept speaking in her native tongue, the words smooth like a whip. "You must, if you were willing to condemn the entire rest of the Ringlands the way you did."

Jädrich shook his head. "I don't hate them. Nothing I did was because of them." He closed the gap between them and stared Aveline in the eye, their height matched with Aveline's hooves out. "I did everything for my people, and my people alone. What happened to your people, or Autumn's or Spring's, was not my concern when my people here were suffering."

Aveline stared at him. Her muscles shook with the rage that ignited in her heart; her jaw clenched. "I was suffering," she hissed. She jabbed a finger into his chest and leaned on it, her face only an inch from his. "I was—Jädrich, without your season, I was trapped. Not on the Seat of Orr. On Kha-Bawaj. I was trapped there nine months of the year as it was, until you came back each year. And then you left for good, and I was trapped there for a *century*." Her pointed finger because a full hand on his chest, grabbing a fistful of his coat's satin. "I was alone. With no food, no nothing. Unable to leave. The sun," with her other hand, she pointed towards the ceiling, as if the sun were right there overhead, "burned me nearly to death when I tried."

Jädrich said nothing.

"My mother died," Aveline rasped, gripping his coat tighter, "thinking I had died. I could see Sekhbal in the distance—I could *see it*—and I couldn't—" her other hand came around and clasped the back of his neck, took hold of it through the thick layer of his hair, "and you say... you didn't even think of them? Of us? Not once?"

It'd have been easier to hear him say he hated her people. Easier by far. But this—

"Who got you off Kha-Bawaj?" Jädrich's voice was cold as the stone that paved the castle walkways.

The frost of the contract didn't have time to pierce Aveline again. In fact, it might not have been able to in the first place, with how her rage boiled in her blood. "Ganaresh," she hissed. "Him and two of his wives, along with a Spring bee and an Autumn fox."

"Why?"

That made Aveline pause, her rage cooled just a few degrees. How much truth was enough to stop the contract's frost? How much was she obliged to tell? She thought she'd test it, by speaking into existence only the very heart of the matter, none of the details.

"To clear a path for moving the seasons again."

The silence stretched between them. Moments passed with ease—and no arrowhead pierced Aveline's heart. No frost seized her lungs. What she said was the truth, the bare truth—and the contract, apparently, accepted that as enough. Aveline could've bounced with glee. A lie, it seemed, was speaking falsehoods—not omitting details.

Perfect.

The sudden crackle of Jädrich's voice made Aveline blink. "It seems you've succeeded."

I have. She'd written it in the contract: Jädrich was to move the seasons again. He was bound to it then; he had no choice, just as she had no choice. *I've done what I needed to do.*

Jädrich's hands came up and cupped her face. Aveline let go of his coat to cover one of his, to hold the ice there against her cheek. He stared into her eyes, searched them, and after a moment, he spoke.

"Forgive me," he said, and just as his magic snuffed the fires she made in the woods, so too did his soft voice smother her rage. His eyes sparkled with what looked like a dozen silver stars. She hadn't seen them do that before. "I cost you something precious. I never imagined someone like you would have suffered what you did when I stopped the Tour of Seasons."

Aveline wanted so badly to accept that apology. But her body tensed as if it had a will of its own, and she muttered, "Someone like me? A mixed-blood, you mean?"

His eyelids shuttered. "A goddess," he said.

That told Aveline all she had to know. Just as he said before, he didn't have any love, or even any care, for the peoples of other nations—so what would half-breeds be to him? Were she a half-Winter, half-Autumn thing, no doubt Jädrich wouldn't have cared a bit. Even as it was—was this a show? This apology, was it real? Something in her stomach twisted and bloomed: a deep, dark cynicism. Still, she had him there, willing to demean himself like this—to apologize. Thanks to such a display cooling her head, Aveline could think better. She didn't want to push too hard and waste the peace he offered. Not when she still had so much use to wring out of him.

"You're forgiven," Aveline muttered. "But never again will you let me suffer like that. You agreed."

"Yes," Jädrich said, and then those stars died from his eyes. "Likewise, you understand what you've agreed to in return."

Aveline blinked.

"You must be this country's Queen and Mother. You must do all you can for its people. You will put them first, even over yourself. Your life is no longer your own."

Every word he spoke had an authority behind it that she'd never heard him use. It was as if Aveline's mind was red hot metal, and his words were the strike of a hammer. She tried to blink away the strange feeling, but it was only when she nodded that she could think clearly.

"Yes, but," Aveline paused, "you don't mind? What I am? You don't mind these?"

When her wings rustled, Jädrich's eyes fell shut. Then, when he opened them again, his stare bore into her with as much intensity as before. "The people can't see those," he said. "They won't understand."

That made Aveline frown. "Yes, but what about you—?"

"My life is also not my own," he muttered, and he took a step back to study Aveline—from her antlers to her face to her wings. "What I mind and don't mind isn't something I've considered since I was a child."

And maybe there was something about Aveline's face then—maybe her expression fell, or maybe her shoulders sank, because Jädrich took her chin and ran a thumb over her jaw, as tender a gesture as she could ever expect. He said, "You are my wife as of this day. You are Queen, and you are Cervora's icon. That is all that matters, and that is all that I, or anyone else in this country, needs to know."

What does that mean? As Jädrich leaned forward to press a kiss against her forehead, his lips hard and cold against her skin, she wanted so badly to ask. *What does that mean?* But it was as if her own lips became like his: stiff, unmoving, cold. She couldn't bring herself to form the words of her question. She couldn't bring herself to know.

"The contract is sealed," he whispered as he pulled away. He smiled and took her hand, though in his eyes was the smallest flicker of magic. "Conceal yourself and come to bed."

Aveline hesitated, but she did as she was told. Her hooves broke apart once more into toes, lowering her under Jädrich's gaze, and her antlers slid back into her skull. Her wings tucked in and fused with the skin of her back once more, until no one could tell they were there. All the while, Jädrich watched, and Aveline wondered.

What does that mean? As Jädrich led her out of the study, she bore the question into his back. *What do you mean?*

Eventually, as they came closer to the north wing, where Jädrich rested his head each night, Aveline resolved to bury the question. She'd succeeded. She won this battle. She hanged this man. That was all *she* had to know, as far as she was concerned. Like a furry Autumn squirrel buried its nuts and seeds, Aveline buried that thought, hoping to forget about it.

Hoping that the dark eyes haunting her mind didn't go and dig it up.

THE MAIN MEETING CHAMBER OF THE SUMMER palace was one where Drakash's sunshine couldn't so easily peek through, and the Summer Council's Head of Diplomatic Relations, Tsevannah, found that unfortunate. Fire was the next best thing in Drakash's absence, and the many sconces along the wall flickered with lively flame, but it made the air taste stale to have no open windows. However, Tsevannah understood it was necessary—a small price to pay for secrecy.

Tsevannah perched on a high cushioned stool beside her husband. One of her fellow wives, Faloorah, Head of Military, sat on his other side. Stationed like this, they could more easily move in the event of an emergency to protect the Sekhran, who sat on a great golden chair covered in jewels and velvet cushions.

Thin, elegant chains dripping with rubies hung from Sekhran Ganaresh's golden horns, his equally golden and wavy hair framing a strong jaw, sharp cheekbones, thick golden brows, and eyes like liquid flame. His robes were light, but no less colorful, intricately embroidered to look like the golden scales of his true and mighty form and accented with reds, purples, and oranges. Even though the chair he sat in was large and extravagant, it couldn't possibly dwarf the most powerful man in the Ringlands.

At this table, they waited for their compatriots to arrive and discuss a frantic message they'd received from their contacts in Winter. It was well past when the bridal competition should've ended, and the news they hoped to hear—that the Winter King was dead—was replaced with something wicked. Apparently, the mixed-blood's unsightly half form gave her a new role to play in that desolate, frozen country: the role of *goddess* as much as Queen. It was so absurd that Tsevannah could've laughed, and she did the night she read that letter with her husband, until she'd seen his face.

Now the enemy is alive, and I'm left without the bride I paid for. That nighttime conversation with the Sekhran left Tsevannah feeling as if she'd been carved of ice herself. *I paid for that bride in feasts we could barely afford to put on—and she sells herself to the Winter King instead. Exalts herself, even. How can I let this go unanswered for, Tsevannah? What would my Father say, if I let such a thing happen?*

Whatever her husband wanted a mixed-blood wife for, Tsevannah couldn't guess, but it was true: for any Yasilan, half-blood or not, to go and make herself a *god* was an affront to Drakash and all his wives. Still, that aside, they knew only one thing: the Glass Witch did not use the tools Sekhran Ganaresh commissioned for her, clearly. And the only thing worse than this was *not* knowing whether she'd also revealed them to the enemy himself—whether she'd exposed Summer to a legal retaliation by letting the King of Winter know of their schemes. Given that they hadn't heard from that Rachfemd boy that took Aveline on as his "cousin," as far as anyone knew, she could've already begun spilling secrets and had that boy killed.

A voice echoed from behind the large palm doors: "Announcing the Empress Feng Souram and her aide, Hana Bante, and the sister of High Priestess Nhale Ba, Odani Ba."

The doors opened, and there stood the Empress in all her red and white finery. Her robes were gauzy and flowing as freely as the clouds in the sky, her black hair shiny and sleek and nearly long enough to reach the floor. Her golden eyes were rimmed with bright red paint, and that same paint dotted her head to look like three falling leaves. Her lips were small, half painted white to blend with her face, and on her head stood an intricate, square-shaped crown full of beads and bells and baubles. Her three black tails wrapped around her like a shawl made of fur any good trapper would kill to get their hands on, and their white tips were like the ends of paint brushes. The aide, Hana, stood in a fine black robe, the only spot of red on her being her hair, her one tail, and the belt that kept her robes together—a robe of mourning for the brother that the Winter King sent back dead.

Walking in beside them was Odani Ba, who, as one might expect of a twin, was the spitting image of her sister. Her body was long and lean, her dark, yellow-striped skin glowing as if covered in Spring dew, and her green dress seemed alive with the vines and flowers sewn to it. Her translucent bee wings draped behind her like a cloak made of crystals, and her long, thin braids were dotted with crystal beads and flowers. Like her sister, she wore no crown, but instead wore a gourd on shimmering pink cords at her waist—just as significant as any crown any of them could wear. On a normal year,

Nhale Ba would use her gourd to gather the first nectar of each country's blooms after the return of their season, an offering to the Great Bear that lumbered along with them in their travels. Every year since, however, there had only been the nectar of the Springlands to fill those gourds—and even that nectar was growing scarce, along with the flowers that made it.

In comparison, Tsevannah felt plain. Her black robes were inoffensive, unadorned. The only gold on her shimmered from her horns, which peeked through her black flowing headwrap, and the golden pin of her station gleaming at her breast. Humility and decorum, that was what was expected of her as Head of Diplomatic Relations; she was never to shine more than necessary, never to remind people of her home and loyalties more than a tasteful touch.

Faloorah, on the other hand, was much more extravagant: her short robes and pants were all gold, red, and black, her headwrap made of tight layers that let the cut of her jaw stand stark against golden, armor-like bangles at her neck, and to keep her wrap secured was a circlet of fine steel, with large circular plates hanging down that covered her ears. Her horns, like Tsevannah's, rose up high from her wrap, but they were straighter and angled more forward than Tsevannah's curved ones— better for charging and goring. Faloorah was dressed, *built,* for the risk of an attack, yet she still looked regal next to their husband.

But Tsevannah didn't complain. There was no reason to. Yes, Faloorah might've been the military muscle behind Summer, her mind built for strategy and her fist one of iron, but when all the wives came with Sekhran Ganaresh to Summer, it was Tsevannah, and Tsevannah alone, that stayed behind to monitor these other Lords. One might've argued that made her more valuable than the military commander, for it was she who knew all the seasons' secrets.

Yet I could've never predicted this mess.

"My dear friends," came Sekhran Ganaresh's deep voice, smooth as the bars of gold in their treasury, "thank you for joining us. I wish we could've met for better reasons, but please—sit. We have many things to discuss."

Nobody said a word as the women came to the table. There were four chairs: one for each Lord or Lady of Seasons. It was where they discussed the yearly changes, the revisions to international policies, the damages and reparations.

In a thousand years, only the Winter King had ever refused his duty. Tsevannah chewed the inside of her cheek. If only they realized then what that meant. What the Winter King was planning to do. Maybe they could've stopped it before that wall came up and blocked the carriages and processions of Spring from coming through. As it stood, the wall was too large, too well defended, for even a fleet of dragons to melt it before Winter's men retaliated. That was Faloorah's estimate, and for *her* to urge caution after a scout with her men told Tsevannah all she needed to know about the situation.

Empress Feng Souram sat down, her aide hovering behind her as the Old Fox's direct descendant lounged in that little chair. She sat across from Odani Ba, whose face never once hinted at her thoughts or emotions; the Spring sisters were leaders Tsevannah admired for the way they kept their thoughts so heavily guarded.

"Thank you for your hospitality," Odani Ba said as palace servants came soon after to set cups and pour fresh coffee. She hardly paid any mind to the young girls as they left a tray of honey-soaked pistachio treats, though she did sip her coffee with care.

Likewise, Empress Souram motioned to Hana to take a treat and nodded, her smile wide. "Yes, thank you. It's been an awfully long time since we've sat together like this, hasn't it? I've missed these treats you have here."

And yet she didn't take a single one, nor did she touch the coffee. She let it wisp its steam in the air as she folded her hands back into her robe sleeves. Hana, in her Lady's place, partook in the Sekhran's minor gifts; she took a single treat and dragged the little coffee cup beside the Empress to sip as she stood.

"I wish we might discuss the new year like old times," Sekhran Ganaresh said. His eyes crinkled with his smile, warm like a hearth's flame. "But today's conversation might be too heavy for such a thing."

Odani Ba nodded, keeping her gaze on the table. "Indeed. If you don't mind, Sekhran, I believe I should call my sister in before we go any further."

"Yes, yes—please do."

The Spring emissary nodded again and took in a deep breath. She closed her eyes and dipped her fingers into that gourd at her waist; when they left the gourd, they were coated in honey so rich that it was almost as orange as a desert Yasilan's eyes. She smeared it across her lips, and it glittered there, full of magic that never failed to fascinate Tsevannah.

On contact, the shimmering honey dripped from her lips and spread down her chin, then pivoted, crawling across her face like a web of golden vines. They covered her face, rooted into her hair, and when they touched the corners of her eyes, Odani Ba opened them wide. Where her eyes were once a blur of yellows and purples, like pansies, they were slowly overtaken with that gold; it seeped in like golden tears and covered her eyes until they glowed with light.

Her body locked up, stiff. Her hands, wide open, began to twitch as a long breath escaped her lips. Across from her, Empress Feng pressed her lips into a thin line, as she often did to keep from frowning.

All was silent a moment longer. Tsevannnah and Faloorah shared a glance through the gold and rubies in their husband's horns. They'd seen this very ritual time and time again, once per year, and yet it never grew any less strange. The Orisi called this ritual some word that, in their language, meant *hivemind*, in which the bees, the women, might share minds and bodies with one another and speak with fellows at long distances. It was the only way Nhale Ba could ever interact with the other Lords when their duties confined them all to the land and made free travel impossible.

"Sekhran Ganaresh. Empress Feng Souram."

With a start, Tsevannah looked to the High Priestess's sister. It was Odani Ba speaking, yes, but Nhale Ba's voice mixed with her sister's. Tsevannah never got used to hearing *two* voices come from one mouth. "A shame we have no man of ice here with us yet again."

Tsevannah glanced at the empty chair across from the Sekhran. Her memories were hazy, but she could still conjure the last of this type of meeting: one where a ghost of silvery, snowy flecks fixed itself across the table to represent the King of Winter. A runestone still sat there, but it was black, dead of the icy-blue magic of the Ismären. It had been that way for a long time.

"High Priestess Nhale Ba," Sekhran Ganaresh said, tipping his head enough to make his rubies swing from his horns. But the woman didn't turn her head to see. "It's a shame, yes, but we're glad to hear your voice nonetheless."

"Yours as well. I understand from your messengers that the mixed-blood failed?"

"More than failed," Tsevannah said, and her husband brushed his hand against hers as she took a few transcripts that she'd tucked into her robe. She tossed them onto the table, free for anyone to pick through and read. "She's betrayed us. Married the Winter King."

A grave silence fell over the room as Odani Ba stayed perfectly still. "I see," High Priestess Nhale Ba finally said through her. "We should assume that diplomacy has been exhausted then, no?"

"No," said Empress Feng, who clasped her hands together and threw her sharp gaze around the table. "There are still options. The mixed-blood—no one has been able to reach her, yes? No one has been inside Winter to verify what she's doing, and now, by the letters the house of Ti-Vaour shared with us," she glanced at Tsevannah, "we don't know what she plans to do if made Queen. She may still work in our favor, if we give her time."

Tsevannah's chest went tight with a building sigh. Finally, the Empress spoke, and of course it was to say the same thing she'd been saying for the past century: that there was *still a way*, somehow, somewhere.

"After all, how are we to know the thoughts of this woman? Hmm?" Empress Feng shrugged, her lips pursing. "How do we know she betrayed us, rather than found a better opportunity to do what we asked her to do?"

Sekhran Ganaresh stayed silent, his hand pausing against Tsevannah's. Then he chuckled. Low and throaty, quiet, it was a little laugh Tsevannah knew well. She kept her face neutral so that no one would know it was the sound of disbelief and barely hidden rage.

"What we told her to do was kill the Winter King—"

"What we told her to do was move the seasons," Empress Feng said. "If anyone told her anything *different,* then they've moved against the spirit of the covenant our ancestors made over a thousand years ago when they became Lords of Seasons."

Something shifted from the corner of Tsevannah's

eye. It was Faloorah, who startled and moved to speak before their husband raised his hand to stop her. Empress Feng's eye cut to the Head of Military, sharper even than the finest swords in the armory, and she continued.

"Don't you all understand? This is a good thing. This is a boon. None of us have any concept of the state of Winter, but this woman, this *Summer* woman, mind you, surely has seen the situation for what it is in a way none of us ever can. She can help the King see what we couldn't from the outside. She can bring him back to his duties in the covenant—!"

"Why do you insist on defending this man, Empress Feng?"

It was the High Priestess's voice, intertwined with her sister's, that cut clean through the Empress's speech. Odani Ba sat as still as ever, as if she'd become nothing but a clay vessel for her sister's spirit, but the words rang just as loud as if the High Priestess were there shouting them.

Empress Feng, however, held the conduit's gaze. She even sat up and rested her hands flat on the table. "Because he is a Lord like us, and it was a mistake to ever think we, even *we*, had the authority to try and forcibly remove him from his station." Then she looked to the Sekhran. "Friend, listen—let us not jump to conclusions. I can send another emissary, perhaps."

For just a flash, Tsevannah met the eyes of the Empress's aide, the Bante woman, and there was nothing but darkness in them as her body tensed into stone. The shadow of death, the memory of her brother, it lingered there in her eyes. And what a grizzly tale it was, when that poor woman first told them the story: how her brother had been what she *hoped* was the last of dozens of dispatched diplomats, such rich talent wasted in Winter's frozen wastelands. The Empress was able to pretend ignorance about something everyone knew, so long as there were no bodies returned. However, it seemed even *with* concrete proof of the Winter King's treachery, with proof of his crimes against the Autumn court, there was Old Feng, still trying to throw sweet words at a monster like *Jädrich Femmel III.*

Tsevannah had served that King before, being Summer's head diplomat. She'd spoken to him plenty of times. She knew firsthand that such a creature registered only what he needed to know to make a decision, and that everything else any creature of flesh would say to him was little more than the tweeting of a bird on its branch to him. Never had Tsevannah met a thing like that Winter King—a thing so silent, so cold, so devastatingly immortal, that even the other Ismären in Summer seemed lively and spirited in comparison. That King was a dead man walking, was in fact no man at all. Despite the century-old Summer heat, Tsevannah shuddered to think of the last time that King's eyes landed on her—ones as milky-blue as the eyes of the blind, yet so undoubtedly focused on her, as if he could see directly into her head.

May Drakash melt the monsters and their King to nothing.

Old Feng nodded. "Yes, another emissary may do, but maybe a different one than—"

But then the Empress startled as something between a groan and a growl echoed through the meeting room; Faloorah slammed her hands down on the table and pinned the fox with her fiery stare.

"Enough with your emissaries, Empress! Don't you see now? Your emissaries are *dead.* The Winter King killed every single one of them!"

Her tails twitching, the Empress huffed, indignant. "We—!"

Don't know that. Tsevannah tried to blink the exhaustion from her eyes. It was what Empress Feng said every single year, at every single meeting: *we don't know that he killed my emissaries.* Yet how could she deny it then? She couldn't, not this time, and that was the only true service that Winter King had done any of them in the past hundred years. With the way the fight drained from the Empress's face as Faloorah stared her down, she knew it, too. So did her aide behind her, who bit her lip so hard that Tsevannah was sure her teeth would puncture it.

"Yes, we do," Faloorah muttered. "The man King Jädrich sent back to you was not some expertly carved replica of a man." She pointed to the aide. "That woman there—Bante? It was her *brother* she watched be carried in like a shipment of ice for your parties, was it not?" The curl of Faloorah's lip as she stood up showed her sharp teeth. "The time for defending that monster is over, Empress."

"Enough now," Sekhran Ganaresh said as he held out his hands. "We're not here to argue what we already know. We're here to decide how to move forward after the mixed-blood's betrayal. High Priestess, have you done as we discussed earlier?"

Odani Ba didn't so much as twitch. "I have."

"Good. That's all that matters."

"Discussed?" Empress Feng clenched her jaw as she looked between the two Lords. "What have you discussed, hmm? Without me? Do tell."

Sekhran Ganaresh sat back and shot his words at the Empress like a poison-tipped arrow. "We discussed gathering our men, Empress. And gather them we have. The Yasilan and Orisi warriors stand ready to storm those ice walls and oust the Winter King ourselves, if no other option presents itself. As of now, we have *one* last chance, and it's thanks to my dear Head of Surveillance. Her son is across those borders as we speak, to fix the mixed-blood's mistakes. Should even *he* fail, then truly, the only option left is to break that ice wall down ourselves."

Empress Feng blinked. Her mouth hung open a moment before she sputtered, "What—no, that—you can't—"

"We are not here to discuss more ways to waste your people's lives," Sekhran Ganaresh said, burning embers lacing every word. "All we want to know from you is: will you gather your archers and your wind-walkers to join our ranks and move the seasons with us, should it come down to that?"

"Sekhran," Empress Feng said as she shot up from her seat, the bells in her headdress ringing like shouts, "please, think a moment. You are insisting upon *war* against a fellow season, war that you cannot even be there to oversee—"

"And that is why Sekhvaah Faloorah is to head the Yasilanri," Sekhran Ganaresh said. "She is, in all the land, second only to Drakash in her strength, an equal in might to me."

"Yes, but that doesn't change what I said." Empress Feng glanced around at all of them, eyes glimmering with golden panic. "War, Sekhran! *War!* It is not the way! Diplomacy—"

"Diplomacy is dead, Empress," Sekhran Ganaresh said, half on a sigh. "The Winter King just killed it and sent its corpse to you personally."

Little Hana flinched.

The Empress stared. She kept looking for anyone that might agree with her, and Tsevannah prayed to the Moon Mother for patience when those fox eyes landed on her. Empress Feng held up her hands as if to beg.

"And you, Head of *Diplomatic Relations*?" Her bells jingled as she tilted her head. "What do you think of that? Do you agree?"

Tsevannah felt her husband's stare like she would

Drakash's midday glare. For all his soft voice that after-noon, and his gentleness with his compatriots, Tsevan-nah and Faloorah knew the real Sekhran Ganaresh Ti-Vaour: a man of flame and gold and conviction no other living creature could ever compare to. A man unafraid to do what every other diplomat, official, and even Lord seemed afraid to do. She knew what he said was true, and he knew she knew it, too.

"My Sekhran's words are final," she said, and that was the end of it for her.

But not for the Empress. She bristled, the fur on her tails puffing until each one was almost as wide as her body, and her ears snapped back as she hissed, "I will not answer treachery with more treachery, *Yasilan.* The Winter King is a Lord, and an ally to all of us, if a forget-ful one! We can still—!"

Sekhran Ganaresh stood so quickly that the huge chair he sat in fell over. He turned on the Empress, his mouth unhooking wider than was natural as scales lined his jaw, and a clicking sound like the smack of hammer against stone filled the room. Tsevannah didn't step away in time, and so she felt the brutal heat on her face as a stream of red and gold poured from the Sekhran's mouth, flame pouring onto the Empress like lava. The Empress's aide leapt back with a yelp as her Lady went up in fire and deep, black smoke.

When the flame finished pouring from Sekhran Ganaresh's mouth, however, what was left wasn't the charred body of a woman. Rather, it was a stump, glow-ing with embers and leaving soot all over the seat. A substitute—a trick of Akerijin illusion. It was sustained by the magic of little Hana, so that she might speak remotely, like High Priestess Nhale Ba did through her sister.

All stayed silent. Nobody so much as twitched until the Sekhran sat back down in his throne. He looked around at all of them, all sense of softness and peace gone from his face; in his bright, fiery eyes were the hard edges, the brutal gleam, of a dragon proper. Tsevannah ducked her head as if signaling to others what was no doubt obvious: the Sekhran's word was the ultimate law in this conference room, his actions the ultimate and final stroke of justice.

And yet, one dared break that silence.

"Now that my Lady is gone," Hana said with a brittle, croaking voice, no doubt drained from having to keep up the illusion around that charred stump, "I can give you this."

Tsevannah bit back a sigh. How exhausting it must've been, to work behind the back of her Empress, knowing the Lady had lost all sense with the Winter King's betrayal. Still, she was a good contact, a fantastic keeper of the spies planted throughout Winter—and a fantastic keeper of the runestone she pulled from her robes. Just like the runestone once used to contact the Winter King, this one was small, black, and carved with a specific sigil in it that was unlike any of the other Winter letters. She went to that empty chair, pushed the King's old runestone away, and set down the new one.

Once she did, a servant came forward from the back of the room with a small vial of what looked like liquid silver. Tsevannah shifted on her stool and wrapped her arms around herself. She knew full well what it was, much as she wished she didn't. Raliyah, the Head of Medicine, hadn't stopped crowing about it since she'd taken it: the blood of that half-Winter woman. Apparently, it was just as silver as any of the grotesque dried jerkies and blood pellets the Ismären took throughout the Seasons to keep their magic strong and vibrant.

The servant uncorked the bottle and put a modest drop onto the runestone. Normally, there would have to be a half-Ismar there like Hana was for her Empress:

someone whose magic, or at least whose vial of deer blood, could activate the rune and channel it properly. With no half-breeds left in Winter and no Ismären capable of surviving the endless Summer, however, this was the first—and best—chance to bridge the gap between Summer and Winter that they'd had in a long time.

After a moment, the drop of blood seeped into the runestone like water into parched earth. Then the whole rune lit up, pulsing its eerie silver light, waiting for someone far away to answer its call.

MARGRAVINE ISOLDE BEURVICH OF TAUBECH was made of ice like all the rest of her people. She knew none of the pains of hunger she'd heard fleshlings once wail about. Certainly, she knew none of the misery of freezing either, though she'd seen it: the way flesh turned black and fell away in Winter's deep cold. Yet still, she thought she might've felt something of the fleshling struggle then, as she stood at the table with her phantom guests: exhaustion.

And the sharp stare needling into her back from the shadows did not help.

In front of her, however, was a much different scene than what lingered behind her. The round face of the Baron of Trevannt swished about above an empty chair, anchored to the table by his respective runestone. He was but a collection of silver dust, a near transparent image born of snow and ice and magic—not really there, but able to speak to Isolde as if he were. It was a type of magic that transcended messages, letters. One that allowed anyone to speak anytime, anywhere, so long as they had a contact's runestone. Then it was a simple matter of setting the runestone down, waking up its effects with a brief touch of one's own magic, and waiting for the other party to see the silver flash of the sigil engraved on it before they, too, connected across the world. Such power her people had, that they could transcend time and space, in a way fleshlings could never conceive of. Such was the power of Cervora and her kin, the white deer. What they had as beasts, the Ismären perfected as people.

"What, then?" The Baron's face didn't move as his voice rippled through the room. "What does this mean for us?"

Bone deep, she'd heard fleshling merchants say. *Tired to the bone.* But she had no bones. Only a soul. One that felt thick, heavy, with a fatigue she dared to say was even deeper than whatever *bone deep* meant.

Isolde rubbed her temples as if she could reach her soul and massage the heaviness out of it. She glanced at her meeting room table there, at the four nobles who, along with Viscount Erik Rachfemd, had put all their hopes on a plan they should've known better than to trust. The other heads of her co-conspirators—the Viscountess of Schirrtel, the Duchess of the East Reach, the Count of the Diamond Hold, and the Baron of Trevannt—likewise floated above their runestones. There was one more runestone, too, at one more empty seat, though it was still dark for the time being.

"It seems to me that it means we remain in our seats, beholden to our King," the Duchess said. Her magical stand-in still captured her thick ringlets of hair and her oddly long lashes, so long they nearly eclipsed her eyes,

as was the fashion of the East. The little head bobbed
about the empty chair Isolde set for her. "And lucky we
are, that your little lordling from Rehrvig hasn't revealed our whole plot to that King. That we know of, at
least. Cervora knows the Duke of those lands would've
never been so stupid as to let things fall apart like this."

Duke Jovann dur Dechem. How Isolde would've
crushed her own hand between her teeth to have that
man on board. What a pity that he wasn't, given his
family's once prolific trade of shadow-red cherries that
brought his lands so much fortune. But try as she might
to hint at such things during balls or other gatherings,
the dur Dechem brothers never once showed any inter-
est in trying to get the seasons to move again if their
King demanded they stay put.

What a disappointment that'd been, finding out how
deep the dur Dechem allegiance ran to the crown. For
so long before the High Summer, Isolde refused the
hands of so many other suitors, hoping one day Jovann
would see the merit in their partnership—he, the master of the fields that produced such valuable wonders
for fleshlings, and she, the lady of what were once Winter's greatest ports—but to discover this cowardice in
him after that great Summer tragedy, she instead closed
her mind to the concept of courtship altogether. She
would be the sole holder of her titles and her lands, and
her *ports,* whenever this damn wall fell and the Ringland
lakeshore was once again open to her.

The Viscountess of Schirrtel's voice scraped against
Isolde's soul. "But that leaves all this work for nothing!
How are we supposed to explain this to our people,
now? How are we supposed to undo all this? Such a plot
is *decades* in the making; no one will forget our truth just
because we demand it of them!"

A valid concern. Even as Isolde tucked her hands behind her back, she flexed her fingers, as she had a habit

of doing after watching her people throughout these past three-odd decades. *The King is a greedy tyrant*, they told their people, stirring them against the Crown they assumed would one day fall, be it by foreign hands or domestic. *The King is a wicked man, who would rob you of your birthright as Ismären.* That birthright being the flesh and blood of Cervora's kin. And so, to prove their lies as truth, they held the meager rations of meat and blood that the capital sent down to them, refused to cull any white deer themselves, and told their people to make do with less and less. They did so until the faces of the people had gone cracked and glassy, until light shined from the souls in the people's heads just like it did from the starlights in the city lamps.

"They'll riot," came the Count's raspy whisper. "They'll crush us into snow."

The Baron barked a laugh. "You think so? No, no, Hefner, I figure they'll be too wrapped up in that *icon* the King's up and discovered. The woman Viscount Rachfemd sent from the Summerlands," his visage sparkled as a stray beam of sunlight caught the ice that made up his magical image, "can you believe it? Her, a mutt, our Mother reborn? Even the merchants and travelers who come through our city from far up north have been going around saying as much: the woman's a fraud. The King's a fool to believe in such nonsense."

"I've heard stories, though," the Duchess muttered. "She's got silver blood. Frost that can reverse the inner melt. Antlers and hooves, even. A spitting image of the Cervora our forefathers wrote about. Deny her as a mutt all you want, but are you telling me you'd deny a wash of frost over someone you love, Lord Fervall? The King has made his foolish decisions, but I do wonder if it's fair to call him a fool in all, especially for this."

Isolde stared at the table. She had yet to tell any of them what she'd heard from the conversation that she'd had with Viscount Rachfemd, the plot he'd cooked up to fix his failures. By the way the talk had turned, as well— the rumors that had grown too far, too widespread, too conflicting, to do anything about—she wouldn't tell them, either. There was no world where Erik Rachfemd's desperate scheme achieved the results he promised; as it was, trusting the fool as much as they did had been a mistake. The other nobles' voices kept warbling in her ears as she melted into her own thoughts, and by the nature of their communications, they thankfully saw her only as she saw them: as a silent, but present head, floating wherever it was that they held their meetings. They didn't see how she flexed her hands, absently appreciating how fluidly they moved. They didn't see how she put her teeth to the velvet of her lip and moved it about, either. As far as they knew, she was as despondent as all of them, their future ravaged with uncertainty.

But Isolde Beurvich, Margravine of Taubech, did not come so far and do so much—starving her own people of magic, watching her once flourishing home on the lake crumble to nothing behind a great white wall—only to give up here.

"I have someone I'd like you all to meet," Isolde said. She glanced at the dead runestone in the corner again, knowing she likely didn't have much time before a separate conversation opened. "Someone else who can help us with this disaster."

"Oh, what, as well as that Rachfemd whelp helped?" There was no hiding the disdain in the Duchess's voice.

But the stare that had shorn down on Isolde this whole time went sharper, and the tap of shoes against the stone made Isolde blink.

"Isolde," the Duchess said, no doubt hearing those footsteps. "Who is with you?"

"Efir Dalmoulah Ti-Vaour," said the creature that

slinked up next to Isolde. He towered over her, a striking thing that was built more like a cat than a dragon,
even under several layers of wool. His skin was a light,
sallow brown that clung to his high cheekbones, his
nose strong and slanted, his eyes all but glowing a venomous green under thick black brows. His dark hair had
been slicked back under a snug leather cap, one with
goggles nestled at the top, and he tugged a thick black
scarf down from around his mouth, which only made
his words that much crisper. "I'm here on behalf of my
father, Sekhran Ganaresh Ti-Vaour, to fix the problem
you face. I understand there's been quite a conundrum
among you and your compatriots."

He was a clever thing, this poison lizard from the
Summer swamplands. He spoke the Ismar language as
if it were poetry, and his accent made each word sound
like the edge of a decorative blade. Isolde waited. Many
a silent second ticked by before someone at her table
finally spoke.

The Baron muttered, "Well, at least we can be sure a
Ti-Vaour will do the job."

The Yasilan smiled at that. He stepped away from the
table and paced, passing Isolde and just barely brushing
his jacket past her back. It made her soul shudder in her
head.

"I bring word from my father: we are at our limit.
The Ringlands must move again, no matter what. If that
means bringing Spring, Summer, and Autumn armies
to your door, so be it. But hopefully, with my help,"
he glanced around at the flickering visages of Isolde's
allies, "I'll be able to snatch up our traitor before such
a thing comes to pass. And I'll be able to personally put
your King's crown into your hands. But I'm also here
to warn you," he paused, glancing at Isolde with such
a wicked smile that she thought she saw a glimmer of
red sparkle off him with her onyx eyes, "that if we have

no announcement of the moving of seasons within one month of you getting the crown, be prepared to see these walls crumble from the outside, in a wash of fire."

Again, silence. Even Isolde could've forsaken everything, to hear such a threat. Fire in Winter again—*dragons* in Winter again, this time truly out to lap up the ice melt her people left behind. She never thought it'd come to this: relying on the very spies and soldiers she would've liked to keep far, far away from her hold. But there was nothing more to be done. There was no more room for error, neither on the Winter side of the border or the Summer side.

I'm sorry, Erik. He'd given her an interesting plan, at least. A plan to make that mutt force the King's hand by holding her for ransom. But this was a safer plan, much safer: one that would guarantee her and her fellows' hands were clean of this mess and that the King, dangerous and unpredictable thing that he was, wouldn't pose a threat to any of them as they seized his crown and the fake goddess he made his Queen. *I can't rely on you anymore.*

Granted, he could try. Isolde would let him try to raise that woman's esteem, to steal her away. That would be his head on the line in the end, and having the supposed icon of Cervora in their grip would benefit them all the more if he successfully convinced the country that this was, in fact, Cervora, despite the circulating slander. But the King still needed to die, and the woman's equally unpredictable actions needed to be likewise dealt with, and Erik had already failed them once. There was no room to fail again.

Isolde raised her head when the silence stretched too thin. "That's all there is to tell you today. Be steadfast, keep to your commitments, and trust that this time, all this misfortune will be corrected for good. When I have more to report, you'll hear from me again."

Then she cut the magic she'd been flowing into each of those runestones, and one by one, the wispy wraiths disappeared. Isolde dropped her shoulders and shook her head. The sudden rush of her magic back into her ice made her hazy, and she grabbed for a small bottle of bloodwine she'd kept on a shelf under the table.

"Are you well?" The Yasilan peered at her as if trying to shear off her velvet with his gaze.

"Fine." The magic stung her throat and prickled in her abdomen as the blood flowed down into her innermost cavities. "Did you mean what you said? About the fire?" She paused before asking her real question: "Will we really face your armies if we don't move the seasons?"

He only smiled at her a moment longer before pulling his scarf back over his mouth and nose. The silence said enough.

Disturbed, Isolde went for the one last rune at the end of the table, the only one that hadn't lit up during the conversation with her allies. "Well, I'm glad you made it safely and found your way here. Did you have much trouble? Making it to me?"

"No, no. I found my way here easily enough; thank you for your concern."

Something about the way he spoke made her magic skitter under her velvet. It was whispery, soft as smoke and just as noxious.

"Good," she said, hopefully sounding as comfortable as if she were talking to any other Ismar. "I appreciate your willingness to give a few words to my allies. They've been understandably unnerved in all this ruckus." Isolde turned to Efir and studied him. "Remember: you have three weeks, according to the announcement the Crown made about their wedding tour. If you can make it to the King *within three weeks*, you may very well be able to put an end to this situation before he and his bride are on the road; it'll save you quite some trouble."

Efir raised a brow and smiled as if holding back a chuckle. "Yes. *Three weeks.* I understand, Lady Beurvich; you've made yourself very clear. You need not worry about how I get from one end of this country to the other in that time."

Isolde stared at him, then blinked her nerves away and nodded. "Forgive me. I just want to impress upon you: the travel here is harsh, and if you can't fly for fear of being spot—"

The Yasilan raised a thin finger to his masked face. "Leave such things to me."

Another moment passed, and despite the nerves twisting knots in Isolde's soul, she nodded and decided, against all the sense in the world, to trust the Yasilan to know what he was doing. "Here." She picked up that one lifeless rune and handed it to him. When Efir took the rune, she said, "That there is what you've asked for. A rune to connect you to your father."

He inspected it, brows furrowing. "It seems dead."

"You need magic to operate it." Isolde snuck past him like a mouse past a sleeping cat and reached into the shelf under the table. A much smaller vial of bloodwine sat in a red glass bottle, a relic from a time when real glassware was still flowing through Winter, and she plucked it off the shelf and handed it to him. "You may be able to find a white deer or so from time to time; save the blood of those beasts when you find them. A drop is all you need to sustain a half hour's connection."

Efir squinted at the bottle, then took it and slipped it into one of the many pockets on his coat. As soon as he did, though, the rune in his hands began to pulse with silver light, and Isolde flinched, knowing full well who was on the other end. He glanced at her with the question written clearly in his eyes.

"Put it down on the table," she said, and once he did, she held out a hand to stop him from pulling that little bottle back out. "Don't waste your bloodwine yet. Let me."

Isolde let her eyes slip shut, steadying her thoughts. Then she willed her magic up from her stomach, its freezing power slipping through her chest, across her shoulders, down her arms, and into her palms. She cupped her hands towards the rune and let her magic flow down as easily as water might from a stream, and when she opened her eyes, she watched as all that silvery stuff gradually took form, spinning and twisting and curling into the perfect image of the man she feared most in the world.

Efir startled. "My Sekhran," he said, bowing his head, and Isolde tapped him.

"He can't see you," she whispered. "Only a still image. Like you saw from the others."

"Efir, my son," came Sekhran Ganaresh's booming voice. Just the timbre of it was enough to strike a scrambling fear into Isolde's soul. This was the man that had let so many of her countrymen melt—and was the man that would give the order to destroy them all again, if they didn't get that crown off the Winter King's head. It made Isolde's soul quake. "What a strange way to see you. I trust you're in the care of our allies."

"I am. This one's done well, this Isolde Beurvich."

"Isolde Beurvich." Even if the wispy illusion of the Sekhran didn't move, Isolde could've sworn she felt those burning eyes start to melt holes into her head. "I'll remember this name. Thank you, little lady, for once again bridging the way between Winter and Summer."

Then the two dragons began chattering to each other in Yasilan. Isolde, having not used the language in a century, forgot most of the words; she only caught snippets here and there, pieces of that throaty, musical language.

Words like "find" and "kill" and "soon" were the only things she could make out, and she wished she'd forgotten those words, too. But she stood there, being a guest in her own home as the two dragons talked, until finally, the image of the Sekhran disappeared, and Efir looked to her again.

"I'll have word as soon as I can," he said. "No doubt this rock works with yours as well?"

Isolde forced back a frown. She didn't want this dragon to be able to call her anytime, anywhere. Not when people might be watching and listening. But this was her ally, too, just as much as any of the others at her table, and she needed to know what was happening from as many sources as she could get. That was why, against her better judgement, she took her runestone and held it up to Efir's, flowing her magic in until they both pulsed and glowed at the same time in perfect unison.

"Do not call unless absolutely necessary, and even then, only after the sun has gone down." When she pulled her stone away, she pulled her magic away with it, and both stones stopped glowing. "When you want to speak to your father, think of him. Call him whenever you need. When you want to speak to me, think of me—and again, only at night."

Efir's mouth was covered, but Isolde still knew he was smiling by how his eyes crinkled at their corners. They flashed in the starlight, and his voice hissed smooth and low.

"I heard you the first time, little Isolde. Be sure that I'll entertain you for as many of those dark hours as I can each night I have something to tell."

Isolde squeaked a wordless complaint, her soul bouncing around her head as she tried to correct whatever misconception got into the dragon's head, but she could find nothing to say. Efir only chuckled at her stupor and walked past her, towards the one cliff-facing window the room had, and he tossed one gleaming look back at her before he crawled out and disappeared into the deep night. Then, and only then, did Isolde manage to relax.

But to relax was to think, and to think was to invite that soul-crushing exhaustion back into her ice again.

SEVEN DAYS CAME AND WENT SO QUICKLY ON THE ROAD.

It was strange to think that just a week ago, Helen was still the head priestess of the castle, the main priestess of the King himself—and yet a week later, there she was, far away from all of it. She was surrounded by nothing but trees and old road and, in that moment, rickety little buildings as the carriage came to a stop. Both her and her carriage driver needed to rest to integrate a new portion of meat and bloodwine before continuing their journey. He'd dropped her off and gone to take their things to the quiet little inn down the road, and Helen was thankful he hadn't questioned her when she said she wanted to meet with the Winter people in the tavern that night. It gave her as good a chance as any to begin scattering her warnings as they worked their way towards not her little hamlet hometown, but the Church of Cervora's main city just before it: Ladensfor.

Helen brushed the snow from her shoulders. Even after a week of travel, it felt strange to be outside without her antlers on her head; the missing weight made it feel like her head would come off her shoulders and roll away if she moved it too quickly. That weight, though, was transferred to her clothing; she still wasn't quite used to the common, heavy furs of traveling folk to keep the snow from crusting to her dresses. It was all wrong, all amiss, and those clothes threatened to pull her down to the ground in her heartbreak—all while her soul still reeled at all that had changed in such a short time.

But there was no time to think about it. There was a job to do, a people to warn, a faith to preserve, and this was the first village they'd come across after so long traveling through the woods and frozen grasslands outside the capital. The night was dark and silent, interrupted only by the faint twinkle of life ahead: a tavern, where fleshlings would once come to make their stinking food, and where Ismären had since taken over, serving what excess bloodwine and deer-flesh they had from cathedral services to the laborers who needed it. Mostly, though, these places were dens of filth, even for her people: places where they would gamble, get loud and wild with one another, and on occasion, even violent. Helen was thankful that King Jädrich took her suggestion to shut the few in Vörnein down to make space for other shops and businesses, lest they fill the capital with their filth.

This tavern wasn't particularly grandstanding. It was a little wooden building with a scant few starlights around its doorway so folks didn't trip on the icy step that jutted up from the ground. A couple of tiny, snow-clustered windows were too dingy and unclean for Helen to make out more than a few moving shapes behind the ice-panes, but as she approached that step, she could hear it: the raucous laughter of the townspeople, the buzzing conversation that became a low hum like Spring bees. It made Helen shudder. This was a logging village, not the castle, and she knew better than to expect the same level of decorum she'd grown used to, but it still scattered her nerves to hear such commotion before she even opened the door. At least her onyx eyes didn't flash red with any signs of danger.

She squeezed her empty hands tight, and she gathered her nerves as best as she could before finally pushing the tavern door open. Her eyes stayed on the floor as if it would suddenly drop out beneath her if she wasn't careful, and she stamped her boots off on the raggy doormat before finally finding it in herself to lift her gaze. Immediately, she wished she hadn't.

Men and women alike stared at her, though the noise and chatter and, in one far corner, the singing and slamming of fists on the table, didn't stop. An old wooden chandelier hung from the ceiling, full of starlights that cast their cool blue light over all the tavern, and the place was clustered with round wooden tables seating four to five people, with barely enough space for the barmaids to get between everyone with little cups of bloodwine. Loggers needed quite some magic to get those heavy trees felled and processed, she knew, and it seemed there was a healthy surplus of Cervora's kin sent here to sustain them, which was good to see. While the noise rattled her nerves all over again, it was the men's stares especially that made her want to back right up out of that tavern and flee back to the castle, on foot if need be. Without her priestly garments, she supposed she was just another woman to them, and that meant their eyes sparkled with something like she'd seen in the glowing eyes of wolves in the forest by the castle. It'd been many, many years since she suffered stares like those.

Helen tucked her hood tighter around her head, the fur rim obscuring some of those stares, and she hurried for one of the few open spaces at the bar. Thankfully, a woman sat beside her, though the way she scanned Helen with a faint, knowing smile didn't make the former priestess any more comfortable than if it'd been a man leering down at her. Especially given that woman had no ring on her finger, and yet the bearded, shaggy-haired man on the other side of her was rather brazenly wrapping his work-chipped fingers around her waist and pulling her closer. It was the first time something struck Helen as truly odd about an Ismar's eyes: the man's were a cheap, clear quartz that only made every crackle of magic from his soul that much more vibrant in them. The woman's eyes were the same onyx as every other's, yet somehow so deep and dark and *empty,* as if they were two holes looking to gobble Helen up.

Is this what people see in my eyes? In all women's eyes? She hoped not. No, it must've been the way the woman's smile curled into a wolfish half-grin that made those eyes seem so.

"What can I get for you, Miss Pip?"

Helen startled at the heavy thud of a hand on the counter. The main barmaid stared her down, her thick braids swinging past the linen shirt she'd pulled off her shoulders. It only stayed in place thanks to the reddish-brown leather apron stained with glitters of silver, as if the bloodwine she served day in and day out became imbued into the very stitches of her clothes. Like the woman beside her, there was something in her eyes— and the hook of her smirk—that made her seem not like a doe, but like a bobcat. The way she loomed, too, was striking—and then Helen realized just how the barmaid had to hunch a bit to face Helen, and how Helen had to look *up* at that other woman. Yes, that was it: they were taller, their faces harsher in their cheeks and the points of their chin, their frame broader and thicker. Built for work, built to last. Not like Helen, carved small and kept delicate for service in the temples from a young age.

"Well?" The barmaid dropped to one elbow to meet Helen's eye and planted the other hand on her rump, as if she were talking to a child. "What'll it be? Cuppa wine?" Then she raked a rough look over Helen's coat. "Maybe take your coat for you? Looks like you're trying to melt yourself, all packed up like that."

It was only then that Helen really understood that this woman was talking to her. Helen blinked. "I—no thank you. I won't be here long. But the snows are thick, and I don't want to ruin my clothes with ice; I'm just traveling."

"Yeah? Where to?"

"Ladensfor."

"Ladensfor!" The barmaid stood up to her full height and pursed her lips as if appraising good craftsmanship, twirling a braid as she glanced at the other people at the bar. They chuckled, and a few whispered to each other before the barmaid said, "*Fancy.* Been a while since a little doe came traveling *to* that place and not out of it. Lemme guess: you're a chapel girl come running home?"

A chapel girl! Of course these bumpkins wouldn't recognize her for who she was, but to see her and think *chapel girl,* hardly more than the earliest initiate into priestly service, and one that would *run* from her duties at that, made Helen's soul shrink with bitterness. Between that and the louder ripple of laughter at the table, the mutterings she caught—things like "aw, poor girl" and "those beast-esses must've run her out," and "think she'll come home with me if I give her a good bed?"—Helen's velvet rippled with prickly frustration. Her nerves went from scattered to singularly focused into a sphere of pure silver, so insulted was she, and stood from the bar and threw her hood off.

"No, I'm not some *chapel girl*," Helen snapped. She pulled from under her coat a silver medal etched with Cervora's antlers and the spiked leaves and berries of Winter's holly: a symbol of her status as part of Cervora's priestesses. When the barkeep saw it, she blinked in surprise, and so Helen turned to the people and likewise flashed that bit of silver around for all to see and acknowledge. "For over a century, I've served as the High Priestess of Vörnein's Keep and ministered communion directly to our very King himself, thank you very much." Then, before her nerves could flake away and take her voice with it, she looked around at the people of the bar. They were staring at her, all those loggers and shopkeepers and barmaids, and a sudden hush blanketed them like fresh snow. Helen lifted her chin and spoke, just the way Clara suggested she do. "I've left the King's castle to give you all a warning, that your faiths might stay untainted by the lies you'll no doubt come to hear soon."

She looked around without seeing, as she feared lingering on any of the faces of the townspeople would rattle the words out of her mouth before she could say them. Before her resolve left her, and with the blissful silence to echo and lift her words, Helen clasped her hands together and delivered her ill news like she might a particularly severe sermon.

"The King has invited blasphemy into our country, my people. Blasphemy. He took up a candidate for Queen—the Lady Aveline Rachfemd—and intends to marry her." *If he hasn't already.* The thought made her soul twist—but then, what self-respecting priestess would write that contract? "However, the woman goes around calling herself Cervora's Icon. She claims to be our Mother reborn."

If the few faces she saw before saying that were scrunched in confusion, they were suddenly wiped blank, eyes wide and lips parted.

"And is she?" One villager by the far wall, an empty cup in his hand, stared. "Is she—?"

"Absolutely not," Helen said with a sharp shake of her head. "I examined her myself, and I can tell you: this woman is false. We've discovered her to be a fleshling with Winter's face: a mixed-blood, and a bastard at that." *Careful. Careful.* To say "mixed-blood" was risky enough. No one knew about the Yasilan blood in that beast except Helen and Clara, and it would do no good for the King to eventually hear these rumors and pinpoint exactly who spread them. Just the thought of what the King would do made her squeeze her hands tighter together. "However, she may come spread her wiles, and she may deceive you with—"

"Hey, now!"

A woman stood up from some table far back in the tavern, tucked into the shadows. The other people near her startled as if they didn't know she was there, and as far as Helen was concerned, she might as well have just materialized from nothing. Her hair was pinned up in a worker's bun, her clothes plain green with a white, unstained apron, and she stood as if she was used to shifting her weight off one leg.

"I know exactly who you're talking about," the woman said, and she pointed an accusatory finger at Helen, "and I won't have you slandering her! That 'bastard' you're talking about saved my life! She *cured my melt!*"

Helen's words were snatched right out of her mouth. She stammered, trying to get them back, "What—well, that's—as I was saying, it's decep—"

The woman rushed past the cluster of people, tables, and chairs to meet Helen there in the middle of the bar. She looked around at the crowd and waved her arms as if she could smack Helen's warnings out of the air. "Forget this nonsense! I'll tell you the *real* truth about the Lady our King's a-marrying: she's Cervora, through and through! Who else could take my leg and make it better? Look!"

The woman tore her shoe off and raised her skirt enough to poke out her leg. After a few initial whistles at the pale thing peeking out from those skirts, a ripple of murmurs spread—because the woman's leg was fine, but her *toes* were slightly misshapen, the velvet a little floppy, yet there was no doubt that the foot was frozen. *Refrozen,* if that lumpiness and sagging velvet was any indication. Helen's soul went alight with prickling anxiety to see such a thing.

"I was fixed! I was *saved,* damn it, on the day I went to the castle to die with a host of Living Waterskins under the King's own hand! And it was the soon-to-be Queen that did it, with a *breath* of frost!" The woman didn't wait to see the reaction of the silent crowd before she faced Helen with her teeth bared like some animal. "And you'd speak against that?"

"Because it's a *trick—!*" Helen tried to say, but the scrape of another chair cut her off, and another voice came from some other shadowy part of the tavern.

"How do we even know you're actually a priestess, huh? For all we know, you just stole that medal! Someone should go check with the priestess here and see!"

Helen wheeled around to protest, only to see yet another face she didn't remember: some skinny-headed thing, his hair a tuft on top of his head. Granted, Helen hadn't been looking very hard, but wouldn't she have noticed someone like—?

"And the *Head Priestess* of the King's own castle, to boot," came a grumble of someone closer, one of the men who'd leered at her coming in. When Helen glanced at him, she caught him tapping his friend's shoulder and chuckling. Then he turned to her and tapped his cup to the table. "That's ambitious, ain't it? I'd have picked a more believable lie, girl, if you're gonna go swinging a stolen medal around."

"What—it's not a lie—!"

"Hey, though, is it true?" Other folks started crowding that girl with her misshapen foot, pointing at it. "Is it really true? Your melt got *reversed?*"

"I swear on my life," she said, her chest puffed proud. She shot Helen a venomous look and let her voice echo through the whole tavern. "And more than that, the woman changed her appearance *right in front of me!* She sprouted antlers like she was sprouting daisies on her head! She had *hooves*, I tell you, black hooves! She was Cervora!"

A man waved a hand. "Oh, come on—"

"It's true! And if you don't believe me, you should at least believe me about the melt! Who else could do that but Cervora?"

"A liar, that's who!" Helen tried again to wrest the floor from that girl. "A fleshling with a convenient mix of—!"

"Of what? What do you suggest she's mixed with, huh?" The girl marched forward, each step an intentional *thud,* and pointed in Helen's face. The rage in her eyes sparkled like stars. "What fleshling do you know that can spit up *frost?* You say you examined her? What'd you find, then?"

Helen blinked. "I—I'm not at liberty to say—"

A roar of protest came up from the tavern, including from the girl as she walked away and threw her arms up, instigating the crowd further. It came so suddenly that Helen flinched and found herself shrinking, as if that would hide her from all those slanted faces, all those furrowed brows and roaring mouths.

The girl whirled around and pointed at Helen.

"You're a liar. And you're trying to steal a gift from these here people! I mean, who here knows someone who was melted?" When she turned to the crowd, she asked again. "Who knows someone who was melted? Or is melting right now?"

Hands shot up as people stood with her, their focus wholly engrossed in that girl's yipping and yelling. Something bumped into Helen and nearly made her yelp, but she looked up to see a man eyeing the girl—and more behind him, pressing closer. His hand was on Helen's shoulder, pushing lightly so that he could get closer, and the *scowl* he dropped on Helen's head when he finally looked down at her shattered her resolve.

"The Icon of Cervora can fix them," the girl called as the crowd pressed in, looking at her leg, even reaching forward to touch it and test how frozen it really was. She beamed as she looked at the crowd, who, as they passed Helen and forced her towards the door, might as well have acted like Helen didn't even exist. Helen watched this crowd ogle that girl, that deceived, lost thing, and all her nerves faded into something so numb that the girl's next words hardly registered. "The Icon can fix them, and she's here! She's here, and she's coming to fix all of us! All of us!"

This is bad. A hollow space opened up in Helen's head, as if a hole had been punched straight through her soul. *This is very bad.*

Didn't these people see? That they were being swept up in lies, in sweet gifts that were actually traps? Couldn't they understand that this "fixing" was a corruption of the real Cervora's glory? Or were they so easily swayed by the promise of fixing their simple ice bodies in such imperfect ways—what with that lumpy foot, those floppy, empty velvet toes? Why did they holler and yip and yell with such joy over what was simply the frost of a bastard half-dragon? And who even *knew* if this "cure" would last—or if it was only temporary, given it was the "cure" given by a creature of the very sun that melted them all?

That last part, Helen hadn't even said to Clara. She hoped, she prayed, that the true Cervora would never allow such a thing to happen again, and that she would sustain this mock-miracle in order to truly save her people. But what an insult it was, that a goddess proper should have to hide behind the miracles of a goddess imposter.

Helen pulled her hood back up. Her priestly medallion stuck to her velvet under her coat; it slid against her chest as she made a sharp turn for the door. She'd lost her temper and spoke before she should've in that tavern, clearly. It was a mistake to think the common people would understand something said in words alone, without the sigil and signature of the Council of Bishops. But Helen would plead her case, discuss her findings—and she would see to it that the Council understood the grave issues coming to plague the Church and its people. If they wouldn't listen to her, those townsfolk, then they would have no choice but to obey the authority of the clergy that still wore their antlers with pride.

She shoved the door open, her silhouette interrupting the square of blueish-white light that sliced through the night shadows. The carriage was some ways down the road. With a soul so heavy that it felt like her head was stuffed with stones, Helen left the tavern and marched for the carriage. This was a failure, yes, but it wasn't the end. No, she refused to let it be the end. For the King's sake, for the country's sake—for *Cervora's* sake—she refused to let this be the first and last effort to keep this country out of the sin of blasphemy.

The Council of Bishops would hear her. The Council of Bishops would help. And if they didn't believe her claims, just as the townspeople hadn't, then she would show them exactly what happened in that conference room. She tapped her breast and felt it soon enough: the hard edges of the runestone she kept in her pocket, near and safe, that only the most trusted and holy eyes would see. The runestone that would fix this, the runestone that would reveal the truth that anyone with eyes in their head could surely make sense of.

The runestone that recorded every word of Clara's findings in that conference room and every moment of the half-dragon's frost on Clara's face.

Karina slumped back in her chair and let her eyes slip shut. She breathed from her gut to keep from gasping and making too much noise, though that didn't stop her heart from fluttering like a little bird in a cage. She kept her teeth gritted tight, too, as by the *gods,* did her head hurt. Yet still, she was alive. She'd done it: she'd spawned and moved *two* separate ice-puppets in a remote location, even made them speak, without having to be close by to manage them herself. And as the sweet smell of bloodwine called her to grab the cup before her, she could only smile. The smell didn't quite match the taste—iron with a tinge of honey—but it eased the shaking in her legs and the beating of her heart, at least.

Such was the beauty of being a *mixed-blood,* as the Ismären sneered at people like her: where she might've needed the help of another Akerijin's magic to support the illusions she'd planted a whole separate hold away, her Wintry ancestry meant she was her *own* help. It meant she could make ice-puppets, not just wood-puppets, and that a steady stream of bloodwine could help her sustain the magic required to operate such things from a decent distance away. Maybe not a whole *country* away, but a hold or two away, absolutely—and that was more than a full-blooded Akerijin could do. Far more. Could even Empress Feng Souram accomplish something like this? Karina doubted it.

"I take it you succeeded?"

Behind her, leaning against the doorway, was Erik. No doubt he'd waited until she was done with her channeling to open that door, lest the recording rune someone planted in the foyer ceiling catch her acting strange. His study made for a good, small place to do her work in comfort; the chair, simple wood as it was, kept her from hunching over during the connection she had to keep with those puppets. Even if there was a rune in the house recording all sounds and sights, it couldn't record much if that study door was closed and Karina kept quiet.

Karina nodded. A sleepy smile stretched on her face. "I did." But the rush of her success didn't last too long. After a sip of bloodwine, Karina said, "We have problems, though."

"Hmm? What? How?" Erik ripped himself off that door frame and towered over her. "What happened?"

"It's as you suspected." Karina sighed and tried to massage the ache from her temples. "I've been watching over that mouse since she was sent packing, and the first time she finds herself in a tavern, she starts speaking all kinds of nastiness against your *cargo*."

It was irritating, having to speak half in code, but Karina understood why Erik hadn't taken that bug from his ceiling yet. The recording rune up there would be better to prove innocence than guilt, should it ever come up in some kind of court.

The sound of Erik's hands clacking against his face made Karina finally turn to face him. He rubbed the hair at his brows and, after a moment, uncovered his face to look at her. Had she not known better, she would've thought Erik was made of flesh, with how his face sagged and his eyes went dull in his exhaustion.

"Well, that's frustrating. Anything we can do to keep the mouse quiet?"

Karina shrugged. "She got laughed out of that tavern easily enough. I doubt she'll be so bold as to try that again any time soon."

"You hope." No doubt, if Erik had any lungs to sigh with, he would've; Karina never saw the man look so fed up with his own people as right then. He shook his head and lifted himself off the doorway, waving a hand as he left. "Well, fantastic work all the same, my friend. Truly, I do not know what I'd do without you." Then he paused and peered back into the study. "You *are* coming with us, I imagine. On the tour around the country."

Karina stared at him. That wasn't part of their original agreement of dealing with the orphan's mess, but if Erik's sharp gaze was any indication, then it seemed this extra service was non-negotiable. Again. "If that's what you'd like me to do," she said, and she did nothing to hide her irritation with how roughly the words left her lips.

Erik didn't seem to notice, though. He only nodded and said, "Good. Now get yourself some rest; the Crown requested we arrive early to the marriage announcement in the morning. We leave for the city square at first light."

Then he left Karina alone. She *did* sigh, if quietly, and she turned her back from where that recording rune was and rubbed her eyes. The piece of onyx in her face felt smooth against her eyelids, unlike her lump of pyrite, and the wrappings around her other eye crinkled against her fingertips.

This is becoming a hassle. Karina chewed her lip. *A downright hassle.*

At that point, it might've been easier to find someone

else to help her secure her mother's lands instead of that fickle lord. He'd been running her ragged, all but trapping her in that room to maneuver her ice-puppets and either dig for or deposit information among the people. Maybe it would work out with Erik still. Maybe all would be fine, and Erik would keep his end of the deal—amended and annoying as it was becoming. But like her father taught her, she would have to be ready at a moment's notice to leave one deal and have something better secured in the background.

Only what was better than this? Karina chewed her lip. Where else could she get authority like Erik's over those lands?

Sniff it out. That would've been her father's response. *There's more than one berry in the woods. Find another.*

The ache in Karina's temple grew sharper, and she banished the thought before it split her head in two.

"T̲HIS IS BLASPHEMY."

Barlan glanced at his squadron partner, Jolenn, who'd been muttering complaints under his breath like that for the better part of the morning. They both stood on old wooden platforms that hadn't been used in at least a couple centuries, by the way they creaked under the guards' weight. All Barlan could do was hope those platforms wouldn't give out as they stood positioned under Cervora's skull and supported it with a steady stream of raw, formless magic: *nedzuring*.

Before Barlan could tell Jolenn to settle down for the thirteenth time, the guard kept at his nonsense: "Cervora's skull should never touch the ground. Never. Nor should it ever leave its place above the throne."

He shook a few loose strands of hair out of his face, and the rest of his hair shook around like a horse's tail. For all he claimed to like efficiency, keeping his hair long enough to reach the top of his back even when tied up seemed to be the only place the uptight bastard allowed himself any leeway. But that look on his face, with his lip curled, brows pinched, and zircon eyes glittering a fearsome, deep reddish brown, reminded Barlan that his friend was as uptight as ever.

"Oh, will you quit your raving?" Barlan put his focus back where it belonged: on that skull. Above him and Jolenn were two manservants tinkering with the massive, near-ancient iron bolts that kept this big piece of bone anchored to the wall. They'd been working on it for the better part of an hour, and yet they'd only *just* gotten the bottom supporting bolts loose. "There's clearly a reason for this."

"I can't see a single reason—"

"And that's why you're not King," Barlan hissed, hopefully quiet enough that the manservant some ways above him didn't hear. Though, no doubt if he did, he wouldn't show it; the maids and manservants never had much, if anything, to say or show the guards. Nobody knew just how much they knew at any given time— which was all the more reason Jolenn needed to shut his mouth. "Trust the King, will you? He must know what he's doing."

"And what he's doing is blasphemy." Even Jolenn glanced at the manservant then. "If he's doing it for what I think he's doing it for."

And by that, of course, he meant the wedding announcement. It was already a little over a week since the bridal competition officially ended, and finally, the King was going to announce his bride—though rumor had it they'd already married, based on how the guards noticed the King and that Rachfemd woman suddenly started going to the North Wing together each night.

Shouldn't there have been a ceremony? It'd been the lingering whisper of the guard barracks: that it was strange to have no big celebration around the King's marriage. *Shouldn't the marriage have been public?* There weren't any guards left from the time before the King, however, and so no one could quite remember how the last royal marriage went. More than that, there had also never been a bride as important as this: as one rumored to be Cervora incarnate. No guard hadn't heard the tale yet—about both the Rachfemd woman and her guard, who spent all week getting re-built and re-shaped after the King's advisor ruined him to see if there was treason afoot.

That's what Ehrwig called it, after telling everyone the brutal details of their findings in Rehrvig and the situation on the way back to the castle: treason. *A wraith,* he'd said. *We have a wraith for a Queen, and a traitor that defends her.* He was an older guard, and he made it seem like they should've all been looking for different jobs with the way he spoke. Different jobs, and, if they weren't made of ice, different countries. *A mixed-blood. A witch.*

Witches. Barlan hadn't thought of such things in a long time; they were from the fairytales, cruel things like *Unseelechs,* except with wicked minds of their own. However, whenever Barlan saw the King and his bride walking arm in arm in the castle that past week, he couldn't help but wonder: where was the flesh of her? She looked like an Ismarrin enough, even if she was carved strangely. There was nothing about her that suggested flesh, never mind *Summer* flesh.

The skull creaked as the bolts finally began to come loose. The manservant above him twisted his magic with all his might, and the creak of iron was a welcome distraction from the otherwise bitter silence. But Barlan had to push extra magic out as the skull began to sag, and as the old brackets it sat on began to moan and pull at their anchor points in the wall. The castle stone crumbled and cracked a little bit. The skull falling down and crashing to the floor was a real possibility with fault lines like those.

"It isn't blasphemy if what the Queen says is true," Barlan muttered. He knew he had to keep focused, but he couldn't help his own sharp words; it'd been a long week of listening to Jolenn whine. "If what she says is true, then what we're doing makes perfect sense."

It's not true, was what Jolenn would've said—but then he'd be crossing into dangerous territory. Calling the Queen a liar and denying the story she and the King were spinning would've made Jolenn a bit dirty with the stink of treason and blasphemy himself, and that would've done the uptight guard no favors in the career he cared so much about. Barlan banked on his friend knowing as much, and sure enough, the guard fell silent and focused on his work.

Eventually, a big iron bolt came out and fell down to the ground. It hit the stone with such force that Barlan was worried the floor below would crack even through the thick carpets they'd put down around the area. However, they didn't have time to stop and check; the people were assembling that very morning, and the skull had to be on the city square's stage to greet them.

But if the Queen really is a—

The skull jerked a few inches down, and the sound of iron creaking and stone crumbling made Barlan panic and shove more magic under the giant piece of bone. It held, but he didn't miss Jolenn's *tsk* beside him. Barlan could've swore at him. Instead, he emptied his head of all these distracting thoughts and stared at the skull—stared into its deep, empty eye socket, so black with shadow that it seemed like the darkness was something he could reach out and touch.

Aveline woke up to a freezing hand at her waist and an icy kiss pressed to her neck. That hand slid over her hips and back up, as if trying to douse every single degree of heat that might've gathered on her body while she slept under her soft rabbit cloak. However, between the cold of her blood and the ice of her bedmate, there wasn't any heat on her body to begin with. And with what Jädrich gave her each night she'd been sleeping beside him, there wasn't any heat *in* her body, either; he'd put all the cold of Winter deep in her belly, leaving nothing but frost where the Yasilanri believed a person's inner fire burned.

With what they'd done, it would only make sense that such a fire would be doused in Aveline, if she ever had any to begin with. What dripped from Aveline each night wasn't the thick stuff she'd seen prostitutes wipe from their legs in the brothel. It was thinner, clearer—like ice water, but shining with silver flecks, as if it were snowmelt that had run down a high mountain. It made her insides feel like they were packed with ice, a delightful numbness, and yet it never froze on her legs as she laid beside Jädrich after having their fill of each other.

"Aveline," Jädrich whispered, and he pressed another kiss to her neck before he continued, "you need to get up soon."

When she opened her eyes, she found the room grey and dingy with the light of a Winter dawn. She pulled her shoulder blades together and felt her spine crackle, then stretched like a cat and curled against her husband. It still felt strange, thinking of him as that—as her *husband.* And it still made her skin prickle to have him so close, even if the eyes of that doe-woman didn't stare so sharply as before. Maybe her madness calmed down, seeing as there was nothing to worry about from Jädrich after all. He knew the truth about her, and yet his touch was still so gentle, his kiss soft.

I'm safe. She could've purred when his hands glided again from her hipbones to her first few ribs. *We're safe.*

Protected. By this man, and thanks to the contract, *from* this man.

As she laid there, though, she noticed how his fingers pressed at her bones, as if seeking them out. He seemed to be counting the ribs as he touched them, then carefully feeling the flesh between rib and hipbone before shifting her skin over her pelvis. She was about to ask what he was doing when he nestled his chin on her shoulder and spoke.

"It's strange. Your bones."

She blinked, then smiled. "What's strange about them?"

"There's all this, which I'd expect of a fleshling," he said as he lightly pinched the skin at her side, making her squirm, "and then your bones are as hard as any Ismar's ice."

Aveline chuckled. "Well, yes. We would be little more than worms without them."

Jädrich stayed silent at that. Then he kissed her jaw and slipped out of bed. "Come," he said as he snapped his eyes back in his head and went for his huge wardrobe in the room's far corner, "we have much to do."

Aveline watched him for a moment. His hair was long and loose and covered most of his back, but she still marveled at the rest of him—how it was carved to look just like any "fleshling's" muscles. The back of his legs, the curve from his waist to his hip—it was like looking at any fleshling man, and yet it was pure, uncovered ice.

When Jädrich turned around and beckoned her to come put on the one dress she hadn't had packed in her trunks, the long, flowing black dress good for travel and moving around, she finally pulled herself out of bed. They dressed mostly in silence, Aveline helping make sure every detail of his coat was fastened just right and him buttoning the wing openings on the back of her dress closed. When they were done, and all was well,

Aveline took one last look at the room—and at the bed, where she knew her snowflake obsidian still hid for whenever she may need it in the future—and left.

Then it was a matter of letting the silver carriages take them down to the city square, as they had for the past three weeks. Except this time, Aveline didn't sit in a cluster of other women. She sat with her prize, and she knew the people down below would be watching no one and nothing but her. Still, though, her stomach flipped as she thought about what she was to do on that stage. Rather than stand there and goad a King, she was to stand there and reveal herself as more, much more, than a Queen.

What if they don't accept it? The advisor, the cursed little runt—even if Jädrich hadn't accepted anything she said, the fact that she could say it at all made Aveline's stomach turn. *What if they don't see me as Cervora?*

When she blinked, the doe-woman's stare reflected her words.

What if? What if? What if?

That doe-woman only unsettled her further. By time they reached the city square, her shoulders went from relaxed to bunched up near her ears, and her hands went from flat in her lap to clasped, fingers twisting up in each other. And neither Jädrich's silence nor the sight of the crowd when they finally made it onto the city square's stage made her nerves any better. In fact, when she got up on that stage and glimpsed the giant thing resting on it, along with all the sets of gemstone eyes focused on it, Aveline tried her best to look at a spot in the distance and simply walk where she was directed.

However, she couldn't help but glance at the crowd, and she felt her stomach tighten with the urge to flee. They watched her without blinking, those people— without so much as twitching. In all that silence, not a single whisper dared mingle with the far-off, howling winds. It was as if someone put dozens of statues in the square rather than living creatures, and it made Aveline's whole body light up with gooseflesh, from her head to the base of her spine. It wasn't natural, their stares. Wasn't right. It was worse than the stare coming from the statue behind her, by far—as that statue of the Winter deer goddess was sweet-faced and full of life.

Yet Aveline was directed to stand there until her cue to move, and so she dedicated herself to doing so: to standing as still and staring as strongly as her people. The only thing worse than the many pairs of eyes trained on her and the dreadful silence, however, was the thing that sat before Aveline on that stage: the huge *skull* of Cervora, devoid of all the soft cheeks and heart-shaped lips and big, shiny eyes that the statue behind her had. It was three-quarters the size of a personal carriage, and those antlers branched out as wide as a tree's limbs did. Whatever Cervora was before her passing—whatever her kind used to be, those white deer—she was a *colossal* thing. Bigger than Aveline realized.

With some effort, Aveline kept the rise and fall of her chest in check: not too rapid and shallow breaths, nor too deep that it was easy to see her ribs expanding. She assumed what she thought the stance of a Queen might be: feet together, hands folded in front of her and laid against her dress, shoulders square, chin up, eyes level. Dignified, powerful, unquestionable—like she'd seen her mother stand when holding firm with an unruly client, or when haggling the price of new jewelry down at the market stalls.

The sound of boots tapping against the stage cracked the silence as easily as a series of thunderclaps. Jädrich finally came to Aveline's side, his stride powerful and sure as he came down from his carriage to stand beside the massive deer skull. He laid a gentle hand on the ancient, blackened antlers, so gentle that it made Aveline's skin crawl, and then he addressed the people with a voice that boomed through the city square.

"People of Vörnein," he started, "no doubt you stand in shock to see the skull of your Mother removed from its place of honor above Orr's throne. However, with all gathered here today, you might see exactly why we Ismären have no need of our Mother's skull anymore."

A little wave rippled through the crowd as the people flinched at the idea. Jädrich turned to Aveline and held out his hand to her, and she kept her chin up even as she took it. She felt so tall then, as she moved to her husband and gripped his hand.

He held her hand up and looked back to the crowd. "Here stands before you your Queen and more than that. The woman you've known as Lady Aveline Rach-femd for the duration of the bridal contest has revealed to me her true self, and in doing so, has bound herself to the Crown in proper, holy matrimony. Now, I invite you all to meet your Queen—and your Mother."

It would've been nicer to hide inside a carriage while Jädrich gave such a ridiculous speech. But Aveline managed to keep her face straight and serene, even as she wanted to gag on Jädrich's words. She slipped her hand out of his and went past the skull of the dead Ismar god, until she stood a fair ten paces away from the crowd. Even the guards, at that point, turned to look at her with wide eyes and tightly pressed lips. Why they were so tense, she couldn't guess; they looked like they thought she might personally tear the skull to pieces with her own two hands. It seemed she never quite won the other guards' favor, if they could still look at her with so much suspicion.

Oh, well.

What they suspected didn't matter. Aveline flexed her feet, her scalp, and she felt her very bones pop and twist into a wholly different form. As the fur sprouted

over her legs, and her feet solidified into hooves—as
her scalp ached with the burgeoning antlers that raised
themselves up high above her head—Aveline kept her
eyes closed. She wanted to reveal every inch of her
antlers, her hooves, before she saw the face of Jädrich's
people, and when the ache in her head finally slowed,
she shook the hair from her face and smiled. Then she
opened her eyes and, to her amusement, caught dozens
of startled, doe-like faces staring back at her.

"Welcome her," came Jädrich's voice, soaring over
them all. "Welcome your Mother."

For a moment, it was as if time itself froze over. Even
the Winter winds seemed to hush, to the point that
the stillness felt practically devoid of wind, of air, altogether. As if to remind herself otherwise, Aveline finally
allowed herself a deep breath—one that stretched her
ribs and flared them wide, and one that rushed out of
her in a loud, whooshing exhale. The sound of that
exhale carried across the city square, over the heads of
the people, and as she loomed over that skull, she let
her voice ring out.

"Ismären!"

How many times had she thought of the words she
would say in this moment? How many times had she
imagined this, hoping to strike the balance just right? To
smile and speak like Cervora might speak?

How many times did her throat fill with bile as she
tried, and failed, to say what she wanted to say: *My
Ismären, my people*?

"This morning, I stand before you all, not the veiled
thing I was a month ago, but the antlered Queen and
Mother that Winter needs." Even as her heart ham-
mered against her ribs, she managed to sweep her arms
out wide. They almost brushed the antlers of the deer
god's skull, and her stomach twisted in a sudden wave of
nausea. "I come home, it seems, to a land broken. To a

people melted, and a nation scarred. I come to heal this nation—soul by soul, body by body, until all of Winter is whole again. And I come to do it beside the son of Orr's sons."

Sick. A cold sweat broke out on Aveline's temples. She gathered herself, but even if her body came under control with a deep breath, her mind wouldn't steady so easily. *Sickening.*

"Bring me your melted, your downtrodden, and I will make them whole again," Aveline said, exactly as she'd practiced in her mind again and again. "I will not rest until Winter shines once more—until all its people are restored."

A pause ballooned in the air. The silence cut so deep—settled so thickly. That kind of heavy silence blanketed her words and didn't even let them echo, and for a moment, Aveline wondered: *do they not believe me?* Her smile stayed plastered on her lips, and yet the cold sweat beaded in her hair, made her skin clammy. She did not dare blink. *Do they not see—?*

"The Icon returns!"

One man, far in the back, shouted; he jumped as he spoke, as if to send his voice shooting over the heads of everyone else around him. That one cry, that ringing voice—it was like the boot over a thin layer of ice, cracking the silence so crisply and ringing out into the air. And with that crowd's silence finally broken, it didn't take long for the rest of the crowd to find their voice.

"The Icon returns!"

"Our Mother! Our Mother!"

"Bless us!" People began to raise their hands, palms open as if begging her to give them something. The people closest to the stage, especially, tried to grab for its edge—though several silver spikes in the ground, and thick chains hanging between them, kept them just a few paces too far to do so. "Mother, bless us! Fix us!"

Aveline's smile grew. She sucked in a deep breath and meant to blow it out, to send all her apprehension riding out into the Winter morning—but her lungs paused, straining against her ribs. Her stomach twisted and turned as she looked at these people; a bead of sweat rolled down her temple.

Don't touch me. Her skin. Again, the crawling feeling under her skin—as if her very muscles were trying to unstitch themselves from her skin and abscond with her bones. *Keep away. Keep away from us.*

Us, us, us.

"To that end," she said, if only to finally release the breath she held. Her voice cut through the crowd's chaos; as they settled into their eerie quiet once more, she looked down to the skull. "You see now why your King tells you: there is no need for this skull anymore. Not when I stand here before you, alive, reborn."

Then Aveline looked to that skull with what she hoped was a tender, open face. However, as she came around the side of it, so people could see her better—as the people in the front stretched out her hands as if intending to grab her skirts and pull her down—Aveline's lips twitched out of their easy smile. Her brows twitched, too, even as she tried to smooth them out; they fought her, desperate to furrow. A sharp pain lanced up through her chest. Even if her mind was only disturbed by this skull, it seemed her body was mourning—and it wanted her to draw near. To fall to her knees and curl against that bleached bone.

She tried to resist it. Aveline came around the front of it with slow, careful steps, and to see the skull again—to see those gaping, empty sockets again—it made her want to flee, to bolt off that stage and disappear into the woods, towards the Seat of Orr. But the eye sockets—they pulled her. As if they had their own force, they pulled her, beckoned her closer. She paused and dug her heels into the stage, but with her body twitching and muscles tugging towards that big piece of bone, it seemed the skull won the battle of wills. Its call was too strong; its sockets were too deep.

Aveline found herself stumbling towards it like a newborn fawn. Her heart felt like it was being filled with air, from how high it soared in her chest, yet still, she didn't have much of a choice but to go to it—and when she tossed a desperate glance to Jädrich, she found no clues on his face. He only watched her, as if there were nothing more interesting in the world than what she would do with that giant piece of primordial bone.

No, the only clue she had was from the bone itself as her legs betrayed her and dragged her closer. Worse, when she was close enough, she thought she *heard* something from those sockets—thought she heard something whispering from within it. Something so familiar, yet so alien. Something her body recognized even if her mind did not.

I need that.

Whatever *that* was, Aveline got the idea in her head that it was essential to her, and she could not shake it: this thing, whatever was inside the skull, it was hers. The animal instinct in her told her so. The doe-eyed thing in her, it insisted on it: this was hers. Like finding a severed finger or a lost tooth, this thing was hers, or rather, it was *her,* and it'd been gone too long.

Give me that. Give.

The whispers in her head hissed and melded with whatever strange sounds echoed from within the skull's shadowy sockets. Aveline got closer still, until she was standing over one socket, and she bent her head to listen. The crowd around her might as well have disappeared as she listened; the world may as well have fallen away and ceased to exist. All she could focus on, like a woman possessed, was this sound. This *sound.*

With her head so close to the skull that she nearly grazed her cheek against its hard edge, Aveline could finally make that sound out. What she heard as she came closer to that cavern of an eye socket was a woman's whispers. They floated on a dry and rasping voice, a voice that she recognized so well it made her freeze.

Murderers. Monsters. Never forgive. Never forget.

Her whole body rocked with tremors, her skin alight with gooseflesh. So powerful a fear washed over her that she could hardly breathe without sucking in a gasp of snowflakes, as she realized then that her throat was snapping, crackling. But even as those whispers grew louder—even as they sank into her mind like rainwater into moss, and even as she squeezed her eyes shut and came face to face with whatever black, gleaming doe-stare had been haunting her for so long—she bent her legs and lowered herself to the ground. The whispers became louder, closer, until it felt like the whisper was coming from her own head. By time she sat fully on the ground and peered inside that socket, until all her vision was nothing but the blackness, she could feel nothing but her thudding heart—*hear* nothing but the whispers from both the skull and her own mind. The whispers melded and fused into one clear, strong, harrowing voice.

Cruel. Wicked. Regret. Nothing but regret—is me, I have.

But her mind was too numb to understand it. Aveline pulled her face from the socket, even as what felt like some invisible hand pushed her towards it; she lurched back as panic gripped her heart, and she couldn't see the many chips and scuff marks in the skull's pale bone for what they were. She saw only depressions, lines and shadows, and it wasn't until a bead of saliva dropped from her open mouth and froze, bouncing off her like a marble, that she jolted. The sudden touch of that little piece of ice startled her enough to remind her of the stage against her shins, the weak Winter sunlight, the clump of people on one side of her peripheral. Of Jädrich on the other.

She still couldn't make words as she fought her own neck and turned to look at him. Barely had the sense to wipe her mouth as she drooled like some frightened animal. But with what scrap of a conscious thought she could make, she figured she might have tried to end this as soon as possible—before people got too concerned. As it was, Jädrich's calm and lifeless face was finally defrosting; he was angling towards her, leaning as if intending to take a step, his brow furrowing as he watched her. So Aveline drew as deep a breath as she could and tried to look like she thought Cervora might, if that doe were to look at her own head. Not the Cervora her mother told her about, maimed and ripped apart, but the Cervora she'd read about in the ice-folk's own books: a gentle mother, a god glad to give herself for the success of her creations.

Aveline tried for a smile, then laid her hand on the bone. Just above the eye socket.

And then there was only snow.

THE WIND LASHED HARDER THAN A SLAVER'S WHIPS. It ripped
at Aveline's hair and split her skin. Made her eyes almost impossible to open, dry as they were; it was as if
they'd been frosted shut, her eyelashes like stiff needles
that tugged against her eyelids in the wind. She tasted
blood at her lips from where they'd burst open, dry
and withered as they were—sweet blood, so sweet it was
almost like honey. And she had no coat, no dress, to
shield her from all that wind.

With some effort, Aveline cracked her eyes open. She
stood atop a mountain, from the look of the rough rock
around her. Behind her, *Unseelechs* circled the mountain
peak like falcons, as if guarding it. Perhaps they were
guarding the gaping cave entrance that laid only a few
feet from her—one that held *something* strange, as there
was a faint silver glimmer coming from deep within.

Aveline's limbs creaked like dead wood as she

reached her arm up to those beautiful creatures. They squawked at her, gurgled, but one swooped down, and she nearly gasped at the size of it; it was as big as her, and it didn't hunch so far forward, like the ones back at the castle. Rather, it stood tall on its wolf-like haunches. Its arms hung forward, talons long and sharp as if it had knives for fingers, and its teeth protruded from its mouth as if there were an icy bramble patch stuck in its face. Still, this thing had no nose, and it looked at her with glassy, empty eyes—but it didn't attack her as it let its winged arms tuck in by its side. And she knew, by the way it tipped its head, that it wanted love.

So she loved it. She laid a petite and pale hand on its head, which was solid and hard, not hollow like the Ismären's. It had no soul, this thing; no *Unseelech* did. They didn't need them to walk and move the way Aveline wanted them. Hence the name the Ismären gave them.

Un-souled.

Aveline went to ask it to fly with her, but she found when she called her wings that they weren't there. Her back flexed and strained, but there was nothing to connect them near her shoulder blades, no skin to lift and spread wide. There was only her bare back, and the wind whipping her hair, tangling it in her antlers. Only the fur at her legs, which did nothing to break the cold as it seeped into her. She missed the rest of her fur, the stuff that covered her whole body to stave off this cold.

When did I have that much fur?

Instead, Aveline wanted to ask that chittering *Unseelech* to take her down to the bottom of the mountain— where white mists covered whatever lay beneath—but she couldn't remember the words. Or, rather, she never knew the words. Yasilan, too, escaped her; in fact, she couldn't even remember what that word meant when it sprang into her head. Where had she learned it? What kind of language was it? Even those questions were hazy, hardly a tickle in her mind.

So she held her hand out, and the *Unseelech* bounced on its haunches, licked her hand. Then Aveline pointed down below, and the *Unseelech* followed her gaze like a dog would. It grumbled. Shrank from the cliff edge. Aveline pointed again and stamped her foot—or, rather, her hoof—which made a *clack* sharp enough for the *Unseelech* to flinch. It looked at her with those big and empty eyes—but could she really say they were empty, when they seemed to shine with some idea it wanted to express? Or was she only imagining that?

The *Unseelech* unfurled its wings and jumped, and then it gripped Aveline's shoulders from above with those huge wolf-feet, but its talons didn't pierce her. They held her rather comfortably as it then dragged her off the edge and sent her soaring through those wicked winds, down into the mists that looked like clouds. Her hooves dangled below her, and her body was far too vertical; this one creature couldn't support her the way she knew to fly, or at least, the way she thought would make sense to fly. She remembered *something* about having wings, even though she knew she'd been a deer her whole life. Her whole life.

When have I ever flown on my own?

Her head started to ache. Just a little, at the base of her antlers.

Soon, they descended into the mists, which brushed against her with such a brutal cold that she could've curled in a ball and prayed for summer. However, she found that it was a thin layer of mist, and that there was empty air beneath it. Maybe it was a cloud after all. But below it was the strangest landscape she'd ever seen, one she'd only ever seen in books: the Iswold.

What's a book?

The Iswold was a silent, lifeless patch before the Seat

of Orr, where there were no trees or vegetation, only a thick blanket of snow and huge columns of ice shooting up from the ground. At first glance, they almost looked like rock columns, but once the *Unseelech* dropped her down into the soft, knee-high snow, she found that those spires were, in fact, ice. And that some had big chunks taken out of them—that some had fallen, cracked from instability in their base. The *Unseelech* chittered to her, then flew away, back to the higher cliffs around the mountain's base; it seemed her babies preferred the mountain to the Iswold.

Aveline loomed over the broken pieces of one ice column. They had holes carved into them, these spires. Man-shaped holes. It was as if a man had been lifted out of the ice like a doll. A toy. Or maybe even a child, a sleeping child, scooped up from—

My children!

The realization hit her, and she felt like a fool; how could she have forgotten about her children? They *had* been lifted out of that ice; she'd carved them with her own two hands, using nothing but sharp stones and thin, stiff picks she'd made with her magic. The *Unseelechs*, too, were her children, but there was something off about them. Why had she made their feet like wolves, when wolves terrified her so much? Maybe because she wanted wolf-things of her own, to scare the *real* beasts off and keep her safe. After all, this body wasn't as fast as her old one, and standing upright exposed her soft belly to anything and everything that could come by and hurt her. She needed protection.

But why couldn't she get these creatures' mouths right, and why did those mouths always become overgrown with such awful teeth? She didn't intend teeth like that. The only thing she'd done right with them was give them those easy-to-move joints, which she'd woven together with a kiss of her own magic, a simple thread-song she'd sung as she carved to keep their parts together and moveable. It was her first way of making children, and it seemed to work well enough. The creatures moved as easily as she did with no need for food or anything else.

But why didn't I do that with my new children?

Aveline huffed as she wandered further into the Iswold. The answer to that question was a silly one: she knew well enough that she just didn't like how it looked. It made the *Kviraeg* feel fake, like they weren't actually alive, and that bothered her. She wanted her children to look like her, not like strange effigies and poorly done representations.

Kviraeg? The word felt foreign, and yet she couldn't remember what else she might've called those winged ice-beasts she called her firstborn. Couldn't remember how she came up with the word, either, but it sounded nice in her mind. Like a two-syllable song. This new mouth, their strange lips—they could make sounds she couldn't ever make before, when her nose was long and her lips little more than skin over big teeth.

Aveline's antlers ached something miserable at their base, but she lifted her hands to her lips, cupped them around, and yipped her calls. Her new children always came with her calls—or, at least, they tried. And as she walked deeper into the Iswold, sure enough, she heard it over the winds: the crunch of stilted steps, the returning yips and hollers. This was a language she understood, one of pitches and notes and music, almost like the birds in the springtime. There was no need for anything else, even if new sounds were fun to make. There was no need for more than the pictures that appeared in her mind, and the feelings that bloomed in her chest, despite all the snow and cold. When spring came, she wondered if her new children would survive the thaw; if so, she could've taken them out to the fields, where the snowdrops would pop up and signal a slightly warmer world for them to explore. Surely, it wouldn't be *that* warm, that these children would melt into the rivers and fade away.

The thought made her chest ache. All that time she spent whittling their jaws, separating their fingers, to look like her new body—all those shiny things she'd found in the cave on the mountain and shepherded into these finely carved bodies, into the empty space she'd hollowed into their heads—they'd be lost if the spring was too strong.

But as a few of her children came hobbling through the snow, she didn't think of it anymore. She instead focused on how her children stumbled. How they teetered, unable to bend their legs the same way she did. They were smaller than her, small enough that she could've lifted them with one hand, and she plucked one small woman-shaped thing from the ground. Her stomach was a fragile point because it was hollow. While these children had no need to eat, Aveline still wanted them to be able to do what her people could do: bear children of their own, rather than having to carve them out of the ice as she did. She just hadn't figured out how to make it work yet.

Aveline wanted this because *she* didn't have a choice anymore; there was no other deer like her, who had wished as hard as she had to become something more than food for more wolves. There were no other deer, the simple, stupid things, who would follow her lead— who would stand up and break her front hooves to pieces, to splinter them into something that made it so she could pick things up like birds did with their claws. And there were none who would make a spine that could lean back, a chin that could tip up, so she could look towards the starry sky.

No, she was alone, but she still had the drive to make

children, and so she made these things to keep her company—these pretty things, incomplete as they were. Along with the women's hollow stomachs, they all, men and women alike, had no hair on their heads, like the *Kviraeg*. Aveline couldn't figure out how to make it grow. And none of them had eyes, either, because she wanted to find something else than just ice to put in their heads, lest they end up with as empty and strange a gaze as the *Kviraeg*. She loved her *Kviraeg*. Loved them. But they weren't *right* yet. They were only a start.

Aveline sat down and let her children hobble over. They smiled, but the ice of their face squeaked, and they didn't sit so much as they creaked, bent, and fell into the snow. Somehow, despite having no eyes, they knew where she was—and she thought maybe it was because of the faint white light that shined in their once hollow heads. Those fuzzy, shiny things she'd found floating in that cave were like some kind of spore, or some little snow spirit; they hovered in the air and blinked with all kinds of pretty colors when she first approached them. She had no idea what they were, but they were alive, she felt—speaking to her in those colors, and even in pictures when they brushed up against her. And for some reason, her children didn't wake up without them. Maybe because she hadn't put any of the magic in them that she did the *Kviraeg*, with their strings of silver thread holding their pieces together and animating them.

Because she'd carved these new children in one piece, though, rather than many pieces, they couldn't move so easily without breaking. But they did look more like her: like real animals, smooth and con-nected, even without skin and muscle. They even sat something like her, with their legs out front. Their feet were strange, though. She thought, since she'd broken her front hooves apart and made herself these useful finger-things, that these children of hers could use finger-things on their legs, too, instead of hooves, and so they had long, rectangular things to stand on, with finger-things at the end that could grip a little like hers could. They weren't perfect, though.

But right then, that didn't matter. She was happy just to sit in a circle with her children, who looked up at her with smiles on their faces. One creaked as it turned towards her. It was a woman, who flinched at the loud squeak from her fragile, hollow belly, but with careful, slow movement, the woman moved towards Aveline's cracked and bleeding hand. She reached out and paused when her shoulder squeaked, then managed to touch Aveline's hand until swiping some of the blood, and then she lifted it up to her face as if she could smell it.

Can you smell? The idea delighted Aveline, though her thought wasn't in words so much as it was in pictures of her father's twitching black nose, the memory of the scent of crushed pine needles. Aveline squeaked with joy. However, her squeaking became mangled in her surprise when that child tasted the blood. Did she not know what it was? Did she think, maybe, that it was some white pine sap stuck to Aveline's hands? It'd likely hardened enough, what with all that cold and the crusty scabs already starting to form on her hands. Still, it made Aveline uneasy when the woman smiled as much as her stiff face let her, when she carefully turned and yipped something without moving her lips. The sound echoed from her head more than it left her mouth.

Before Aveline could think too long on it, however, heavier footsteps crunched through the snow. She recognized these steps: they were those of Aveline's firstborn of this new batch of children. He was bigger than the rest, as she'd been carried away with her first one, but he still only barely made it up to Aveline's hip when she stood at her full height. He was also, in her biased opinion, the prettiest one she'd made, even for all his imperfections. Yes, his nose was crooked, and his head was a little too long—yes, his chest was a little too broad and out of proportion with his narrow hips, his legs a little too long in comparison—but he was still First, and that made him the Eldest Brother, the best one.

Though that day, he didn't come sit with the others to start their singing as they always did. Nor did the others look very interested in Aveline, or any of the fun magic tricks she might've tried to show them despite their lack of eyes. Rather, her First kept walking towards her, taking slow and careful steps to avoid further cracking his knees. They'd already taken quite some damage, and she'd already fixed them; she'd patched them with snow and saliva and magic quite a few times. It seemed he respected that, because his steps were slow enough that Aveline thought her First might take a century to reach her.

But reach her he did, and he put a biting cold hand to her thigh. He brushed the fine fur there as if comforted by it, and Aveline was glad to see him smile, even if it put a few more fault lines in his sharply carved face. Then he tilted his head up to her, and he raised his hands up, begging to be held by his mother. One hand was held in a fist, and it seemed like he might've been scared to release it, lest his fingers crack off his hand.

Still, Aveline smiled back at the pleading thing. She could never refuse him. Unlike the others, small enough that she worried about crushing them, this one was big enough that Aveline could comfortably lift him and tuck him against her, letting him use the breasts her strange new form gave her to prop his head up and look at her. She held him close and studied him, though she wondered if perhaps she'd still come too close to making these creatures look like *Kviraeg*, what with those bald heads. At least they had ears, though, and noses

something like hers—things that actually poked off their
face—

Pain.

Her mouth went dry as something stung her deep,
just below her ribs. Without thinking, Aveline flung
her precious First away from her and scrambled back,
desperate to get away from whatever made a pain *that*
sharp, *that* deep, *that* wicked. All her movement, however, and all her breathing, only made the pain worse,
until she steadied herself on her hands and knees and
found something sticking out of her.

A sharp piece of gray stone. One dripping with her
kin's silver, magic-laced blood, the blood that no winter
could ever freeze.

Why? There was no reason for this. Maybe it was an
accident. Yes, an accident—because her children would
never wound her, the way the wolves would. Her children were *not* wolves; they were like her, looked like
her—they were deer—

"*Maeg blote,*" said one of her children, though she
didn't understand what the sound meant. She didn't
quite speak with them—only pointed at things and gave
them names, things that sounded nice with the strange
sounds her odd form's mouth could make. Aveline
didn't have a clue what they'd been doing with those
sounds while she had been off on the mountain, looking for more fuzzy things to illuminate new children's
heads with. Were they always able to make such sounds?
The fuzzy things? "*Maeg blote; lav trintem!*"

Aveline didn't like how that sounded. The call, the
strain of it. Since when did her children ever sound like
that—so scary? The pain still ached in her stomach, and
her breathing was difficult; it felt wet, her lungs, and she
coughed as she tried to stand, coughed up silver that
disappeared into the snow.

Bleeding. She was bleeding, heavily—to the point

that when she got up, her legs were shaky, and her vision swam. Her First stepped forward with his hands outstretched, and she wanted to think he'd help her—wanted to think he'd make her pain stop, do something about that stone—but she would never forget that it was his hand who put that stone there. No, she would never forget. Just as a deer never forgot the smell of a wolf, or the spot where one of their own had been attacked.

So she ran. As fast as her wobbly legs would take her, she ran. Bounded away, clutching that stone in her stomach as she disappeared into the spires of the Iswold. Her panic made the pain fade, but the stone was so slippery. So slippery, so *bloody*. Worse, everywhere she ran looked the same; everywhere was white snow and tall ice spires, so tall they descended into those pale mists above. The forest had to be somewhere, though—if she chose the right way to run, she'd find them, the dark pines, and she'd hide—

Something tangled her legs and tripped her. She went sprawling in the snow, and she bleated as that stone felt like it'd jammed deeper into her with her fall. So deep, so painful, that stone knocked the breath out of her, and she coughed harder, though each cough only made it worse. A terrible cycle, pain and coughing, until her ribs ached and she felt she was choking on air, her vision hazy. Her legs were going numb. Her ears were full of sounds of her own agony.

That was why she didn't hear the footsteps as her vision blurred. As she grabbed for the edge of that slippery stone, her magic snapping around her while her blood continued to leak around its edges, there was suddenly a hand at her arm. It closed its frozen digits around her arm, yanked it up to the point that her own hand sliced open on that stone.

Then there was a bite.

Ice-teeth sank into her arm and split her skin,

stretching and tearing it before ripping into her flesh. That alone was a pain so wicked that it made the stone feel like just a dull discomfort, but she was weak by then, too weak to kick the attacker away—to even turn her head to see it. She squeaked, hollered—her eyes stung with tears that froze on her face—but the more she thrashed, the more other hands came to grab her, hold her in place. And then there were more bites that went clamping down on her, separating skin and muscle from bone and tendon with such fiery pain that she was nearly sick. More hands, more bites—skin tearing, tendons snapping and shooting up her bones. She went to scream, but no sound came out, as she could hardly even draw in a breath, lest she vomit. She could see nothing then, her eyes focusing on nothing—nothing but a pair of legs, then knees as the thing sank down—

And then a face, an eyeless, hairless face. Rather than translucent ice, clean ice, though, there was silver dripping from its lips. Silver swirling through its body, down to its stomach, as if her blood had spilled into water.

Why?

Her child reached a bloody hand for her, but by then, there wasn't so much feeling anymore. She felt cold in a way she never had. There were sounds that rang in her ears—brutal cracks, the squish of wet things and a few shocks of duller and duller pain here and there—but she didn't understand what it was anymore. Her head was too fuzzy, her vision going too dark. All she could make out properly was that eyeless child, who frowned at her before something else got her attention. Someone gave something to this child, who Aveline knew was a woman by the shape of the chest and the hollow spot in the abdomen. Tha was where Aveline once thought children could somehow grow. But someone offered the woman something, and the woman took it.

It was a hand. By the light gray spots on the back of it, the slight fuzz from where there'd once been fur, it was Aveline's hand. And a bite had already been taken out of the palm of it, just under her thumb. From the mangled stump, little bits of skin and tendon hung, dripping with silver blood that would never freeze. The bone was jagged, splintered. The marrow, sucked out.

Why did you do this?

There was such an emptiness to her. A lightness, as she stared at that hand. As if her body no longer existed, but her soul remained tethered there a moment longer, making a throne of her antlers. Then, and only then, did Aveline regain her sight—as she sat atop her own antlers. Then and only then did she feel no more pain as she blinked, drifted up—as she looked down at the things she'd carved with her own hands and called her children.

You are the wolves.

But where her pain faded, something worse bubbled up. Something so cold and dark, deeper than the darkest night of the year. Because she watched them. Watched them pull her body apart, covering it like flies covered dead animals in summer. In the snow laid gray things, gray rope—her organs—and as she'd seen the *Kviraeg* do with rabbits and foxes, so too did her own children stuff those bits into their mouths. If only she'd had her *Kviraeg.* They would've protected her. But she never thought she'd need protecting from her own children. The squelch of their chewing reached Aveline even as she drifted higher and higher, away from her body.

Wolf, wolf—you! And you!

And the darkness grew deeper. Colder. Until her children were nothing but a speck, and she herself was nothing more than some vague impression in the wind, atop the Iswold's spires. From there, she could see the black wood that she'd meant to escape to, and the mountain she'd taken her children's essence from, those fuzzy things that blinked with pretty colors and drifted to her like living snow. A bird flew by—a snowy owl. And somewhere far away, a wolf howled.

Why? Aveline's entire mind focused on that one question, dark as it was. The answer that sprouted in response was just as dark and so very cold. *Mistake.*

Within a moment, Aveline was in the sky, looking over what felt like the entire world. It lived, it breathed—and she knew then, as she felt every life, and every breath, that she did not. Just as her body ascended and became something unlike her father, mother, and all her herd, so too had her soul ascended in that moment—brimming with more than just an animal's one life.

Within her body, she'd discovered creation, and she'd made lives outside her own. Outside her body, she'd discovered a second life, and things outside her body she'd never understood before, never even thought about. She'd discovered, in that moment, the darkness that was her regret, her shame. The freezing, life-sucking winds of her rage soon followed, and it was so cold, so bitterly cold, that even though she no longer had a throat, or lungs—that those organs swam somewhere in the belly of the wolves she'd entrapped in ice and called her new kin—she screamed. Aveline screamed for what felt like a thousand years. She screamed and wailed sounds that were not words, but nonetheless carried a wish—a curse.

Let all things die. The trees, the birds, the wolves—let all things freeze.

The sky cracked as she wailed. As she mourned and raged, voiceless and without form, she shook the heavens themselves. She frightened the moon and stars that had once answered her prayers for *more*. It was them, the moon and stars, that whispered their secrets to her while she chewed pine needles with her herd. And it was them, grieved by Aveline's wrath, that guided her soul up, as if coaxing it to become a star like them.

But Aveline's wrath was too great. She cursed the stars, those onlookers. How dare they sit and watch in that sky as she died so miserably, the cowards? No, Aveline found power there, in her thickening, blackening rage. She had no hands, no arms, and yet she found it in her to reach her essence up to the sky and *pull*—to steal from the heavens, to wrest their weapons from them and take them as her own.

Die. All things. All things, die.

Aveline grabbed onto something in those heavens and pulled until they came loose. In that moment, she took those things and hurled them down, wholly focused on completing her curse. The things that shot down past her were huge and dark; they were some massive collection of rocks that, as they hit the ground, pocked the earth and kicked up snow and frozen dirt alike. A punishment, yes, for those creations that did this to her—that was what she stole from the stars. This was what she threw, despite the moon's attempt to slow them and pull them back up.

Die. Die. Die.

The moon's mercy was not stronger than her wrath. Slower came the rocks, but they still came. And with all her screaming, all her howling, all her shrieking, she also managed to fill some of those rocks with glittering, icy shards of some bright gem. Pale, milky blue stones, pretty stones that ate up her hurt and became unbreakable, unforgettable. As the stones hit the earth, they glowed in the ground like fire so hot that it burned blue. It was the fire of her words as they ripped from her soul and echoed around the world.

Die. It became as much a command as a curse while

her wrath rained down. *All things, die. The fish. The ferns. The children. Die, all things, as I've died.*

With that curse laid in the sharpest anguish, she discovered one more thing: hate. A hate so deep, so bitter, that it would cover the world in death—silvery as her blood, blue as the densest, hardest ice. Just like those pretty stones in the rock.

"—line. Aveline."

Her ears rang. Her throat ached. Aveline clutched her head and clawed at it to the point that her fingers were tangled with hair, and her stomach lurched so violently that it felt like it was about to escape her body, flee out her mouth. It was only a dry heave, but it was enough of a pause that something strange washed over her: not a sound, but the lack of it. She couldn't see anything; she could feel the wind as she whipped around, hear someone calling her, but she couldn't see a thing. All was black still. Her hands crawled up her head and grabbed the base of her antlers as if they would steady her. Dizzy, Aveline finally saw one shape in that blackness that shone like snow in the sun.

It was the animal part of her. The vision of instinct made flesh that had apparently taken over as her body moved—though where to, Aveline didn't know. But the animal woman, the doe woman, she didn't look as she always did, with Aveline's face and body, and simply black eyes instead of blue-gold ones. No, she was like the rotted dead, chewed apart and missing chunks of her body. Bone showing from her leg. A hand missing.

All things. The woman's jaw was missing. So too was the skin and hair, the rest of the flesh at her face. It was just the skull.

All things—gone.

And there was no body anymore, either. In another blink, there was nothing *but* the skull, with something shimmering pale blue from deep inside the empty sockets.

All things, dead.

"Aveline."

All things, frozen. Stopped.

Then there were freezing hands at her face that held her in place, and the skull of that doe-wraith blinked out of Aveline's sight. It said nothing else as it disappeared, though Aveline could still feel it digging under her skin, into her muscle; it was attached to her like roots were attached to rich earth, anchored there and refusing to let go. And Aveline knew, by the eerie feeling in her bones, that it was staring at Aveline's very soul as if it could freeze her spirit solid. Still, Aveline screamed her silent scream. She screamed even as she tilted her head up, as if her screams would reach the heavens; the doe-wraith's grip on her mind loosened. She screamed without sound, the air hissing from her broken throat—and as she ripped her eyes open, she saw it: the *sun*.

No clouds blocked it. No haze dared hamper its shine. Its light kissed her skin, warming her cheeks; it hung there in the sky, bright enough to erase all the stars and even the moon from the bright blue expanse of the heavens. Drakash. Drakash Ra-Kedaar. He was there, making his presence known. He was there, exerting his authority. He was there, doing what the moon and stars could not: bringing that doe-wraith to heel. At least for the time being.

Drakash. Aveline raised her hand up to the burning sun, to the god she never dared pray to until then. Her hissing breath slowed, exhaustion settling into her lungs as if she'd taken a deep breath underwater. *Drakash. Help.*

Hands grabbed her face and forced her head down.

The glory of the sun left spots in her vision, and yet she still startled—because there it was again, that color. That wicked color. That icy, pale blue shade of anguish, of betrayal, of crystal clear *hatred.*

Pale blue diamonds—the two blinking, frosted eyes of the Winter King.

Oh, no.

Karina's ears rang with the sound of that woman's screaming, even through the cloth wrapped around her head. She and Erik both stood there in shocked silence as it happened: as the orphan seized with some inexplicable force and became little more than a statue. It wasn't until the screaming started that she and Erik glanced at each other, and by then, there was nothing to do. Nothing at all as the wild woman ripped her hand off that skull and clutched her head. She grabbed around the base of her antlers as if she could tear them off, all while sinking to her knees and shrieking worse than any *Unseelech.* That scream would no doubt ring into the distance for days.

No one could do anything, either, while the King simply stood over her and watched until she screamed herself hoarse. It felt like a year passed before he finally called her out of whatever nightmare she was clearly stuck in. Once the orphan's hands dropped from her antlers, her whole body slumped, and she fell over into the King's arms. He simply picked the limp thing up and carried her to the carriage they came in—as if she were a dead bride.

And the people. Karina glanced at the people, and all their cheers, their cries—they'd gone so silent. As if the orphan's screaming swallowed those cheers forever. The faces—the wide eyes, the glancing back and forth—

There goes all my work in this city.

"Lord Rachfemd, Lady Vilnach," one guard said, and the sudden sound after such silence made Karina flinch, "please make your way back to the carriage for the beginning of the tour."

"What—?" The word slipped from Erik's mouth, hardly more than a puff of sound. He glanced at Karina one more time; his brows were knit tight enough to crack his face. Erik looked at the long-haired, flat-faced guard that had approached. "That's not—"

"This way, my lord," the guard said.

He motioned towards the back of the stage, where the carriages were stationed. The King was already settling the orphan into his, at the head of the line. Karina didn't have a choice but to let herself be herded on. The others on that stage, the guards and that little seamstress, were also marching (or, in the seamstress's case, *being* marched) towards their carriages. So Karina walked—and she tapped Erik's arm so that he, too, might unstick himself from his place on that stage and get moving.

They lied. She said that to him with one long look, and she hoped he understood. *This is dangerous.*

Erik's eyes flashed with twinkling silver magic. It clashed with all those gold flecks in the otherwise deep blue of his lapis lazuli. But he said nothing; he only pressed his lips together and offered her his arm.

She took it, hard and cold thing that it was, and together they went for their carriage. With no supplies, no trunks, no nothing, they had no choice but to steel themselves for a long two months on the road.

EFIR'S TALONS ACHED. THEY'D BEEN WEDGED in the rock of
the cliffside for the better part of a half an hour as he
watched the sparse clouds and prayed for Malouçe to
hide her great shining face. Blasphemous prayers, yes,
but the merciful Mother would understand: he couldn't
so easily climb this cliff and slip into the Winter King's
castle with the full moon's light shining down on him.

His black scales helped him in the shadows, and
his thin and wriggling body, more wyrm that dragon,
was easy enough to coil up and hide in corners. But all
of that depended on there being shadows in the first
place. For a land where the sun was blotted out nearly
every moment of the day, he'd hoped for at least *some*
clouds to be able to likewise eat up the moonlight, but it
seemed that the clouds in this land only had contempt
for Drakash.

In Summer's Northern Swamplands, though, the

moonlight got lost in the trees and vines. It didn't reflect
so well off waters covered in algae and reeds, either. In
the desert, it was easier to see under the moonlight, but
at least there, the cold sand was something he might
wriggle in and hide under. Out here, however, in Winter, there was nothing: no refuge in that limb-killing
snow, and no chance of it eating up the moonlight. It
did the opposite; it shone so brightly that one might've
thought the moon was a second sun, reflecting off the
snow in a way that every single thing was visible, and
that trees and buildings even cast shadows. It was as
if Winter were some upside down, impossible world,
where day was night and night was day, where the living
were wicked and the dead—or the fleshless, never alive
in the first place—were holy. Efir's teeth bared at the
thought. Winter was a haunted land, wretched in every
way, and the sooner he was done with it, the better.

Another moment passed. Another two. Three. Efir
thought his talons might rip clean off. Either that, or
he would freeze, given the heat stones strapped to his
arms and legs were beginning to lose their warmth.
He wouldn't last even five minutes in his dragon form
without those. A string of curses wove through his
mind. This was his punishment for thinking arrogant
thoughts, for believing the Isolde woman to be a wor-
rywart. Three weeks seemed like far more than enough
time to reach the castle, and yet there he was, a week
and a half later, seeing civilization for the first time in
days and desperate to finish this wretched job. Had he
not gotten lost in the deep, dark wood on the way up
to the capital, and again in the woods around the castle
itself, he would've been able to be here right when he
planned: when the moon was hidden away, not watching him and his murderous plots. *Please, Mother,* he
prayed to that moon, clenching his jaw tight enough

to send sharp pains shooting through his head scales. *Please. Hide me.*

At some point, when the clouds still didn't pass over that moon, Efir began thinking of ways to slowly crawl up the castle wall without flying. Maybe, if he was careful, there was a path he could take over the face of the castle that would lead him to the King's chambers. Those chambers were on the farthest, highest point of the castle—of course they were—but maybe he could transform and slip past—

Just as he was about to climb up and consider it, the sky darkened. All the light shining off the castle from the snow faded, and Efir looked up at the sky. A large, thick grey cloud, one threatening a nighttime storm, blotted out the moon and threw the Winterlands into darkness. Not for long. Only for a few moments. But that was all Efir needed.

He launched himself off the cliffside and dove down into the great trench separating the castle from the rest of the city, then shot up like an arrow as if to embrace those very clouds. His paws throbbed where flesh met talon, and his shoulders cracked, stiff with how hard he'd had to hold onto that cliff edge. Still, how good it was to spread his wings and slice through the air to find his mark.

In the darkness, shielded from moon and starlight alike, with the monotone night vision his eyes afforded him, he was easily able to navigate towards the back of the castle. The sound of waves beating on rock filled the silence as he drew closer, creating the perfect cover for him to beat his otherwise silent wings and land on the rooftop. There were guard towers on this roof, yet from what Efir could see, no guards were posted towards the back. There may have been one or two in the guard tower towards the castle front, but they were difficult to tell apart from the other structures and spires, what with how the guards themselves were little more than ice statues.

Efir didn't waste more than a moment looking for them; he only needed to confirm no eyes were looking in his direction as he climbed from the roof onto the wall. He was careful not to leave holes too deep in the wall as he gripped the stone. The goal was simple: melt the King and leave unseen. If Winter didn't know who destroyed their King, they couldn't very well march in on any one country of the Ringlands; they'd have to blame it on their own people. From what Efir understood, there were many folks willing, for whatever reason, to do away with their own King and bring the full cycle of seasons back to their lands. Maybe they knew they were unnatural things, those Ismären. Maybe they wished for the true god's light to liberate them—a melting kiss from the Sun-Dragon that sustained all life in the world.

A large balcony overlooked the sea. Efir slipped down onto the railing and peered inside, keeping just out of sight of anyone who might've been there. This was the place his informants assured him it would be: just under the final spire, with a massive, undecorated bed and sparse furnishings, as if the King had no more need for items than a doll did. The only thing that signified this room was even being used were the two people-shaped lumps under a thin white sheet, which struck Efir as the same kinds of sheets the Yasilanri used to cover their dead for embalming. But all that aside, the main things Efir saw that confirmed the place were the balcony doors themselves: the handles were special, the only ones carved with little wolf details in the center of them. Why only the King's doors had that, Efir didn't know— nor did he care. This was it: the chambers of the King of Winter.

His scales rippled along his body, then fused together

and melted back into skin. His bones cracked and popped as they rearranged themselves in his body, and once sharp black talons became smooth, pinkish-brown fingernails. His clothes reappeared, too, emerging with his man-body in his transformation, and the warmth of those layers returning made Efir let out a quiet breath of relief. The sprouting of hair from his reshaped head made his scalp itch, but he resisted the urge to shake it out and instead pulled his lockpick set from his pouch. The lock was a simple one, to Efir's disappointment. Had he been a graceless and stupid thing, he might've even just smashed the balcony doors; they were made of nothing but glass. Granted, his own father's palace wasn't any more protected, what with the open throne room exposed to all manners of beasts and wind and sand.

It was true that the idea of killing a Lord of Seasons was unthinkable, and so maybe his father thought he didn't need any such protection—but that didn't mean that there wouldn't be a day just like this one, where the son of one Lord went to undo another. These were strange times with stranger problems. Strange problems called for even stranger solutions. The fact that this King could've been so careless about his security, even *with* known assassins in the country, therefore, was nothing short of stupid.

And this is the man that ruined the rest of the Ringlands?

The lock clicked open after a moment of Efir's fiddling. He supposed stupidity wasn't so surprising. The Lord *had* gone and abandoned his forefathers' promise to continue the Tour of Seasons, after all. But as Efir slipped inside and crouched low, following the wall to the shadowy corners of the room, he still found it so disgraceful. A Lord of Seasons was only a half-step off from a god. No one with that kind of power could afford to be so careless, or so cruel.

From the shadows, Efir glanced around. There was no one else in the room that he could see, even when the clouds parted and finally let Malouçe's light come back down to the world. There was only Efir, the Winter King, and that traitor, the latter two being huddled under a sheet on that mattress. Once he crouched down, all he could see from the bed was the covered profile of the King: the straight nose, the curve of the forehead. Efir found it odd that the King would lay a sheet over himself and his bride like that. What did an ice sculpture need to cover itself for? What was the witch doing, playing along with this strange behavior?

Like a cat, Efir stayed low to the ground and crept around the side of the bed, hidden by the height of the mattress. He wasn't sure what ice sculptures needed mattresses for, either, though from what he knew, it was a relic of times when fleshlings would stay in the country. A thing of fashion, of social convention, not of necessity. Why they kept the tradition was anyone's guess, and it was one Efir didn't care to understand. He unsheathed his obsidian dagger and came around to the King's side. Fire, it seemed, could kill these monsters even when trapped in things like ash and obsidian, which meant even a flameless wyrm like him could bring an ice-man to melt. Though what it took for fire-glass of any kind to affect them wasn't something anyone had tested before. Did it need to be plunged into the body? Was only a scratch enough? Efir wasn't sure, and so he did what was safest.

He stood up, then held the blade in both hands and prepared to plunge it down into the King's face. After that man melted, he'd take that traitorous witch and drag her out by her hair if he had to.

"You're awfully warm for a Swampland wyrm, boy."

Efir's body moved on years of practice: he shot away from the bed and towards the room's shadowy part, out of the range of the moonlight. When he looked towards the source of that voice, there in the doorway stood a short woman with hair cropped so close to her chin, cut so harsh at her brows, that he could've mistaken her for a small boy. Her clothes were simple, too: a white tunic with bronze and black embroidered edges, a simple belt, and white pants tucked into black boots. A completely unassuming thing, that woman. When had she opened the door? How long had she known he was there? He didn't know, nor did he have time to ask, because half a moment later, something shifted behind him. Before he could even begin moving to escape whatever else hid in the shadows, though, he found his arms twisted behind his back and his knife snatched. A cold, hard boot kicked the back of his legs and sent him to his knees.

A quick tug told Efir that there would be no escaping this grip—not even if he thrashed with all his might. It sobered him immediately to realize that the hands on him weren't holding him with muscle, but ice that felt harder than diamond; there was no negotiating with unnatural, inhuman strength like that. When he twisted around, he saw a guard, clad in that same black armor as the many guards he'd seen all along the towns and forest edges and the wall of Winter itself. His eyes were a toxic, banded green, flickering with some silvery phantom starlight that made Efir's hairs stand on edge. A moment later, there was the sound of fabric rumpling to the floor, and then this guard that seemingly materialized from nowhere was joined by his comrades— likely the ones pretending to be the King and the witch.

What? He couldn't understand it: the black armor, the missing King and witch, the fact that Efir hadn't noticed this man hidden behind him. More, how could they have ever known he was coming? That he existed at all? *Where did—?*

A freezing, yet velvety hand bit his jaw with its cold, and he flinched as the hand forced his head back towards the door. The little woman—there she stood. But he'd never heard her take a step. Never even felt her presence. Not the best assassin of Summer could've concealed their steps, their scents, or the thrum of their living flesh *that* perfectly. But what did he expect?

These things weren't people. They were dolls. Mockeries of life. Ones animated by the magic of some dead god who hadn't checked them and their unnatural ways in centuries.

The woman bent her head closer to Efir, and he couldn't move away with how strong her grip was. As she came closer, he noticed something strange: the stitches in her face. Between the velvety feel of her fingers and the thin strands of silver woven across her face, like thread made of snow, Efir wondered what exactly it was that covered this woman. It was like seeing a doll with a stitched, silvery burlap skin. The thought made him shudder.

"Don't be scared, wyrm," the woman cooed, and Efir's spine lit up with how guttural the Winter language was off her lips; each word she spoke sounded like the grind and crunch of twigs and crusted snow underfoot. It sounded like the growls of beasts in the cold underbrush, like the hiss of Winter winds and the squeak of ice just about to break. Even the other Ismären he'd listened to didn't sound so harsh. The woman grinned, showing off a row of ice teeth, and her pure black eyes—black as holes, as the deepest abyss—glittered with that same light the guard's had. "We won't kill you. We will take this, though."

The other guard came around and pulled the dagger out of his hands with surprising gentleness. Maybe a little cut *was* all it took to ruin an Ismar with fire-glass.

That guard then handed the dagger to the woman, who appraised it with eyes full of that crackling silver light.

"My, what an ugly weapon," she whispered. Her teeth tapped her lip. "Terrible. What were you hoping to do with this, hmm? Who were you looking to plunge this into?" She gestured around the room and smiled as if chastising a small child. "Only the King and his bride sleep here. Surely a wyrm wouldn't dream of driving this little thing into a Lord of Seasons, would he? That'd be ridiculous, I think."

The words took a moment to register in Efir's mind. Once the confusion settled, and the dread had shivered its way down his spine, he set his jaw as if his teeth were the walls of a great fortress keeping all his secrets locked inside. What he should've done, if he didn't fear the consequences of leaving an armed Summer body in the deepest pit of Winter, was keep a suicide pill tucked in his cheek for this exact moment. It was his duty to die before spilling a single secret to enemies like these dolls.

But he had no pill, and he had no strength with which to break free; he had no flame to melt these things, either, only venom that would be all too easy to trace back to the Summer Swamplands and wouldn't do much to ice in the first place. The only option he had was to stay silent. If he was lucky—which it seemed he wasn't—he would find a way to kill these people that had seen him and escape. Otherwise, he could only hope he wouldn't have too many broken bones and bruises by time the ice-folk were done trying to pull answers out of him.

The woman's smile slipped. Her lips pursed as if she were a child disappointed in a pet that didn't spin on command, and she shrugged as she turned away.

"Well, I'm sure I don't need you to tell me what you're here for. I'm sure I can guess accurately enough. After all, it doesn't seem like much coincidence to me that a wyrm appears only shortly after that half-dragon whore."

Efir didn't dare so much as twitch, even if his heart fluttered with the first crackling embers of panic. It seemed he didn't need to do or say anything, though. The woman peered over her shoulder and grinned, and only then did Efir think to reset his face. Sure enough, his brows fell down and his eyes slipped half shut, erasing his look of surprise far too late. He'd been caught with that face, and both he and the woman knew it.

"You know about her, don't you?" The woman turned on her heels and tucked her hands—and the dagger— behind her back. Then she bent towards his face, so close that their noses nearly touched. All he could see were those deep, silver-speckled black eyes. The way the silver flashed across them, it was like watching dozens of stars be born, only to wink out a moment later. It made him dizzy. "You know the half-dragon I speak of."

Stay silent. Silent.

"Something must've not gone as planned for you to be here trying to stick this dagger in my King. What would you have done, though, when the half-dragon woke up? Hmm?"

A sharp sting lit up his thigh, and a part of his pants went damp. He didn't need the woman to back away to know it'd already begun: the little cuts and bruises and scrapes they'd try and use to needle one word out of him at a time. But they were fools, these Ismären. They didn't realize that all Efir's life, he'd been prepared for moments exactly like these. If he let himself get lost in the black, star-flecked eyes long enough, he could've pretended he was looking up at the desert sky again, all while the bite of a whip split his back open and the searing pain of hot pokers laid scars along his skin. He'd been through every pain there was and proven his mouth a fortress no creature could breach.

"Hmm." The woman backed away. There in her hands was the dagger, glistening with the slick of Efir's poisonous blood. It steamed there on the obsidian; it seemed even the "cold" blood of the Swampland folk wasn't *so* cold that Winter couldn't shock it still. But the way the woman stared at him made his blood run cold enough to numb him from head to toe. "Assassins are good at keeping their secrets, hmm? That's fine." Then she looked to the guards behind her. "Bring him to the infirmary. Dr. dur Verdem can find a back door in his mind, if he won't let us use the front door of his mouth."

Embers of panic flared in his temples. He knew better than to loose his tongue even an inch, but he couldn't stop his thoughts from racing. What did that mean, *a back door*? What could these things do to creatures like him?

The woman stepped forward with one hand outstretched. Her finger suddenly lit up with a silver light, and her face split again into that artificial, doll-like grin.

"Sleep now, wyrm. You've come such a long way."

He struggled, but the guard held him so firmly that he thought his arms would pop from their sockets if he tried too hard to escape them. The glowing finger brushed his temple. It tingled as if he'd been brushed with frost and mint—and there was a smell in the air just as sweet that he couldn't understand the source of. None of it mattered, though. From one second to the next, his vision blurred, his mind went hazy, and he found everything sliding into a deep, empty blackness.

"Move!"

Clara shoved guard and maid alike out of her way as she hurried down the castle halls. With her arm finally frozen and reshaped the way it was supposed to be, she no longer had to think about how it would swing and toss her off balance if she went too fast, and that alone made her feel like she could *fly*. And well she would, because what she'd seen in the mind of that Summer lizard made her soul want to scream loud enough to crack the ice of her skull.

Two guards trailed after her, and one said, "Lady Ronterweis, slow down! We can search for you; you don't have—!"

"I will see that damn box with my own two eyes! Now look with me or look elsewhere!"

She raced into the hallway of the guest quarters, where Rachfemd spent her time during that bridal competition. Clara could've cursed herself. She was the King's advisor, and yet she didn't *advise* her King against that mistake of a competition. How could she have, though? When King Jädrich was so insistent that it was time to take a wife, how could she have refused him? There was no argument to be made; it'd been a century of endless Winter, and King Jädrich couldn't have very well stayed unwed and heirless forever.

But he picked that snake, *that wretched woman—!*

Clara all but broke the door down to Rachfemd's old quarters. She shot to the center of the room and pulsed out a wave of her magic, screwing her eyes shut and letting the magic do the searching for her. It picked up on the basic shapes in the room: the furniture and the balcony door windows, the places where the walls and floor met. But it didn't pick up any shape of a box, so Clara had to look around herself. She looked *in* things her magic wouldn't have been able to do, like inside the empty dresser and around any potentially fake panels under the bedframe, but still there was nothing. Nothing in there.

Don't tell me she took them.

From that branch of the Sekhran's whelps—those

sneaky ones, the spies—came a box, according to what memories Dr. dur Verdem could hook from that fleshling's squelching brain. Clara had never seen something so horrid: all that pink, gooey stuff, *that* was where a fleshling's thoughts happened? In a bag of filth and blood and who-knew-what-else, under some hard bone-cap? It was enough to make Clara want to crawl out of her velvet entirely, thinking about how the doctor inserted his probe-sticks into that pink stuff and spoke a long, complex runespell to weave the pulses of that flesh into something understandable. With an Ismar soul, it was easier, so much easier, to get clear memories to project up from the probe-sticks like some kind of detailed moving picture, but what they got from the lizard, even with all the doctor's skill, was fuzzy, vague. Warped by time, as if even their memories were made of nothing more than flesh and could wither like fruits on a Summer vine.

Where is it? Clara all but tore the room to shreds, nearly ready to start drilling her magic into the stone itself before she got ahold of herself. *Did she take it? Did Rachfemd take those damn things with her?*

By time any guards even made it to the room with her, Clara was positive Rachfemd's room was a dead end. She turned around just as two guards reached the door, and she snapped, "This room is empty!"

"Yes, my Lady, we know," one said, one with short hair and a broad, flat face that made him look stupid enough without that wide-eyed, gawking expression he had on that moment. He blinked, his jaw jerking as if he forgot how to speak, and before Clara could yell at him to get his thoughts in some coherent order, he said, "We found a box. In the King's chambers."

Clara stared. Then, without a word, she hurried from Rachfemd's old quarters and back to the North Wing, to the King's chambers. All she could hear were the clack of her footsteps against icy stone as she ran, with all her might, to see what horrible thing the castle guards had found. If it was what she thought it was, then she didn't know what she'd do or what she'd feel.

"Where is it?" Clara shouted as soon as she was in earshot of the King's chambers. She almost hesitated to cross the threshold, even as a long-haired guard poked his head out of the doorway, that hair nearly slipping from a sloppy, tied up lump on the back of his head. But Clara didn't have it in her to nitpick anyone's appearance right then; there were more important things. Like the oddly colored box that guard showed her. She steeled herself and went inside the King's chambers for only the second time in her life.

How terrible, that the first day she'd ever seen these chambers was the day she'd caught some venomous wyrm skulking about. Clara once dreamed, before the High Summer, that she might see them as the Queen— but fate was a cruel thing. Cruel and unjust and not very funny at all, to tie so glorious a man as Jädrich Femmel III, a near spitting image of the sketches of Orr still found in the oldest archives, to some creature playing at being Cervora.

Clara knew. Clara knew the whole time, what that frost was. Especially after reading the notes found in Berlund Rachfemd's home. Maybe the King's wits were compromised, with whatever dangerous game he was playing without consulting her—as how could he have guessed? How could he have guessed that he would, in fact, need to lie about when he intended to leave on his tour with that half-breed? That he would have to lay a trap like this?—but Clara's wits would never be so clouded. Couldn't be, not if she wanted to protect that King properly from others, if not from his own self. And sure enough, there in her hands was exactly the confirmation to the fuzzy memories Dr. dur Verdem dragged from the goop in that lizard's head: a box of wood Clara hadn't seen in a hundred years. Coconut wood.

The guard that found it handed it to her, and it felt so smooth in her hands. Before she opened it, she looked around at those guards and whispered, "Where did you find this?"

The long-haired one pointed at the bed. "Under there. Under a stone."

Another guard, one with a hard-edged face and a head shaved bald, was kneeling by the bed. He beckoned Clara over and, when she knelt beside him, showed her the hole that was somehow just the shape of the box. A brick had come loose, and it'd clearly made the perfect hiding spot. But why would Rachfemd leave something like this behind? Something so *damning,* so terrible?

Unless—

That barely-formed thought was enough to finally shake Clara from whatever fear she had of the box's contents. She gritted her teeth and flicked that wicked gold clasp open, and to her relief—to her horror—there were two shining black eyes lying in plush purple cloth. Had those two black marbles not been marred with patches of scraggly white, she might've thought they were eyes like hers: onyx. However, with the way they began to radiate a terrible red thanks to the warning signals her *real* onyx eyes sent, she knew: these were fake eyes, ones made of *obsidian.* Volcanic glass potent enough to melt an Ismar to nothing. They must've been given to Rachfemd to put in the King's head, by the spikes on the back. Must've been made for the purpose of melting the King to a puddle. And it could've only been the other three Ringland Lords that sent Rachfemd on the quest to do so, the selfish beasts.

"Why didn't she take them, my Lady?" The bald guard whispered his question as if saying it too loud would send that box flying out the window and into Rachfemd's hands, wherever the snake was. He eyed the box as if it were a letter of war—which may have made him smarter than he looked, because that was exactly what the damn thing was. "Why did she leave them here? Where they could be found?"

"Does it matter? Clearly she didn't think they would be found," *the stupid animal,* "so we should just count ourselves lucky that the fool wasn't so careful. But," she snapped the box closed, and the sound was so sharp that even the two guards with her flinched, "we did find it. And so we need a message to go to the King. Immediately. I'll put one together, and then you drag that lizard into my personal study."

The long-haired guard blinked. "My lady, are you sure? I don't think that's safe—"

"I didn't ask what you think," Clara snapped. The tap of her shoes as she left the King's chambers, the click of her heels against the stone, they were just as sharp and crackling as every syllable she spoke. "Just get that thing in my study and bind him right, and it won't be a problem."

A pause hung in the air before the guards' voices followed her: "Yes, my lady."

THERE WAS NO FORGETTING IT: THAT SCREAM.

Aula huddled up tight in her carriage, which was thankfully still for a moment. They'd been on the road some three days already, and there hadn't been a single village yet. It seemed the space outside the city was sparser and more desolate than Aula ever imagined, which would make how long some merchants took to get her materials to her understandable. All she could see outside the window of her carriage were trees, snow, rock—and at one point, the smooth rock of the roads even disappeared, making the already uncomfortable carriage seats that much more unbearable with how the carriage rocked and bumped along. The only thing that made the drive even *longer* to whatever their first village was, was the fact that Aveline had to eat and drink, and it was the guards who had to go fetch things from those woods for her.

But by Cervora's velvet, that *scream.* That endless, air-shredding scream. Aula had been there in the crowd with Erik and that strange friend of his when it started. The fact that the King would drag out the very skull of Cervora into the open air like that was already such a shock—and one could only wonder if it was Aveline that demanded it—but what *happened* to her? To make her lose her composure like that? To make her scream herself hoarse and clutch her head as if something were trying to burst out of it? To make the King have to whisk her away and shove her into the carriage like an animal? It was only that moment that Aula realized that the tour was beginning, too, because the guards around her similarly herded her, Erik, and Karina into their own carriages and locked them in.

I want to go home. Aula knew Aveline needed her, and she'd committed to making this journey—after all, it was only two months, only two short months, that she'd be away from her husband's memory in her house— but as she sat in that still carriage alone, her head still echoing that scream, she could only wish for her home and all the safety and simplicity of it. The familiar workroom, full of her fabric scraps and pin cushions, her mannequins and her mirrors. The little sitting area, where patrons would come out to show husbands or fiancés or whoever else their new clothes and twirl around with such a smile on their faces. The bedroom, where Aula still remembered her late husband.

"In position!"

Aula hardly twitched at the sudden shout. She'd grown used to it: the calls of the King's guard as they organized the several carriages and started the whole bumpy journey towards the first village again. She pressed herself into the corner of the empty carriage and watched its door. At some point, another guard would come in and sit there in silence for another stretch of the way forward. Some three had rotated around already, each one another black-armored thing that reminded her *far* too much of the ones that took her husband's broken body away. All of them had that same blank look, those same frosted-over eyes—just like the ones that—

The door swung open, and a guard Aula hadn't yet seen climbed the steps. All these guards explained why they had so many carriages following them out of the city square a few days ago.

"Alright," the man whispered, apparently to himself, "off we go again."

Aula watched as he shut the carriage door and plopped into his seat. The guard sat back as if he were finally able to relax after a long day's burden on his ice, and his shaggy hair drifted all about his face and shoulders like snow blown around in the wind. His eyes were cheap blue lace agate, a stone more suited for women looking to measure their lovers' favor and get a marriage band than a guard. What he was doing with eyes like that was anyone's guess.

Those banded blue eyes swiveled towards her, and the guard sat up just as the carriage lurched forward. He leaned over with his forearms resting on his knees, his face closer to Aula than she would've liked. She tried to erase all thoughts from her head, all moods from her mind—offering him only an impassive stare as he studied her. His brows quirked anyway, lips lifting in a small smile.

"Too slow," he muttered, and he shook his head. His smile grew, as if he meant to tease her. "Far too slow, Ms. Seamstress."

She frowned. "It's Ms. Verrinson, thank you."

His eyes snapped back to her, and she bit her tongue before she said anything else. But this guard—Cervora's velvet, she hated the way he looked at her. It pricked her with the needling sensation of her own irritation: the smugness in that smile, and the way he lounged as if he didn't have a care in the world.

Seems a little loose for a guard.

"Ms. Verrinson," he said. "I apologize. Have you been treated well so far? By the other guards?" Only then did his smile slip as he studied her. "Because—"

"I know what your eyes are made of," she snapped. "Don't you think it's rude to peep at a lady's emotions before you even know her name?"

The guard paused, then grinned and sat back. His arms crossed over his chest as he stared at her—specifically, as he stared just above her head. "I don't decide what I see, or how much I see," he said. "You may as well be shouting your thoughts from the rooftops."

Aula squeezed her teeth together. Then she muttered, "You're in an awfully good mood, aren't you, guard?"

"Ristef Gürrensig, you mean," he said, and annoying thing he was, he winked at her. "And I wouldn't say I'm in a good mood, no. Just not a bad one."

This *Ristef* put his hands behind his head and stared at the carriage ceiling, as if he were going on some vacation rather than doing his job. It certainly didn't say much about palace security. Aula studied him a bit longer. She could feel her face pinching the more she looked at him; she knew she was scowling. But she couldn't help it. What a menace, this guard.

He glanced at her, and Aula quickly looked away—but no doubt, when he chuckled, those peeping eyes of his saw whatever glimpse of her irritation she couldn't hide. She tucked herself tighter into the carriage corner and tried her best to ignore him, like she'd ignored every other guard so far.

"So you're the one who makes Aveline's dresses?"

Aula whipped around and gave the guard as harsh a

look as she could. "That is *Her Majesty,* our Queen and Mother, thank you—"

Ristef's smile made her words fizzle out in her mouth. He only kept staring, waiting for her to answer his question, and if for nothing else, it made her pause.

"Are you," Aula blinked past her surprise, "are *you* the guard that Aveline had? Erik mentioned a guard that defended her."

A guard that was much too comfortable with her. One that was casual enough to be frank with her, and apparently, even call her by her first name when he thought no one was listening in on his conversations with Aveline. But Erik was always a bit stiff about things like that.

Ristef nodded. "I am. She told me to call her by her name, and who am I to deny an order from the Queen?"

Aula felt her face open as she considered him; the tension left her bit by bit. "So you must've kept her company, then? During the bridal competition?"

He nodded again. The easy smile never left his face.

"Then, yes." *He seems kind, if a menace.* "I am the one who makes her dresses."

Ristef sat up. "They're very good. Interesting. And she seems to like them a lot."

Aula nodded, but she didn't say anything else. She let the conversation fizzle there, even as Ristef occasionally glanced between her and the carriage floor. Eventually, when the silence was thin enough, she looked back out the carriage window and watched the trees rumble past.

"Do you think she'll be okay?"

The question startled Aula. She turned back to him and saw him staring at his folded hands, hunched over with his elbows on his knees.

"What do you mean?"

Ristef shrugged. It didn't take blue lace agate eyes for Aula to see the concern in his face: the pinch in his brows, the way his jaw shifted as he thought, the downcast stare.

"You were at the city square. Something happened." Ristef looked out the other carriage window. "Something happened to her, but only she knows what."

Aula sat silent. She was at a loss as to what to say; she didn't know what happened any more than anyone else. All she knew was that Aveline's scream was something no creature would do if they were right and well. What that meant, though, was anyone's guess. What Aveline saw there in that skull—as the guard said, only she would know.

The silence stretched on until Ristef sat back and plastered a smile back on his face. "Well, we'll see. We should be arriving at our first village soon. No doubt Aveline will have had a good few days of rest to put her back to her old self."

We'll see. He said it so simply, as if Aveline hadn't suffered more than a chipped foot. Aula knew, though, by the twitch of his lips, that it was more a polite close to an unpleasant conversation. The guard was a menace, yes—but he was apparently Aveline's companion, and he very apparently cared for her very much. Aula could only be glad for Aveline, to have someone lively by her side like this guard. It must've made it easier to be in that castle for three weeks.

Yet both of them, it seemed, still heard that terrible scream echoing through their heads.

All was dark. Everything. When Aveline first fell, and all was so black and silent, she thought that perhaps she'd finally know peace and escape that doe-wraith—but fate itself apparently had no love for her.

In the black, empty nothingness, the skull of that

doe-wraith hung over her. It no longer felt like the animal instinct Aveline always harbored—something she thought came from her being half a thing of blood and bone, half an animal, as her father's people saw fleshlings. That thing was only ever instinct before: it knew to be scared, knew to be wary, knew to push even when her rational mind knew it was useless. It knew a bad choice from a good one, even if it couldn't express why; it knew who to trust and who not to trust, even when her rational mind overrode its sense. But it was always, *ever,* Aveline. It couldn't have been anything *but* Aveline.

Until the moment Aveline touched Cervora's skull and invited this thing into her body. No, as Aveline stared at this apparition, she knew: this instinct fit into the wraith like a missing piece of treasure in a dragon's great, meticulously maintained hoard. The instinct was not, and was never, Aveline. It was this—this thing. A neutered thing. A shadow, a whisper of something more—something outside Aveline. And it'd always been hidden there, like a parasite, in Aveline's bones. Watching. Waiting.

There was something wicked in that cold, horrible—and for the first time, the voice she heard come from that skull, that animal, was hardly a voice at all. As the cold dug into her skin and threatened to crack her skull, she heard only the wind whispering in ancient sounds too old to be words. Yet Aveline understood them nonetheless, clearly and perfectly:

I will not die again. I will not serve them again.

Its one intact hand reached up, and its fingers went sharp and terrible as those of the massive *Kviraeg—Unseelechs*—whatever they really were. A shining silver line of magic suddenly glowed there in the dark of Aveline's mind's eye. It came from Aveline's chest, and it moved around, circled from behind her, as if something was tethered to her—some outline of a man. A man? A man.

Aveline.

Someone called her, but she couldn't register it. She could see nothing, and no one, but the doe-wraith, who stood there clicking its sharp talons together. Then, above it, the moon and stars shone down, so bright it nearly blotted her out, as if they were trying to erase the skull; their light was like spiderwebs, sticking to it, encasing it in a white sheen. Something happened to the moon, too, as those webs reached down. It flickered as if blinking, and the stars twinkled as if alive. Aveline knew without knowing, her being of half the blood of the Sun's own people: it was not just the Moon and Stars. It was Malouçe and the other wives of Drakash, those softer Summer gods.

The moon cannot bargain with me again. The words echoed from the skull, different from the half-coherent yippings Aveline heard since her near-starvation on Kha-Bawaj. It had a sharpness to its voice like a well cut and polished stone, a dreadful clarity. With it came a freeze so deep that even Aveline couldn't breathe. *The moon cannot soothe me this time.*

And again, some voice rang in the distance: *Aveline.*

I will not tolerate this. The doe-wraith suddenly appeared right in Aveline's face, as if it refused that little voice's influence, and it hooked its finger under that silver line with the full intention of severing it. *I will not be bound to my killer's kin.*

Something touched her, and she jolted—both her and the doe-wraith. Startled, Aveline understood then, the shape of the man, the long hair, the strange spires rising from its head: Jädrich. Jädrich! And the line, then, the line was—!

"No!" Aveline snatched the wrist of the doe-wraith and *howled,* because its skin and bone were colder even than Jädrich's body. So cold that it felt like it could kill the flesh of her palm in but one moment, rendering it black and frostbitten beyond repair. Still, she held on, and she fought it as it tried to catch that line of magic. When she'd gathered herself, she hissed, "No, you stupid beast! You *stupid beast!* This line keeps us alive in this country!"

The doe-wraith paused, but it said nothing.

"This keeps us *out* of their jaws! It's keeping us alive! Leave it!" Something crackled in her mouth—frost, she thought, her frost—but it felt too warm on her tongue. Far too warm. And it shone, too; it made *light.* Golden light. "Leave it!"

As she shouted those words once more, the light lit up the darkness; the doe-wraith stood against a backdrop of red and gold, and in that light, it recoiled. It hissed, pulled its claw away.

"Leave it!" Aveline kept shouting, as if it were a spell she could banish the creature with. "Leave it, leave it! Leave it!"

I will take your strength.

Even as the doe-wraith shrank, its voice thundered in Aveline's head and threatened to split her skull in two.

I will take it one day. Yes, dragon, I will take it.

It strayed farther away as it hissed its promises—farther still, until it was but a shining speck somewhere against all that red and gold.

I will not be prey again.

"Aveline," came that voice again, but this time, it sounded clear and close—even through Aveline's groggy mind. The blackness cracked as her eyes began to open, and she found herself curled up in a carriage, her knees hugged tightly to her chest. Across from her sat Jädrich. He stared at her with what she might call concern, given the way he frowned. When she finally looked at him, he sat at the edge of his seat and reached out to put a hand on her shoulder. "Are you well?"

Aveline stared a little longer, then rubbed her stinging eyes. She went to speak, only to wince and clutch her throat. It felt as if a cat had gone and shredded her throat to ribbons. But she managed, after some fight, to rasp, "Fine. I'm fine."

It hardly sounded like her. Still, Jädrich produced a small bottle of a watery golden liquid and held it out to her. "Evergreen sap and water from under a deep river," he said. "Drink."

She did, and to her surprise, the water was fresh and cold. That and the sap both soothed her throat and made it easier to breathe, even if it hurt to swallow. When the bottle was empty, she gave it back to Jädrich and sat up. The ache in her bones made her wince.

"We're still a day from the first town," Jädrich said. "It's been a few days already. Will you be able to speak when you arrive?"

"I think so." Already, that sap coated her throat and made it more bearable to try.

"Good. Then we'll begin our work right away." Jädrich's face smoothed out, though he still studied her. Eventually, he said, "Tell me what happened."

Aveline blinked. Then she shuddered. Even if her voice hadn't been nearly gone, Aveline couldn't have spoken a word about what she saw, nor of the thing hiding in her bones, like some deep rot that threatened to spread. She simply didn't have the words to explain what she'd seen. She couldn't even figure out where to start.

"Not now," was all she said. "One day."

Jädrich stared at her longer, and Aveline braced herself to argue. Of course he would want to know what happened. Aveline would've wanted to know, too, if she saw someone scream themselves hoarse the way she did. But no matter how much she tried, it was as if both her mind and her body had betrayed her; they both froze, paralyzed at the thought of explaining the pain of tendon tearing off bone, or how she knew a word like *Kviraeg,* or what that doe-wraith said before slinking into the deep, forsaken parts of her being. Aveline's hand went for her neck as if she would find comfort there, just as she had all the weeks prior—but damn it all, she knew she'd find nothing. She knew her mother's bell would not be there, and she knew she couldn't have it there, either. She knew, staring into that doe-wraith's bleached skull, that her mother's memory had no business being attached to a monster like this.

"Fine," Jädrich said. The one word shook Aveline out of her thoughts. When she focused on him, he only nodded. "One day, you will tell me. Until then, rest. Later, we'll bring you something from the woods to eat."

"Gods above, every single one of them," Erik muttered as he climbed out of his carriage.

The guard that sat with him and Karina left the carriage last, watching Karina carefully as she descended its steps. Erik held up his hand to her and guided her out. He couldn't help but rub his thumb over her skin and press the strange flesh that hung on her bones; it simply didn't feel the same as velvet over smooth, hard ice. She shot him a look for it, though; her brow quirked and her mouth pursed in a silent question.

Before Erik could say anything, their guard hopped out of the carriage and stared at them with eyes of deep forest green. He was a younger guard; Erik could tell by the way he kept those eyes so open, as if showing them off. Perhaps they were the first set he ever afforded on his own. But the short hair of an early, practical-minded recruit and the hard edge to his brow made Erik think he couldn't have been at the job very long. It made him wonder just what kind of security the King thought he was taking along for a prize as valuable as Cervora's icon.

Makes our mission easier in the end.

"Lord Rachfemd, my lady," the guard said, standing stiff as a board with his hands straight by his sides, "allow me to escort you to your place of stay while we're in this village."

Village wasn't quite the right word for it. As Erik and Karina followed the guard over the paved path, he looked around and found that the "village" was more of a town proper, what with how many houses there were. They were simple houses, yes—small ones built of wood, the beams stretching across the white painted exteriors, and clustered together with no alleys or gaps to be found—but the people had infused their white homes with sap-paints, covering them in purples and blues and greens like a Spring artist covered their canvas. The paintings were of flowers, the ones that dotted the Winter ice plains and could handle the endless frost. There were even still flower boxes in the windows full of moonblooms.

This was only a mining town—at the inner edge of the territory of the Baron of Trevannt, no less—and yet it seemed as well maintained as any other city, which surprised Erik. Given how the Baron was in on the plot, he expected the village to be a bit more run-down, what with there being less venison and bloodwine getting into the hands of the people per their agreement. However, it seemed he prioritized these lands getting any resources for their magic. It made sense, given this was one of the first towns to find after the desolate roadways between the capital and the rest of the country; it would be all too easy for the King to see a problem from here. But no doubt, as they kept going south, the fault lines in the magicless men and women would begin to show.

The guard led them to a great house that seemed to be made of mostly logs. Unlike the other houses, so nicely painted, this simple, undecorated, yet massive thing was clearly *old*. It probably stood first among all the houses in this village, and it was clear right away that this was the guest house of the Baron himself, as the only decoration on it was the black and green shield above the porch's entryway. On it was the image of an eagle, along with the silver stars of the Northeast Sky.

And in fact, the Baron was there to greet them. He was a strangely carved man, no doubt—one carved thick in his middle, his arms round as tree trunks and his legs bulky enough that his pants never seemed to fit him right. His neck was thick, too, practically blending his chin into his chest. It was as if his parents thought he'd one day be a prize logger or fighter instead of the head of his house. But the silver hair that grew in a thick bush and mustache on his face, as well as the short crop of hair at his head, covered the awkwardness of his carving enough to make him look rather friendly—especially when he smiled as he did right then.

"Ah, welcome!" The Baron tipped his head and extended his arm as if he meant to hug Erik, but that arm swung around and motioned to the house's huge door. "Come, come! It's good to see you, Lord Rachfemd, and a beautiful day to see the King and his Queen as well."

As Erik came closer, he pinned a smile on his own face—and he did not miss how, the moment the guard passed the Baron, that cheerful face became something more pointed. Those squinted eyes opened wider, piercing Erik with their deep blue sapphire stare. It was as clear a message as any: *why are you already here?*

Erik could only flash his eyes and tighten his smile in response. *I don't know.*

Within a moment, that cheery smile came back up,

eyes obscured in the Baron's goodwill, and he bowed his head deep to whoever was behind Erik.

"Your Majesties," the Baron said, "welcome, welcome. Thank you for choosing to bless this here village first with your presence."

Karina gave a quick pinch to Erik's coat sleeve and stood aside in the doorway with their guard, and Erik followed her, turning to see that Aveline and the King were coming down from their own carriage. Aveline again wore a veil; her face was obscured behind a layer of black gauze, her clothes likewise thick and dark as if she were wearing a mess of blankets instead of a dress. Her antlers and hooves were hidden away for the time being, but as Erik glanced around at the street, he found that did not stop her from drawing any attention. People were clustering in doorways, in windows; they were pausing their walks across the village, stopping their errands, to stare. They wanted to see this Queen, no doubt. Erik could only hope that it was only their curiosity clustering them together, and not any other unsavory rumors.

Would anyone have been able to come here faster than us? Erik had to consciously smooth his face as Aveline and the King passed; he forced himself to bow his head low as they came through and entered the manor first. *Would anyone here know about that disaster performance Aveline put on?*

"Rise, Lord Fervall," the King said. His voice was so deep and dark that it could've made even an Ismar like Erik shudder. "We appreciate your hospitality. Please settle us, that our Queen Mother might begin her duties right away."

"Of course, yes—this way, Your Majesties." The Baron nodded and pushed the door open, and all waited until Aveline and the King entered before following.

As Erik and Karina trailed behind, and the sound

of guards pulling trunks from carriages echoed in the village silence, Erik found another hand pulling at his coat. He turned around to see Aula there, tucked towards him like a small child. The recluse hadn't left Vörnein in decades, and that uncertainty was carved into her pinched face. Then, as the shrieking cries of Aveline's *Unseelechs* pierced the air, and as they fumbled and crashed about in whatever old carriage they'd been locked in, Aula flinched. Erik did, too, at so wretched a commotion. After, though, he could only absently pat her shoulder as they walked, because his mind was soon miles away—from Aveline, from Aula, from the Baron's house, from the entire hold of Trevannt.

Gods. His ice felt heavy, too heavy. *I have to warn Isolde. I have to fix Aveline's mess—deal with those damn beasts she brought. I have to get the rumors under control. I have to get ahead of the news of Aveline's outburst. I have to figure out how to—*

And so went his thoughts, whirring on and on through the list of things he had to do to keep his idiot "cousin" from ruining her ransom value before it began to truly shine.

Couldn't he have given me a day to rest?

Aveline's bottom still ached from laying in that carriage for so long. Jädrich said they'd settle her things, but she'd hardly been able to put her things down before she'd been whisked back outside and into the carriage alone, and she'd barely more than sat down before that carriage lurched forward towards the cathedral. The belfry of that cathedral loomed over the village like a watchful guardian, its big silver bell shining in the soft light like an Ismar's magic-laced eye. As Aveline's carriage rumbled towards it, she couldn't help but feel *that* was the real god of this place. What else could've had the power to draw people so close with just three rings of magic-molded silver?

Aveline had been lucky so far: she hadn't had to step foot in one of these things her entire time during the contest. It seemed the services were only held once a month, with a mandatory ration of meat and blood given to all the people a church could service—something like fifty to a hundred depending on the size of it. This village was big, a fair collection of quaintly painted houses and old, weathered roads with the occasional cobblestone missing. It was apparently a mining town, with a stone quarry and a silver mine keeping people there in the first place, but Aveline hadn't been out to see the mines just yet. With how tight the schedule was for her going about the country, however, Aveline wondered if she'd even have the time to.

You're to bless the people, Jädrich told her when they were alone in the room that Baron showed them to. *Bless them with the gift of frost, and when all who wish to step forward have come to you, we'll go on to the next town.*

He made it sound so easy.

However, the new scenery, the emptiness of the carriage, made it easier to focus than it had been in what felt like a century. There was no room to worry about the flashes of wicked images, or the darkness lurking in the shadows of her mind; there was only the people and their endless stares to worry about. Even though the bell hadn't rang yet, the people were already outside and tracking every turn of her carriage's wheel. Some even *reached* for the carriage like some pack of desert ghouls from the horror stories her mother told her. Thankfully, Aveline had the privilege to shudder and hide in that carriage, with no King riding along to chastise her.

Just as the carriage came to the cathedral, the bell started its triple chime. The sudden, deep call of that silver thing made Aveline flinch; from directly below that belfry, it sounded like the booming, eerie voice of a metal giant, speaking a language Aveline didn't know. Worse, the relative silence of the townspeople made it seem like Aveline wasn't about to enter a sacred space as much as she was about to be sacrificed to that giant, and this whole torturously slow ride had been her funeral procession.

Slack. Her throat squeezed at the thought; her skin came alive with needling tingles. *Save your frost.* Some heavy weight sat on her shoulders, as if a person were trying to stand on her neck and crouch to whisper in her ear. *Slack.* There were no words, though. There was only a feeling. A conviction so deep that it seemed to sprout from the very marrow of her bones—as if the shadows had rooted there and were threatening to bind up her body in their terror. It erased her mantras and stole her voice, her mind, her very sense, to insist a terrible thing.

They'll sacrifice us.

The feeling of freezing teeth biting her skin apart made her flinch and clutch her ribs. A metallic tang tainted her mouth from the back of her tongue.

Again.

The carriage door swung open, and the sight of Ristef at the foot of the carriage steps sent those thoughts scattering, if only for a moment. He smiled at her with such softness that she almost forgot he was ice and not flesh; his eyes, despite being so pale a blue, seemed almost warm as they sparkled with whatever emotion laced his soul. With a nod, he reached a hand out to her and spoke.

"Your Majesty," he said, "please show yourself. His Majesty will soon join you."

So formal. But the way he projected his voice made it seem that this was some marker of ceremony—made it so the words skated right past her, as if he wasn't talking to her, but someone behind her—and so Aveline sat frozen for a moment. The echo of the cathedral bell still haunted the air, too, disorienting her further. *Who is this?* For a moment, she didn't recognize that uncanny dimple in his ice, or the smooth hand that she'd held all those weeks in the competition; something crawled under her skin at the sight of him that seemed desperate to escape out the other side of that carriage and disappear forever. *Who are you?*

"Aveline," Ristef whispered as he leaned closer, his smile becoming a teasing grin, "come on. Don't just sit there like a dove."

Oh. As if a spell were broken, Aveline blinked her fugue away. Ristef. Her Ristef, her friend, her trusted confidant—one that would never rip her flesh from her bones or pull her entrails from her stomach, of course—that was who reached for her. Nothing to worry about. Nothing at all. As she tried to convince the shadows in her bones of such a thing, she pursed her lips and swatted his outstretched hand.

"I'll sit like a dove all I damn well want," she grumbled, but they both found themselves chuckling. For at least that moment, the tension disappeared. She gathered her courage and took that earnest fool's hand; she let that man in shining black armor lead her under the dull light of another Winter day.

And when she got out, tempted as she was, she didn't look at all those people and their silent, outstretched hands. She knew better. Her nerves were a carefully assembled tower of stones; it wouldn't take much to topple it and create a mess in her mind all over again. Even their whispers, she let herself pretend were only the wind—and she looked up at that cathedral instead, at the belfry that would've cast a wicked shadow in stronger light. The clouds hid the burning sun, great

Drakash, in a way that strained her eyes, and yet she could still make out two very important figures around that great spire: the outstretched wings and flowing silver hair of her babies. They seemed like they were trying to hide behind that belfry, flying so high up.

So Aveline yipped. Like a Yasilan shepherd, she yipped her call to her two-creature flock, and she raised her hand to make a snap of glittering silver magic that they knew well. It only took a moment for them to notice her and breach the boundary of that belfry; another moment, and they answered her yips with high, piercing shrieks that sounded like the squeak and moan of ice about to break.

Then, while the people shifted in Aveline's peripheral and their whispers became uneasy murmurs, her babies descended like arrows on the tail end of their deadly arc.

One landed at her feet with a *thud* on that tattered road; its talons scraped along the old cobblestones, and its head knocked into Aveline's calf as a sign of affection. The other, however, careened towards her and only *just* pulled itself up early enough to avoid knocking into her chest; its glassy eyes sparkled with whatever thoughts an *Unseelech* could have, and its teeth gnashed in pleasure as it settled into Aveline's open arms. Its great feet settled against her stomach, talons delicately pressed against her ribs, and it draped its wings around her shoulders as if trying to cover her in an icy blanket. Aveline smiled at the sweet thing and held it close like she might a young child. Past it, though, she caught Ristef's wide-eyed stare as he stood by the cathedral doors waiting for her.

What are you doing? That's what stare said to her. *Wrong! Wrong!*

And yet it was Aveline's decision what was right or wrong—or did a goddess not get that privilege after all?

With her children at her side, she finally found the last bit of courage she needed to look at that crowd—and no one could've understood her delight when she saw not outstretched hands, but recoiling ones. Not faces open and seeking, like her *Unseelechs,* but ones scrunched in the unease that had threatened to poison her just moments ago. *Yes,* she thought, from the very marrow of her bones, *stay back.* She knew how she must've looked: dressed in her most comfortable dress, a loose thing so black it seemed made of the shadows that haunted her, and wrapped in beasts the Ismären so pitifully disdained. *Fear me. Come no closer.*

Had Cervora had these with her, then maybe whatever mess she saw after she touched that skull wouldn't have happened.

"Come," she said instead. When the people fell silent and stayed still, she blinked. *Am I not your Queen? Should you not obey?* But it seemed only the King's crown could command as forcefully as she'd have liked. She'd need something more than a Queen's crown, and more than a King's, too.

So she heaved a great sigh—one that made not a few of those wide-eyed townsfolk startle. The gush of her breath mixed with the distant roar of Winter's quiet. She kicked off her shoes and, with another breath, she flexed her scalp, condensed the bones of her feet, and let the pop and crack of her joints smash that silence to pieces—let her bulging legs peek through the slits of her skirt as they rippled with silver fur.

With her antlers rising up in place of a crown, and with her hooves lifting her higher than any such ridiculous shoes ever could, she barked again: "Come. Or do you want no blessings?"

Without waiting for their response, she moved for the doors of the cathedral. Her hooves clopped against the stone with such crisp snaps that seemed to echo over the whole town, over the whole next league, and she couldn't tame it: her beastly grin that bared every tooth. Delight and satisfaction coiled in her gut like sister snakes; her bones were warm with something, someone's, approval. Maybe Drakash's. Maybe her mother's. Maybe her own.

And yet, as those doors creaked open with her approach, she found herself soon buffeted by some awful stench: the smell of stale air barely hidden by some strong, sweet fragrance. It clung to her nose with every breath in, as if she were sipping spoiled wine, and her throat closed as if to reject the smell outright. She paused, and in the meantime, she looked around at that cathedral as she coaxed her throat back open.

It was a stone monstrosity with great panes of stained ice-glass in dizzying patterns of blue, green, and purple, a place lined with wooden benches that all faced towards an altar and a great statue of Cervora under a soft halo of starlight. Sconces of starlight likewise hung from the many columns that supported the building and all its high ceilings, and bright white moonflowers sat tall and proud in their silver vases on either side of the two blue doors towards the cathedral edges. Maybe they were other exits, or maybe they went somewhere else; Aveline couldn't have imagined a building that looked so big and bulky on the outside would be so narrow on the inside. Unlike the airy, open temples of Drakash, where the sun was meant to touch all angles of the sacred space and where there was room for worshippers to sit and pray on all sides, this long and skinny cathedral felt more like a closet. A tight, cramped closet that hid everything and everyone from the outside.

Aveline frowned at the thought. She'd never been much of a temple-goer in the first place; she had no love or praise or song to offer to a burning hot god that clearly wanted to erase her from this world. However, she would've preferred to feel the Winter light on her face in such an open temple rather than be caged in this stone closet. And as she walked forward with one baby still resting on her hip, taking tiny sips of that tainted air, she found a grey carpet runner underfoot, the same color as the stone, that would eat up the sound of her steps all the way to that white-clothed altar.

Where is Jädrich? He'd stayed behind to speak with the Baron, but she expected to see him in that cathedral soon after she got there. *Am I to do all this alone?*

She would if she had to. But as she walked, she could feel it more than hear it: the press of people at her back. Their stares bore into her before she ever heard the shuffling of their clothes and the hissing whispers they shared between each other—ones so quiet that she *still* couldn't make anything out.

Anything except one sharp snap. As Aveline came to the front of all those pews, someone came too close to her other *Unseelech* as it stayed by her legs; the little creature squeaked a complaint at the foolish girl that invaded its space and earned a wicked, cat-like hiss in return.

"Ugh, *wraith.*"

Her brows were bent in such fury, her mouth curved into an ugly little frown. But as Aveline stopped short, and the *Unseelech* clung to her leg, the woman looked up and immediately wiped all expression off her face. Whatever she saw in Aveline's eyes, it was enough to make her sink slowly into her seat and bow her head in a silent apology.

Aveline had antlers, but seeing that woman bow her head like that, they may as well have been a dragon's horns. She let her other *Unseelech* down and barely hid her smile as it scampered up to that woman, studying her for a moment before cracking a warning snap in the back of its throat. Both creatures flanked her as she climbed the couple cloth-lined steps up to the altar. And how the people shrank in their seats when her *Unseelechs* flanked her there, too—when they hopped up and sat on either side of her, their feet leaving gravel and dust on that otherwise pristine white altar cloth.

Good. Yes, these creatures would've served Cervora well, had they been with her. They were fearsome things. Aveline would've hated to be on the wrong end of their teeth. *Stay back.*

In the back, on the other side of the main entrance, Ristef leaned against the wall. He caught her gaze and lightly shook his head. Maybe he was disappointed with the creatures. They chittered and crooned in her ears and bumped their hairy heads against her chin, but she didn't care. They were hers. And this altar, too, was hers. She decided then, answering her own question: this place was hers. And these people were simply allowed in it for the time being. It seemed they knew that, too, by the way they stared at her with those wide eyes and balled their hands up in their laps, silent and waiting for her to speak.

They've sinned.

The thought sprouted in her mind like an early Spring snowdrop. It was a strange thought, and yet as she looked around at that cathedral full of sullen faces, she could only agree with it.

They've done wicked things.

Aveline blinked and saw an open sky bordered by blackish green pines. She blinked again and saw a bald, glassy, ghoulish face hover over her, a face devoid of any and all emotion, a face that did not know love. A face that had actively let love rot in its empty stare.

Terrible things.

Aveline blinked the images away and sucked in a breath. She was just about to speak a word or two of welcome when the sudden snap of steps appeared by the main entrance, and a few moments later, Jädrich appeared. The moment his steps hit the cushion of the carpet, the people stood and turned to face him. Aveline cocked her head to see it: how they gave such deference to him and honored him like that without his having to say a word. Maybe they just didn't know what to do yet to honor her—in which case, she'd tell them. In fact, her bones would tell them, her blood would tell them—the dark shadows of that doe-wraith that clung to her very soul would tell them—and tell them happily.

Jädrich approached without saying a word to Aveline; he hardly even glanced at the *Unseelechs* she had up on the table with her. It was almost disappointing, how little Jädrich showed in his face and manner. If he cared that she was dragging around these creatures he, himself, considered vermin—that he, himself, was fine ordering the destruction of—then no one could've guessed. Was she really able to do anything she liked? Anything at all?

"People of Weiharten," Jädrich said as he faced the packed cathedral, "thank you for receiving us—I, your King, and my wife, your Queen and Mother. You see her," he turned to her, hand outstretched, and Aveline took it, "antlers taller than any crown, hooves harder than any ice. You see her: Cervora returned to us." Jädrich turned back to the crowd, and Aveline had no idea if he noticed how her body rocked with a shudder. "She comes to heal your melt and lift your spirits. We will be here today and two more days after that, so all who wish to be cured should meet with your goddess reborn."

Only then did Jädrich glance at Aveline, and despite her dry mouth, she said what Jädrich coached her to say: "I'll be waiting for you, my children," her stomach knotted, and the threads of shadow in her bones tried to pull her hand out of Jädrich's, as if they could work her like a puppet—but she stayed firm and swallowed the bile that rose in her throat. "I'll be there from sunup to sundown."

Which, thankfully, wasn't so long in Winter.

"Now," Jädrich continued, "please meet your Mother for healing. She'll care for you all one at a time, in the basement, where it'll be easier to queue and keep your privacy. Any who can't make it down the stairs will be treated in the cathedral, after all others have left."

Knowing there was a basement made her shoulders sag. She didn't even realize they'd been so close to her ears in the first place, and the sudden loss of tension made her huff in relief. A basement, yes, one like the underbelly of the castle—she could do such work there with this many people. She was used to that. It would be easier to move about there, without unnecessary eyes watching her; it would be more intimate and relaxed— less public, less exposed. If she were to fix these people, it would not be up there in front of that cathedral, on display like some circus beast. No, that was what the statue of that ruined, hacked up goddess was for.

A sharp twitch bit her cheek at the thought and made her eyes sting with tears she quickly blinked away.

Aveline swallowed another wave of bile and kept her head high, kept her throat open. She cast her stare over those people like a mantel, and she raised a hand, crooked a finger.

"Come, you melted ones" she said, and this time, several people stood right away, ready to follow. Aveline kept a smirk off her face. "To the basement we go."

"Now, Lady Ronterweis, I wouldn't," said Headmistress Klassech. Her voice crackled through the King's study, which Clara rooted herself in those days while waiting for her King to end his ridiculous tour with that beast he called a goddess. "Killing that wyrm would give some room for legal retaliation from the beasts outside the Winter Wall."

Clara laced her frozen, perfectly re-shaped fingers together and rested her flawlessly formed chin atop them. Even after a good couple weeks with her body renewed, it was still a novelty to be able to do such a thing. But as she stared at the unmoving image of the headmistress, a collection of wispy white and blue shapes taking the form of a stern-faced woman, she found her thoughts more focused on the problem at hand: the wicked things she'd distilled from the mind of that lizard that had crawled past Winter's wall.

"Then the people need to know that their King is being hunted," Clara insisted. "Both outside and inside Winter. By their own Queen."

"And they will—but their King needs to know first. Haven't you had a conversation with him already?"

Clara gently rubbed her chin over the top of her hands. "I tried, but he didn't give me much time to explain. Nor did he say much. In fact, he didn't seem concerned about it at all."

A pause. Then, "I see."

"Do you? Do you see the situation we're in?" Clara got out of her chair and paced behind the desk with her hands tucked behind her back. "We have the fleshlings at our door, and our King doesn't have directives for how to handle this obvious breach of international law!"

"Well, international law *is* a bit of a bygone conclusion, isn't it?" Headmistress Klassech chuckled, then said, "The other three nations could catch us for as much as we could catch them for, I think. I'd be surprised if the King still thought any of our neighbors would side with him, if he were to take this to international court. He must have some other plan in mind."

That made Clara pause. In fact, it sobered her. When she'd called her King, he only let her get as far as telling him about the Summer intruder with obsidian blades before saying *good work; keep record of it* and disappearing. Clara wondered if maybe her King just hadn't heard her right. Or hadn't understood her. Maybe missed the implications of what it meant for a dragon to be hunting him in his own home.

But then, maybe he knew perfectly well that the beast he paraded around was little more than a murderous mutt, and he was only using her for the frost that could cure even someone as wretched and half-gone as Clara. Maybe he was planning something, telling her to keep record of the beast. Clara already had with the runestones they'd planted in the King's chambers that night; she'd been suspicious as to why the King would leave earlier than announced, and her intuition had not led her wrong. Rarely did.

Nonetheless, all this she understood well, and had her King told her that was his plan, she would've happily gone along with it. But he hadn't. He didn't tell her, the most trustworthy person he had by his side, what any of his *real* intentions were, even though he'd let her know about other preparations. So why hadn't he told her the full extent of his plans? Surely he trusted her, his aide. When had she ever given him a reason not to trust her with anything he could be thinking?

"Where is that dragon boy now?"

The Headmistress's question snapped Clara out of her thoughts. Clara pressed her lips together. "He's in the dungeon. Why?"

"Secured? No way out?"

"Secured and recovering from the poking and prodding our surgical doctor did to get all this information, yes. *Why?*"

The blank stare of Headmistress Klassech's apparition bore into Clara. A long silence passed before her voice echoed through the room: "You must understand now, Clara: I do not say what I'm about to say lightly. Nor do I say it with the intention of treason. In fact, I say it with full intention to save not only our people, but our King, and I hope you understand this, given it was you that contacted me for advice and support."

Ugh, you menace. Clara chewed at the velvet on her lips and glanced at the *other* runestone on the desk: the one that radiated with magic, recording everything about the room: the sights *and* the sounds. No doubt if Klassech used such a tool to capture that mutt's odd behavior, she might've guessed Clara would use it to keep this conversation contained. A shame that she couldn't somehow cut that bit out.

"What do you intend to say, Headmistress?"

"That you should use that dragon boy. To both correct this situation and save Winter."

Clara paused. "How do you mean?"

"Bring him out. Send him to follow the King's tour south. Use him to expose his countrywoman before King and people. Then let the King do what he wills with the beast."

What an idea. But too dangerous, far too dangerous. "You understand, Headmistress, how we found him, don't you? In the King's chambers, poised to strike. The beast will try for our King's life the first chance he gets."

"Not with my help, he won't." Headmistress Klassech's apparition stayed just that: an apparition. And yet, the smugness in her voice made Clara believe she could just see the barest hint of a smile. "No, Lady Ronterweis, with my help, he will be the perfect tool. I'll send you something via *Unseelech* carrier by tomorrow, with instructions. You'll see. It'll be excellent."

Clara crossed her arms and shook her head. That tone in the Headmistress's voice, the strange thing she was suggesting—no. This woman never could've been Queen. These scholarly types were a menace, with that special sort of madness they had. But with little other option, Clara could only hope that such madness would work in her favor.

"Fine. I look forward to receiving it."

She was here. The Queen—the Mother. She was here. And maybe—the old miner hardly dared to be hopeful—maybe she could fix his sins. Make them right. Keep his family whole. Snatch their son out of the clutches of that wicked sun's heat.

But what if they're right—?

Elsfvor shook the thought right out of his head; he tossed it out so quickly that he might've heard it clatter on the ground, as if it were a chunk of raw silver. No, the people that frequented that tavern and had the bad sense to mix holly and sap into what meager rations of bloodwine the mining town got—what did they know? With their souls jammed up by that holly, they no doubt said all kinds of things they didn't really mean or believe just to cause trouble. And trouble they caused. There'd been enough arguing over rumors to make that tavern less a resting spot and more a place to brawl— verbally and just about as much physically. Elsfvor knew which side of the argument he fell on, even without going to the tavern anymore. The Queen was no *wraith,* even if she had *Unseelechs* at her heels. The Mother was no *half-breed.*

Still, Elsfvor's hand hesitated on the wood of the cathedral's basement door. Something stirred in his soul that made him pause, but he couldn't have told anyone what. He glanced around the corner to the main altar, where the statue of Cervora stood with her arms outstretched as if inviting a child to run to her. Her smile was sweet, her eyes dark, her antlers high and mighty, and her body was soft and round, not a harsh edge to be found from her legs to her shoulders. A picture of motherly love, a true, pure heart: that was their goddess.

So there's nothing to be afraid of.

"Papa?" His son, Luka, tugged at his pant leg. "Why aren't you going in?"

The tiny voice made Elsfvor blink. It took only half a moment to steel himself before he looked down at his son. When Elsfvor did look, though, no amount of preparation made it hurt any less to see the poor boy:

he only had one eye in his head, one of his grandfather's old galena spheres good for seeking out silver veins in the mines, because the other half of his face was nothing but a smooth, shiny crater. It'd melted so far that it wouldn't be long before the boy's soul was exposed in his head and begging to leak free—and Elsfvor had no one to blame but himself. He had, after all, married a woman with a melted foot.

It'd just been a touch. Just the very tip of her toe. He didn't think that would transfer to a son; he didn't think a blight so little would even count as a curse. Damn it all, he hadn't even believed the little spot on her toe was melt in the first place, given it looked more like she'd just chipped that toe hitting it on their hard stone stairways. And yet, by time the water of his love crystallized in her abdomen and passed from her, that toe became a foot—and that was enough that no one could doubt that the curse of flame was in her body, nor could they be surprised when their son was brought into this world with a little spot of wet on his face.

Elsfvor squeezed his teeth together tight enough to make them squeak. A little more and they'd break. But he pulled them back apart just before that. He reached out to pat the poor boy's fuzzy head, and he managed to speak with what he hoped looked like a smile and not a grimace.

"Don't mind it. Are you ready?" He crouched down so he was eye level with Luka and looked around the corner, to that big statue. Then he pointed to it and said, "Ready to meet her?"

A big grin bloomed on the boy's face just as a drop of water rolled from that melting cavern down his cheek. "Yeah!"

Elsfvor didn't dare let his smile falter, even as he watched that drop roll down to the boy's chin. He nodded and whispered, "Alright, then, let's go see her."

And then he stood and went to push that door open—only to find it locked. For a moment, his soul squeezed with panic. Wasn't the Mother already there? It was early, yeah—her service wouldn't begin for another hour—but he knew she got there early. He'd seen her coach take her from one end of town to the other that early on the morning prior. It seemed this was the last day the Mother would be in town before she moved on to the next, just to catch stragglers like him that waffled on a choice so obvious, and that itself was a mercy that cut him deep. Yet the door was locked. Maybe she didn't want visitors yet. Or maybe she wanted to wait until the official sessions began, where people clustered about the cathedral and came one by one down these stairs to beg for her healing frost. But what kind of Mother would ever lock the way to her?

Had it been just him, Elsfvor might've doubted too much and turned around. He might've let his stubbornness replace his faith, even. After all, the boy's face was so melted; what would even be the point of fixing it? *Could* it even be fixed, with such a deep curse? And he certainly didn't make enough money to hire a Body Sculptor, nor was he good enough at snowing and carving to make his child look the way his father and father's father did. Would he curse his son a second time, to forever holding the memory of his melt?

Better not live at all, then. That's what Elsfvor would've decided for himself.

But his wife insisted that the memory of a curse and the life of an Ismar was better than an active curse and no life at all. They'd fought about it every night since they heard about the King's tour around the country, and it only got worse once the Mother actually came to grace their little mining town. The argument got *so* heavy that they finally put the question on the boy himself that previous night to settle the argument once and for all. And by Cervora's velvet, how it stabbed Elsfvor's soul when Luka told them he wanted to see the Mother and take the "ache" out of his face.

Yet the door was locked. No way in. With his boy there, though, there was no choice; he had to at least try. As it was, he'd still kept his son away from those first services, if only because he couldn't stand the way people looked at him and his wife and his son whenever they were outside. That was yet another sin he had to atone for: letting the whispers of the people keep him and his family away from the cathedral. His pride—how he repented that pride in the hours before daybreak. He *had* to try then, for his son and for his own soul, if that repentance was going to mean anything. So he knocked three times on that door, his fist heavy on the wood.

A moment passed. Then another. Elsfvor's soul quivered; it buzzed with worry in his head, already thinking of what he'd have to say to maybe make his son's disappointment a little softer. But just as he raised his fist to knock again—*answer, please answer*—the lock clicked, and the door cracked open. No sound came from downstairs, no call of welcome. There was, however, an odd squelching sound, and the squeal and screech of something else downstairs. Elsfvor paused, and as little hands clung to his pants, he didn't have to look at his son to know the poor boy was scared.

"Hey, now." Elsfvor decided to put on a brave face and pushed that door open. At the other end of the stairs was the bluish white shine of starlight. *Someone* was definitely down there. "Nothing to be scared of. She's our Mother, remember?"

The hands at his pants tightened. Luka's little voice quivered, but he said with as much certainty as a boy could have: "I remember."

"Then let's go. Come on." Elsfvor guided the boy down the first couple steps. "It'll be okay. You'll see."

As they came down the steps, something clattered at the far end of the basement—and something scratched against the stone. Something gurgled, then squeaked like the pop of ice. Elsfvor's own soul quivered and condensed in his head, what with sounds so... *unfriendly.* His nerves told him to get out of that stairwell and go right home like nothing ever happened. Tell the boy everyone was crazy, that the Mother never came, and that he'd be doomed to melt until he was home free on the Seat of Orr again—that this life was only ever meant to be a short break from the legendary caves full of Ismar souls for him.

But his shame and guilt sat so heavy on his shoulders that it nearly sent him tumbling down those stairs and taking the boy with him. He steadied himself, and just before he kept marching, he heard a woman's voice—a harsh, raspy, yet sharp voice, one that scraped along the cathedral stone.

"Did you get lost in that stairwell? Come down, now; come down."

That voice, those words, they did *not* match the statue behind the cathedral altar. Rather than a sweet and loving mother, that call invoked a picture of the old tavern harpies, the women rough and jaded enough to make any man feel small with little more than a sharp stare. The ones he'd seen leave with stupid, single men to the inn down the street and send them home the next morning with a glaze in their eyes like they'd had their soul pulled out through their mouth. It made one wonder who was really the hunter and who was the hunted, with harpies like those.

No. Elsfvor didn't even let the question come back as he coaxed Luka down the rest of the steps. *They're idiots, those tavern-dogs; they're wrong about—*

But when they reached the foot of those stairs, and Elsfvor laid his eyes on the one that called to them, there was really no other way to describe what he saw except for that nasty title the tavern folk gave her: the Wraith Queen.

Where Cervora was always depicted unclothed, her whole body on display to remember what their ancestors ate, this woman was clothed in a huge, heavy-looking pile of black fabric that was rolled up to her elbows and that cut far down her chest in a v-shape. It made it so Elsfvor could practically count her ribs like the rungs of a ladder. Where the statue of Cervora had a head of very thin, straight hair, this woman had a thicker curtain of silver cascading to her waist, the slight wave in it making it seem that much more unruly. Where that statue had soft hips, smooth and almost plump arms and legs, and a sweet, round face, this woman was nothing but sharp angles on a slender, lanky frame: elbows that could've smashed a man's head right open, a torso that seemed longer than was sensible, and a face so sharp at its chin and cheeks that Elsfvor was convinced it could've cut cloth. Where Cervora had the black eyes of a doe, this woman had deep blue eyes flecked with gold, as if the entire mystery of the night sky sat in her gaze. And where Cervora's antlers were carved nice and blunt, with a smoothness that made them almost seem like curling vines more than anything deer-like, this woman's antlers were jagged like the branches of a dead tree.

And sharper. So much sharper at their points. As if made for goring creatures.

Elsfvor squeezed his eyes shut as if he could crush the thought between his eyelids. When he opened them again, the Mother had sat down in a plain wooden chair and draped her spindly arm over the table behind her. It was only then that Elsfvor noticed the stained white rags behind her, white cloth covered in a shocking *red,* and it was then he noticed the pink stains around her mouth. They were on her fingers, too; as she stroked her long throat and stared at the father and son before her, there was no mistaking the pink stains creeping towards her knuckles. Elsfvor's soul shuddered, and he didn't *dare* glance past her at the source of whatever was gurgling and squelching at the dark side of the basement.

"Oh, goodness," the Mother crooned. With her raspy voice, though, it sounded more like the scratchy rumble of a bobcat. She crossed one leg over the other, her black hoof shining in the starlight like the black ice weapons the guards carried around, and she pursed her lips as she looked Luka over. "Poor boy." Then her expression dropped so fast that Elsfvor thought he might find it on the floor somewhere. She cut him a ferocious look from under her long silver lashes and muttered, "What took your father so long to bring you to me?"

Elsfvor immediately lowered his gaze. The shame hit him like a hammer and knocked all the unease right out of him; there was no room for it under the timbre her judgement took. But Luka, brave Luka, he let go of his father's leg and took a few steps towards the Mother.

"I don't know. But I'm here now. Can you fix me?"

"Luka—!" Elsfvor snapped his head up to hiss at his son for his disrespect, but before he could, the Mother's crackling laugh echoed through the basement.

"Of course I can. Luka is your name?"

"Yeah."

"Then come, Luka." She stretched her arms out like the statue—only her fingers were too bony, her nails sharp like talons. "Come let me see you, and I'll fix you right up."

Luka hesitated, but he eventually came closer, until she had his face in her hands. Her nails disappeared into the fuzz of his hair, and her smile curled tight on plump, silver-grey lips as she looked him over. Her thumb brushed the melted side of his face, and for a moment, Elsfvor relaxed. That was a Mother's smile, at least. A kind, gentle smile, the goodwill in it holding up even to those sharp cheekbones.

Once she looked into that melting cavern in Luka's face long enough, she nodded. "Ready?"

"Yeah."

No, she's no monster. Sure, the Mother looked harsh in this life, but what did that matter? *She's no wraith, no half—*

Then she stood and towered over the boy, and something in her throat began clicking. Her mouth opened—so much it seemed to unhinge—and she hovered that huge mouth near Luka as if she meant to bite the boy's head clean off. Luka shook in her grip, and the clicking continued until something poured from her mouth: a cloud of powdery frost.

Luka yelped. Squealed. Tried to flee from the Mother, as if she were hurting him. But she held him tight until he was completely awash with frost—until Elsfvor couldn't even make him out, as if he'd stepped into a white-out blizzard.

The last time Elsfvor saw a living, breathing, flesh-made creature do *anything* like that was during the High Summer. Only it wasn't frost that showered down from its lips.

"DID YOU HEAR?" ONE MAN, A LOGGER in simple leathers and linens, with a thick crop of hair sprouting along his upper lip to match the short hair on his head, clacked his hand against his friend's shoulder. That friend startled, his neck squeaking as he looked too quickly towards the logger. He was a younger man, and his hair was patchy on top—a sign of a man who worked a lot with his magic. "The Queen—I couldn't believe my ears!"

Weak bits of starlight flickered and threatened to wink out in the old frozen sconces of the tavern, which were the only decorations on old stone walls. The counter of the bar itself was pitted with dents and knife-wounds, each pocket and hole collecting deep black shadows. The stone floors of the tavern were scuffed and laden with dirt no broom could properly sweep up. Chunks of ice rattled against wooden cups that were warped and worn with age. What should've been the pure and milky blood of Cervora's kin was something more like half-frozen slush that smeared on the men's lips, blood mixed with pine sap to make the tavern's meager supply last a little longer. Bertrine, the barmaid, hated that they had to sell such watered-down muck—but what other option was there, when the King decided that the people further south weren't worth the effort of supplying like the capital was? All they had left to sell in these taverns, where laborers sometimes had the funds to pay for extra blood, were what they had to hunt and what scraps the Church gave them, and it seemed each month there was less and less to go around.

When was the last time I even had a bite of meat? Bertine was only half listening to her patrons' conversation. It all sounded like garbled chatter to her after several hours there behind the counter. Little sparks of pain lanced through her body, always at her fault points: elbow, ankle, shoulders. But like the others in that tavern, she'd just learned to live with it. Her earnings, plus her husband's, barely got them a good couple cups of *undiluted* deer's blood every month on top of cathedral service, and so they had to stretch their magic out. Her husband, though—what a difficult man. Even though he worked in frost silver smithing, and he had no choice but to use more of his magic, he refused to drink the watered-down bloodwine. Said it was rotten blasphemy that Bertrine even sold it, never mind that people drank it. But without her work, there would only be less pure blood for them to drink.

So Bertine atoned for the work her husband hated and got by on a half a cup a week. A quarter cup on a particularly busy week for her husband. And it made her body feel so fragile, what with all those pricks of pain every time she wiped one end of the counter down to the other. Better to be fragile, though, than to be melted—like her husband, who, over the past century, lost his left leg up to the middle of his thigh.

"I can't believe it, either." Another man, with a missing arm and a flapping, empty sleeve to show for it, came up and slammed his cup down on the counter to cozy up beside the other two patrons. He shook his head and clicked his tongue against his teeth. "I mean—to have *Unseelechs* crawling around is strange enough, but to be a *mixed-blood?* And how about that mess in the capital? Heard about that?"

"Ah, well, I don't know about her being some mixed-blood," the logger angled towards Bertrine, who polished a cup with pine resin and made sure not to make eye contact with them, "but I'll tell you what: I heard the Queen can fix the *innernfröscherl!* Isn't that something?"

Huh?

Bertrine made the mistake of pausing, and the men noticed. They fixed their eyes on her like she was a little squirrel amidst a cluster of owls, and she tried to pretend she didn't notice how hard they stared, even as she watched them from the corner of her eye.

The logger leaned towards her. "Hey, Trine, what do you think? About all this?"

She stilled her hands and held her chin high, hoping to seem unbothered by such a wild claim. "I think you should finish your drink, Van. Been workin' on it a whole hour now."

"Ah, I'm getting there," he said, his voice booming even as the other men clapped his back and laughed. "But what'cha think? About all that? I figure maybe you might wanna take your man up and get that bum leg of his fixed up right—"

"Nah, no need, no *need,* you hear? She's coming *here!* To us!" The third man that'd come over turned around to the rest of the tavern, where the wealthier men were sharing a single skinny venison steak, and where other folks were fishing the ice out of their water-thinned drinks. The man hollered loud enough that Bertrine thought he might rattle the old frost silver chandeliers from their weak and rickety supports in the rafters. "The Queen—she's coming here! To fix us all! I hear she's in Weiharten right now, with the Baron himself— only a few days from here!" Then he turned back to Bertrine, Van, and the other man and said, much quieter, with a fierce gleam in his eye, "And if she can really fix that melt, then I don't even care if she's half *lizard,* or if she drags a whole parade of *Unseelechs* through here."

Bertine gripped the cup even harder. Hard enough that she might've cracked her hand, were she not careful. She rubbed ever more resin into its wood and kept her face straight, even as many thoughts went shooting through her mind.

Could Järvur get fixed? Could a new leg get put on, even? She polished the frost silver rings binding the cup planks together, too, circling each little bolt in the rings. *But what of the King? The Baron said—we were told the King would have to answer for leaving us without like this, without the meat and the blood—but Cervora? Cervora's* icon? *The Queen?*

It was too much for her head right then. Too much. Especially with all the shouting and arguing in that tavern, the men all making noise about whether the Queen was some savior of their people or some ugly, half-wild wraith come to disgrace their King with lies. Sure, Bertrine went to the cathedral service each month like anyone else, and that's where she got the bulk of her blood rations from—that was the Church's job, after all—but for the Church to ask her to believe Cervora's icon was returning in *her* lifetime?

No, it didn't seem real. Didn't seem right. What was special about this era, that Cervora should come back in it? What was different about this year than the year before? Why wouldn't Cervora have come a century earlier, when the High Summer struck? Her husband was lucky to only have had his foot melted by a too-strong ray of Summer sun while he and Bertrine were bringing frost silver further north, to other holds. Others, when they came back home, were found to have been missing entire family members.

Why now, a century after all had come to terms with this horror? Why not then, when people needed her most?

"Cervora's gotta be back!" That overexcited man waved his empty cup around, looking around at the crowd. He seemed emboldened by the people who nodded along with his raving. "Who else could fix the melt?"

Another man sitting in the back shouted over the noise of the crowd: "But it's the *way* she fixes the frost, you hollow-head! What deer *breaths* frost?"

"She's a goddess! She could piss frost, and I'd drink it!"

"Well, she ain't supposed to be *pissing* at all if she's coming in some shiny new body, like the Church says!"

The arguing, the yelling, the ridiculous back and forth, it all sounded like little more than the roar of mountain winds to Bertrine as her focus faded from her customers. She just kept polishing, kept scrubbing, kept thinking—kept pouring cups of watery white blood whenever someone asked—and she couldn't help the needling within her head. The anger.

Where were you all these years, Cervora? All those years we needed you?

Her knuckles squeaked, then stung. She paused her cleaning and set the cup down, cradling her fractured fingers under the counter, and she kept her eyes trained on her knuckles. Rather than listen to the arguing of these men, she decided to hear only the roar of the whipping, whistling Winter winds. At least until another customer came and asked her for more thin, spoiled blood of a god that, for whatever reason, decided to live again.

"Ristef, you're not eating again?"

One young guard, Jolenn, snapped Ristef out of his thoughts with that question. The other guard, Barlan, hovered his fork before his lips as he watched Ristef, waiting for an answer. The barracks of Baron Fervall's guesthouse were dark, with only one starlight floating in a wall lantern. It wasn't enough to chase away the shadows that clustered around the place. It was like someone colored the stone with all the pencils left in Winter, so dark that even the night might get jealous.

Ristef sat at the chipped old table with an empty plate and an empty goblet. The thought of taking even a single sip of bloodwine made his ice feel tight around his soul, and he didn't understand it. Even if Aveline was Cervora's icon, that didn't mean that he didn't need that holy flesh and blood to function; he could've eaten half his weight in white deer after he'd been dragged back into the palace drained of all his magic. He would've done it out of her sight, of course, but he would've eaten a whole deer before it'd even been slaughtered. Would've bit its jugular open and poured all that blood directly down his throat.

So why was it that he didn't want any meat for the past week since he'd watched Ronterweis get showered in frost in the King's conference room? Or, rather, a better question would've been: why didn't he *need* it? The feeling he got looking at that meat, it wasn't some personal issue with it. Nor did he feel anything watching his fellows stack their plate with slivers of flesh and shove it in their mouths.

"Ristef?"

No, rather, the feeling he got looking at that meat—like eating it would make his body feel too tight, too small, too alight with magic—was the feeling he only ever had once, when he'd been able to eat and drink to his heart's content during the first year of endless Winter and thought the excess magic in his body would break it into pieces.

Ristef shrugged and pushed the empty plate away. "I just don't need it, is all."

Jolenn peered at him. A beat passed, and then: "Have you been drinking from the Queen? Is that it?"

"I—what?" The question made Ristef start. He didn't know what to say; he only shook his head to the point that his hair whipped him across the face. "No! No, I'm not doing anything of the sort!" Ristef set his perfectly opaque, magic-filled hands firmly on the table, and he didn't dare mention the bloody wrist Aveline held to his mouth that day the King had gathered them all in the conference room. "I'm just... not using my magic as much, clearly. So don't speak so casually about Cervora's icon like that."

Jolenn and Barlan exchanged glances, but they only shrugged, and Jolenn said, "I see. I only wanted to ask because, well," he cut Ristef a sharp glance before staring into his half empty tankard, "I've heard that you've been close to the Mother. Very close. And I just wondered if—"

Something thumped under the table as Barlan shot Jolenn a harsh look. A snap of bright red hovered around the boy's hair: the color of alarm. At least one of these boys seemed to understand the concept of rank and manners to their higher-ups.

"—if maybe you could teach me how to not lose so much magic," Jolenn quickly said, though a flash of red snapped off him, too—a darker, more sullen red, the

color of irritation bordering on anger. "I seem to lose
magic just walking, so it'd be good to know what tips
you might have as a more experienced guard."

Ristef watched the colors shift around Jolenn's head.
Orange bloomed there, bright as the sun on a rare clear
evening, and it chased the little snap of red away. It was
the orange of suspicion. Jolenn didn't believe Ristef for
a second; that much was obvious. But it was the truth.
Ristef's magic wasn't draining, and he couldn't begin to
guess why. Was it because he drank from Aveline's wrist?
There was no way to know, given that it wasn't like
anyone drank from Cervora's icon before, and the last
people to drink from Cervora herself were long gone,
centuries gone.

"Maybe soon," Ristef muttered, hardly even understanding what he said as he got up from the table.
He was too lost in his own thoughts, too disturbed by
Jolenn's accusation. If he could think that of Ristef,
then what was stopping anyone else from thinking it?
What was stopping the King from thinking it? "I need to
return to my patrol now, though."

And by "return to patrol," Ristef really meant that he
had to find the King. He would know what to do about
this. He would know how to best protect Aveline if anyone else were to find out. He didn't hear whatever Jolenn and Barlan whispered to each other as he hurried
out of the dining hall and into the streets of Weiharten.

Even with the clouds, the light outside was bright
enough that his vision momentarily left him. He saw
nothing but white for a moment as his crystal eyes
adjusted to the sudden brightness, so he had no choice
but to stop until they did. Once his vision came back, he
looked around at that village and felt a pang in his soul,
a dull and heavy headache born of that potent mix of
nostalgia and grief.

This village—it was so much like his own. Even down

to the quaintly painted houses. He stared down the old cobblestone road, watching as little boys carried baskets full of good stone to sell to artisan carvers or beat each other with frozen sticks, pretending to be in the King's Guard. And the little girls, their hair kept neat and out of their face, were out twirling and dancing with each other like they were at some grand ball, squealing when a little snow devil kicked up in the wind and buffeted them. All the sunny yellows and light blues of their joy and concentration clouded around their heads, unspotted by anything else. As it should've been. As it always should've been.

Nothing, however—not even this sight—could've made him forget about the colors he saw when he returned home from that first, and only, Tour of Seasons. The greys, the deep pitch black, hung around what few survivors his village had like smoke. Grief and hopelessness became so thick around those people that he could hardly even make out their faces. He'd never seen that before, and he hoped he never would ever again.

At the end of the road, before it split off into two paths that led through the forest and curved around towards the plains out to the east, was the cathedral and the village's municipal building. That cathedral wasn't as grand as the capital's, sure, but it was a good building, all sturdy stone and stained ice windows, with a great clocktower that made sure no one forgot the hour even all the way down the road. And the belfry on that cathedral steeple was pretty big for a village this size, which made it seem grander than it was on the outside, at least. The other guards were right: this was really more of a town, maybe even a small city, and Ristef wondered if it was because it was the Baron's main residence—and the village closest to the capital.

Ristef shook such thoughts out of his head. Politics wasn't his strength, anyhow. He marched down the road, his mind set on other things. The King might've known something about the mystery around Aveline's blood already, given he'd been around Aveline more than anyone these past few weeks—but then, when would he have ever thought to bite down on his wife and find out for himself?

Before he could think of an answer, a boy ran in his path and hopped up and down. "Mister Knight, Mister Knight!"

His friends soon followed, all carrying sticks that were battered and chipped from their play. One boy had a hand stuck to the waistband of his too-big pants, likely hand-me-downs from an older brother, and all of them could've easily blended in with the dirt road with how filthy their simple clothes were in the first place. It seemed even after endless Winter, some things didn't change, and most common folk still couldn't afford the washing salts and dyes needed to keep rowdy young boys clean and their clothes brightly decorated. They all stared up at him with massive eyes carved of simple river stones, smooth and matte grey, and so the only color on them came from the bright yellow haze of joy that haloed them, and the occasional snaps of excited, curious pink that shot out of the yellow.

Ristef smiled at them as they huddled around his legs, but it was tough to keep that smile up the more he looked at them. The boys were beginning to bald; their jumping and running was shaking hair loose from their heads. And underneath those dingy clothes, there were the earliest signs of fault lines. Through the haze of their childish delight, too, Ristef could see clearly: their faces were beginning to show little cracks from all their shouting and grinning, their cheeks going glassy with lack of magic. He glanced up at the municipal building and wondered if the King ever saw them, too—these urchins who, despite not being disgraced by the need for food, water, and warmth that cost fleshlings all their gold, still didn't seem any better off. Seeing them, he didn't have the heart to tell them that he was only a guard, not a knight.

"Mister Knight, can we see your sword?" One child, the tallest yet thinnest of the bunch from years of clearly uneven snow-packing for his growth, rapped his knuckles on Ristef's armor. "Can we see it? We've never seen a real sword before!"

"Yeah, yeah! I wanna see!"

"Me, too!"

"Alright, alright, now," Ristef said as he crouched down. The boys surrounded him like Spring geese, noisy and clumsy things, and he couldn't help but remember his own boyhood—how he, too, was once just a child with a stick, dreaming of the day he'd hold a sword and stand by his King. These poor things didn't know just how much of that job involved standing around and waiting for something interesting to happen, while also hoping *nothing* interesting happened. "Listen here. I've got some things to do, but you wait out for me later by the spinner lady's wheel there," he pointed to what looked like the local tailor's house, what with its big decorative spinning wheel outside the heavy wooden door, "and I'll come back and show you the sword. And maybe," he reached out and tapped one of those mucky sticks, "a thing or two about swordfighting, too, yeah?"

The sparks of pink erupted off those boys like a blizzard as they squealed and bounced around him, nearly overtaking the yellow of their joy. Ristef patted one hopping boy on the head, and he almost cringed when yet more hair fell away from the boy's head. Then he slinked past them and hurried off. They were still shouting in the street behind him, little peals of *a real sword!*

and *we're gonna be knights!* and other such things ringing in the distance.

What good spirits Ristef had from a moment with the children evaporated when he made it to the municipal building. Inside, the weak daylight barely made a dent in the shadows, and the municipal secretary had only one starlight hovering over her shoulder. She sat behind a little counter, the thing covered in papers of who-knows-what, and while she seemed to be better off than those children with her deep blue dress and single silver ring, her thin hair was tied back as if that would make it less obvious that she was losing it. They were such subtle signs, so little—as children weren't so prioritized for receiving Cervora's kin in the first place, and in a mining village like this one, no doubt the laborers took the lion's share of the rations—but this was the Endless Winter. Everyone should've been able to get enough of Cervora's kin to sustain themselves, shouldn't they? If Ristef hadn't found himself in so strange a position with this seemingly tireless magic, he would've vowed a hundred times to never again complain about the rations he and the other guards got.

"Miss," Ristef said as he clapped his hand on the counter, and he felt only a little guilty when she startled and dropped her pencil, "is His Majesty still here? I need to make a report."

She blinked up at him, then pointed to a door on the left. "He's down that way, but he's with the Baron right—"

Ristef darted off, leaving her to sputter and call for him to wait. He didn't have time to wait, though; he'd gotten distracted enough with the children. As he opened the door, he saw there at the end of a long corridor: the King, sitting at a table covered in papers, with the Baron looming over his shoulder and pointing at something. They spoke too quietly for Ristef to make anything out until he was practically in the doorway, where the Baron waved his hand over the papers as he spoke.

"—and so it's become an issue of conservation, you see. We can't afford to keep culling the white deer when—"

Ristef knocked on the doorframe. "Your Majesty, I have an urgent report."

The Baron, a rather round man dressed in a black and purple suit, with a full and thick patch of silver clustered at his chin, looked at Ristef and frowned. Clearly, between his face and the snaps of reddish-brown frustration shooting from his temples, he wanted to chase Ristef out, but he knew better than to speak before the King could.

King Jädrich lifted his head and barely looked in Ristef's direction. He looked like he wanted to wave his guard away, until he saw that it was Ristef. Then an otherwise clear head frizzled with hints of bright red, of alarm, even though his face never changed.

"Is something wrong, Gürrensig?"

Is Aveline in danger, was the real question the King asked, and Ristef shook his head. "No, but I do have a concern regarding Her Majesty."

That made the Baron's head blink. Snaps of lighter, paler orange—less suspicion, more curiosity—overtook the angry brown tones. "A serious concern—?"

"Leave us," King Jädrich said. Despite how smooth and low his voice was, there was no doubt about the severity in it; his command cut the Baron's words right off. Once the portly man nodded and hurried out, Ristef closed the door behind him, and the King's voice struck him next. "What is this concern?"

How could he start to explain it? Ristef peered through the crack in the wooden door's planks, and when he was sure the Baron hadn't stopped to listen outside, he drew a rune on the door with his magic just in case. It was a combination rune, its shape fusing the words for both sound and lock, and when Ristef spoke the accompanying word—*Låseleitum*—it shone a deep, bright, and powerful silver. It was more powerful than any version of that confidentiality spell Ristef had ever cast, because he had the magic to waste on it.

"Your Majesty," Ristef said as he stared at that rune, stunned by the shine of it, "please forgive the redundancy of my question, but when Lady Ronterweis presented the letters that day in your conference hall, no doubt you witnessed it: how Her Majesty the God-Queen gave me her own blood to drink?"

When Ristef found both the discipline and the courage to face his King, he clenched his jaw. Such angry red sparked only once from the King's head, the color of murder. It was a much deeper, darker shade than the red of the King's alarm, yet not at all the muddy color of frustration; it was a color Ristef hated to see more than any other on any person, and it nearly broke his resolve to see his King shoot that color in his direction, as if his thoughts were arrows ready to fly and crack Ristef to pieces.

But it was gone as soon as it came, and King Jädrich nodded. No colors clouded him at all then. For the most part, outside this whole bridal competition and discovery of Cervora's icon, King Jädrich's soul was much more disciplined in its expression than most of the people Ristef had ever met. It was one thing to tame a face into a composed mask for a crowd—and an entirely different thing to tame a soul.

Ristef chose his next words carefully. "Since that day, I've noticed a difference in my magic. I find that I don't need to take my rations of meat and blood anymore. In fact, I've noticed that to eat them makes me have too much magic, to the point of some kind of illness that

I've only ever felt once before—when I accidentally took on too much magic from my rations."

King Jädrich's face didn't change, but he did blink. He stared at Ristef, but by the sudden glaze over his eyes, the lack of focus in them, and by the gradually increasing flurry of crystalline white sparks from his soul, Ristef knew his King understood him. Those crystal flurries from the soul were the flurries of deep thought, of understanding, of pure clarity.

Eventually, the King said, "Why did you say nothing earlier?"

"I," Ristef flexed his hands, "I didn't realize such a thing could be possible until just now. I came to tell you as soon as the idea occurred to me." As King Jädrich stared at him, Ristef couldn't help but ask, "Have you ever heard of something like this, Your Majesty? From the records of the Originals, maybe—?"

The King gave one sharp nod and leaned over to rest his head on his hand. It seemed like he, too, hadn't had this idea occur to him, by how he stared straight through Ristef. His mind was somewhere else entirely, and Ristef didn't need his blue lace agate eyes to see that. Then he shifted in his seat and stared at those papers in total silence.

"Does anyone else know about this? Or suspect it?"

Ah, damn. Ristef shifted and tried to find the perfect words. He didn't want to bring any bad attention on his fellow guards' heads. Nor did he want to explain the nature of their suspicions, not to the King—Aveline's lawful husband.

"Does anyone suspect this, Gürrensig?"

King Jädrich's question bludgeoned Ristef, and even though no color at all flashed around the King's head, his stare alone could've cut clean through Ristef's armor. Could've cut him in half. Knowing the King's emotions was terrifying—but not knowing them, especially when the King wore that face, was even more so.

"They wonder why I'm not eating as much," Ristef offered. "They wonder why my magic doesn't run dry like theirs."

It wasn't a lie; it just also wasn't the full truth. King Jädrich stared at him a moment longer, as if trying to carve Ristef's head open just with a look and see all the thoughts hidden in Ristef's soul, but after a long pause, he spoke again.

"And no one questions where you might be getting this excess magic?"

Jolenn's questioning echoed in Ristef's head. But how could he explain that? King Jädrich hadn't taken kindly to seeing Aveline always stuck to Ristef's arm as it was during the bridal competition; the sheer memory of those murder-red arrows flying off his soul when Aveline ignored him in the gardens was enough. Murder-red arrows, every time, and once, they lingered long enough for Ristef to notice a deep, murky green haloing the King, too: an ugly stain of envy.

Ristef was so lost in that memory that he didn't notice the King move until his broad hands were on either side of Ristef's face, holding his head tight enough that Ristef realized, with a wash of horror, how easy it would be for the King to free his soul from his head with a simple squeeze. Those blue-grey eyes crackled with currents of his magic, flashing like strips of silver lightning; it was all Ristef could see.

"Answer me."

"Your Majesty," Ristef cursred his voice for trembling, "please let me reiterate that I have not, and never will, be anything more than a guard for Cervora's icon, both to her and to myself."

So much magic crackled in King Jädrich's eyes that

Ristef couldn't even see the color of the Femmel diamonds anymore.

"But... yes. They ask me questions. I believe they think," *careful, careful, careful,* "that Cervora's icon favors me. Takes pity on me." When all the shine suddenly died from the King's eyes, Ristef quickly added, "But I don't think they realize that taking blood from her is any different from drinking a cup of bloodwine; they don't know that the magic lasts indefinitely."

Had Ristef ever lived through a moment longer than that one? Where all he could see was blue-grey, and all he could feel were two hands clamped on either side of his head? Perhaps he would meet his melted family soon. Ristef wondered then, if he prayed to Cervora for mercy, if it would be Aveline that would hear it.

"Good," King Jädrich suddenly said. It was a quiet word, yet Ristef felt it echo off his own lips. As the King's hands left Ristef's head, and as the King drew himself up to his full height, he looked at his guard with such a cold indifference that even Ristef, made of ice, felt a chill. "Tell no one."

"Yes, Your Majesty. Of course."

Ristef bowed, not quite registering what he'd agreed to. Though he wouldn't have told anyone a secret like this anyway. He could only imagine what these magic-starved people would do if they knew that one bite of Aveline was all it would take to cure them of the stiffness and lack of magic forever.

"Leave me now." King Jädrich went back to his seat and stared at those papers.

"Yes, Your Majesty."

Ristef nodded once more, but the King didn't see him. He was too busy scanning those papers, his elbows set hard on the table, a hand covering his mouth. The crystalline flurries were back, racing around his head like the snow devils whipping around outside. Something about the sight made Ristef uneasy. He wanted to ask what the King planned to do with this information, but of course, he had no right to know the thoughts of the King. Ristef could only do his duty as a guard and keep his Queen safe.

With effort, Ristef tore his eyes off the King, undid the runespell, and forced all his worries deep down into the cavern of his gut. There would be no reason to worry. The King was just and righteous, and Aveline, wild and holy Aveline, she no doubt had the people's health and happiness in the forefront of her mind, too. So whatever the two of them did with this information, Ristef knew it would be for the best.

Ristef left, and glancing at the clock ticking above the door of the municipal hall, he realized Aveline would still be in that cathedral basement another good three hours, at least—and that she had plenty other guards stationed there at the cathedral entrance and inside. She didn't need him right then; his post was elsewhere. So he made it a point to go find those children and hope their parents wouldn't be too upset about him showing them what a real black ice sword looked like.

FRANZEL AND DIEVEN GLANCED AT EACH OTHER as they stood before a silent Lady Ronterweis. They'd been called in ten minutes ago, and after giving their report from their castle rounds, they were met with nothing but silence. Lady Ronterweis didn't look at them the whole time they spoke, and she didn't speak for a long time afterwards. Neither of the guards could leave until they were dismissed, though, nor could Franzel leave without delivering the mail addressed to the little woman, so they stood waiting for her to say something.

In that time, Franzel studied her as much as she studied whatever spot she stared at on the King's desk. It was strange, seeing both of her hands functional, seeing her face properly shaped. Almost a full couple weeks had already passed since the King and Queen left for their wedding tour around the country, and in that time, even the advisor's hair had grown in more.

Franzel even dared to say that the little woman looked *pretty*. She had a face that wasn't so round as other women's, but more like that of a Winter fox: sharp, clean, graceful. And her hair framed that face nicely, with bangs cut to her brows and light waves just coming past her chin. Whatever lumbering thing she'd been just a month ago was long dead, and anyone could see it when they looked into this woman's deep, thoughtful gaze.

"The King says to prepare for the moving of seasons," Lady Ronterweis said.

She said it so suddenly that Franzel hardly registered it. Dieven was the one who started and sputtered, "To move—the King intends to restart the Tour of Seasons?"

"He says to prepare the horses," she continued, as if Dieven hadn't spoken at all. The way her eyes stayed glued to the desk made her seem more a madwoman than a King's advisor. "The Virdensals. And to take full stock of the armory."

That made even Dieven shut up. Franzel went still, too. Virdensals weren't the types of horses that went on the Tour. They were powerful beasts, ones meant to carry grown men in full suits of armor. Carriages— that was what Franzel's elders said always went on the Tour of Seasons. Carriages, guided along by guards on foot, to make an agonizingly slow procession meant to spread Winter's chill over every corner of the next country they went to. There weren't many reasons to use Virdensals. Or to check the armory.

"My lady," Franzel started, and he gave Dieven a sharp glance before the oaf could interrupt him, "is there something we should know about this year's Tour of Seasons?"

"Nothing more than what I've said. Prepare the horses. Check the armory." Then, for the first time since they walked in, she looked up and stared them down. "Do you have any correspondence for me, Hervonder?"

Franzel nodded. Only then did he untuck his arms from behind his back and produce the letters that had come up through the castle courier. Their magical seals remained perfectly intact, even with how desperately Franzel wanted to unravel them and read whatever secrets came from outside the castle. Despite the relative seclusion of his position, and the fact that the Wraith Queen was miles and miles away, he still felt her presence in the castle—still heard the *scream* she let off for what felt like hours. Sometimes, he thought he could still pluck shards of that scream out of the empty air in the gardens. And he wanted to know, since the discovery of that Summer lizard, what that wicked woman could've possibly been planning in this country.

A century. His thoughts were punctuated by the soft rip of Lady Ronterweis's letter opener. *Peace lasts a century before it begins to unravel, hmm?*

Lady Ronterweis read without dismissing them. She scoured those letters, given how close her face was to the paper, and yet the pure black of her eyes never indicated where she was looking. It seemed to Franzel that she was looking at the paper without seeing—until she sat back and frowned. After a moment of tapping her foot, clearly stuck in her thoughts, she went ferreting through those letters again, looking for yet more news. Franzel glanced at Dieven, who stared at the corner of the advisor's desk with something of a sullen pout forming on his lips. The fool. Franzel lightly tapped his boot, and the expression dropped off his face like a mask.

The sound of ice clanking made Lady Ronterweis look up. She stared in their direction and said, "Is something wrong?"

"No, my lady," Franzel said with an easy smile. "Is

there anything of note that the castle guard should be aware of?"

Lady Ronterweis blinked, then looked back to her letters. "Nothing more than you've already been made aware of."

And by that, she meant the letters she'd shared with the guards. The ones from Rehrvig. If Franzel had any doubts about the ash-talk that poured from Ehrwig's mouth, it all died with each stroke of those old, nearly crumbling letters Lady Ronterweis let everyone read. There was no denying it: the Wraith Queen was, in fact, a mixed-blood with a Summer mother and a Winter father—and yet somehow, she was walking around pretending at being Cervora incarnate.

Franzel prodded Lady Ronterweis with a seemingly innocent question, "Am I correct to assume these things we've been made aware of should stay confidential? Or should the maids and servants also know?"

A smile spread on Lady Ronterweis's lips, and she soon looked up at Franzel. "It should stay confidential, yes. What a smear on the Queen it would be if the servants here, or the people down in the city, thought that there was anything wrong with our Queen." She tipped her head to Franzel and peered at him through her lashes. "What a shame, if people learned what you know and doubted their Mother while she was away."

Politics. Franzel tipped his head, the message received loud and clear. While it wasn't the most honorable work Franzel had ever done, it wasn't the most *dis*honorable, either. Lady Ronterweis had him and Dieven sprinkling little questions and secrets around to the merchants and other such folks who came to and from the castle, and over the past week, the city guards reported that they were catching whispers of people's discontent. Surely, that morbid performance the Queen herself put on before leaving for her tour with the King made a good seedbed for all those little ideas scattered from the castle. *Ever the politics.*

"I understand, Lady Ronterweis," Franzel said.

"I'm sure you do. Now go." She waved a hand. "Back to your posts."

Without a word, Franzel and Dieven turned on their heels and left. It was only when they were far enough down the hall that Dieven muttered something—though he muttered it so low that Franzel could barely hear it, and he was walking right next to the man.

"I don't like this."

"You were the one sneering just two weeks ago about the half-breed," Franzel muttered back. "Don't tell me you've had a change of heart so suddenly."

"No—but there are better ways of going about this, aren't there? Than spreading rum—"

Oh, Cervora's velvet—

"No." Franzel stopped and grabbed Dieven by his shoulder pauldron, then put his face so close to Dieven's that all he could see were the man's purple eyes. "There is not. I need you to understand something: we are on a knife's edge, where all is legal and illegal on one side and the other. However we slip off this damn knife is yet to be seen."

Dieven blinked.

"I understand your principles, friend," Franzel said, softening his voice just a touch, "but you cannot have it both ways here. You want to see this situation resolved? Then you do what you can to help us end up on the right side of that knife's edge—even if it's just tap the floor hard enough to shake its handle. Do you *understand?*"

The silence that settled between them made Franzel's soul squeeze. It'd been two weeks of this: of Dieven grumbling and muttering over their unofficial duties, of him letting off quips and comments about how it wasn't just when he thought only Franzel could hear. Worse, he'd let his thoughts be written on his face for anyone walking by to see—and if anything would cause a problem, it was being as tactless and indiscreet as that. Words could be misinterpreted or drowned out; faces, not so much.

Eventually, Dieven whispered, "What do you want, Franzel? What do you think about the Qu—?"

"I think that whatever happens, we should find ourselves on the right side of it, for the sake of our jobs and our *families*" Franzel said, and then he patted Dieven's pauldron as the naive man's eyes went wide. Yes, there it was: the fear for his family's safety. No doubt, if they gambled and lost on these duties, the charge of treason that would follow would extend farther than just their own heads. That would prove a better lock on him than the fear for himself. "Now let's leave it at that and get to our post."

How has it been eleven days already?

Already, nearly half a month had gone by. The carriage rumbled along, and Aveline found her thoughts rumbling with them. She was coming back to the guesthouse of a new mayor, in a sweet new town called Firtuchs: a quaint place not quite fit for a King, but not offensive to one, either. Or at least, so Erik said.

Her bones ached, and she rubbed her eyes to see if she could rub some of the burn out of them. Hours and hours, she'd spent in that cathedral basement, and her throat was near-frozen as a result. All she wanted was to lay in bed for a good day or two, which she figured she'd earned, given how much work she'd done already. After all, they'd already seen much of Trevannt, little hold that it was; they'd gotten through Weiharten pretty

quickly, then another town, then another two hamlets—
all more or less the same to her. Whether the towns had
big buildings with brightly lit windows full of dresses
and hats and other fine things, or whether the villages
had bumpy dirt roads and only a few houses scattered
along a road before a tiny cathedral, Aveline's scope of
it all stayed the same. As far as she was concerned, every
village, town, city, or whatever else was only as big as its
cathedral and as its local authority's manor, where she
and Jädrich rested their heads after another long, mo-
notonous day.

Though, given every day looked the same as the one
before it, it was only natural that all those days would
blend together into one long smear of greys, blues, and
silvers. The routine was simple, too. So mind numbing,
throat shredding, yet *simple*.

Wake up.

Sit in the bowels of some cathedral.

Eat in the near-dark. Freeze the Ismären until sundown.

Eat again in whatever local lord's house.

Climb into bed with Jädrich.

Lay with Jädrich—if her eyes didn't sting too much
from exhaustion, and her back didn't hurt too much
from hunching over people, and her throat, tongue,
and teeth didn't ache from the continuous frost that she
poured from those little glands.

As the days passed, however, such pain became more
and more common, while something that became
increasingly more rare, more elusive, was sleep itself.
It wasn't that she didn't want to sleep. It's just that she
didn't trust herself to.

Eventually, the carriage came to a stop, and Aveline
was escorted out to the room she'd been sleeping in.
Jädrich wasn't there yet. He often came late, very late,
doing whatever it was that Kings did. So she threw her

clothes in a pile on the floor and slipped into bed—and then she stared into the darkness of the guesthouse, hoping resting her muscles would soothe her where she couldn't rest her mind.

Even though her eyes burned and begged to slip shut, she couldn't let them. The darkness was just as black with her eyes opened or closed, but at least with them open, she could ignore the sensation that had been creeping deeper and deeper into her mind the past week. She could avoid the flash of something bright in her peripheral that only happened when she went to sleep; she could pretend that the shadow-strings pulling at her bones, tendons, and flesh were just twitches of her nerves. She could ignore the "animal" part of her— which, ever since touching that skull, she realized was never really *her* at all.

Aveline.

It knew her name. Whispered it sometimes, so vividly that Aveline often snapped her head aside to see if anyone had crept up on her and whispered right in her ear. Rarely did it say more than her name, though, as if Aveline already knew what it wanted. And she did. Though she couldn't bring herself to speak it, she did know what it wanted—and that she didn't know what it would do if she let herself sleep too long. Didn't know if it would twitch her limbs into action while she laid unconscious and move her body somewhere else, somewhere it wasn't supposed to be. Didn't know if—

Her thoughts whirred for so long that Jädrich eventually did come in and quietly slide into bed beside her. Aveline rolled over and wrapped her arms around Jädrich's, and she pressed her forehead against his shoulder. The ice against her chest and head shocked the thoughts from her mind. Her eyes burned so much from her exhaustion that she closed them, just for a moment, and she thought she might've drifted off just a moment later. However, she could see it in her peripheral: that eerie shine, as if some phantom sunbeams were coming through a window and shining off something stark and pale as bone. It was no longer something that stared at her directly, this doe-wraith; it was something that only ever stood behind her, and its stare bore into Aveline's back—made her shiver with apprehension, as if she were waiting for a knife to come lodge itself in her spine and twist.

"Don't hold onto me if you're too cold," Jädrich said.

The sudden sound of his voice made her startle. "I'm not cold," she muttered, and she winced as the words skated past her raw throat. She swallowed a mouthful of spit as if it would ease the burning soreness, but it only sharpened the pain for a moment.

Silence laid as heavy on them both as Aveline's thick fur blanket. The town mayor fetched it from who-knew-where in the guesthouse, this musty bearskin thing, but the weight of it was pleasant on Aveline's bones, even if the cloth underside was a bit rough on her bare skin. She squeezed Jädrich tighter and curled up into herself under that blanket. Moments ticked by, so slow that Aveline could count them like pebbles falling in a pond.

After however long like that, Jädrich pulled away from her and got up. A single blue starlight bloomed in the room's one old sconce, and the sudden light made Aveline squint until she could barely see. The clank of his boots, the fluttering of his coat, and the *click* of him reinserting his eyes sounded around the room, and Aveline could've groaned when he spoke.

"It's time to rise."

Aveline's outstretched hand laid flat on the cotton sheets. Her mouth felt as if it were full of that cotton, and her bones felt so brittle, enough that she couldn't fight the weight of the blanket. "I'm tired."

"You slept all night."

I didn't. I laid there. Though what was the difference to someone like Jädrich, who only ever did just that?

"My throat hurts."

That made Jädrich pause. "Can you still make frost?"

"I think."

"Good." Again, the sounds of cloth crumpling and silver clanging echoed in the dark as Jädrich finished getting ready. "Meet your people, then. I'll arrange for more sap for your meals today to ease your throat."

Aveline felt as if she were sinking into the bed. "I need rest, Jädrich. Rest." When he didn't say anything and simply kept getting ready, she croaked, "You said no harm would come to me. In the contract."

He buttoned the top of his coat and turned to her. Something glittered in his eyes as he studied her— something sharp and bright, his magic like shooting stars across the blue diamonds. Then he sat on the edge of the bed and said, as gently as if speaking to a child, "We don't have time to rest. This tour is quick as it is. We need to help as many people as we can before we return home and move the seasons again. I'll do everything I can to ease your discomfort, but you need to endure just another month and a half. Can you do it?"

Discomfort. Of course Jädrich didn't understand what it felt like to puke up frost for hours on hours every day. Aveline didn't, either—not until this gods-forsaken tour. Every shard of ice that ripped up her throat made it seem as if a creature's talons were raking it to ribbons, and the cold would get so deep by day's end that she thought she'd lose feeling in her throat, lips, tongue, even teeth, forever. *A month and a half more of this?*

But then, hadn't she suffered worse? She'd starved for decades on a mountain, all alone; she'd survived on so little, slept on stone floors with not even enough fat on her body to cushion her. She'd nearly burned alive in the sun and nearly died to the teeth and claws of mountain lions. If she could do all that, then surely, a couple months of this kind of pain wasn't so bad. If it meant Jädrich would protect her and give her a life worth living in Winter, then she could—

Aveline.

That voice echoed against the inner walls of her skull. There was an unspoken offer in the way it whispered her name, a promise to end her exhaustion and her pain right then in a way Jädrich could not. In the very marrow of her bones, the rotting wish of this thing still pulsed and echoed, and it was a wish so terrible that Aveline never wanted to put it to name; she never wanted to hear its wretched wishes ever again.

Aveline clutched her head and curled into herself. *Go away,* she shot back into her own head. It felt like she was a step away from hissing it out loud, as if her real voice would banish the thing.

Aveline.

Her eyes squeezed shut, and there it was, out of the corner of her eye again: the glow. Her hands gripped her hair so tightly that she thought she might come away with two fistfuls of it, and she conjured that word in her head with all her might. *Away. Go away.*

A freezing hand landed gently on her shoulder. "Aveline."

"Go *away!*"

Aveline's body sprang into action before she could stop herself. She knocked the hand away with such force that it made her wrist smart, then cast her blanket aside and scrambled off the bed. The blanket caught her legs and made her stumble until her back hit the wall. Her heart thudded in her chest, and she sucked in a deep breath as if the extra space in her ribs would accommodate the beating thing.

Jädrich stared at her from across the bed. With all

but his crown and cloak on, he struck her as more of a prince than anything else—including with the way his brows pinched and his lips parted before falling into a small frown. The King she knew was stoic and expressionless, but this man looked at her as if she'd punched a hole in his chest.

"You've come to dislike me so much already."

Her stomach twisted. There was a knowing, a *knowing,* about his words that she could not put into speech. Bile clawed up and sat in her throat like a well of Swampland poison. There was the twitch of her fingers as she tried to keep them pressed flat against the wall—a crook in their joints, as if they meant to sprout a dragon's talons and dig brutal trails into that man's ice. But her heart twinged at that face. Her lungs crumpled, unable to breathe in.

"It's not you," was all she said on what breath she had left. Then she forced a deep breath in, one that ripped over her aching throat and made her wince. "It's—Jädrich, it's not you. I swear. That wasn't meant for you."

The speed with which his face smoothed out startled Aveline. "Then who was it for?"

For the beast in my head. It was what Aveline wanted to say. However, even if her throat *hadn't* closed right that moment and corked her words, she couldn't possibly explain what she meant. How was Jädrich ever supposed to accept the thing she saw in that skull's darkness? That question alone was enough to make her head spin, and while she couldn't speak, she could fight the shadow-strings holding her to that wall. She dragged one arm up, even as it suddenly felt like it weighed a hundred pounds, and she tapped her temple. Tapped it again and again. Stared at Jädrich, hoping he would understand, as she dug her nail into the skin on her skull.

The beast. The skull. The doe-wraith.

Another voice rose to meet hers like a taunt.

The goddess.

Jädrich, however, didn't seem much impressed by her attempts to tell him. He only blinked and cocked his head. She caught how his eyes swiveled; clearly, he was thinking something, but he gave no hint as to what it was. After a moment, he turned away and took his cloak from where he'd draped it, on an old velvet chair nearby.

"Get dressed," he said, as if nothing happened. "We've taken long enough."

Then he left her alone. It took Aveline all her strength not to slump against that wall and slide to the floor. Jädrich made it clear with that dismissal: there would be no rest for her until she got home. But she had a home. He gave her a home. So long as he gave her that—and the protection that came with it—she could weather the weight of her duties. At least, that was what she told herself as her bones went heavy.

Aveline refused to listen to the whispers that came from deep in those heavy bones.

18

War. The word was foreign in Tsevannah's head. In fact, the very idea of it hadn't crossed the mind of a single soul in the Ringlands since before the Pact of Seasons.

"Sekhran Ganaresh, your blacksmith reports a low reserve of iron and charcoal. He estimates needing another two shipments of what we last sent him to fulfill your orders."

"Tell Kershet he'll have it soon. Tell him to keep working in the meantime."

Tsevannah perched on her husband's empty chair. The table, circular and fashioned from solid sandstone, adorned with lapis lazuli and gold, was made to chart the constellations that Drakash's many wives made in the sky. Laid across it was a large map of the Ringlands, covered in small gold pieces that represented the places Ganaresh and his men would attack, with oil-coated swords and plumes of Drakash's glorious fire. In bronze were pieces signifying where the High Priestess's butterflies would infiltrate and destroy the Winter Wall, and where they would root themselves after certain cities fell and ensure the steady stream of supplies into Winter.

War was a hard thing to prepare for, especially when the supplies—the weapons, the food—had to be built from the ground up. After so many centuries of peace, there were only so many swords to go around, and most were decorative scimitars for palace and city guards in the first place. Her husband stood towards the door, surrounded by fast-talking men covered in soot and sweat, ones that had sparks flying from their tongues. At his side was Tsevannah's fellow Council Member, Faloorah, who looked over the detailed lists the men handed to her while Sekhran Ganaresh spoke to the palace's keeper of inventory. The keeper was a tiny thing, old, his beard stark white against his weathered face, but he nonetheless wrote with cracking speed, faster than Tsevannah could write. All the while, Tsevannah, the Head of Diplomacy, sat in silence. Her talents were unnecessary for the first time in ages.

Her husband turned to face her. Even with all the chaos, his orange eyes were bright, focused, like two torches in the night. The gold chains swung about his horns, the gems catching the room's soft lantern light.

"My wife," he said as he strode towards her with bold, sure steps, "what impression did the Empress give you?"

The Empress? Feng Souram was a wily thing, never to be trusted where the Winter King was concerned. Their seasons were the seasons of the dead and dying, and they protected each other's interests, even though the life and abundance brought by Spring and Summer were better for all things with beating hearts. Still, it seemed even the Empress saw reason, especially after

Sekhran Ganaresh made it clear what her options were at their last meeting together.

The Winter King cared nothing for those born of flesh. Even an ally as dear and close as Empress Feng Souram, he cast aside. No matter how much the Lady of Seasons wanted to align herself with the ice-folk, at the end of the day, she was flesh like the rest of them. When Tsevannah went to visit Autumn, to follow up on their last meeting together and extend an apology for her husband's rash behavior, the Empress spoke to Tsevannah with the rasping, hungry notes of someone who knew the limits of her own skin and bone.

It helped, too, when Tsevannah came with seven crates of fruits, seeds, and grains. The Autumn palace's storeroom was scant. No doubt the rest of the Autumn-lands were worse off. Summer had what Winter could not, and would never, provide. By the look in Empress Feng Souram's eyes, and the gauntness of her cheeks that she'd hidden so well through her illusory body at the last meeting, it seemed she'd finally accepted this.

"I don't think she's sent any message to the Winter King, my Sekhran," Tsevannah said with a dip of her head. "Her aide seemed adamant that no more diplomats would ever cross into the realm of Winter while Jädrich still sits on the throne."

Sekhran Ganaresh's jaw shifted. He nodded as he kept those burning eyes on Tsevannah, and then he turned to Faloorah, his tone clipped. "All the more reason we should paint the soldiers' leathers for night cover. The less we give those ice-folk to see, the better—"

"Sekhran! Sekhran Ganaresh!"

Tsevannah clutched a fistful of her robes to her chest at the sound of the young messenger's shouting. Faloorah, the strong thing that she was, caught the messenger as he tried to run in and held him around the neck. He flailed, nearly kicked the blacksmith's men as he tried desperately to loose himself from Faloorah's grip, and Sekhran Ganaresh clapped his hands so loud that Tsevannah flinched.

"Relax, man! Find your head! Faloorah, let him go."

Faloorah's arm flexed and choked the man a moment longer before she dropped him to the floor. He sat there panting, the crunch of paper nearly hidden by his breath, but the Sekhran bent to snatch whatever he held.

"What is this, hmm?" Sekhran Ganaresh stood up and opened the letter. "What has you so—?"

"It's," the messenger boy coughed and rubbed his throat as Sekhran Ganaresh read the paper, "the Winter King—he's—"

Tsevannah's scalp prickled under her veil. *What about that snake?*

Her husband crumpled the paper in his hand. Then he laughed, just once. A little hiccup. Sekhran Ganaresh rubbed his temple and handed the paper to Faloorah, who smoothed out its freshly wrinkled face and squinted at it.

The prickling of Tsevannah's scalp only got worse. Her throat clicked with sparks. "What? What is it?"

"Come look," Sekhran Ganaresh said as he planted a hand on his hip. His robes shimmered as they caught the light, and when he turned, his smile was just as vibrant—though his eyes burned with a silent fury Tsevannah was all too familiar with. "Look, Tsevannah."

"Um," one blacksmith's servant helped the messenger up, then peered at his Sekhran, "my Lord, should—?"

"Get out. Go, all of you," Sekhran Ganaresh said. "Tell Kershet I'll come to speak to him myself first thing tomorrow morning."

"Yes, my Lord," the servant said, and then he, the other servant, the inventory man, and the messenger boy were all gone, scattered like sand in the wind. The

Sekhran slammed the doors behind them and paced, his robes swirling around him as he rubbed the golden stubble on his chin.

Tsevannah slid off the chair and hurried to Faloorah's side. Her grip was vicious on those papers, tight enough that Tsevannah was worried she'd tear them, but she didn't have to have them in one piece to see the silver ink that glittered off the pages, or to recognize the great silver wolf that made up the Femmel house's crest. That, and the intricate silver border on the stationary, told Tsevannah the worst news: this was a letter from the Winter castle. From the King himself, personally addressed to Sekhran Ganaresh Ti-Vaour.

"Are you reading this?" Faloorah spit the words out like shavings of sharp metal as she angled the papers to Tsevannah. "Are you—?"

"I am."

Sekhran Ganaresh Ti-Vaour, the paper started, *it is the pleasure of both myself and the Queen to announce our resuming of the Tour of Seasons.*

As the voice of Winter, alongside our newly reborn goddess, the White Doe Cervora, I declare the calendar moves forward once more. Winter will come to Empress Feng Souram's lands within the next two months, and so begins our Tour again.

I wish you the best of luck in your seasonal preparations.

The Winter King's signature swirled along the bottom, taking up the last of the white space with elegant lines of silver ink. Even without touching it, Tsevannah could feel the cold of it, the wicked and deathly magic of the ice-folk. Whatever it did, Tsevannah didn't know; she only knew that every single letter was filled with magic, as if this letter were already carved into the Face of Malouçe, inevitable in every way. And the message itself, it made true what their Winter ally's frantic ball of silver magic said when it exploded into the palace some several weeks ago: the Winter King did, in fact, marry the Glass Witch, and she was, in fact, committing such incredible blasphemy.

"That woman," Sekhran Ganaresh rasped as he came to tower over Tsevannah and Faloorah both. Sparks glimmered in the back of his throat as he smiled and ran his tongue over his teeth. His eyes shone with fury, enough to make even Faloorah pause. "That half-Winter runt. What does she think she's doing? We pull her off that mountain, feed her, give her strength—and instead of paying for it with the King's life, she puts on a circus like this." The Sekhran shook his head and rubbed his chin. "I will burn that creature myself."

No, no, no.

"She is the wife of the Winter King now," Tsevannah said, her tone sharp. "There will be no burning anyone unless you want to find yourself on the wrong side of international law. The best we can hope for is strong relations between her and her King, the land of Winter itself. But this is good. She is still paying for those feasts, husband—with the moving of the seasons. We can hold off for now, on all this talk of war."

"International law," the Sekhran mused. "What does that matter to the Winter King?"

Tsevannah paused. Her stomach twisted at the thought, but it was her duty to be the voice of reason—even if reason seemed more and more scant. "Precisely, my Sekhran," she said. "We don't know what it matters. But I don't doubt he would still appeal to it to defend any retaliation, should we make any moves against a diplomatic solution now. In fact, you should call your boy back from Winter and hope he returns unseen; there's no reason to have assassins after the Winter King if he's finally doing what we've been begging him to do for decades."

Sekhran Ganaresh only tipped his chin up, as if she'd said something sly and treacherous. It was how he always looked at her when he hated her counsel; she'd grown used to it. But if he was wise—which he was—then he would take that counsel.

Rather than agree with her, though, he turned on his heel and left the room. "Call for the Seer, Tsevannah. Faloorah, come with me."

"Oh, Drakash's scales," Faloorah muttered, so quiet only Tsevannah could hear. She followed their husband, tossing a sharp glance over her shoulder as she left. Tsevannah, too, held in a sigh until both of them were far enough away.

The Seer. Just the thought made Tsevannah tired, but she picked up her robes and hurried down the corridor anyway, in the opposite direction of her husband and Faloorah. *Always the damn Seer.*

The Head of Faith, Shayazeri, to be precise. The one wife Sekhran Ganaresh always turned to when he hoped to bypass all of his Council's advice and go directly to the Moon Mother Malouçe for wisdom. Tsevannah could only pray that whatever the Seer spit up this day wouldn't be nearly so rash and recklessly divined as the last message one century ago.

Once Tsevannah hurried her way into the bowels of the palace, down sandy, twisting steps and through dark corridors where the sun's light did not shine, she came upon one richly painted door. It sat all blue and gold and decked with little speckles of white paint that, in the orange sconce light, seemed to twinkle. This was the bottom floor of the palace, all the way in the back, facing the endless desert and the sea beyond it—and there was a certain something lingering in the air that made Tsevannah's hair stand on end. A certain eeriness, a sense of a place between the world of the living and the dead, as if she were stepping into a tomb.

At that door was a single guard who stood as stiff as a corpse. Tsevannah sometimes wondered if the guard stationed down here hadn't been mummified long ago, and if Shayazeri hadn't simply propped him up there to look like she was being guarded—but as she came closer, he nodded to her, and when Tsevannah told him to, he promptly slid open one of the door's small windows and asked the Head of Faith to prepare for visitors.

Not long after, the Sekhran arrived without Faloorah, and the guard hardly so much as blinked as he opened the door to the Seer's isolated chamber. It wasn't the first time Tsevannah had been exposed to this chamber, secluded as it was, and yet it seemed she never grew more used to seeing the place—or the Head of Faith herself.

Shayazeri was a strange woman; no one could've disagreed with Tsevannah about that. Yet it was that strangeness that gave her the sight no one else had, and the connection to Malouçe no one else understood. As Head of Faith, the woman was draped in fine silks that looked like the moon's own silver light. She had moonstone and lapis lazuli hanging off her ears and piercing her nose, as well as wrapped around her fingers and throat in tight bands of silver. Moreover, with hair prematurely white and eyes blue as if struck by blindness, her youthful face seemed all the more peculiar, as if the great moon goddess refused to let this woman age a day, never mind die.

Incense coiled up from a brass burner. In the moonlight, little was visible of the Seer's room but the arch of Shayazeri's small window, the cushions she laid on, and the pot of coffee that gleamed in the nighttime's silver shimmer. Unlike her fellow Council Members, who always had books and papers strewn about in their great offices, Shayazeri needed nothing o the sort. She only kept enough room to admire the sky through the window—only wanted enough space to listen for the sound of the ocean lapping at the shore behind the palace.

Tsevannah and the Sekhran sat on the opposite side of Shayazeri's reading table as she sipped the last of her coffee. She'd poured her husband a cup, too, a small cup, which the Sekhran already sucked down nearly to its end. A little bit of liquid was necessary for the Head of Faith to work her skills. As she drank her own last sip, all was silent.

Then came the sharp *clack* as Shayazeri overturned her cup onto the plate. A moment of moving the cup in a circle over the table later, and she then put it all down, picked up her cup, and peered inside at the lines and patterns the grounds left behind around the rim. After, she took the Sekhran's cup and did the same, but she didn't look at his just yet. She stared into her own cup for what seemed like a thousand years, all while the Sekhran waited with a stony face. Tsevannah would've rather been anywhere except in that room, with how thick the silence was as Shayazeri frowned.

"You hothead, husband—you quick actor." Her pale blue eyes, pale enough that Tsevannah often wondered if she would one day go blind, still managed to land exactly on the Sekhran. "I wish you would've come to me first, before you sent the doe back to its butcher."

Tsevannah caged a sigh. Worse than all of Shayazeri's oddities was the way she spoke in metaphors and riddles. But her husband, ever patient with the Seer lest he drink up Malouçe's own flavor of wrath, only nodded.

"We did what we had to."

"Mm, no. You did what you wanted to. And now look," she said, clucking her tongue as she pointed to lines of grounds only she knew how to interpret. How Shayazeri mastered this craft so accurately was just as great a mystery, and that was what gave more credence to her skills in communing with the gods above. "The doe—she's awake. Mother Moon put her to sleep, hid her memories in bone and gave her good dreams of

Summer, and now she's awake again in the frostlands. She's awake, husband, and she wants justice."

More riddles, and yet more riddles. Still, these riddles were laced with something cruel and terrible, wicked enough to make Tsevannah tremble if she didn't keep a tight yoke on her body. As the half-moon filled their space with light, though, hanging in the sky and ruling over the desert in Drakash's absence, Tsevannah felt she shouldn't open her mouth. Perhaps she shouldn't have been even thinking her own thoughts, given Malouçe hovered right above them as if she, too, were a direct part of this meeting.

"My Priestess," the Sekhran said, bowing slightly, "the seasons haven't moved for—"

"I know, yes, I know. Because you didn't bring Father Sun all the way to the white mountain in the far north, like Mother Moon said to. Now look what you've done."

Tsevannah bit her cheek. This was why she hated these meetings: the way Shayazeri spoke to their Sekhran, the son of Drakash's sons. That, and the way her husband even bowed to her, as if being a priestess was higher in rank than being the very Lord of Summer. But if Shayazeri noticed Tsevannah's shifting, or the clearing of her throat, she made no sign. She only peered into that cup as if the contents of it were whispering to her, and she shook her head.

"Ah, no. No matter how many times I look, the answer is the same: the doe wants justice," she said again. "No, hothead, no—you've put yourself worse off than you started. This doe comes for you now. For all of us. Until all of us are like the Mockeries."

Tsevannah raised her brow at the slur. *Çelvedrari.* Not even beasts and brutes were called such a word, nor had the Ismären been called such a thing to their faces while they walked through the streets of Summer. It was a word only for them: the mockeries of life.

"My Priestess," the Sekhran tried again, though his hands clenched tight enough in his lap to go white at the knuckles, "the King of the Mockeries wishes to move the seasons again. Do we let him? Or do we extend the endless Summer yet longer and prepare for war? Please ask the Moon Mother for us."

Shayazeri glanced at him, then nodded and set her cup down on the table. She then leaned over and plucked his overturned cup of coffee from the table, along with its saucer. Then she peered into the cup and froze.

Tsevannah blinked at the woman, how she'd just locked up and gone slack-jawed. "Shayazeri?" She reached out to tap the Seer's arm. "Shaya—?"

"You will have war if you act," Shayazeri whispered, her face falling into a grim, dark frown, "and Winter if you don't." Her hands trembled as she held the cup. "You will have Winter if you don't—as will all other nations. A cold, deep Winter to restart this world, one so deep it'll feel like death."

Sekhran Ganaresh and Tsevannah glanced at each other. The words seemed like good news, but it was the way Shayazeri said them that made the hair on Tsevannah's neck stand up. She turned to the Head of Faith and chose her words carefully.

"My Prie—"

However, no amount of care mattered when Shayazeri refused to listen. She clutched the cup and rasped, "Get that doe, husband. Get that doe, get that doe!

"Whoa, whoa," Sekhran Ganaresh said, though Shayazeri jerked away when he tried to lay a comforting hand on her, "hey, now—"

"Butcher it! Skin it!" Her bright eyes turned on them both, shining with the same ferocity as the moon in the sky, and her voice died to a whisper. "Do not let it have a second chance."

Then she dropped the cup onto the saucer and fell into her pillows, as if her prophecy had drained her down to the last drop of her energy.

Efir's head ached as if someone drove an axe into it. His throat was so sore that he thought some rodent might've crawled in it and scratched it all up from the inside; his lips were dry enough to split and bleed the second they pulled back in his grimace. And even though his feet were squarely on the ground, his ass squarely in a chair, he couldn't help but feel like he was spinning—spinning endlessly, to the point that he was dizzy just from sitting still. There'd been many times where he'd been conditioned to take blows to the head and still get up and walk, but this? No. This wasn't at all the same. This was something else entirely.

"Awake, now?"

He flinched at the sound of that woman's voice, more out of surprise than anything else. Still, that movement was enough to make it feel like the phantom axe in his head only got pushed in deeper, and he lost control of his face as he tried to bear it with a snarl. One of the most important lessons he'd learned was to never let the enemy see the results of their torture. Yet this was a pain he'd never felt, a whole-body disruption that he wasn't quite sure *pain* even covered.

"Ooh, look at you," crooned that woman. When Efir managed to pull his head up enough to see her, he could barely make her out; his vision was washed out in shades of white and blue, as if his eyes couldn't adjust right to whatever lights they had floating around. "Poor thing. I'm sure you're feeling like a downright mess."

Efir didn't respond. He tried to keep his breathing steady, but every breath in made it feel like he was

inflating his head until it would pop. The woman, or
what he could see of her, made some jerky motion,
and then there were freezing fingers at his temples. He
jerked, tried to escape the touch of whoever was behind
him, but it was only then that he realized that he was
strapped to that chair with a generous helping of snow-
rope, which was only sapping what heat he had left in
his body. At this rate, he'd freeze to death—that much
he knew.

The fingertips returned to his head, and it seemed
that freeze would start in his skull, with the cold that
washed over him. But rather than freeze, he found a
cooling sensation like mint, one that tingled in his skin
and cleared whatever fog hung over his mind. The pain
eased away, the nausea subsided, and the breath he took
felt crisp, clear. He blinked the last of the fog away and
looked up to see some staunch man behind him, one
with a silver goatee and a shiny bald head, as well as
a white coat lined with silver buttons and plain white
slacks. Had Efir not known any better, he might've
thought he was seeing a ghost. The man only turned his
nose up at Efir, and then he went to sit in a chair by the
edge of the room.

A strange room it was. Small, yet so meticulously
organized that it felt like it could've held a world of
materials inside. Each bookshelf that lined the walls behind the woman's small, thin-legged desk was perfectly
stocked with tomes, every inch of space taken up by just
the right book, and the two empty chairs on the other
side of the room were nestled into the corner in such
a way that they looked like they'd been built into the
stone. A large circular tapestry full of silver, blue, and
black swirls took up nearly the entire floor, and from
the ceiling hung a cage full of what looked like cold blue
stars that shimmered and lit the whole room.

Efir blinked at those stars, then gave his arms a

good tug. It was no use. Those ropes were solid, and he
doubted his venom would melt snow so easily. It could
melt all the flesh in the world, but against snow, he
could've only wished for his father's lava-like plumes
of flame. As he struggled, the lady at that desk watched
him with unnatural stillness, her hands folded before
some box.

Wait.

He paused his struggling and took a closer look at
that box, and then he really was sure he'd freeze to
death, because whatever warmth was still in his blood
left him then. It was coconut wood. The coconut wood
box, with the—

"What is that?" Efir cursed to the deepest trenches of
the Sunless Sands and back. Still, he kept his voice low.
He twitched his brows, his face becoming a mask of
mild curiosity to cover his rising panic. "What's in that
box?"

"Mm, what *is* in this box?" The woman stared at him
with those deep, glassy black eyes, so uncanny that he
could've crawled out of his skin after just a moment under their gaze, and she smiled in a way that only made
the stitches in her face more noticeable. They pulled
against her jaw, the stitches straining against her sharp
chin. "I'll be honest, wyrm, I don't think I know any
more than you do." Then she reached over and flicked
that gold clasp open. "Would *you* like to tell me what
these things are? What they're for?"

Inside were two pieces of snowflake obsidian. The
very same that his father had fashioned for that Winter
woman. But if this woman had them, and both King
and his wraith "Queen" were nowhere in sight, then it
could've only meant exactly what his father feared: the
Glass Witch had fully betrayed them. Efir knew what the
Sekhran's response would be. The dragons that would
cross over the ice wall would be not the children of the

Head of Surveillance, like Efir, but the sons and daughters of the Head of Military and all golden dragons under those captains' commands. Granted, that would be the case *if* Efir left that room alive and was able to give the Sekhran his report.

Stop, stop. Maybe they really don't know what they are.

Efir hardly knew. He didn't let any of his nerves show on his face, more because the state of his nauseous body made it impossible to anyway. He could hardly keep his eyes open as he looked at them. After licking his dry, chapped, near frozen lips, he tried to make words.

"I don't," talking made it sound like the words were echoing in his ears, "I don't know."

"Oh, come now." The advisor stood up and plucked that box from the desk, then came to Efir's side and showed it to him. She patted a frozen hand on his shoulder; the ice bit his skin. "Surely you know. Is this not coconut wood?"

As she shook the box, he muttered, "It is."

"And that's only found in Summer, no?"

"Yes."

Before he could wonder what was making answers slip so easily from his lips, that advisor made two quick steps in front of him and crouched, until all Efir could see were those endlessly deep black eyes—just as black as the obsidian. Somewhere deep within, a pinprick of silver light sparkled in each one, like some faraway, distant pupil. Another wave of cold sweat broke over Efir's scalp as he watched those little lights flicker around in that well of darkness.

"Then what did you wyrms send our *dear Queen?* Hmm? Out with it, now." She gripped his chin with a hand as hard and cold as steel, so hard he thought she'd crush his jaw to powder. He never would've expected that kind of strength from a tiny thing that didn't even have any muscle in the first place. Worse was the way her words seemed to push into his mind like needles through his skull. "We already saw your mind, boy. We know you and your little poison-tongued sister are the ones that put these things snugly in their velvet casing, *Efir Dalmoulah Ti-Vaour*. So tell. Me. What. They. Are."

They what? It didn't make sense, what she said, but hearing her say his name made his already aching mind nearly split with a sudden wave of thoughts. They looked inside his mind—whatever that meant—and they knew his name, found the box—what else did they know? With a deep breath, one that felt like he was inhaling knives in that frozen castle, he decided not to give them any more than what was patently obvious.

"They're gems. What of it?" Efir shook his head, or at least tried to, and it made his temples throb. "Jewelry, maybe. I don't know."

The woman blinked. Her lips quivered as if she didn't know whether to ask more questions or curse him to dust. But before Efir could say anything else, the woman looked up at the castle guards and that man in the white coat.

"Would you leave us a moment? I think maybe this one is a little too shy to speak in front of an audience."

Efir blinked as the sound of the men's footsteps tapped out of the room. The door clicked behind them unceremoniously; not a single one so much as grunted, never mind complained or objected to leaving the little woman alone with a prisoner. The only times a person *would* ever excuse other people, though—other witnesses—would be to begin some kind of torturing. But surely a woman this small, even with her unnatural strength, couldn't possibly think to begin torturing him for answers. Work like that was reserved for the folks who loved tools and tears more than open air, sunlight, or society. This was clearly a high-ranking woman, one close to the King and in good esteem of the guards, so—

"Låseleitum."

A hiss of wind and the smell of a wickedly cold Winter morning suddenly whipped through the room, and then there was silence again—until the woman came back around to him. Her footsteps were light and slow, and eventually, she stood in front of him again with all expression wiped from her face. Something about that blank stare was worse than any smile or scowl she'd given before then, because she looked so stiff, so unreal.

She stared at him in complete silence for what felt like an hour, not so much as twitching all the while. If Efir looked hard enough, he could've sworn she wasn't even there in the first place; she simply blended in with the rest of the white, grey, and blue room, the outline of her shifting and fading into stone and silver as his head throbbed. It made his skin crawl in a way nothing else ever had.

How many times had he and his siblings joked with each other about the Winter people? Agreed with each other, again and again, that things made of ice instead of flesh couldn't really count as people, or even animals? Too many times in the past century. Far too many. And yet looking into that woman's face, wiped clean of all expression, of any life at all, left no room for jokes. All the beatings he'd taken in preparation for times like these, all his siblings skilled in torture that did everything to terrify information from him—even feigning indifference and coldness to his pain—they were nothing compared to the true indifference in her face. Or maybe it was something worse than that, something even more alien. Whatever the word for it might've been, Efir knew: the stiffness of her, the emptiness in her black eyes, the silence, it only confirmed a bitter, terrifying reality.

These Ismären were *not* people. Not the way the people of Spring, Summer, and Autumn were. No, these folks were replicas of people: similar in shape and size, able to walk and talk and build and fight and govern. But that face, those eyes—there was no spark of anything reminiscent of life. Even Efir's mother, distant and disciplined as she was, had some shimmer of life to her that this woman, this *thing,* did not have in that moment.

Eventually, the woman moved, and Efir startled. She turned around to put the box back on her desk, and then she leaned against that desk, half-sitting on it as she reached her short legs out. It looked like she would've sighed if she could, but there was still nothing but the most uncanny silence from that ice-woman. Her head lolled side to side as she studied him, and then, finally, she spoke.

"It'll be war, you know. One way or another."

Efir's tongue felt too thick to make words. He was starting to lose feeling in his fingers, too, and it wouldn't take long before his toes also became nothing but numb stubs. Still, he only tilted his head in silent question.

The woman shrugged. "I kill you here and send your frozen body back to your Lord father: war. He'll have a reason to come melt us all. I find out the truth from you that your thoughts and memories didn't fully reveal to us: war. King Jädrich has had more than enough of you meddling fleshlings trying to steal our peace away. And truthfully, I think even what we *do* already know— about the mutt you sent over our borders, about *you*—is enough to bring an ice age over the Ringlands."

Despite how cold Efir had been that entire time, and despite him knowing far better than to even twitch under enemy eyes, he couldn't help it; that last line made him shudder from deep within his bones.

She saw that shudder and pinned him with that deep, empty stare. "Do you want war, little wyrm? Do you want to watch the Ringlands break in half like that?

Torn apart across solstice lines? Do you want to watch our country melt while every man, woman, and child in yours freezes into statues?"

The best lies have a little truth mixed in. So said his mother. Efir braced himself for whatever threats and coercion that ice-thing could've thrown his way and spit out, "No."

She stared at him, then nodded, as if resigned. Then she kicked her feet and studied her shoe. When she looked back up, it was there for the first time: a glimmer of something small, something fragile, below the surface of her icy face.

"Then I have a job for you. I'll even give you back all your funny little toys if you say yes—those knives and odd cannisters and other things you had. Wouldn't want you to go about this job completely unarmed, of course. How about it? Will you do it?"

Job. Something about that word snapped in place in his mind, like a key clicking as it turned in its lock. *Job.* It snatched his attention, cleared his mind of all thoughts, all pain. He barely noticed that he didn't have his waist-pack full of "toys" and "cannisters," as the woman called them—the special bombs that activated with a Swampland Yasilan's venom instead of fire. *Job.*

Only Drakash could've known why he sat up—why he so quickly and easily nodded.

It was the talk of the town that morning in Firtuchs. As Tannel swept the snow off his front step, he listened to a few passing women chitter and chatter like Winter squirrels searching for frozen pine nuts.

"My husband said so! The Bishops are coming!"

"The Bishops! The Bishops never—!"

There were four of them, walking arm in arm, with their leather heels barely saving those thick wool dresses from dragging on the pavement. With all their dresses either black or blue or both, and all of them wearing matching black dockenbaretts with blue and white feathers, Tannel could only assume they belonged to some club or organization closer to the inner part of town. Many of the townswomen, whether in some social club or not, came around these parts for the shoemaker at the end of the road. Why that old man never moved his shop closer to the city center, Tannel could only guess.

"I heard they're here to investigate the Queen."

"What? No! They're—what is there to investigate?"

"Well," the four of them stopped short and clustered closer to one woman, leaning in for her whisper, "she is rather strange, isn't she? Have you seen her?"

"Of course we have. I don't think there's anything strange about her, except maybe her *pets* or whatever she calls those beasts she had with her."

"Yes, that's one thing, but have you seen her up *close*?"

By this point, Tannel was done with the front step, but he was curious, so he busied himself tidying some of his walkway and the sides of his step. He hadn't had any reason to visit the Queen; none of his family were melted. It was only on the service she held that, in the town's big and overly crowded cathedral, Tannel ever caught a glimpse of her—and from what he could tell, she didn't look all that odd, even if her dress was more like some big lilac robe instead of a dress proper. The two skulking, long-haired *Unseelechs* sitting on the altar table also didn't give Tannel the opportunity to feel the excitement and joy he maybe should have. But she had antlers proper, none of the fake ones the priestess did, and she clopped about on big hooves. Who could've doubted she was anything other than what she said she was?

"There's something strange about her," that woman said. "When she went to fix my hand, she just didn't have the countenance I'd expect from a doe. And I expected her frost to be a magical application, not... breath."

An uneasy silence fell over the space, only broken by the sound of a straw broom on stone. Tannel hardly even wanted to sweep anymore; the silence was so thick that his busywork felt like an intrusion. A moment passed before another woman spoke.

"I wonder if what they're saying in the south is—"

"Come along, now." The tapping of heels against the stone picked up. "We'll discuss more over cards. If we keep babbling out here, we'll miss our appointment."

Tannel wondered, too. He'd heard what the south was saying. Who hadn't? One merchant or traveling artisan comes through looking for a tavern to get a cup of sap-diluted bloodwine, and then the tavern knows everything discussed in the past ten taverns before it. The Hopping Line, people called it—that way information hopped from tavern to tavern along someone's route. And boy, did the Hopping Line have some nasty news to share about that Queen—news that surely made the whole town pack themselves into that cathedral just to see if those rumors were true.

The Wraith Queen. An Unseelech-*lover. A mixed-blood.*

The first two could maybe be chalked up to people being heretics, or even refusing to understand whatever Cervora's icon wanted them to know by dragging those beasts around. But the last? Cervora's icon, a mixed-blood? What could she possibly have been mixed with?

Breath. Tannel set his broom against the wall and knocked his boots against the side of his step. *Her frost is breath.*

He shoved all those thoughts out of his mind. Better he lived a faithful fool than let those ideas evolve into heresy.

Or so he chose to believe.

Aveline paused with a berry just a couple inches from her lips.

A plate of raw river trout, berries, and some almost-frozen treat of hazelnut meal and crystallized sap rolled into little balls sat beside her. It was as good a breakfast as she'd get without cooking it herself, and she found it a perfectly pleasant meal, even if one of the townswomen ducked her head in shame when she served it. But for people who didn't eat anything in the first place, the fact that the town's mayor could scrounge up this much was impressive, and the little dining area of the mayor's house was cozy even when Aveline ate alone. Big windows let in the hazy grey light, plush carpets of bear fur lined the floorboards and nestled under the small table for four, and little bookshelves lined a couple walls around a big, dead fireplace, all of which *almost* gave the place a sense that it was lived in.

And she would've been perfectly content to enjoy her plate and the cozy quiet, if not for the way that quiet was interrupted. A wave of sharp, stinging gooseflesh erupted across her temples, down to her chin. The words she'd just heard didn't make any sense.

"What do you mean, the Bishops want to *verify* me?" Her heart fluttered as if it were the tiny, fragile heart of a mouse. "What is there to verify?"

Jädrich took slow, deliberate steps towards her. He never broke eye contact with her, even as Aveline's *Unseelechs* rumbled a warning and clustered around her legs. Their hair tickled her bare feet.

"Aveline," he started, "you understand that anyone can claim to be Cervora's icon."

"Can they?" Aveline clopped a hoof against the ground, and one *Unseelech* startled at the sharp sound. "Anyone? You're telling me there are others with hooves and antlers and frost to heal this country?"

What if they realize I'm—?

"Not that I know of."

Jädrich towered over her and let his stare rest heavy on her shoulders. Her *Unseelechs* yowled like cats, complaining at how close he'd come—but they knew. Poor things, they knew what he could do if they so much as scratched his boots. Aveline put her berry down, snatched a couple pieces of fish, and held them under her seat until the yowling stopped and the frigid lick of their thin, ribbon-like tongues nudged the fish from her fingers. All the while, Jädrich watched, but if he disapproved of her feeding her babies in front of him, he didn't show it.

Aveline huffed and said, "Then what reason do they have to 'verify' anything?"

He stared at her a moment longer, then quirked his lips into a smile that didn't meet his eyes. "Are you worried they'll learn something about you?"

Her breath caught.

Jädrich's smile grew. He shook his head and said, "You have nothing to worry about. I promise. Now come," he held out a hand, "they'll be looking to meet you in the cathedral."

"They're already here?" She glanced at the food left on her plate; her heart fluttered as her lungs tried, and failed, to suck in a deep breath. "I haven't finished eating."

"We should be there before them to prepare your examination. You can eat later."

When is "later"? Aveline stared at him, frozen to the spot. That smile he'd tacked on dug under her skin. "I'm hungry now. I want to eat now."

"I'll have the same plate prepared—"

"Jädrich!"

The thump of her fist on the table surprised even her—as did the rattle of the plate and the silverware. However, her body wasn't being pulled by the shadow-strings in her bones. Not right then. All of this—the squeezing in her chest, the prickling heat at her temples, the tension in her muscles—was her own doing.

She rose slowly, so that she might gather her thoughts more, and when she stood near eye-level with Jädrich, she spoke so low that her words sounded more like a rumble of faraway thunder than a woman's voice.

"You already denied me any rest from these duties until we get home. Do not come and interrupt my meals on top of it. The Bishops can wait until *I* decide I am ready to see them. Do you understand?"

I am the Queen. I am the Goddess. Aveline held Jädrich's stare and repeated those things over and over in her head, as if they were some mental shield against his crown and his presence. *I am the highest in the land. I am Queen. I am Goddess.*

And then, something snuck into her mantra—made her blink, made her thoughts stutter.

I am the Dragon. My teeth are sharper than yours now, wolf.

"Aveline."

She flinched and cursed herself for it. Her mantra tumbled out of her head as she refocused on Jädrich and caught a crackle of magic flash across his eyes.

"The Bishops and the Crown are in a careful balance of power." He spoke so gently. "If anyone has the power to derail you in this country and deny you your rightful title, it is them. Should they feel disrespected, or that there's even a single thing amiss with you and your behavior, it'll cast suspicion on you. You surely understand how long the Ismären have been waiting for you—and how many may find your arrival too good to be true." He took a step back, then another, making a careful path for the door. "However, yes, I understand. Please eat. I'll find a way to stall the Bishops in the meantime."

Aveline opened her mouth to say something, but nothing came out. It was as if a tight fist were closed around both her lungs; her breath would not fill them, nor would any breath leave them to let her speak. She watched, heartbeat quickening, as Jädrich left the room and closed the door shut behind him. The tap of the door nestling in its frame made her blink.

Aveline.

Her hands flew up to clutch her head. She squeezed her eyes shut and sank to the floor. Two soft, firm things rubbed against her arms—her *Unseelechs*—but she couldn't even hear them gurgle or chitter as she focused on the echo of that voice in her mind.

Aveline.

That was all this thing in her head said for the past few days. Her name, over and over, with that unspoken offer hanging off the last syllable. *Stop,* she hissed back. *Stop it. Shut up. Leave. Leave me.*

The tightness in her skin and the deep ache in her bones were her answer. *No.*

Something thin and cold lapped at her face, and only then did she wrench her eyes open. She stared into the glowing glass eyes of one of her babies; it squeaked and crooned at her, and its needle-teeth gnashed in its concern. It hooked its one wing-talon on her wrist as if trying to pull her hand away from her head. The other one forced its way under her elbow, then jerked its shoulders to pull her other hand away.

"Oh, you two," she muttered. They croaked as she stroked their hair; the sound of their contentment made it easier to drop her tense shoulders and take a deep breath. "You two. Let's finish eating. Then we'll go."

And that was what they did. As difficult as it was to rush through frozen foods, Aveline managed to stuff the rest of her evening meal down and herd her babies out the door. It didn't take long before one of the mayor's footmen greeted them, and even if he looked at the *Unseelechs* with barely hidden horror, he did allow them to ride in the prepared carriage with Aveline. It was the first time they'd ridden with her this whole tour, and they bounced about the carriage like dogs looking for scents on the wind. Aveline watched them, desperate to keep her mind as blank and relaxed as possible as they rocked along towards the cathedral at the other end of town.

Firtuchs was the biggest town they'd been to yet—though not quite big enough to keep anyone exploring for more than a day, so maybe Aveline wasn't truly missing out on much by not being able to wander the streets for a bit. The best thing about the place, though, was that it was near the other end of the Baron's territory. Soon enough, they'd be in the lands of some Margravine, and that'd mark the halfway point of this wretched tour. For the time being, though, they were still traveling south, going through ebbs and flows of villages and towns, freezing people along the way before rushing off to the next place.

As if I'm just some tool.

That wasn't her thought. Aveline caught it then—the slippery way those words leaked into her mind, like a snake in a crevice. That wasn't her thought, even if it was her voice, but it was fine pretending it was her. It was fine pressing that thought on her, urging her to think it was her own—and that the feeling that came with it, that bitterness, was hers, too. Aveline noted it, but she didn't say anything against the thought; there was nothing *to* say, nothing to think, that would win her any ground with the doe-wraith lurking in her tendons and bones and blood.

Eventually, the carriage came to a stop, and the driver opened the door for Aveline and her *Unseelechs.* She let them go first and hopped out after them; they stayed so close to her skirts that they nearly got swallowed in the heavy fabric. The carriage driver tipped his head to her before getting back on that carriage, and there he sat, staring straight ahead, waiting for everyone to return. It was so mechanical, the way he sat and stared. So uncanny.

And the cathedral itself didn't do anything for Aveline's nerves. This was a bigger one than most—one covered in vibrant stained glass, with a great rose window above the huge silver-gilded doors. Inside were two rows of long pews, big enough to hold twice the castle's residents, and plush blue carpets for the wide aisle down the middle. Great starlight lanterns hung from the stone pillars that supported the cathedral's high ceiling, and flowers clustered anywhere there was an empty space, always stuck in huge silver vases. Instead of a statue of Cervora, there was a great painting of her that took up the cathedral's entire back wall—one where she was casting blue diamonds from her hands that looked like pale tears. As always, the Cervora the Ismären imagined had a sweet smile, a round face, huge black eyes, and a body perfectly plush and untouched. Even her antlers seemed soft, round, harmless.

I am not harmless.

Aveline shivered from deep within her bones.

The basement door to the left was closed, but as Aveline came down the aisle and approached that door, she heard the faint warbling of someone's voice. When she pushed that door open, the words became clearer.

"—assure you of her legitimacy, on my word as King. So too do these witnesses, who have personally been blessed with our Queen Mother's mercy."

Her hooves clopped loudly enough to echo on the stone steps, and if anyone down there was going to reply to Jädrich, they stayed silent. Her *Unseelechs* stayed a step or so behind even as they scrabbled about, just as she'd taught them, so they didn't trip her as they had in the castle on several occasions. Just before Aveline reached the end of the staircase, she drew in a deep breath, and with her *Unseelechs* behind her, she steeled herself to face whatever nonsense these *Bishops* had to throw at her.

Once she left the last step of the cathedral basement, she held her head high and hoped her hooves and antlers would speak for her. The Bishops sat at the long table where Aveline did her work each morning. There were five of them, spread out on one side of that table, facing off with Jädrich and four others: Erik, Karina, Ristef, and Aula.

Witnesses. Aveline's gaze settled on the middle Bishop, whose big silver hat was shaped something like a spade. *I'm on trial.*

The Bishops' hats were embroidered with glittering blue thread as if imbued with magic. All their robes were similarly decorated to the point that under the basement starlights, they seemed to glow like moonlight off snow, what with that silver-blue sheen their satin gave off. Their faces were smooth and relaxed of all expression, their hair as long as Jädrich's and carefully braided into a thick rope that hung over their left shoulder, and their eyes all sparkled the same shade of red—a shade Aveline hadn't seen in Ismar eyes. But the blunt, almost red-orange color told her it was jasper in their heads, bright and burning red jasper.

"This is her?" The center Bishop, to his credit, didn't break Aveline's stare to look at the *Unseelechs* that raked their talons into Aveline's skirts. "The one who claims to be our Mother?"

Before Jädrich could answer, Aveline said, "I am."

As the Bishop farthest to the left stood and came around the table, the main one folded his hands on the table and said, "May I ask why you didn't come with the King?"

"I was finishing my evening meal."

That made the Bishop stare. The other Bishop came up to her and inspected her antlers and face. Up close, the many bands of sandy golden agate swirling across his otherwise red eyes were the only thing that distinguished him from any of the other men at that table. They could've all been copies of each other, with the meticulous way they dressed and the uncanny likeness in the carve of their faces; if Aveline was to tell any of them apart, no doubt it'd be by their eyes.

"Your Majesty," this Bishop said with a slight incline of his head, "please allow me to inspect your build. Just an arm will do."

That made it sound like he wanted to take her arm off and carry it back to the table. Maybe her *Unseelechs* thought so, too, because they growled at that Bishop as he stood close to her—though good things, they didn't swipe at him. They sat still and kept close to her, just as she'd trained them to do, and the Bishop didn't spare them more than a glance before swiveling those agate-scarred jasper stones back towards her. Still, Aveline's hips and thighs went tight—and as she saw more of the detail of this Bishop's long silver-blue cloak, and saw all the motifs of deer and holly and stars woven into it, she found that her body wasn't tight with the urge to bolt. No, from deep in her blood and bones, she—or rather, her body—wanted to rear back a hoof and put a hole in this man's chest.

Slack. More than her throat, it seemed her whole body needed to settle. Aveline kept that one word in her head as more of a command to her body—and whatever hid in it—than a mantra. *Slack.* Then she lifted her arm and held it out to the Bishop, even as it felt that some invisible force was trying to pull her away from him by her hips. *Slack.*

As the Bishop took gentle hold of her arm, squeezing the meat of her forearm and testing the pad of her palm, the middle Bishop once again spoke: "Might I ask what you typically eat as your evening meal, Your Majesty?"

"Might you make magic for me?" The Bishop closer to her whispered it, as if afraid his voice would knock the other Bishop's question out of the air.

She didn't pay him much mind, even as the freezing magic slid from her stomach, up her chest, to her shoulder, and down her arm, until it appeared as a silvery light shining up from her palm. Her only focus was that middle Bishop, whose stare could've ripped her in two, and gave him an answer.

"Fish. Berries. Nuts. Snow."

"I see." The Bishop stared at her a moment longer, then sat back and shuffled through a few papers on the table in front of him. He looked it over for a moment, then said, "Your Majesty, might you tell us your earliest memory in this life? So we might understand exactly when it was you may have come to us?"

The question made her clench her teeth. But at least that other Bishop finally put her arm down. He nodded to her, whispered "Thank you," then returned to his seat.

All the while, Aveline tried to figure out how she would explain her first memory: the memory of something shiny and silver jingling in the market stalls of Sekhbal, the only silver thing in a box otherwise stuffed with gold and copper rings and pendants. The silver pendant was pointed, like a star, and in the middle was a shockingly blue gem. She saw it from high up, from her mother's arms—and it was the first thing Aveline's mother ever bought for her, that little star pendant. The silver tone looked strange against her mother's bronzed skin, her tone so clearly more suited for gold, but in Aveline's ghostly hands, it made sense. The chain gathered in a way that looked like starlight had come down to pool in the snow. A shame that she'd lost that pendant some years later.

"Starlight," she finally said, because what else was she to answer with? So long as she focused on that pendant, and not all the sand and stone and heat and market noise around her, they would never guess she'd made this memory in Sekhbal. "I held it in my hands: a star. A silver star, with a blue gem."

As she spoke, the Bishop that prodded her leaned aside to whisper to the other Bishops, who leaned in to listen. The middle Bishop kept glancing between his peer and Aveline, and once she was done speaking, he nodded.

"I see. And those creatures beside you there," he glanced at the *Unseelechs,* "can you explain these creatures? Why they have the magic of your kin in their ice?"

"They're my children," Aveline said, quickly enough that her answer clipped the end of his last question. "The magic I give them completes them."

Those Bishops glanced behind her—no doubt at Jädrich, whose stare she could feel in her back. Still, she wanted to make her point, so she yipped to her *Unseelechs,* and like the good babies they were, they clawed up her skirts and into her open arms. With one nestled on each hip, their talons carefully clawing into her dress or resting on her shoulders, their icy heads nestling under her jaw, these creatures did in fact feel like children.

Would a true Ismar child feel the same?

"But Your Majesty," that middle Bishop started, "these creatures are unclean."

"According to who?"

"According to *you.*" His voice pierced her more than his stare did. "Your revelations to your priests and Bishops and Saints after your death told us as much: that these creatures were fit to be suitable for little more than pulling carriages or delivering letters, if even that. 'They are flawed and unworthy things compared to the art that is my true children'—so you said in your Revelation to St. Vard of Histelheid."

My Kviraeg. Something bubbled up her throat. Something thick and dark and hot, as if her stomach were a volcano full of tar. Her very bones seemed to burn as the word she'd learned from her memories stuck to her mind. *Kviraeg.* And even though her heart was still, her eyes stung with a film of tears as the memories from that great deer skull flashed in her mind's eye: memories of the *Unseelechs* that so faithfully carried her up and down the Seat of Orr. Her body shuddered with a grief she didn't know personally—an old, inherited grief, a bitter tar of regret.

"Your St. Vard of Histelheid," Aveline muttered, forcing the words past that bubble of tar that threatened to silence her, "was a liar in my name."

That made the Bishops pause. They leaned towards each other to whisper whatever little things to each other, and then that middle one narrowed his eyes.

"Interesting. We'd never considered that one of your Saints might be a liar." His lips twitched into a tight smile that faded a moment after it came. "Your Majesty, as you do make the claim to be Cervora incarnate, and as you claim that it's possible the holy men and women who have served you—"

Liars. Murderers. Unholy.

"—could have received *incorrect* revelation from you, then I suppose we should review all of our understanding of you. This is a process that may take several weeks of questioning, and as we understand you have your duties to attend to on this tour, we might very well ask you and His Majesty your permission to visit in the future. Until then, however, might you please give us your true, direct account of why you decided to die the first time?"

Decided?

The word rang in Aveline's head, screaming past the visceral memories of teeth at her thighs and arms and waist, of the *tear* of her skin and the *squelch* of her flesh between those teeth. The searing pain as a tendon tore from her bone and snapped up her leg. The howling—the howling, the screaming her throat raw, just as raw as it'd been the day she touched that skull. The dizziness. The slip of her hand on all the blood leaking from the puncture in her side. Every time she blinked, she saw another moment of that murder—*felt it,* and flinched with each new reminder.

Decided?

Again, that word bounced around her head. Only when its echo bounced back to her did she realize that her mouth had opened on its own—that the word born deep in her blood managed to escape her lips.

The Bishops flinched at its loud ring. She shook her head as if to banish those wicked visions of murder, squeezed her lips shut, and hugged her babies closer; her heart fluttered from her carelessness.

"Holy Bishops," Jädrich said as he stepped beside Aveline, "this seems to be a question better asked when our Mother isn't so weary from her duties. Perhaps now, she may instead demonstrate for you her capacity for miracle, and you may hear from her witnesses."

His hand pushed her hair aside and rested on the nape of her neck. The cold of it soothed her, and so did the gentle coos and chitters of her *Unseelechs* as they put their mouths closer to her ear. It seemed like they, too, were trying to soothe and settle her, the sweet things.

"Very well. Your Majesty," the Bishop on the right of that middle one nodded and leaned forward, "may we see an example of your miracles?"

Her heart fluttered again under the stare of those five men. But as Jädrich slipped his hand off her, and as her arms grew tired to the point that she had to let her babies back down, she steeled herself. No one said anything about her frost yet—at least, that she knew of—and so hopefully, these Bishops, too, wouldn't recognize it for what it was.

"I'll show you the stuff that has re-frozen those with melt," she said, and when the Bishops nodded, she swallowed the last of her nerves.

Then she squeezed her throat, and it clicked. Each click snapped through the silence and echoed back to her, too, just as it had every day she'd been stuck in some basement, surrounded by half-melted things. As it clicked, a pool of such deep cold settled in the back of her throat that it stung her flesh—and when enough of it gathered there, she pushed a heavy breath from deep in her belly. The pool of condensed cold became a stream of white frost as it sailed on that breath and left her lips. That frost was as thick and white as a blizzard, and as it fell to the floor, it left what looked like a light dusting of fresh snow on the stone.

One Bishop, the one farthest to the right, got up and hurried to that frost. He bent down and reached a finger out to trace a line through that frost, then plucked some and rubbed his fingers together. His brows knit as he studied the stuff, and then he looked to his peers and nodded. Once he'd returned to his seat, the middle Bishop folded his hands on the table.

"Impressive, Your Majesty. We've never seen a creature of flesh make snow." Then he looked past her, to Aula and Ristef, and said, "And one of you has had your melt healed?"

Footsteps rang against the stone, and then Aula stood beside Aveline—far enough that she was in no danger of brushing up against Aveline's *Unseelechs,* who clung to her legs again. Aula clasped her hands together and nodded.

"I have. I'm Aula Verrinson, the seamstress for our Queen, and I made her dresses for her bridal competition. She breathed this frost on my melted fingers and face, and since then, they've been just as hard and firm as the day I was first born into this world. I've been able to sew again without any handicap, and my fear of the melt is gone. This our Queen has done for countless others, but it's my honor that she's done it for me first."

The sincerity in Aula's voice surprised Aveline. Knowing what a snappy thing the seamstress could be, Aveline couldn't help but wonder if some of that wasn't an act. But what she said was true. Aveline remembered it was Aula who even gave her this idea to masquerade as a god, who begged her to be showered in that frost.

"Come, my lady," the Bishop to the left of the main one said, his hand outstretched. "Let me test the strength of your ice."

Aula nodded, then hurried to the table and stretched her hands out to the man. The middle Bishop watched for a moment, then turned back to Aveline.

"I understand there's a second miracle, as well."

Aveline blinked. *What?*

"Young man," the Bishop said, looking past her to Ristef, "might you come give your testimony and explain this second miracle?"

The heavy step of boots crunched over the stone, until Ristef stood where Aula once did. He glanced at her and smiled; his eyes crackled with a stray snap of magic. *It's okay,* that look seemed to say—but Aveline only stared in return. Surprises—she told Jädrich once that she wasn't a great fan of surprises.

"Holy Bishops," Ristef started, "thank you for giving me the opportunity to reveal this miracle. My testimony is simple: in my efforts to defend the Queen from the threats of others, I found myself drained of magic and broken. It was our Queen who saved me in a way I could not anticipate." Again, he glanced at Aveline, studying her as if she were some priceless jewel. Then he turned back to the Bishops and said, "She fed me not with the blood of her kin, but with the blood from her own veins. It ran as silver as that of any white deer, tasted just as sweet, and restored my magic nearly immediately. And better yet, it was *her* blood that did what no white deer's blood ever has: it has permanently sustained my magic."

Her heart thudded in her chest. Its beat echoed in her head, too. So loud that she could think no thoughts.

"I haven't had to eat or drink in weeks, and yet my magic is as strong as if I'd just had a full ration. More, when I *did* try to eat, I became sick with excess magic. I cannot eat anymore. I have no need to eat anymore."

"I confirm the same," said King Jädrich. "To explain the potency of our Mother, I tasted but one drop of that blood, and I, myself, have yet to need even a bite of Cervora's kin. This was several weeks ago as well."

Aveline's chest felt as though it were on fire. Her lungs didn't quite work right; they didn't let her take a full breath in. Her mind could form no thoughts, but the question screamed in her bones, her blood, her tight and quivering flesh.

They want more?

A sound warbled in her ear. Ristef was speaking again, but her ears started to ring, turning all his words into some muffled sound, and then drowning them out altogether. Aveline blinked, and in her mind's eye was one single flash of bone. Bone and antler.

They want to eat us again.

Aveline caught Aula's stare. She still stood at the Bishops' table, and when her eyes locked on Aveline—those huge, shining black eyes, just as deep and dark as the ones that had haunted Aveline for so long—Aveline tried to speak. Tried to scream. She wanted to tell them that not a single one of them deserved another drop of her, not a single one—and she wanted to turn and run, too. Turn and run, flee, disappear.

They're going to eat us.

Aveline made the mistake of blinking. Her eyes stayed shut this time, squeezed together. And in her mind's eye was one socket of that deer skull, one empty, black pool of shadows. It stared through her, even as her head began to spin and her body felt as if it were moving. Moving, she was moving, all while that doe-wraith stared at her, a single word hovering near.

Aveline.

A sharp pain burned through her knees and hips, and only then was she able to wrench her eyes open. Her palms burned, and when she looked down, she noticed how her hands clutched the stone steps leading up to the cathedral. Her knees and hips had cracked against the stairs' edges, too, and her wrists smarted as she lifted her hands up. Her chest rose and fell so rapidly that she thought that half the air in the stairwell had simply disappeared. Behind her was a sharp, screeching sound—so close, and yet so far away. Something scrabbled beside her. A wolf-shaped foot made of ice. Her *Unseelech*—at least one of them. It screeched, then spread its wing out wide just as she wanted to turn around; it blocked her view from the Bishops' table.

"She springs away like prey," came the drawl of that middle Bishop. "At the mention of bloodletting, she flees. Can she provide such a miracle in such a state?"

No, no, no, no, no—!

Aveline turned for the door at the top of the stairwell. The bright light that leaked into the cathedral made it impossible to see anything past the doorway; it was one large silver square in her mind, and she reached for it. Desperate, heart thudding, she reached for it.

Aveline.

It couldn't be. It couldn't happen. She tried to climb another step and hissed as the pain flared through her bones. But still, her arm reached for that doorway. She reached as if she could close the gap between her and the door with just a wish.

Aveline.

They wouldn't. They wouldn't suggest that I—

"Aveline!" The word hissed in her ear just as a freezing hand closed around her wrist. "Enough! What's the matter with you?"

Whoever grabbed her pulled her back enough to force her to look away from that doorway, and she found herself staring into eyes just like hers: lapis lazuli things of deep blue and gold. Erik frowned at her with enough intensity to kill her right there.

"Get up," he hissed. "Get up, and don't you dare move a muscle. We'll handle it from here. Just stand there and look like a god."

Look like a god. Aveline's entire body shuddered with such hot, bitter, wicked energy—energy enough to tear through the stone itself. And yet Erik's hand and words choked it. Before she knew it, she found herself standing again—not at the stairs, but at the table of Bishops. It was as if she'd never moved. In fact, she didn't remember how she even made it there.

She only knew, as the voices continued to warble around her after that, that the doe-wraith was peering at her from deep within the darkness of her mind.

Aveline, it whispered, in the form of her organs squelching from stress and her tendons twitching like puppet strings. *Aveline.*

No, no, they can't, they can't—

Aveline. Over and over, in a thousand different ways, the doe-wraith beckoned her.

Surely they don't mean—surely they won't ask me to— Aveline.

"L‌ord Rachfemd, thank you for joining us today." The newsman, a skinny-headed, patchy-haired youth in an ill-fitted black coat with simple stone buttons, fiddled with what was no doubt a stack of runestones in the drawer of his old, chipped desk. "Especially after you just arrived in town yesterday. I'm sure you're still getting settled, so I'll try to make this quick for you."

Erik nodded and stayed silent. He sat in a plain wooden chair, nestled in what felt more like a dungeon cell than anything else, what with the plain stone walls and the bare stone floors. Most newsrooms he'd been in before, especially in the early days of the bridal competition, were ones more suitable for lords to come through: ones that had thick velvet curtains, plush blue carpets for the floors, fine smelling sap sticks tucked in between bouquets of Winter flowers and fir branches. However, even if this new town of Hauslof they'd come to a day prior was bigger and more equipped than most, it was still no Rehrvig, and certainly no Vörnein.

Once the newsman had a suitable rune, he sat back up and set it on the desk between them. A little of his magic drifted from his fingertip to the stone like fresh snow, and it soon came to light, magic blooming like a moonflower from its surface. From that moment, it was recording all sound—and when the newsman spent a little more magic, that flower stretched up by a thin silver stem and pointed in Erik's direction. It sparkled from its center, and Erik knew it was recording his features, as well. The newsman released his magic, rubbed his glassy fingers together, and nodded before focusing his greenish-blue eyes on Erik. Aquamarines, no doubt. Most newsman and newswomen had such stones to better communicate with interviewees and the public alike.

With a smile, the newsman said, "So, again, Lord Erik Rachfemd of Rehrvig, welcome! Your cousin, the Queen and Cervora reborn, continues to make her first healing tour through the country. I understand that just a couple days ago, the Bishops verified her as well. You must be thrilled with the good news, yes?"

Erik arranged his face in as pleasant a smile as he could. "Of course," he said. "I always knew my cousin spoke true, but to have it verified by the Bishops is a reason for us all to rejoice. Our Mother has returned to us, truly."

Did she really fool the Bishops, though?

After all, her behavior didn't quite match the criteria of a soft and sacrificing goddess. It did match that of a doe, though—the way she scrambled at the mention of her own blood in the mouth of another. But Erik supposed it didn't matter. What did matter was that Erik get these news-runes out, and get them out quickly. The pace in which the merchant and traveler talk was spreading was alarming, to say the least, and it didn't seem that anything Isolde was doing was slowing it down. All along this tour, Erik took every opportunity to speak with the newsfolk who would then play these runes for the townspeople, so that all, whether able to read or not, would know the version of truth that Erik carefully crafted.

The newsman nodded, smiling wide. When he nodded, a few hairs fell from his head. "Truly! And please, do tell—what is this we hear about a new blessing from the Mother? She's gone around the country giving her frost to those affected by the melt, but we hear there's something else she can do."

Erik's soul squeezed in his head. He kept his smile tacked onto his lips, but he didn't know how much longer it would stay in place. The stunt that King devised was nothing short of a nightmare, and it made Erik want to wash his hands of all of this nonsense and run for Autumn, warmer weather be damned.

"Our Mother has come to cure our melt," Erik started, and he paused as he gathered how to speak without giving away too much. "However, as she's come through the lands, she's noticed a different problem. One where her kin are routinely slaughtered to the point of scarcity, and where both the Winter people and Winterlands alike suffer for this imbalance. But with growing populations and expanding cities, what other choice did we Ismären have, save to continue culling those white deer? Some domains even began to farm them like cattle, against every advice and warning of the Church."

It was a good lie that the Baron came up with. A scarcity of beasts. An overharvesting for a growing population. Yes, a good lie, and one that hid the rations that the southern and eastern nobility were sitting on in an effort to drive up hostility for the King. The only problem was that the King, for better or worse, was not one to sit on a problem and let it fester.

*If only he wouldn't have made such a mistake with the End-
less Winter.*

Erik composed himself and continued. "However, the
further we've gone along this tour, the more we've seen
the results of this scarcity. That's why our Mother has
decided to bless us further and give us the gift of eternal, everlasting magic."

Even the newsman blinked at that. His big smile fell
away, his mouth agape as he stared, awestruck. When he
gathered himself, he said, "Eternal? Can such a thing... is
that possible?"

"It is. Already, two have received such a blessing.
Their magic never fades, and they never need to eat
another bite of Cervora's kin. In fact, to eat it causes
sickness: an *overflow* of magic, if you can believe it."

"I... Mother forgive me, but I hardly can, no. How can
people come into this blessing?"

"Easily enough." Erik's soul quivered in his head
at the very thought of what Aveline was doing; it was
almost enough to make him choose a glassy, cracked
body over a magic-imbued one, thinking of bringing such a sullied cup to his lips. "Whenever she stops
to give a sermon in a town or city's cathedrals, bring
yourselves and all your family. The cups of communion
bloodwine she will bless there will have what you seek."

The newsman leaned further and further over the
counter while Erik spoke. It took all of Erik's focus
to keep his cadence even and his face composed; he
focused on the magical flower above the runestone as
much as possible, even as the newsman's bright eyes
hovered nearby.

"Thank you, Lord Rachfemd," the newsman said. He
spoke so quietly that Erik almost didn't hear him. "I'm
sure the people will be thrilled to hear this."

A moment later, the magic in the runestone condensed once more. The flower closed its petals and

settled into the runestone, locking all it had recorded away to be played at a later date. No doubt the newsman would make copies and distribute them to other towns, as well, with an announcement this large. However, as the newsman snatched the runestone with those glassy fingers, Erik couldn't help but wonder of the repercussions. The newsman's patchy hair stood out, as did that desperate stare as he cradled that runestone. It was right then, too, that Erik noticed the fault lines appearing by the newsman's lips. Thin, hardly noticeable fault lines that would soon expand into deeper, uglier cracks.

Too much. He stood to excuse himself, though everything he said to that half-hearing newsman was also little more than a warble in his own ears. *We've done too much.*

But at least this would secure Aveline as a valuable ransom to trade for the throne.

One drop per cup. That was how much of Aveline's blood she had to mix into each person's ration that came through the doors of the cathedral. That was how much would permanently replenish each and every person of their magic, so they might never have to eat the white deer again. That was it. That was all she had to give: one drop per person.

According to the last census, there were nearly eighty million people in Winter. Did she have eighty million drops of blood? Would she be able to make that much in her lifetime? Wouldn't the Winter people's population only continue growing as she filled vial after vial with blood, all while the doe-wraith raged in her bones and tried to stop her from bleeding altogether?

Aveline couldn't think of it then. She could only stand there at the cathedral's altar, before what looked to be the entire town of Hauslof, packed there in that one little space. However, she knew that the place could only hold a little over a thousand people in the pews, and that there wasn't much standing room on the side, so packed as it was, there couldn't have been more than fifteen hundred people. It was far less than Hauslof's total population, far less. Which meant she'd have to do this for several days.

"Ismären," she called, still unable to call them *her* Ismären, "welcome. On this morning, I invite you all to partake in something wonderful." Her mouth filled with bile as the words clawed past her throat; she'd barely had enough rest to stave off the sting that all her ice breath caused her flesh. Still, she lifted her hands high— holding back a wince as her altered, tightened sleeves pulled against her bandages—and she let her raw voice ring out across the cathedral. "Your Mother has seen your woes. I have seen you melted, and I have brought you healing frost. Now I see you thirsty, and I bring you something good to drink. Here before me," she gestured to the table, then plucked a vial of her own blood off it and held it up, "is my blessing to you. One drop in every cup. One drop of my blessing in every cup, and you shall never thirst again. Are you ready, children of the Iswold? For such a blessing?"

Applause crackled through the auditorium. So many people clacking their ice hands together at once made it seem as if the entire cathedral had come under a furious hailstorm, and it made Aveline's skin twitch. Her hands twitched, too, with the urge to crush the vial. Her muscles even tried, that old beast in her bones worming its way up to take hold of her body once again.

No.

Aveline closed her eyes and saw it—the edge of that doe-wraith's bone face. She put all her will into that word: *No.* And she let it know—in images both from her memories and her imagination—just how much more they'd have to suffer together if she lost even a drop of what she'd already spilled.

Yet all that she felt in response was that offer. That wordless offer, so tempting and sweet. That promise of survival, that vow for justice.

Aveline.

She forced her eyes open and picked up the communion cup. It was already half full with the first ration of deer blood. With all her thoughts vacated from her head, and all feeling numbed from her body, to the point that her bones felt as if they were made of iron, Aveline poured the vial of her own blood into that cup. It mixed together right away. Within a moment, Aveline couldn't tell any difference between the silver that ran in her veins and the silver that bled from those beasts out in the woods. The thought left her mouth bitter.

But the ratio of the first cup was complete. This cup alone would meet the lips of dozens of people that morning, just one sip per person, and then that would be that. No longer would any of those people need to destroy the white deer for their own magic. A strange pain lanced through her chest at the thought, but she ignored it and raised her hands over the cup. A little crackle of her magic flickered from her palms and dusted the cup—just for show, just so the people would think she actually did some kind of alchemy there, what with the mixing of blood and the casting of miracles— and Aveline spoke again.

"By the might of my name, Ismären, I bless you. I free you from your fear of the sun and all its heat with my frost, and I release you from the bonds of your bodies with this cup." She stopped her magic and lifted it up high. "This is the blood of my kin, sanctified, purified, and made complete. Never again shall your bodies crack for want of the life it brings you."

Aveline's tongue felt thick. Her lips felt bloated, fleshy, clumsy. Yet she didn't dare let herself trip on the ridiculous script that Jädrich made her rehearse in the dead of night. Nor did she let herself blink away the burn of exhaustion that still stung her eyes. She said her script, set the cup down, and then, hardly registering the rows of ice-folk, she lifted her arms like a mother inviting her children to her.

"Come, now," she said, more to the cathedral air than to anyone sitting in the pews, "claim this miracle."

And so they did. One by one, sip by sip, minute by minute and hour by hour, Aveline continued the charade in the cathedral, followed by another several hours in the cathedral basement, washing her frost over yet more dilapidated people. Where she once felt something for the people that came to her—and especially for the children, with their eyes missing from the melt, their arms little more than icicles in early Spring and one or both of their legs ruined—by that point, she hardly registered the things she was showering in frost as people at all. They were all just shapes to her—silvery shapes that moved and warbled and wailed when she refroze their cursed bodies. Moreover, by that point in the tour, even if her throat still ached from constant frost, it didn't seem to hurt quite the same way. It was as if her throat were growing scales on the inside, so as to defend her flesh from a cold so deep that it threatened to bite her flesh dead. She never thought she'd grow used to a cold deeper than that of Winter itself.

When the last woman to see Aveline in that basement was frozen again, her arm a lumpy, yet perfectly solid limb, she'd squealed something and hurried up the stairs. Aveline didn't catch what she'd said; she'd only smiled and let the girl run off. That girl's one thick braid swung as she ran, and her old wool skirts slapped her legs as she rushed off to whoever she had to share good news with.

Meanwhile, Aveline rubbed her throat. It ached. The muscles were tense, the flesh dry and cold to the point that breathing in felt like she was swallowing razors. Her stomach, too, twisted with a sharp pain. It'd been hours since she last ate. And even though she had a cup of snow nearby, swallowing down an icy lump of stuff wasn't the same as drinking water proper. More often than not, that bowl of snow sat mostly untouched, and her throat suffered for it—as did her dry tongue and her aching head.

Something hard and cold bumped her ankle. When she looked down, there were her two *Unseelechs*, laying quietly at her feet. One looked up at her with eyes so full of light that it seemed like it had two full moons in its head, and it made a soft chittering sound through its needle-teeth, as if asking her: *are you okay?*

"I'm fine," she said as she stroked its hair. It was thick, soft, and so very cold. "Just tired. Tired, my baby."

"I imagine you'll want to go straight back to the manor to rest, then."

Aveline startled so hard that she hit her elbow on the table. It sent a sharp arrow of pain shooting up her arm, and she hissed and clutched it close. Her *Unseelechs*, too, startled by both the voice and Aveline's sudden movement, shot up and flanked her on the table. They spread their wings wide and hissed, only to then crouch and cower next to her as they saw who it was that spoke.

Jädrich adjusted a button on his shirt cuff as he approached. His footsteps were silent, quieted by the magic in his boots, and it seemed as if his very presence were muted. Whatever he did, it made it so once again, Aveline—and even her babies—didn't notice him coming. She cradled her elbow and narrowed her eyes.

"You don't have to sneak around like a rat."

"Nor must I announce myself to an audience of one."

Aveline frowned and pointed to her *Unseelechs*. "Three, you mean."

Jädrich didn't respond to that. He only stared at her, waiting for her to join him so that he could bring her back to whatever guest house they stayed in. But as Aveline held her smarting arm, she studied him—looked for any sign that the contract was affecting him in any way. After all, he signed her terms: agreed to never let her come to harm. And there had been harm. Plenty of it. Yet somehow—

After a moment, Jädrich said, "Is something wrong?"

She blinked her thoughts away and chewed on her words before spitting them out. "I just wonder what it feels like to you—when our marriage contract activates. When it punishes you for not upholding the terms you agreed to."

He blinked once, then said, "I've upheld my terms, so I wouldn't know."

That made Aveline blink, too. In what world could he say that with a straight face? Was an accident like she just had not considered harm? Was the raw, aching pain in her throat not considered harm? Was having Karina cut her wrist not considered harm?

Aveline.

Her flurry of questions, of prickling nerves, seemed to have nudged that doe-wraith again. She could feel it in her bones: the essence of it, hiding there, leaking its sentiments into her blood and her flesh. Every beat of her heart translated the feeling that settled deep into her gut like some slimy black rot.

He's wicked.

Aveline held up her arm and yanked back the sleeve of her dress. She winced as the tighter fabric scraped over the bandage. That sting in her skin was familiar, and sure enough, a little spot of silver suddenly soaked through the bandage.

"This doesn't trip your end of the bargain? Did you not agree to protect me from all harm, Jädrich?"

He went so still that Aveline thought he reverted into a lifeless, soulless ice doll. Those bright blue eyes pinned her with their icy chill. Seeing them in the starlight, seeing that shade of blue, it reminded her of where they came from—of what they were made of. It only made the rot in her stomach spread further through her body.

"I agreed to put my country above all other things," he said. Each word was calm, slow, and yet it sounded like the warning growl of a big cat. "You, too, agreed to be the Queen and Mother your people need you to be."

"Yes, but I can't be that with my safety at risk."

"Your safety is not at risk," he said, as if his word was the deciding factor in what separated truth from lie. "You have not come to harm. If you wanted to bind me to protect you from *every* danger, even from bumping your arm against a table or losing a few drops of blood, then you should've written so in the Faun's Tongue. It would've made your demands more tangible."

Each word was measured, slow, as if Aveline were but some stupid child having common sense explained to her. Still, her already ashen mouth went so dry that she had nothing to swallow. The cold air whipped past her raw throat, stinging it with every breath, as she turned those words over in her head.

Should I have written in the Faun's Tongue? But she couldn't. The damn doe-wraith—it wouldn't let her write or speak it. *Does that mean my contract isn't as—?*

"Come," Jädrich said, and he held out his arm to her. "You have your evening meal waiting for you in our guest room. I'll come to bed with you and stay until you fall asleep."

Her mind raced. *Am I safe? Am I protected?* The rot in her gut became something of a beast of its own, chewing at her stomach, twisting it in knots. That was the only thing making all this exhaustion and pain worth it: the promise of safety later, of a place to rest and be at peace. *But do I really have that? Am I guaranteed protection if I didn't write my demands correctly? Am I—?*

"You're not going to stay?" Aveline blurted her question. "In bed, I mean. You won't stay the night?"

Jädrich offered a small smile and shook his head. "Not tonight. I have work to do while you sleep."

What other work? What are you—?

"Come," Jädrich said again, his hand outstretched. That one word scrambled Aveline's thoughts enough for her to focus on him. "You're tired. Let's get you the rest you need."

But what—?

Aveline squeezed her eyes shut and snuffed her thoughts. They would only drive her into a frenzy; that much, she knew. But as she closed her eyes, she once again caught sight of the beast that lived in her bones— the sheen of its skull, the eerie, ghoulish glow of whatever phantom light radiated from its body. It stared at her as if it, rather than Jädrich, was expecting Aveline to come closer.

Aveline.

She shot to her feet and wrenched her eyes open. Then she drew in a deep, painful breath and blew it back out. Without another word, she took Jädrich's hand, and as her *Unseelechs* followed behind them, she forced every thought out of her head. Forced her mind to be so purely silent that she had nothing to focus on except the stairs and stone directly ahead of her. Yet still, in the deep corners of her soul, there was that one sweet, beckoning call ringing out to her.

Aveline.

THE PINE TREES WERE GROWING THINNER AND THINNER. Soon there would only be the pockets of forest on the other side of the near-eastern cliffs that had any trees at all, and once they passed over them, that was it—they'd be halfway through the King and Queen's first healing tour.

But that second healing miracle—

Ristef shoved the thought away. He stared out the carriage window and counted any trees he saw among the houses of the town. He wasn't sure what he expected on this tour, really. Maybe spending so many years working in the castle made him forget what the rest of the Winterlands looked like. Maybe he expected the towns to look more unique than they did in each hold. But no—every town looked about the same. White houses. Brown beams layered across them. Slanted, shingled brown roofs. Oftentimes, flower boxes in the windows. All set tightly together on cobblestone roads.

The only things that stuck out to Ristef as they rushed
from one place to the next was whether a town had a
little stone fountain in its center, or whether it had a
massive statue of Cervora instead.

Villages, as they came through, were often full of
plain, squat white houses and dirt roads, only a handful
of people in each one. Those were easier to get through.
Oftentimes, their carriages didn't even set up to stay
a night; Aveline would be taken up to the cathedral,
where she would freeze whoever needed freezing, and
then she would get back in the carriage, and off they'd
go again to the next place. Ristef didn't see her all too
much anymore, but when he did, he knew she was tired.
Her face seemed so much longer, and she never had
those dark patches under her eyes before. More, she was
wearing higher collared dresses, as well as dark leg-
gings that hid all parts of her save for her face and hair,
which she started to keep tied up and out of her narrow,
sharply angled face. It did nothing to hide the shadows
that pooled in her eye sockets or the way her shoulders
sagged when she thought no one was looking.

Hold on, Aveline. It was a brutal tour, yes, but a necessary one. And a short one. Only two months. Others
wouldn't be so fast paced and demanding, surely. No
doubt those miracles she did for the people took a toll,
but if anyone could make them happen, it was her. *You
can do it.*

And already, the results of her efforts were spreading.
After the Bishops confirmed Aveline as Cervora's icon,
the plans to distribute her blood discreetly began, and
the King was certainly right to keep the source of that
infinite magic a secret. Whatever Aveline's cousin did,
that slimy viscount, it had people practically beating the
doors of the cathedral down to receive their blessings
from Aveline. Maybe that was why she bolted for the
stairwell the day the Bishops questioned her—because

she knew the frenzy people would get into. If they'd
known the blessing came from the very blood in her
bones, would they have—?

No. No, our people know better. Cervora's icon was supposed to be inedible, anyway. Untouchable. *But... didn't I
drink from—?*

Again, Ristef shook the thought away. If he thought
too long, he'd confuse himself; that much he knew.
Theology was for the people in robes and surrounded
by books, not people like him. But it seemed to be
brightening things, at least. Where people were once
more curious than reverent, now people came in droves
to see their Queen and Mother, and they came smiling and calling for her, arms outstretched—as it always
should've been. Aveline always deserved a welcome like
that, rather than the silent stares she used to get. All was
going well. All would be okay. Ristef knew that, because
he had complete faith in Aveline.

"We're here!"

The carriage came to a stop, and Ristef glanced at
Aula, who was looking from one window to the next
as if that'd help her see where they were any better. It
seemed that they were tucked under the awning of a
bigger building, and as Ristef helped Aula out, he saw
that the building was a storefront. In the windows were
mannequins in fine dresses, hats, and other such things,
all frilled in lace and studded with gems and silver and
even pearls.

"Ristef, I hope your arms are up to snuff," Aula said
as she dug into her bag and leafed through a little
journal. It seemed the bag was made of fabric scraps,
given it was a patchwork mess of all kinds of different
colors and textures. When Aula looked back at him, she
beamed. "You'll be holding onto all the samples and
things I grab."

Ristef's brow quirked. "What if I need my hands free to defend you from danger?"

That made Aula chuckle. "Danger? Are you worried the store clerks will make a pin cushion out of me?"

"You never know."

Aula swatted Ristef's arms and shook her head. "I think I know enough. Now, no more chatter! We have a lot to see before we can get back to the mayor's home. Maybe a new dress will make Aveline feel a little better."

They both paused at that. Aula's smile faltered, too. In that room with those Bishops, truthfully, Ristef wondered if maybe he shouldn't have said anything at all about Aveline's blood—either to the Bishops or the King, whose idea it was to share that secret with the head of Winter's faithful. The way Aveline reacted to such an idea—the way Aula reacted to Aveline, the horror carved into her face—Ristef couldn't unsee either of those things. It was only with much assurance that Aveline's health wouldn't be jeopardized that Ristef could even get Aula to speak to him after the inspection was over.

"Well," Aula said as she pinned that smile back on her face, "let's quit wasting daylight! Come on!"

She didn't wait for him as she hurried for the fabric store's door. Ristef didn't hurry after her, either. While it was his job to keep her safe, he was fine taking his time and getting away from the same wooden walls of the mayor's house or the same stone streets outside the cathedral. It seemed that was all his life was in the past few weeks: a life of standing and staring at nothing, more than his usual duties at the castle had him doing. The King was with Aveline, as were the other guards; Ristef didn't need to worry so much about whether or not she'd be kept safe. He only worried if she'd stay rested enough, which no guard could help with.

Once Ristef made it inside the fabric store, he stayed

by the door. The clerk at the shop, another young woman with an apron full of needles and pockets of threads
and thimbles, was hurrying to tie up her mass of messy
hair as she chatted with Aula and led her between several tables full of all manners of fabric. Shiny green fabric,
dense, dark blue fabric, fabric whiter than snow—so
much lined those tables, and then along the walls were
dressers full of things that the clerk pulled out to show
off: buttons, beads, pearls, and more. On top of those
dressers were spools of different patterns of lace, which
Ristef overheard were made in house by skilled bobbin
lace artists. All the while, Aula listened with such focus,
the kind of focus she only seemed to have when she had
a needle between her fingers.

There was only one time Ristef ever got to see Aula
in her element. On a day where Aveline needed a new
dress fitted, Aula flittered around her like a songbird,
snipping threads, pinning things, measuring fabric and
adjusting sleeves. Her face would pinch when she focused like that; gone was the light hearted, mischievous
thing, and in her place was a soldier who could draw
taught a thread like a soldier drew a bow.

I wouldn't mind being assigned to Aula more. It was a joy,
seeing her work—and it passed the time quickly, quip-
ping back and forth with her. Like he had with Aveline
during their walks around the castle together.

Another thing that fascinated Ristef was that, by
the things Aula created, she had both the means *and*
the money to dress herself in something flashier, too,
but looking at her and the clerk together, it seemed
seamstresses didn't do that. They both wore plain grey
dresses, simple cloth like any peasant would wear, full of
makeshift patches and pockets for storing yet more little
bits and pieces for their work. They devoted so much
time to their passion and their craft, and it puzzled
Ristef as to why they wouldn't adorn themselves in the

same kind of quality work. He figured it would've been
a good opportunity to advertise their skill. But then, if
Aveline wore Aula's work, he supposed that was all the
advertising—and all the work—she'd ever need.

"And we have several selections of patterns on black,
if you're looking for something more..."

The clerk began showing Aula around the corner in
a different room, and Ristef was compelled to follow.
He kept his distance, so as not to crowd the women and
make them uncomfortable, but he had to keep eyes on
his charge at all times if he was to do his job correctly.
No one could be trusted at the end of the day. Not the
most innocent store clerk. Not even Aula. Though he
imagined, by the way the yellows and pinks of joy and
excitement flashed around Aula's head, that she was just
a seamstress that loved her work and loved the opportunity to dress her Queen in it. He could only hope that
she was right—that a new dress would make Aveline feel
better, just as it made Aula feel better to make one in the
first place.

Karina had no one to share her thoughts with, and so
she bet with herself: that orphan would not last.

There'd been no time for the poor fool to process
anything. In fact, if Karina remembered correctly, it
didn't seem like the orphan heard a word after she'd
been pulled back to stand before the Bishops. The men,
those men—they were the ones there, talking about
how they might distribute bits and pieces of the orphan
to the people, like some solstice roast, while Karina
and that seamstress girl stared in shock at the whole
ordeal. Karina could still see it in her mind's eye: the
way Aveline scrambled for the stairs like a rat, desperate
to escape all those gemstone eyes and their unsavory

thoughts, and the way her strange creatures tried desperately to shield her from all onlookers with their big wings, their hissing and their gnashing teeth. After witnessing that disaster with the Bishops, then coming to begin this new horror of a "miracle" right after they'd reached the next town on their route, Karina felt for the orphan for the first time. Felt a deep, gnawing pity that threatened to pull her heart down into a dark pit.

At the bottom of that pit was a single thorn—a prick of guilt. Because Karina was the one Erik argued to have presiding over the bloodletting Aveline had to do.

A row of six empty bottles sat on the table, along with a bowl of untouched berries, a tiny, ancient white candle with only a bit of wick left to light, and a roll of gauze much like what Karina used to wrap up her ears and flesh eye. Each could hold something like two thousand drops of blood, according to the doctors they'd taken the bottles from—enough to bless twelve thousand people. Karina had already filled three with Aveline, and yet one had already been drained, and more was needed. Of course more was needed. As it was, twelve thousand drops—that wasn't even a fraction of Winter's population. If Aveline were to stay by that King, no doubt she'd find herself bled dry within a year.

But that was why Karina was there doing this morbid task—to monitor Aveline's health. Erik told the board of Bishops it was because Karina had extensive training with Cervora's kin and knew how much damage creatures of flesh could bear before their bodies started failing them, but of course, it was really because Karina was a creature of flesh herself. One who wouldn't be tempted to take a bite out of Aveline, like no doubt any magic-starved Ismar would be, should they know exactly how their communion cup would be "blessed."

Karina and the orphan sat together behind the closed door of the guest room, which Aveline didn't seem to be getting much sleep in, if the dark circles under her eyes were any indication. They sat in silence for a long time. Long enough that Karina was able to take in every detail of the quaint room—the darkly stained pine furniture covered in fine silver-blue cloth, the thick wolfskin rugs and the silver candlesticks that hadn't seen candles in them in over a century. The bed itself was one with a dark wooden frame and a fine, light blue canopy, with thick blue curtains tied up to the bedposts in silver cords. One large window led to a balcony where one could watch the hustle and bustle of the town's main square—but by this time in the evening, the sun was already long gone, and the only light coming through that window was from the starlights from down below.

Aveline fingered the handle of a little cup on a saucer. It was half full with snow, which she'd been eating with a spoon as if it were a treat and not simply a more ridiculous way of getting water in this frozen country. However, she stared into that cup as if it would open some hole she could escape through, the way a mouse might scurry behind the walls to find a way outside. Her eyes had those dark gray bags underneath them, and her hair was stringy and disheveled in a way that suggested she hadn't brushed it in at least a day. And she still looked far too thin for someone the King claimed to be feeding.

Karina's voice finally shattered the silence like a plate hitting the ground. "Well, shall we get started? Sooner we're done, sooner you can rest."

Aveline's fingers curled tight around the cup's handle. Her shoulders tensed, and her lips turned into a hard frown. It only made that gnawing, dark feeling in Karina's chest grow all the more potent, because for a moment, it seemed Karina wasn't talking to a woman, but an animal. And what animal liked to have its skin split? See its blood leak free?

Fool. Karina could've sighed, but she kept it tight in her lungs. *You fool. You took such a terrible gamble, placing bets on that King.*

But it was too late, too late by far, for the fool to begin having the regrets that painted themselves onto her face. Karina slipped a hand into the folds of her thick woolen dress and produced two things: her long unused flint and steel and a small paring knife she always carried around. Even if fire were illegal in Winter, Karina kept her flint and steel handy when she traveled so she might cook whatever creatures she caught. She kept the knife for the odd string she might've had to cut off her cloaks, and once, she kept it to peel the occasional apple she bought from the markets, but now, it was as good as anything to open the orphan's veins. The ease with which Karina made shallow cuts on their first bloodletting was proof.

Karina lit the candle, and the orangey light of the flame ate up the eerie blue starlight. It flickered and crackled for a moment before settling into a small, still flame. Karina then held her paring knife over the flame, making more of the blade go black. There was no way to get a whole pot of water to boil in a land where even this candle flame could've landed Karina in prison, and so this was the best Karina could hope to do to ensure her knives wouldn't cause Aveline's flesh to rot and fill with pus.

When she was satisfied that the knife was clean, Karina blew out the candle and held her hand out. "Give me your arm."

But Aveline kept staring into that cup. Her frown cut her face so deep that it looked like a child scrawled her lips on in charcoal. Her hands shook, and her brows twitched as if she were fighting her own face from crumpling into tears.

Oh, goodness.

"Aveline," Karina started, "you need to—"

"I'm trying!"

Karina blinked. What did that mean, that she was *trying?* All Karina could see was the orphan's shoulders getting closer and closer to her ears as she hunched over, and her fingers twitching against the cup. But her skin flushed a greyish-silver, and it was clear that she was making a great effort to move—only to go nowhere.

"Just—" Karina shot her hand out and snatched the orphan's wrist, careful not to grab where she'd already been cut, then dragged her arm over—but it was like dragging an ox with one hand. The strength in that seemingly frail woman was enough to make Karina nervous. "Just give me your arm."

Aveline squeezed her eyes shut, then took one long, deep breath. As it slowly hissed out, her fingers finally unwrapped from that cup, and Karina was able to pull her arm closer bit by bit until finally, the orphan re-laxed. Her hand dropped against the table, right in front of Karina, and the rest of her breath gushed out.

Karina undid the gauze. Already, her shallow cuts were healing, but they were still scabbed and tender. She inspected the orphan's wrist for more of those silver-grey veins and muttered, "You don't need to be so afraid. I'm not going to butcher you."

The orphan's fingers twitched. Then she whispered, "I know."

"Okay. Good." Karina gathered the bottles closer, then pulled the stopper from one and picked Aveline's arm up. She positioned the orphan's wrist over the bottle opening and held her knife up to it. "Are you ready?"

"Yes." Aveline's gaze didn't lift from the floor. "Just hurry up."

Karina watched the orphan a moment longer. With brows so tightly scrunched and a tooth chewing her lip nearly to ribbons, Karina would've thought that Aveline was being asked to bleed her firstborn dry rather than just lose a little of her own blood. The only time she dragged her eyes up was when Karina's blade touched her, and then she was staring at the door as if waiting for someone.

With a bit of pressure and a quick pull, Aveline's skin split. She flinched and flexed her wrist, which only made the silver blood that pooled there gush out faster, and Karina was careful not to let any spill. There could be no room for waste, for the orphan's sake. Yet as Karina held her wrist steady, it felt like she was holding a wrist made of rock; the orphan was so stiff, her breath so sharp, that Karina could've scolded her for being so dramatic. Had she never known injury in her life, to be acting this way? Karina found that hard to believe.

Aside from that, though, the two women stayed silent until the last four bottles were filled. Once the last drop fell into the bottle, Karina quickly turned Aveline's wrist and wrapped it tight with gauze. The cut wasn't too deep or too long, and so Karina didn't doubt it would close up soon.

Karina glanced at the table and hooked that little bowl of frozen berries closer. Then she pushed it towards Aveline. "When was the last time you had something to eat?"

Aveline pulled her arm away the moment Karina let it go. She tucked it into herself and stared at the table, ignoring the bowl. "This morning."

"What was it?"

"Fish," Aveline muttered with a shrug. Her eye snapped to the bowl, but only for a moment. "Berries."

For every fox's tail. The old Autumn expression flitted across Karina's head as she sucked down her sigh. She pushed the bowl even closer to the orphan. "You need more than that. Especially if you're out here bloodletting for these people now."

That got the orphan to finally look up from the table. She blinked once, then twice, and her jaw shifted before she whispered, "I know. But," Aveline shook her head, "I'm tired. Too tired. It makes me sick—to eat too much."

Karina sucked her teeth at the excuse. "Then you'll either faint or die. If that's what you want, then—"

"It is *not* what I want."

That silence Karina shattered came right back down upon them, like a thin layer of ice over a pond's surface. It wouldn't take much to break it, Karina knew, but the way the orphan hunched into herself, Karina thought better of it and kept her mouth shut. There was nothing she could say to the poor fool that would make this situation she got herself into any better.

May the rebel lords be kind to you, Karina thought. Whatever happened to this half-Summer thing wasn't Karina's concern afterwards; only the results of the ransom and the rights to her home were. But still—*still.* In the shadows under Aveline's eyes were memories of Karina's own sleepless nights and near-empty store rooms, of "fires" that were barely more than live coals during the era where the King's men would patrol the forests for fleshlings in hiding. Yes, Karina thought it best to leave the woman be, and so she gathered her things—the knife, the bottles, the candle, the firestarter—and tucked it all back into her dress's inner pockets, then got up to leave.

"Karina," the orphan started. She eyed Karina head on, and the gold flecks in her eyes seemed to sparkle.

With a blink, Karina said, "What?"

"That knife," Aveline nodded to it, "can you stab me with it?"

Karina almost laughed. She only didn't because she saw how tight that orphan's face was—how much that request was not a joke. The orphan looked up and pinned Karina with that starry-eyed stare and waited, though by the tightness in her lips, it didn't seem she waited patiently. Karina blinked.

"Why would you want me to do that?"

"Just to see something. Please. Can you stab me? Not to kill, just to injure. At the very least, you could run at me like you're about to stab me." The orphan stood up, her stare never leaving Karina's face. At her full height, she seemed even more lanky, more unnaturally lithe. "Go on. Do it."

"I," Karina shook her head, "no. I can't do that."

"Karina," Aveline snapped. Her hands balled into bony fists. "Please. Just try. I need to see something."

What are you—? Karina shook her head. "No. I won't. I don't know what game you want to play, orphan, but I'm not playing it with you."

Aveline stared. In such dim starlight, her typically deep blue eyes seemed nearly black, save for the golden flecks in them. As they stared each other down, Karina found her mind wandering to distract her from the prickle creeping up her neck. *Are her eyes stones? Or flesh? How did they get like that?*

Finally, after a few long and quiet moments, Aveline let out a breath and deflated. Her hands opened and her shoulders dropped. Her face went long and gray, too— though not with any kind of peace.

"Go," Aveline muttered. "Leave me be for the night, please. I should sleep. So I can be up early enough tomorrow."

She didn't even wait for Karina to respond. The orphan went right to her bed, still wearing her clothes, and climbed onto that mattress. Karina didn't even think of anything to respond with before some glitter of silver magic came and flicked every wrapped cord off the bed's curtains. The thick fabric dropped into place, and then Aveline was sealed off inside.

"You should eat those berries," Karina said, but her words practically bounced off the bed's curtains. There was no response.

So with nothing else to say and no reason to stay staring at blue cloth, Karina shook her head. Then she turned and left the guest room, hurrying off to her own quarters, where she could once again get to work with her puppets. Like Aveline, she had a job to do—but unlike Aveline, that job wasn't entirely draining her of her will to live.

Not yet, at least.

With a huff, Karina shook the thought off. She dodged a couple maids, took a corner too fast, but none of it mattered, as she was focused only on thinking up a new idea for her next puppet tricks. New ideas, and new things to tell the people about their Queen through them. Things that were not so crass and threatening as their Queen could really be.

*W*HY IS NO ONE ANSWERING ME?

Efir did everything the ice-woman said to. He'd poured the silver blood on the runestone. He'd thought of his father, and all the sunshine and warmth that surrounded him. Then he'd waited and waited as that runestone pulsed on a rock in the snow. Waited so long that his joints ached as the deep cold pushed deeper and deeper into the fabric of his clothes. Waited so long that he almost forgot what warmth and sunshine even felt like. All the while, he begged for someone to answer him, as if his thoughts could reach as far as the Ismären's magic.

But the runestone blinked its eerie silver glow one more time, then fell dead.

Efir stared at the blood-crusted thing. He'd used about all the blood the ice-woman gave him; there wasn't more than a couple drops left in the bottle. She

said he could hunt more of those white deer they ate—
but he hadn't seen a single one in this entire nightmare
of a mission. Two drops, maybe—two tries—that was all
he had left if he wanted to contact anyone at all.

I need answers.

The thought pierced him as if someone were spear-
ing a needle into his skull. It was as if it were trying to
go from the back of his head through his eyes; it *killed,*
that need for answers.

Someone has to answer me.

He hadn't wanted to call the ice-woman. In fact, he
had no intention of ever contacting her again; had all
gone as it was supposed to, then the King would be
dead, the witch captured, and the country doomed to
whatever fate his father decided for it. But she—that
ice-woman—

Did she know?

She insisted so heavily on *three weeks.* So heavily.
Perhaps she knew the King would leave sooner and
meant to have him trapped by that vicious woman in
the castle. Perhaps this whole cooperation between
these rogue Ismären and the rest of the Ringlands was a
farce. Perhaps an Ismar was an Ismar after all, and they
truly never cared about the other seasons, and this was
all a ploy to gather evidence so that Winter could legally
retaliate against the rest of the Ringlands.

*Legal right or not, the Mockeries have done enough to
warrant their death.* In the end, three countries against
one would prevail, whether legally or militarily. *No, that
woman would be a fool to try such a plot.*

And yet, as Efir stared at that bottle, covered in
sparkling silver crust, he knew there was only one way
to find out. She said to only call her at night, so Efir
decided it was night. Truthfully, whether it was day or
night, Efir didn't know; he'd been crawling through
thick woods for what seemed like years, and the pine

trees blotted out what little light this country got. All he knew was that his head was beginning to *ache,* as if it were being split in two, and that one thought was the axe driving down on his skull.

I need answers.

So he rubbed the blood and crust off the runestone, flaked it off the bottle, and poured one more drop onto that little black square. Then, as it lit up, he focused with all his might on the ice-woman's black eyes, mousy face, and strange hat with three points.

The rune's shine began to blink. It pulsed there once, twice, three times—and Efir braced for yet another dead end. In the distance, a tree branch snapped, and birds flew away.

Answers. All Efir could see was white and grey—snow and stone. *I need answers.*

"I told you not to call me during the day."

Efir flinched at the sudden voice. He looked up from the runestone and saw it: the apparition of that ice-woman, as if her ghost had come to him. She didn't move at all; she only stared ahead with those empty eyes, a hollow, doll-like thing. His father was the same way that one time he'd managed to speak with him.

"Isolde Beurvich," he said—though the words didn't feel like they'd come from him. Nor did he know why he said them.

The apparition was quiet for a moment before the woman's voice sounded again. "Are you well? What happened? Why are you calling me?"

"To find something out," he muttered. He shifted his jaw side to side, then stretched it, as if to confirm that his mouth was *his,* along with the words he spoke. "I can't reach my father. Have you been able to speak with him?"

Another pause. "I haven't had a reason to try."

"Hmm." Efir stared at the two dark spots in that

woman's face. Those eyes reminded him of the black beads used for the eyes of stuffed children's toys. "Even though things didn't go as planned? With your King?"

"I've," the ice-woman hesitated, "I've been trying to prepare myself for this unexpected turn of events. I'm sure all can work out still—"

"Did you know the King was going to leave earlier than you told me?"

"No," she said, right away. "I did not. None of us did." Before Efir could say anything else, she added, "And you? Are you following him back along this trail?"

"Trying to."

"How close to the capital did you get before you realized he was already gone?"

A haze settled on Efir's mind. It made his thoughts thick like syrup, and it made his tongue feel heavy. His own voice seemed muffled in his ears, as if someone stuffed them with cotton, but he knew he was speaking—could vaguely feel his lips forming the words.

"I got into his chambers."

It was getting hard to focus. Efir needed to sleep. He needed sleep and running water—no more just eating snow from the ground. He needed a hot bowl of soup. More than all of that, he needed an afternoon sunning himself. A warm sand bath. He needed anything other than this hellish Winter land.

"Did anyone see you?"

Efir blinked as if it would make some of the haze leave his mind. He didn't want to admit that he'd been caught. More for his pride than anything. But maybe the ice-woman could help him, if he told her what happened. Ever since he left that castle, he hadn't felt right.

Specifically, he hadn't felt *alone*.

"A lady," he muttered, though his tongue was so thick that he almost couldn't get it out. He had to fight to say it. "Guards. They did something—do you know what they—?"

Suddenly, the ghoulish image of that ice-woman cut off. It disappeared as quickly as it came, and the rune died down to a lifeless black rock, as well. Efir stared at it. Despite how bleary his gaze was, and how much his bones ached, he couldn't help but stare at it. His lungs tightened with a breath he couldn't release, and the haze lifted from his mind until he could see it so crisply—that *damn square*. All the while, another thought echoed in his mind and then winked out, like the ember on a candlewick after the flame had just been blown out.

Isolde.

The crack of stone and the shattering of glass echoed in Efir's ears, and then there was only the crunch of his footsteps over long-dead pine needles as he continued his march south.

Aula plucked scraps of silk and gauze and tulle from the things she'd bought a few days ago, but none of it seemed right. None of it. All the blues, purples, silvers—none of it inspired her. What kind of dress could she make that would take any of the exhaustion out of Aveline's face? Or the pain from her bandaged wrists, which Aula mended her dresses to hide? She rubbed her hands against her face and shifted the velvet over her perfectly frozen ice. Even a good month later, she still couldn't believe that her face was solid again. How could she, when she'd been so used to it getting softer and softer over the course of a century?

I have to try. Aula peered through her fingers at the scraps of cloth, even as her imagination failed to bring any of them to life. *I have to try to cheer her up.*

Especially since Aveline was capable of so many

miracles—more than Aula even thought possible. As grotesque as it was for her to have to bleed herself for the Ismären's sake again, and as horrible as Aula felt watching Aveline's panic overtake her reason, she was truly a divine creature, wasn't she? Who else but a goddess could do things like Aveline did? Maybe, if Aveline could freeze Aula's melt and permanently enrich the people with magic, then she could melt the King's resolve, too. Could make the seasons move again. And maybe, *maybe,* Aveline could find some way to un-shatter, un-freeze, and un-kill Aula's long-dead husband, too.

It was a stupid thought. But she still thought it. After all, if Cervora could revive herself, why couldn't she revive anyone else?

I don't even know where his pieces are.

She squeezed her eyes shut. Memories of that day filled her head: the day the town guards came to drag out the last fleshlings hiding in Winter. After the King's decree to stop moving the seasons, the mass deportations began. Many of Aula's friends and neighbors were rounded up from the city and driven south. Only a bold few tried to hide and wait out the King's irrational decision, and Aula's husband was one of them. He didn't want to leave, even when Aula warned him what Winter would do—refused to leave, no matter how much she begged him to save himself and get back to Spring.

But he didn't, and eventually, that black day came. The same day that had been repeating for four years at that point: a bleak day, the grey clouds casting their dingy color over a grey city. By that point, even the colors of Aula's fabrics had started looking grey to her, what with no sunlight to bring out their color. Starlight didn't do any of her fabrics and designs justice, no matter how much she tried to match her designs to that silver light. It never worked. None of it worked.

And neither did the blankets, after only one month of the endless Winter. Neither did blankets, neither did three pairs of socks and gloves, neither did layers and layers of furred coats. None of those things worked for her husband, Amadi, that gentle Spring butterfly. In a country where fire was banned outright—even just the coals that he used to keep his separate bed warm enough in their Winter home—what was there for him to do, except go to sleep one day and never wake up?

Aula spent hours at his bedside, waiting and watching over her beautiful husband. Even in his deep sleep, he looked like a prince: his dark skin shimmered with patches of rich orange, and his black-orange wings laid under him like a king's cape. His hair, too, was frozen in perfect shape, each thick black lock framing his sharp and high-boned face. Even though his lips were frozen, they still looked so plush, but every time she went to brush her lips against his, she found them just as rigid and hard as her own. How terrible that she couldn't even try to brave a fire in their dead hearth, if only to bring some life back into his face. She could've made him his favorite tea. Could've prepared something, even just grilled vegetables, no matter how much magic she might've wasted to set the pots and pans shaking and stirring themselves. But smoke from her chimney would've been a dead giveaway that something was off, and as it was, it was difficult to stay focused for patrons, knowing her husband had been asleep upstairs for hours, days, weeks, *years*.

Aula would've hidden her husband forever if she could've. She would've waited for when the King finally *did* announce the Tour of Seasons again and allow all the torn-up families to unite again. But it simply wasn't something she could bear any longer: looking at a face so close to death, yet so far. The Orisi, those beautiful people, they could survive a deep freeze like this; they could hibernate, preserved forever in frost, and thaw into new life the second the weather warmed. Aula hoped for it. Every day, she hoped for it. But by year four, it seemed she'd been too frazzled. Too distracted. Too quiet.

So someone left an anonymous tip, and then there were three of the town guardsmen at her door, sharp maces of packed ice in hand. He was too heavy for Aula to move, and she couldn't hide him from the guards that came to her house with a warrant to search it. One guard held her while she shrieked and flailed, one contained every snap of magic and blocked every runespell she tried to weave, and the last disappeared up the stairs of her house, towards the bedroom.

Then there was the sound of ice smashing, and the guards put all those pieces of Amadi in a bag and hauled it all away.

They had the gall to tell her it was a mercy that they didn't arrest her, then a grieving widow instead of the hopeful idiot she'd been. She'd hoped, prayed, wished for Cervora to change the King's mind about that endless Winter all the while, but it seemed that wasn't in her husband's stars, for whatever reason. And every time Aula saw Aveline, she found herself too tongue-tied to ask why.

With a clap of her hands against her thighs, Aula resolved to quit her morbid train of thought. Thinking about it like that wouldn't bring Amadi back, nor would it make Cervora—Aveline—do anything for her that the poor thing wasn't already doing. She shook her head as if she could shake the thoughts loose, dragged herself up from her table full of fabric, then turned on her heel and left the city mayor's conference room. That day, Aula transformed the room into a giant tailor's workshop for the sake of making Aveline a dress to celebrate the end of this exhausting healing tour. Maybe, once

the healing tour was over, Aveline could do what she'd
originally come to do: get those seasons moving again.

Though what an end to this circus that'd be, Aula thought
as she hurried down the stairs of the mayor's home.
*Refreeze all these people, then announce that Summer's com-
ing back in six months. That'd go well, I'm sure.*

Though who knew? Maybe it would. If their god in
the flesh was back and could fix their melt, then maybe
people wouldn't be so afraid anymore. Anything could
happen. Anything except what Aula wanted most, apparently.

Stop it.

Aula shook the thoughts loose again, muttering
curses at herself as she burst out of the house. The weak
Winter light was hardly any different from the starlights that lined the manor hallways. Aula walked out
to the town square, where a long-frozen well sat full of
snow, useless. She marched past it without really seeing
it—marched all the way to the cathedral without seeing
much, really—and kept marching without seeing the
person she bumped into by the cathedral door. She did
so hard enough to stumble back and nearly fall, and she
would've fallen, too, had that person not reached a hand
out to grab her arm and steady her.

"Whoa, hey, now," said a familiar voice, strong and
clear as the cathedral bell. "Careful."

Aula blinked up into the softly smiling face of that
guard: Ristef. His smile slipped as he studied her face,
and Aula knew it was because of those damn stones he
used for eyes; he was a cheater, a snoop, clearly looking at all the emotions she had swimming around her
head. She should've guessed he was using them during
the conversation that eventually bloomed during their
first carriage ride together, when he so easily hooked
her attention and had her chattering away like they
were some old friends. And she did find him easy to talk

to—so easy, the man himself a real charmer in a way Ismar men usually weren't—which made it all the more dangerous to be so open around him. Kind face or no, a guard was a guard, and Aula was—at least at one point—a conspirator in the potential murder of the King. There was no world where a member of the Kingsguard took that well. So she stood up straight and pulled her arm from his grip, all while she closed her mind up and wiped all thoughts of her dead husband out of her head.

"Thank you," she said as she patted her skirt smooth. "You're the watchman for Aveline today?"

"That I am."

He smiled as if proud of that fact, which was odd given that he was the one whose testimony made Aveline's wrists into ribbons. It was wrong for her to deny Aveline a chance to share her miracles, yes, but the way she ran—the way she *ran* from those Bishops—it hadn't settled right in Aula's soul, even if Aveline eventually came around and agreed to give the people her blessings.

Ristef glanced at the cathedral. "Going to see Aveline?"

"More just going to sit for a while." Aula tapped her head. "I'm out of ideas for a dress. Need a moment to think."

Then she walked around him, off towards the cathedral for that quiet moment alone. Though what peace she might've found in a cathedral was a mystery to her, what with the god the cathedral was built for up and walking around like anyone else. If she wanted to pray, might she not have just talked to Aveline?

Can she hear the prayers I still make?

Heavy footsteps crunched in time with hers. Ristef came alongside her and said, "I don't think she has anyone there right now. We can visit her together."

"Is that a good idea?"

The question flew out of her mouth before she could stop it. Both she and Ristef stopped short on the carpet leading to the altar, and as the question rang out, she did her best not to shrink under Ristef's stare.

He blinked and frowned, clearly confused, before he said, "Why would it not be?"

"Well," *how do I say this?* "You *were* the one to suggest… you know. That she do what she's now doing. And she didn't seem to take it so well, so—"

"Oh," Ristef's smile broke his sharp expression, and he waved a hand, "no, no. You heard her: she was just startled by old memories, is all. She knows we would never mean her any harm like that. And she's been fine since she started doing all that, too, so it must not be so bad for her. Come on—before someone else comes to have their melt fixed."

She couldn't argue with a man that chipper and sure of himself—even if she had her doubts about the shaky way Aveline reassured the Bishops and the King that day they all tested her. After all, Ristef could see one's emotional state just fine. No doubt he saw what was going on with Aveline, too, so he must've been telling the truth.

There's nothing wrong. She wanted to believe it so badly, even as the memory of Aveline scrambling away was still so vivid in her mind. *This is fine. Aveline said so: this is fine.*

Aula nodded, and they both carried on. She kept her head down as she and Ristef headed towards the back of the cathedral, to the basement door. It was a habit from mass, though without a veil on her head, she still felt naked under the high ceilings. *Shame on you*, her mother would've said for her entering a cathedral uncovered— but there was no one there to see her save for Ristef, anyway. It was quiet in there, and the air was thick with some suffocating holiness that seemed to cling to every surface like a fresh powdering of snow.

The cathedral was a decent one. Not nearly so grand as the massive one in the capital, but not as small as the ones in the little hamlets they'd passed by, either. It was respectable, full of stained ice paintings and beautiful moonflowers, with fine white silks hanging off the altar and well kept wooden pews. There was no statue of Cervora anymore—why bother having a statue of a living woman?—so Aula had nowhere to focus her eye except forward, as they marched on towards where Aveline sat for the day.

As they got closer to that old basement door, though, some voice whispered from behind it. Aula and Ristef paused, wondering if someone was down there with Aveline after all, but as Aula listened closer, she found something strange about the voice—and the fact that she couldn't make out the words. Moreover, there was a hiccup to those words. A sickening hiss, and then a grunt—a beastly sound. Then the singing resumed, the voice broken and quivering.

Aula stared at the door. There was no sign of danger; nothing shone with that hideous red color that suggested she should run. Her eyes weren't directing her any particular way, either; no silver threads showed her what she should do to get away from that singing. So she glanced at Ristef, whose face was once again pinched in a tight, wide-eyed mask of concentration, and when she noticed his hand already drifting towards the doorknob, she snatched it instead and threw the door open.

They went quickly, but carefully, down those stairs. The closer Aula got, the more she heard the throatiness of whatever was being sung, the trills of a rolling tongue and the hissing quality to the ends of phrases. It was no Ismar language, that was for sure, and Aula paused. Who else could it have been but Aveline? Who else would speak a language like that, all snapping and hissing like the embers in a dragon's mouth? That's what that language must've been: Yasilan. Aula hadn't heard it in so long that she'd all but forgotten what it even sounded like. Hearing it then, her soul prickled as if full of frost needles.

Ristef, too, paused as he listened and said with a frown, "Is that—is she speaking—?"

She hurried ahead of Ristef as her panic flared; she fully intended to run in there and give Aveline a fright. Later, she thought she'd give Aveline an earful for speaking a language that would get any other Ismar running to the King in half a minute—and she could only hope Ristef wouldn't run and tattle himself—but what she saw when she made it to the bottom of the stairs made her freeze in that basement entryway.

Aveline sat in a chair, arms unbandaged and freely bleeding, and her shoulders rose and fell with quick, dramatic jerks. In her hands was a long and slender knife, one from an empty plate of berry pits and fish-bones that sat beside her.

Her head lolled back and her singing trailed off, even as her hands kept trying to slide that knife over her already split skin. However, all that blood was just leaking away, wasted; she didn't even have any bottles there to catch the silver stuff. She stared at the floor, and what a picture it was: Aveline, antlers practically weighing her head down enough to snap her own neck. It was a wholly different picture than the goddess Aula grew up reading and hearing about. In fact, right there was no goddess at all—not one Aula recognized.

"Aveline," Aula whispered, all while an eerie smile stretched over Aveline's lips, "what are you doing?"

Aveline whipped her head up and chirped, "Jädrich?"

"Ash and sand," Ristef snapped as he rushed past Aula. He dropped to one knee before Aveline and took a gentle hold of her wrist, then swore again. "She's—Aula, do you have anything to catch this? It's going to waste."

Waste? Aula stared at him as he fished around for something to put under Aveline's arm. Then he gave up and simply scattered the things off her plate, wiping it clean with a spray of magic and holding it under her bleeding arms. *What—you're worried about the—?*

Aula moved without thinking. She rushed for Aveline, all while ripping scraps of her own apron off, and she pushed Ristef out of the way to wrap those scraps tight around Aveline's wrists. Aula moved quickly, slippery as Aveline's arms were, and she ignored both Aveline's hiss of pain and Ristef's complaining.

"What are you doing?" Ristef took Aula's shoulder, but she brushed him off. "You're getting it all soaked in that fabric! We need to catch all that—!"

"She's dying, you idiot!"

Aula's voice rang off every wall in that basement, and the volume of it alone seemed to knock Ristef off balance. He blinked, but she didn't have time to wait for him to get some sense. Aula returned to Aveline's wrists and saw that her apron scraps were already soaked through.

If Aveline's singing earlier made Aula's soul needle with nerves, seeing all this made it feel like her soul was getting sliced to pieces by that knife. Aula wanted to turn tail and run, like the good little doe she was supposed to be with her stupid onyx eyes. She shouldn't have been the one to see this. Or deal with it. She was a seamstress. Yet there she was, watching her living god start looking more like she was about to fade away into nothing but snowflakes and sparkles; Aveline's eyes were slipping shut, and she was wilting faster than any of the delicate blooms after a freak snap of frost in early Spring. It was only because of Amadi that she knew anything about fleshlings, how their bodies worked, but she didn't have a clue as to how to handle all this blood loss. She only knew she had to help, and quickly.

So she wiped the smears of silver off her hands and pulled herself together enough to pool her magic into her finger. Then she let it come out the tip like the beginning of a fine silk thread. Aula was a seamstress; closing something split was what she did for a living. But never in her life did she want to go sewing up a *fleshling* like this. Still, what else was there to do, while her goddess was halfway to leaving them all behind again?

Had that actually happened, and Aula didn't do anything to try and help, she'd be more than crushed and melted. So she pulled the makeshift bandages back off, then slipped that icy thread through the split skin, a simple and unremarkable bit of *nedzuring,* and closed the wounds properly until no blood could even try to bubble through. Then she took another scrap of cloth from her apron—until hardly anything was left of her apron, her good one with the deep pockets, *damn it*—and tied those wrists up again.

"Take her," Aula snapped to Ristef, who stood there in stunned silence. "Take her and help me get her someplace where we can find her something to eat."

RISTEF DIDN'T UNDERSTAND.

Sneaking out of the cathedral, his goddess in his arms—the Yasilan his goddess spoke, the language of Winter's destroyers—the fact that his goddess was apparently dying—none of it made sense to him. Yet he kept moving out the cathedral's basement door. Kept following the seamstress towards the thick woods that sheltered old Hauslof's edges behind the cathedral. He focused on the path ahead, even as Aveline murmured small complaints while half asleep. Snow crunching under his boots was the only noise apart from those murmurs, and the rhythm kept him from thinking too hard about it all. He would have time to ask his questions. He would have time to understand—if anyone could explain all this to him.

"This way," Aula whispered. She pointed to the left,

where the dark, thick forest broke and the white snow seemed to glow in the daylight.

They kept going, at one point trudging through a decent pile up of snow. Aula had to raise her skirts to her knees to get through it. In the clearing itself, though, the occasional glimpses of sunlight seemed to have melted more of the snow down, and it made it a little refuge in the forest, a place soft enough to set Aveline down yet clear enough to easily walk. He knelt down right away and gently laid Aveline on the ground, and that was when he caught a glimpse of it again: the greyish marks along one of her arms, from scars of small cuts to dots of scabs from previous cuts. The bandaged arm was sticky, wet with sweet-smelling blood. Her skin itself, though, seemed strange. It wasn't pale—she was always pale—but it was somehow flat, almost dingy, with dark circles so stark and obvious under her eyes.

"What's wrong with her?" Ristef didn't know what disturbed him more: the Yasilan he'd heard or the odd color Aveline had.

Something hard swiped at his head and sent his hair flying about.

"Are you an idiot? What do you mean, 'what's wrong with her'?" Aula loomed over him as he knelt, face twisted in a murderous scowl and hand raised to swipe him again. She gestured to Aveline, whose chest was rising and falling much more noticeably than Ristef had ever seen it do. "She's lost quite a bit of blood, Ristef. That kills fleshlings, if they lose too much!"

Ristef startled, then looked back to Aveline. It was *blood loss* that killed fleshlings? But she hadn't lost too much, had she? How could she have? Surely she'd known how much she could lose before something like this happened. He didn't know much about fleshlings, but surely Aveline knew herself enough.

She speaks Yasilan. Why does she speak Yasilan?

He tried to push the thought from his mind; there were clearly more pressing things to take care of. However, no matter how much he tried, he couldn't shake the thought. He could only hover over Aveline, as if that would do anything for her, and wonder.

The letters in her father's house were lies. Somewhere along the way, it seemed he really had convinced himself that those notes he'd found in that abandoned house in Rehrvig were, in fact, fake. That they were planted by someone as dishonest and ruthless as that Clara Ronterweis. Not once did it occur to him that Aveline might've ever *actually* been of the very people that nearly destroyed Winter in the first place. No, surely, the letters weren't true. Surely not.

"Come quick," Aula said, suddenly sounding much farther away. Ristef looked up to see her speaking into a glowing message orb and pulling at the velvet on her lips with her teeth. With her free hand on her hip and her hair a bit disheveled from walking through the forest, she didn't look like just a little seamstress anymore. "We need help. Blood loss. She's dying."

Dying. Ristef just couldn't understand the word. Surely his goddess knew better than to die; she'd only so recently come back to the Ismären at all. And she was working hard for the people—helping the people get what they needed, to never hunger and thirst for magic again. What was there to die over? What reason did she have to be so careless with herself?

A snapping made Ristef look up again, and there was Aula, shuffling around and looking for big sticks to break into pieces. She cracked them with the sheer force of her magic and gathered them under her arm.

"What are you doing?" Ristef sidled closer to Aveline and took her limp hand.

"I'm gathering wood." She looked back at him, face hard, lips pressed tight. "For a fire."

That made Ristef stand up. His hand went to his sword without even thinking about it. "You know that fire has been outlawed the entire past century, Aula. What do you—?"

The way Aula stopped and stared up at the sky made him pause. It was like she was looking for some revelation from the blanket of grey clouds. When she did face him again, it was with so hard an expression that Ristef could've broken a rock on it.

"She needs to *eat*," Aula bit out. "She needs to *drink*. She needs to *recover*. She cannot do that with berries and raw river fish and snow; she needs something *warm*." Then Aula took one of those sticks and pointed it at him. "Why don't *you* go make yourself useful and catch something for us to cook? Instead of hunching over her like some dumb beast?"

Ristef's hand stayed on his sword. They stared at each other a moment longer before Aula pointed that stick towards the woods.

"Go! Now! Catch something, anything! If it's small like a squirrel, catch five! If it's big like a fox, one'll do! Now get going, unless you want to just stare until she dies there!"

Who is this woman? Everything was wrong. What language Aveline spoke, the sudden ferocity in an otherwise sweet and plucky Ismar woman, the message orb, the secret helper on the way—nothing made sense, and nothing he'd seen or heard in the past ten minutes explained anything, either. As a guard of the King, he was more than just some oafish officer; he had a duty to uphold the law perfectly, because it was his Lord's law, the *highest* Lord's law. He couldn't just walk away and let Aula melt herself trying to start a fire. Even if Aveline could fix her, the law was the *law*.

Does the King know Aveline speaks Yasilan? That she might be a mixed-blood after all?

Those were outlawed, too.

A moment later, Ristef found his hand slipping from his sword hilt anyway. Found his legs moving towards the tree line. It wasn't even so much that he wanted to let Aula make the fire. It was that he was still hoping, somehow, he might come to understand what he was seeing: a dying, possibly half-blooded goddess, a secretive and snappy seamstress, a mystery person she knew to call. There were too many things happening, none of which could be solved with a sword or a pair of icy chain-cuffs. So he went off to the woods to think—and also to wait. Maybe also to hunt.

It didn't take him long to find things to kill. With one eye removed, he could see the heat of life in many little creatures: squirrels and rabbits and foxes and such. Like Aula suggested, he took five rabbits, three squirrels, and two foxes, and he strung them up together with a rope of magically-bound snow to carry on his back. Then he sent a flicker of magic into the runes under his shoes, the silencers, and he crept towards the tree line to watch Aula and wait.

Aula knelt beside Aveline, trying to get her to sit up so she could wrap her shawl around Aveline's shoulders. Aveline's head lolled to one side; it didn't seem like she was conscious at all anymore until her mouth moved. Whatever she said, though, Ristef was much too far to hear.

A few moments passed, and Ristef wondered if the mystery person wasn't simply Lord Rachfemd. They knew each other, after all; it wouldn't have been outlandish. It also would've meant that Lord Rachfemd might've had trouble tracking them in the forest. Ristef had half a mind to go out there and help the viscount find the way, especially as another long couple moments stretched by—but then, something fell from the sky, into the clearing. A person.

The bandaged woman.

"What happened?" That woman fell like a meteor, kicking up a cloud of snow as she landed. She hurried to Aveline's side, sliding to her knees, and took a strong hold of Aveline's shoulders. Then she spat some word Ristef didn't understand and dumped a brown sack off her back. "Who did this?"

Aula tossed her hands up and let them fall back onto her lap with a *clack*. "She did. We caught her bleeding herself."

The bandaged woman paused. "Who's 'we'?"

"Me and her guard. I sent him off to find something for her to eat. But help me build a fire now; she needs to warm up. I think." Aula cocked her head. "She's cold all the time, so maybe that won't help?"

"It'll help." The bandaged woman got up, then planted her hands on her hips. She watched Aveline a moment longer, and then, her chest expanded—and she *sighed*, a long, deep sigh. "Stupid girl."

A moment later, she was fussing with the fire pit, stuffing it with needles and smaller sticks, and soon after, smoke rose. But if Ristef was puzzling over her *sigh*, he thought his head would roll right off his shoulders when he saw her lift a hand and create a vacuum: a *wind tunnel*. Akerijin magic.

"Hey, hey!" Aula shot up and dispersed the wind tunnel with a puff of silver magic, then created a dome of ice that stretched up high to catch the black stuff. "I don't know when the guard's coming back!"

"People will see the smoke! We're not that far from town!" The bandaged woman clucked her tongue as drops of the magical dome dripped into the fire and hissed. "It'll stop smoking faster if you don't have something melting above it!"

"Then make whatever thing you conjured *smaller*,

Karina! For the love of every god, don't make it so obvious!"

With a frustrated huff, *Karina* went making another wind tunnel, smaller, and fixed it under a small cave of snow she'd packed together. Had Ristef not been watching, he might've thought they'd done some clever Ismar magic to lure the smoke into the snow hole. But he had been watching, and his soul was beginning to squeeze with the sharp pain of confusion—and the panic that came with it.

That's a fleshling. A mixed-blood. One that looked enough like an Ismar to walk around and hide in plain sight. How many more of these things were in Winter? How many more were hiding from the deportation officers, the guards? So many thoughts started running through his mind that he thought they might crack his head wide open.

He stood. While Karina and Aula went fussing with little stone bowls and packets of dried leaves and berries, he released the silencers on his boots and let his footsteps crunch loud enough to catch their attention. They snapped their gazes to him, and Aula blinked at the haul on his back, nodding with a surprised, if approving purse of her lips.

"Well, then! Look at that!" Aula stood up with a bowl full of snow and herbs. "Caught a good few things, didn't you?"

Ristef didn't say anything. He only dropped the animals by Karina's foot and kept clear from the fire— though he swore he could feel it nip at his ice even from a good few feet away. She glanced up at him with one eye that looked no different than Aula's—clearly onyx—and yet all Ristef wanted to know was what was underneath all those bandages.

"In fact, you might've caught too much," Aula mused

as she came around. She poked a dead fox with her foot. "I don't think Aveline can eat all of this."

"Then maybe the half-fox can eat it, if she's fine eating her own kind."

Never had Ristef heard silence so deep. Not even the crackle of burning wood could pierce it. His eyes locked on that one shining black sphere in the half-fox's face. For a long moment, neither of them moved, and he imagined the half-fox didn't breathe, either.

Then he was rolling aside in the snow and raising any type of shield he could. He'd hardly had time to register the dark shape that flew at him, or the sound it made as it whistled past his ear. The half-fox was fast, however. By time Ristef steadied himself and prepared to fire something back, she was gone. Aula stood there with her hands over her mouth, the bowl of snow and herbs tossed aside, all while Aveline sat there shaking her head and trying to raise her soaked, bandaged arm.

Ristef wasted no time dropping his shield and rushing to her. He picked her up like a bride and said to Aula, "You..." *You're under arrest. You're coming, too. You're going to explain everything.* "You better hope I don't find you when I come back to look later."

She squawked a wordless complaint, but Ristef would hear nothing from her. He looked at the animals he'd killed, then readjusted Aveline and squatted to grab one, so he might butcher it for Aveline back in the village. These were red-blooded animals; surely they'd feed Aveline just fine, cooked or not. One of the three foxes he'd caught should've been enough for one person, maybe—

Three foxes?

His hand almost closed on one, and to his shock, the lump of white fur jumped up and snapped at his fingers. Three crunched off with a shock of sensation that made Ristef nearly drop Aveline back in the snow.

The fox dashed around him and moved to jump on his back, maybe to bite his neck, but he pushed hard and found himself sliding—with Aveline still in his arms—to his right. The fox slipped off him and growled, slowly prowling closer, and Ristef held Aveline tight against him with one arm, then used the other to form a small spear of ice just above his palm. From this range, he could easily—

"Stop," came a little breathy whisper. Aveline's hand crept up his breast plate. "Stop it."

Her other hand twitched towards the white fox, and the creature gave it a quick lick. It fixed one golden eye on Ristef, the other eye nothing but an empty socket. Everything seemed to pause in that moment; the whole world stood still and crashed its silence into Ristef's head.

And then the fox stood up on its hind legs and, in a great burst of wind and snow, stretched and lengthened until fur became skirts, skin, and hair. The full half-fox woman towered over him, her bandages gone, and while her golden eye seared him, her one empty socket was a well of shadows. Looking at her, though, Ristef wondered how he never saw her features for what they were: the roundness of her face, the tiny blunt nose, the small, heart-shaped lips. Without the bandages, her white hair fell lush and straight, shining like running water in the sun, and her ears, though hairless, were long and pointed. She was half-Akerijin, no mistake.

"Guard," she spat, "you heard your *goddess*. It does no one any good for you to fight and cause chaos."

"Me?" Ristef cradled Aveline closer as the half-fox tried to take her from him. "You're—you're not supposed to be in Winter—!"

Something hard bounced off his head and scattered his thoughts. Only then did he notice the blurry shape in the corner of his eye: Aula, with another rock ready in her hand. Her face was pinched tight, her head ha-loed by light blue determination. However, he knew by the bright red snaps in all that blue, and by how her hands trembled, that she was scared.

"Shut up, Ristef!" Aula's voice was raw, splintering between higher and lower registers in the way only Ismar souls could do when desperate. "Enough! Enough with this guard charade of yours!"

While he was distracted, Aveline suddenly disap-peared from him. He grabbed after her, but between how fast Aveline moved and the fact that his hand was suddenly much shorter with its missing fingers, he caught only empty air. Aveline floated on a cloud, out of his reach. Karina looked at him viciously enough to melt him and hurried towards the then roaring fire.

What is this? With the half-fox by the fire, and Aula looking at him like she were a rabbit and he a wolf, he had no choice but to pause. *What is—?*

"You," he muttered to Aula. She flinched at the tone in his voice. "Explain. Explain all of this. Right now."

"What, so you can run to your King with it all?" Karina's voice carried over the clearing; its tone was light, clear, like a glass bell. A cloud appeared under the animals Ristef killed and carried them over to the fire. "Maybe *you* should explain first. Explain why you would *ever* talk Aveline into whatever mess she's in now." The half-fox turned and snapped, "*Why* would you tell the King and Bishops about her blood?"

Ristef stood as still and silent as he could. For a mo-ment, he thought maybe if he didn't talk, the question would pass him by, and he could pretend he'd never heard it. It was hard to think straight, what with all this chaos and commotion. But Aula stared at him as if will-ing an answer from him, and the half-fox didn't let him get away with staying silent, either.

"Well, guard?"

"I—what do you mean? She could save all of Winter, forever! Why would I not tell?" Then he ran his hands through his hair and motioned to the near-lifeless goddess. "Aveline agreed to it!"

"Agreed to what, *killing herself*? Gods, Ristef. We were all there. We saw how she ran. You say it was just *instinct*?" Aula threw her hands up and motioned to Aveline. "Look at her! What if *this* was what she was afraid of, back then?"

He didn't want to look, but his head felt as if it were filled with rocks, with how hard the guilt hit him. Guilt like that gave him no choice but to look, and so he did—and he saw Karina there, tending to an ashy Aveline, trying to get her to swallow some kind of tablet or whatever red thing Karina had in her hands. Once Aveline ate it, Karina took a knife from inside her layers of robes and got to work dressing those beasts, ripping fur and skin clean off the meat.

"Aula, you don't understand," Ristef said. He marched over to her, and it felt as if someone punched a hole in his chest when Aula flinched and shot away from him. She looked at him as if he'd personally cut Aveline's veins open, her teeth bared through her frown. "The King commanded this—so that *our people* might be spared what we've seen in all these damn towns! And again, she agreed to do it! To make a Winter where no one is breaking into *pieces* for lack of meat and blood-wine. Don't you want that?"

Aula stared at him. It was as if everything he'd said just rolled off her back and disappeared into the snow. After a long, roaring silence, Aula muttered, "But what about *her*?"

Ristef squeezed his teeth together so tightly that his ice ached with the pressure.

"What about *her*, Ristef?" Aula's arms fell limp at her

sides. "As if our Mother hasn't already been butchered once for us."

"No one is butchering—!"

All his frustration, all his confusion, all his head-needling panic, it all shot right out of him when he caught Aveline's gaze. She was finally sitting upright, eyes fully open, and they drilled holes into him. Her face, too—it had none of the beautiful smile, none of the soft lips he knew. It had only tight lines carved around a deep frown. As Aula walked away, towards the fire, Ristef wanted to pull her back, but Aveline's stare practically cemented him in place.

Nothing is right. A half-fox, a half-*dragon*, a—

"Wait," Ristef unstuck himself as things began connecting, too; he moved a few paces closer to the fire, until he was sure he could be heard without risking melting his armor or his face. Aula stood a few paces away from him, but she didn't look at him. "Aveline. Those Yasilan silks you asked me for a couple weeks ago—were those yours all along?"

Karina paused her work; a rabbit hung half-speared on a sharpened stick. She glanced at Aveline, then shrugged, and Aveline swallowed—winced.

"Yes." Her voice was a broken rasp.

Ristef paused. "So what I heard, then—you do speak Yasilan?"

"Yes."

"And the letters," his voice grew soft, "the letters from your father's house... they were real? Your mother is—?"

Aveline blinked. "Yes."

Ristef didn't want to believe it. He stared at her, then muttered, "Then someone should tell the King—"

"He knows."

What?

There was no way. No way his King could know such a thing and not cast Aveline out, in that case. Something had to be a lie, and he hoped he'd just been hearing things this whole time—both the Yasilan language and Aveline's confessions.

Before Ristef could really deny it all, though—before he could start to tell himself that she was lying or simply out of her mind—she sucked in a deep breath and hunched over. Then something sprouted from her back. Two large, leathery white things, like the cloth of sails. They stretched up, massive, and then they folded in to drape behind her like some delicate leather cloak.

Wings. Dragon wings.

Neither Ristef nor the women spoke. They only stared at each other as the Winter silence shrieked far off in the distance. Whistling winds from miles and miles away—that was all Ristef could hear as he tried in vain to make sense of the odd scraps of leather hanging off his goddess's back.

"But," Ristef shook his head, as if he could simply will those wings out of existence, "but you're Cervora's icon. You're our goddess. Not some—"

Not some mixed-blood beast. That's what he would've said, had Aveline not let her eyes slip shut like a disappointed mother and heaved a massive sigh. That sigh completely deflated her; from her head to her shoulders to her wings, everything drooped and sagged as if she were melting. Ristef faltered; no more words could even form in his soul, never mind leak from his lips. It was him that should've been scandalized—and he was!—yet it sat heavy on his chest, seeing her stare at the snow with such a deep frown on her face.

What right do you have to look so disappointed? Maybe he could will his thoughts into her head if he couldn't make his mouth speak them. *I nearly shattered to defend you, and yet—*

"Take Aula and go back to town," Aveline rasped. "If

anyone asks for me, don't tell them where I am. Just tell them I'll be back soon. That I'm safe in the forest."

"But," he spluttered, "you can't just—!"

"Go!" She shouted so harshly that it sent her into a coughing fit. The half-fox leaned over to put a hand on her back and shot a sharp glare at Ristef. Aveline clutched her throat with one bony hand and said again, quieter, "Go. Leave me."

Footsteps crunched through the snow, and a small hand slipped over his arm. Aula stood there, her eyes stormy with the flickers of her magic, her mouth carved into a sharp and tight frown. While she didn't say anything, she did shake her head and tug his arm, and that said enough to him. He didn't need the deep, angry maroon around her head, or the occasional black flashes of despair that ran through that maroon like lightning, to understand that he was utterly alone in his own crushing despair.

She's not a goddess, then. Without a word, Ristef took a tight hold of Aula's hand and all but dragged her away from the forest clearing. *She's a mixed-blood, and she's lied to us all.*

But every step made him so keenly aware that he walked so smoothly and painlessly by the grace of her blood. And the grip he could have on Aula's hand, which she'd told him was once soft and partially melted, was by the grace of Aveline's frost. The two greatest threats that ever faced his people—who could cure them, if not a goddess?

So went his thoughts, round and round, as he dragged Aula along in silence.

Karina sighed. Her eye was still somewhere in the snow. With luck, she'd find it. Should've been easy to find something so dark and shiny in bright white snow, anyhow. Her whole body felt as if it'd suddenly turned to stone, what with the way she'd had to transform with no preparation, and her mind was just as heavy, even as her hands worked to separate limbs from torso on the foxes. Soon enough, she had legs roasting on the fire, other pieces of meat laid on hot stones near the fire, and all was sizzling away just fine. That only left the squirrels, and *those*, she knew from plenty of experience, were much more irritating than bigger animals. So much easier to contaminate and mangle. The foxes were a dream in comparison.

"Eat my own." What a fool. Unlike the Ismären, stupid things that they were, the Akerijin were under no impression that some regular old fox was at all the same as them—as a *person*. Just because he couldn't tell the difference between a normal fox and a transformed Akerijin, didn't mean nobody could.

A flash of movement in the corner of her eye caught her attention, and she turned in time to see Aveline flop over in the snow. Karina nearly threw the knife into the fire with how quickly she flung it away, but before she could go and check if Aveline hadn't up and died right there, she found the orphan hiding her face in her hands.

"It's all a wreck," she whispered, her voice even hoarser than before. Then she brushed her hair back and turned over to look up at the sky. Under her eyes was a light blue color, as if her eyes were bruised from the tears that leaked out and rolled down her face. "It's all in ruins, all of it. All of it."

What am I worried about? The orphan was alive, the bleeding stopped. Maybe she was weak, but if she had the energy to whine like that, then she couldn't have been doing so badly. Still, Karina's chest ached, looking at that pathetic heap of bones and dragon wings. It wasn't so long ago that she thought she, too, might be able to stake herself in Winter with enough work.

Studying the language until her voice was hoarse as Aveline's.

Fitting the always in-fashion eyes to her empty socket, hiding the other behind patches and bandages.

Always wearing hats to cover her ears and tucking her tail under all her layers of robes.

Never eating where people could see, unless it was what swallows of bloodwine she could stomach without retching.

None of it worked. None of it made the Ismären see her as anything more than a mistake—even her own family. Mixed-bloods weren't the greatest thing one could find in their family across the rest of the Ringlands, either; Karina's father warned her of that much. But in Winter, it seemed any such occurrence was nothing short of an insult to their god. Pure ice: that was all these "people" would accept, and goodness, did they never miss a chance to tell her so. Karina learned this long ago, but to watch it play out on this foolish woman's face—

"Hey," Karina whispered. She didn't want to dirty Aveline with fox blood if she didn't have to, so she kept her hands away. "Quiet, now. Shh. You're fine. Your guard is just an idiot."

"No," Aveline whispered. She swallowed the thick lump that always comes with tears like that, and her chest heaved with a massive sigh. "It's Jädrich too."

Karina paused. *Jädrich?* "What do you mean?"

"He tricked me."

It took all Karina's effort not to sigh. Karina stayed quiet and waited for Aveline to keep talking.

"He," she wiped her eyes and swallowed again, "he—I don't even know how to say this. In our marriage contract—do you know about Ismar marriage contracts?"

Oh, gods. Don't tell me. "I do."

"Well, he wrote—or I think, I *think* he let me write in a way—that nothing I wrote stuck, but everything *he* wrote, everything *he* put on it, I was chained to. And that means I have nothing, Karina. This?" Aveline held up her bandaged arm. "I—what I wrote was that he would defend me from all injury, of any kind. And yet with a wound this deep, gods above, with a would *this deep,* he never came. He could've let me die from this easily. And I think he might've, if not for—"

For what you can do for him and his country. Aveline didn't need to say it for Karina to understand, or for a fresh wave of tears to bead at the corners of Aveline's eyes and escape. Karina shook her head, then motioned with a still-bloody hand to that bandage.

"What was that, then? A test? Of the contract?"

She nodded.

That made Karina wonder. She tended to the fire, then said, "Is that why you asked me to stab you earlier this week?"

"Mm-hmm."

"And your husband there, he really didn't do any-thing after you carved yourself up?"

"Do you see him here?"

"Hmm." Karina sighed and went to rotate the pieces of meat. "That's fair. Well, I could've told you it would be this way."

The silence told her to stop talking, and so Karina did. For a long time, she sat beside the orphan and simply went about cooking, cleaning her hands in the snow, making more tea for the half-bled thing, and star-ing into the flames. The meat was just cooked and ready to eat when Aveline's raspy voice once again broke that silence.

"I want out." She cleared her throat. "I want out of this place."

Karina took the meat and found some clean plates in her bag to set it on. She cut the pieces and muttered, "What, you want to burn up in Summer again?"

"No. I want out of it all. The whole Ringlands, I want out."

Hearing that, Karina paused, then quickly kept cutting. She had a job to do. She had a contract to uphold with Erik, a reputation to maintain abroad. It wasn't as if she could do anything about this idiot orphan and her poor choices.

"Do you know how to get to the Melded Isle, Karina?"

Shit.

"Do you? Could you take me there?" Her pale hand ended up on Karina's wrist.

Karina stared at the lump of meat on the plate and tried, with all her might, not to see that hand right next to it. The meat was nicely cooked. Juice was already running out on the plate, and it was enough to make her stomach squeeze, looking at it. It'd been a good couple days since she was able to get out and eat anything other than frozen fish and berries.

"Please? Surely you must know how to get there?"

"I can't take you there, girl."

Karina pushed Aveline's hand off her wrist and put the plate of meat in it. Aveline didn't move, even as the steam of that meat swirled in her face. Neither of them said anything for a moment, and then came the orphan's one question.

"Why?"

"Because I'm working." With what Karina hoped was a serious and unquestionable face, Karina looked that orphan in the eye. "I'm keeping my word to your cousin. That's why. I don't go breaking contracts just because someone decides to have a fit in the snow. And I won't hear anything about you trying to escape, either," Karina said, pointing a sharp-nailed finger in that girl's face. "It'll be easier to find you than finding a cardinal in an empty field."

Karina should've looked away right then, but idiot that she was, she stayed staring into Aveline's face. She watched it wither, until what was before Karina wasn't a girl at all, but a witch from a fairytale, all sharp-eyed and frowning hard enough to cut wicked lines into her jowls. And then, Aveline's eyes slipped shut, and her shoulders rose and fell with a great breath.

When she opened those eyes again, they were dark. In them was nothing: no emotion, no thought, nothing. They were as hollow as the eyes of any Ismar woman she'd had to speak to in the past century, except somehow they were *colder* than that, darker. So dark that the blue of them almost seemed black, and all the gold flecks of them were dulled into little points. It was like looking into a sky full of dead stars, and it made Karina shrink. And with the antlers and the hooves out, the *wings* out, it was a sheer corruption of any of the photos Karina had ever seen in the books about Cervora.

"Fine," Aveline said. "Fine, fine. I'm sure Erik sees you as an Ismarrin. Just like he sees me as one. Right?"

Karina's stomach twisted. "That's not the point—"

"And I'm sure the Akerijin see you as an Akerijin, too. Just like the Yasilanri see me as a Yasilanah. Right?"

"That's—!"

"And I'm sure that they truly do care if we keep our word about anything. I'm sure they think it's noble of us, to keep contracts with us that serve them more than they serve us. Right?" Those empty, soulless eyes cut deep into Karina. "I'm sure sacrificing ourselves for lands that don't care if things like us die one way or another is worth it. Yes, you're right, your contract and reputation are so important. So is mine. Yes, of course."

Karina blinked. There was something about her words that dug their way into her mind like a worm dug into a ripe fruit. Her heart stirred to hear them, too—as if it strained to echo those words, to amplify them. But the orphan didn't understand. It wasn't just about maintaining her reputation with people she knew saw her as a mutt. It wasn't about being seen as some noble thing, some good citizen. It was, plainly, about gathering enough favors to make sure that, no matter what happened, she might have the connections to rise above, start over, and not only survive, but flourish.

Without Erik's protection and aid, she wouldn't have even been able to keep her family home, never mind live in it. She was gambling on all of this turning out in a way that she could once again rightfully, *publicly,* announce herself in that home and live in Winter, the way people had before the Wall went up, so she could resume the many trade opportunities that would no doubt grow again. Aveline was putting herself first, trying to leave—and Karina was putting herself first, trying to stay.

Aveline stared at her with those empty eyes. "What if it doesn't work out?"

What if what doesn't work out? Karina wanted to ask, because there was no way this orphan was reading her thoughts—though that stare needled her so deeply that she couldn't help but wonder. After all, how many times had Karina asked herself that exact question? How many times had she calculated the risk, wondering what to do if she happened to fall on the sizeable chance of failure? How many times had she asked herself if it was worth it, to keep a contract she knew worked her like a dog with only a scrap of hope behind it?

I could take the orphan and run. She'd gotten in and out of this place with ease. No one would ever know. *We could run for the Melded Isle. No one could follow us there. We could wait out the nonsense games of these Lords there and start over again once the dust settles.*

Tempting as it was, there was something off about that orphan. It seemed as if there was something deeper behind those cold eyes, something more than just a stupid wildling's desperate pessimism. In fact, the more Karina matched Aveline's gaze, the more she thought she saw *two* sets of eyes looking at her. Karina's skin prickled with unease. Two sets of eyes—two layers of eyes. Both peering at her, watching her, waiting for her to say what she, *they*, wanted Karina to say. But surely that was ridiculous; if anything, Karina knew well enough that this look was the look of a woman who already decided her course of action. She was being given a chance: take this opportunity to run with the orphan, or risk everything trying to stop her. And the math on this risk—if that face the orphan wore was any indication—worked out even worse for Karina than the risk she'd already taken following her contracts this far.

You need to sniff out another berry, her father would've said. *This is the berry.*

"Wait until we're near the border before you try anything ridiculous," Karina muttered. "When we're in the territory of Margravine Beurvich, we'll be able to escape much easier. Much, much easier. And then I'll show you to the Melded Isle."

Aveline didn't answer. She only took the sizzling fox meat in her bare hands, and the juice ran down her face as she ripped a steaming chunk of it off between her teeth.

THE DAYS BEGAN PASSING SLOWLY AGAIN—far too slowly.
Aveline sat on the edge of her bed as Aula pulled glittery
fabric after scratchy tulle from a basket she'd brought
up to Aveline's guest room.

"How about this for a skirt?" Aula held up a sparkly
purple thing. "Do you think maybe—?

Aveline's eyes burned with exhaustion, and her wrists
smarted every time she so much as twitched her fingers.
Her back ached between her shoulder blades from
hours of freezing people, and she thought she would've
liked someone to break her spine in half just to relieve
that pressure. They were once again in a new town, a
much smaller one than Hauslof that took her only two
days to freeze and bless with blood, but it was the last
one before Aveline could get free.

"Aveline?" Aula's hand landed on Aveline's. She
flinched, not realizing how close the seamstress had

come, and Aula startled, too. She looked up at Aveline with those big, black doe eyes—looked so oddly like that doe-wraith once did—and it made Aveline's stomach turn. "Should I leave you for now?"

Aveline stared at the woman. The events of the past few days were little more than a smear; the only thing out of the ordinary was that day in the woods, when she finally had something hot to eat, and when she'd secured a way out of this Winter nightmare. Every other day was the same as it'd always been. This entire tour, the whole almost *four* weeks of it, felt like one long, unpleasant dream that she couldn't shake herself awake from, full of hazy memories that she couldn't even pull apart into separate days.

It'd all been the same. Day in and day out, just more of the same, until it felt like she was stuck in one endless loop of the same day altogether. The same agonizingly, mind-numbingly slow day.

"I'll—yes, I'll come back," Aula said when Aveline stayed silent. She stuffed those fabrics back in her basket and tucked it by her hip. "Maybe tomorrow—"

Aveline ignored her stinging arm and reached out to touch Aula's shoulder. She stared into that basket, saw nothing but light blues, light purples, even a shimmer of deep emerald green, and shook her head.

"Black," she said. "Gold. That's what I want. None of these Winter colors." Then, as Aula frowned and considered her basket, Aveline whispered, "A Summer dress. I want a Summer dress. Or something close to it. Do that for me."

That made Aula startle as if Aveline shouted at her. She blinked, and her mouth opened to protest, but then she closed it and nodded. "I'll—okay. I'll see what I can do. You get some rest now. Lots of traveling to do tomorrow, right?"

Aveline smiled and patted Aula's shoulder. "Right.

You too, Aula. Don't torture yourself over a dress. There's no rush; you've already made me so many."

Aula returned Aveline's smile, though it was a tight one, as if the velvet on her lips was being stretched thin. Aula was a fast worker. She'd only gotten faster after taking in a drop of Aveline's blood. Refrozen and permanently imbued with magic—what a dream that must've been for an Ismar like her. No doubt Aveline's command to take her time would skate right over her head. Still, Aula nodded, then gathered her things and hurried off without another word. Only when the door shut behind her did Aveline let her smile drop.

She flopped onto the bed and sighed. Another day of travel waited for her, yes. They were finally about to be off to Taubech, the port city that marked the midpoint of the tour. It felt like it'd been years since the tour began, and Aveline wondered how she was ever supposed to survive another month of this—how she was supposed to do this more than once over the course of her life. It would've killed her eventually, yes. Would've drained her until she was nothing more than a husk of skin and bone. Just like she'd nearly become on Kha-Bawaj.

Maybe that was the point. That contract popped into her mind. *Maybe Jädrich intended to break me like a horse.*

Her skin rippled with a silent rage, and her hand came up to her chest, where she once wore her mother's bell. When her bandaged wrists brushed her chest, they stung all over again, and her sore throat cinched as her fingers brushed nothing more than the high collar of her new dresses. That bell was miles away in the capital, in a little jewelry box in the guest quarters. Maybe someone found it already. Maybe they hadn't. Maybe they never would. After all, who checked a jewelry box in an unused room? All Aveline knew was that it didn't matter either way, because horrible daughter that she was, she had no intention of going back to the capital to look for it. And without her mother's bell there, tinkling around her neck, she knew she was rightfully alone in that little bedroom.

Alone save for her two *Unseelechs.* They were curled up on the ground under the window like sleeping dogs, but Aveline knew they did no such thing as sleep. When she forced herself up and slid off that bed, she wasn't surprised at how fast they scrambled to their feet and crowded around her ankles, gurgling and squeaking.

"Shh." Aveline crouched to them and ran her hands over their hair. They made soft coos as she pet them, like pigeons nesting on a building, and then she looked up at the open window. Moonlight poured in and washed everything in soft silver light. Jädrich wouldn't be back all night, likely—he didn't often rest with her the night before they moved onto a new city—and so, as she basked in that moonlight, she wondered if she couldn't take her babies and clear her head out there, in the town. Aveline looked at her *Unseelechs* and whispered in Yasilan, "Will you keep me safe out there tonight?"

Their coos became crackling snarls and croaks, and they stared at her with those bright, glassy eyes. It was enough of an answer for her. So she snatched her rabbit skin cloak off the bed, then fished in her to-be-packed trunk of dresses and found a mint green dress she didn't often wear. It was one from her first few weeks in the bridal competition, a tight one that made quick escapes difficult. With a huff, Aveline crackled her magic from her hand and neatly cut the dress into a long strip of fabric. Then she took that scrap and wrapped up her hair in it, the way married Summer women would do, until all her hair and even her ears were hidden. With no antlers or hair, she hoped it would be harder for people to recognize her.

The thought made her look at her *Unseelechs* with a heavy heart. If anyone were to recognize her, it would be because she had her babies by her side. She crouched down to them again and said, "You'll keep me safe best by staying here, I think. Making noise. Making people think I'm here. Can you do that?"

They bounced on their haunches and grabbed at her legs, as if they wanted to climb up and perch on her thighs. Whether or not they understood her, Aveline doubted she'd ever know. All she knew was that they followed all the way to the big window and made their funny little noises as she undid the latch. Like most guest rooms she'd been in, this one, too, had a tiny balcony to stand on, but unlike the others, it didn't face the city square. It faced the little city gardens behind the mayor's townhome, where a frozen fountain towered over a garden of little more than snow patches and pots of moonflowers.

Aveline hurried out and closed the door before her babies could follow, and they squawked as the window bumped into their flat faces. Their talons tapped against the windowpanes as they tried, and failed, to get out.

"I'm sorry," she whispered, even though she knew they couldn't hear.

Then she pulled herself over the balcony railing and jumped. A burst of her magic softened her landing; no doubt hitting the ground straight from that height would've at least fractured, if not broken, her legs. Still, she was outside, and in her cloak and headwrap, under the light of a bright and beautiful Malouçe, she knew she would be safe. Safe enough, at least.

So she turned from the snowy garden and went down the alleyway on the side of the manor before appearing on the cobblestone street of the town. This was a textile town—one that, unlike the other shops they'd been to, *specialized* in all things needle and thread. What a shame, that Aveline only just gave Aula any direction for whatever new project she wanted to start. No doubt the little mouse would be out there first thing in the morning, trying to search for more fabric before the carriages left. In fact, she may have already run out into the night to find an open shop. The thought of her scrambling about rows of fabrics in a store made Aveline smile.

As Aveline walked down the street, her soft shoes padded against the stone. They weren't meant to be worn outside, only to keep her feet protected from the floorboards and carpets of the manor, but she was too focused on all those shops and things to care. It wasn't even very late yet, but in Winter, the sun faded so quickly that it covered the land in what felt like eternal night. Moreover, the bright silver moonlight washed out the blueish glow of the starlights, and even though many shops were still open—even though a good few people still came in and out of them and hurried on home with arms full of bags and stuffed baskets—it felt as if the town were haunted rather than inhabited.

Aveline glanced around. She watched people shop, watched them read books at the tables outside little bookstores, watched them admire mannequins with elaborate costumes in the storefront windows. And she caged a sigh, knowing just how much of Winter she'd never get to see. As it was, this glimpse of a lively town was more than she'd been able to explore the entire tour, given Jädrich's breakneck pace. All she'd wanted was to maybe take his arm and stroll around, like they had that one day they went to the observatory—but it seemed that the King she knew in that competition was not the King that presided over Winter.

Those little moments of indulgence were temporary. They were an outlier from the true life of a Lord of Seasons. And he would've been content to make them an outlier for her, too, never letting her step too far away from a cathedral, never letting her leave the castle grounds. As Aveline walked along and recognized the people that visited her for blood and frost the past few days, she realized that stone was stone and grey was grey—whether in the form of a rough-hewn mountain cave or carefully carved castle rock.

He never intended to let me walk free, did he? Her shoes provided no support, and she felt the crooked edge of every stone she stepped on. *He never intended to let me be any more than the "Queen and Mother" his people needed.*

Fool that she was, that thinking being a goddess meant anything in a land of god-killers.

A wave of gooseflesh rippled down her spine, and her hands tingled with the urge to squeeze into fists. They might've, if not for the way her skin tugged when her forearms flexed and threatened to rip her wounds open. Still, the sensations in her skin whispered a clear message: *I told you, I told you, I told you.*

Aveline reached the town square and sat down at a frost silver bench under a massive, bare-branched tree. No doubt, it once would bloom, make leaves, and then drop those leaves with the turning of the seasons—a better seasonal calendar than any paper chart could ever be—but a century of Winter made it dormant, if not dead. Aveline stared up through its branches; the leafless twigs looked like black cracks against an otherwise deep blue, starry sky. As she looked, her lips twisted in a rueful smile.

You did tell me, didn't you?

Something skittered along her nerves like a colony of ants. Something rumbled in her stomach, filled her heart with ice. Something flooded into her eyes and made it feel as if she wasn't the only one peering through them. Something had come to the surface, from deep in the refuge of Aveline's bones, and it climbed into her conscious with gnawed, mangled fingers, with chipped hooves and a face made of bone.

I did, all that sensation said. The way Aveline's hair stood up on her neck told her quite clearly: *it's dangerous here. Always was.*

Mm. Even if the doe-wraith only spoke in instincts, Aveline could respond in words. *Seems we need to leave.*

Her body stilled. Even her heart seemed to skip a beat. Then a twitch in her right eye snapped: *justice.*

We'll have it. Yes, we will. Aveline rubbed her arms as if she could soothe her body, and the sharp pain in her scabbed skin underscored her next words. *But not if we stay. Only if we leave. Leave this land for good.*

Leave. Her legs twitched with the urge to bolt. *Leave.*

Yes. We should leave. But, her eyes slipped shut, and sure enough, there it was: the doe-wraith, all chewed up and gaunt, some phantom light shining off its skull. It stared at her with nothing but dark, empty sockets. *We need to free ourselves first.*

Aveline didn't have to say much more than that. Just like the day she stood on that stage in Vörnein, she saw it: a thread of blueish silver, one that stretched far into the blackness of her closed eyelids and showed her the direction her husband was in. And just like that day in the capital, she saw a sharp bone claw reach out and hook that thread.

Aveline shuddered. Stupid as it was, her heart ached and twisted, as if it could wrench that thread away from the doe-wraith's claw. *What if,* she wondered, *what if I'm overreacting? Making a mistake?* After all, Jädrich never outright *said* he'd tricked her. Never admitted that his part of the contract was a lie, and that he wasn't bound to it. Maybe she was safe, and she was just letting her exhaustion get in the way of her judgement.

Then her arm stung so sharply that her eyes flew open, and she looked down to see that her cloak had caught on her bandages—tugged them enough to dislodge a scab and make a dot of silver dampen those bandages. Aveline tucked the arm deep under her cloak and hoped nobody passing by would smell the stuff they'd gorged on for centuries.

Never safe. That bead of blood sobered her. *Never.*

There wasn't any choice. Karina already laid out an escape plan for her: apparently, that Margravine Beurvich was to host a ball, and her sweet cousin Erik intended to take her hostage to get back at the King—to force Jädrich to give up his crown. And then who knew what would happen to Aveline? Who knew what prison she'd find herself in, and what they'd do to her? Maybe Jädrich's contract held, and he'd lay waste to such treasonous fools to protect her—or maybe he'd protect her by giving up his crown when they had a knife to her throat. But then he wouldn't be her keeper anymore; other lords would be. Either way, it was clear: there was no way out of this mess except past the wall of Winter.

So Aveline closed her eyes, and there it was again: the claw, the thread. It hesitated there, that claw, as if it were waiting for Aveline to change her mind and force it away again. As if waiting for whatever bright orange stuff crackled in Aveline's throat before, in what felt like a bad dream so many weeks ago. But Aveline didn't shout. Didn't scream. Didn't even cry.

She only nodded, and her chest emptied of all feeling, her mind of all thought, as that claw sliced clean through that contract thread.

Clara fiddled with the contraption Klassech gave her to pilot that lizard boy, but it resisted her every twitch. It was a ball made of frost silver, with little nodes of runestone conducting the magic Clara poured into its hollow base. On top was a larger runestone, one connected to the fragment of runestone implanted in the creature's brain, that let her see everything through the eyes of that lizard. The other nodes were to let her influence him—to get him to maybe turn in a certain direction, look a certain way, and most importantly, think certain thoughts—or even put certain thoughts at the forefront of his focus.

It was a horrifying contraption, one Klassech had been testing on rabbits and wolves for apparently quite a few years, and Clara wondered if it wouldn't have been possible to save a few of those butchered diplomats from Autumn for the headmistress to play with, too. After all, even if the fleshlings were little more than beasts themselves, their minds were certainly more complicated than that of a rabbit. Piloting them, therefore, according to Klassech, meant not just pushing them in certain directions, but overriding where they were trying to go, too—and unlike rabbits, the fleshlings would begin to wonder why their brains seemed different.

Not too much, Klassech had warned. *Don't influence too much.* But how could Clara not? The thoughts she'd gleaned from this creature were alarming, the murderous intent palpable. She tried to focus his intent on only the mixed-blood, but there was this sense of rage, thick and black as the lizard's own venom, that was directed towards that southern Margravine.

That was irritating. Clara would've preferred the Margravine to stay alive for a bit of testimony about their so-called *goddess*—the conspiracy against the King, the foreign and domestic enemies that wanted to see Orr's line crumble. Yet every time she used her magic to send forth impulses of *justice, law, Crown,* into that lizard's head, the murderous intent only grew. It expanded beyond the mixed-blood, beyond even the Margravine, and stuck like sap to the very idea of the King.

Damn it!

Clara sparked her magic into the main runestone and looked out the beast's eyes. All she saw was what she'd seen the past several days: more forest. The damn wyrm, he kept to those woods like the animal he was, and it made it impossible to gauge exactly where he was in relation to the King's route. There was no doubt that he was trying to reach the south, but without knowing exactly where he was, Clara could only hope to delay him by manipulating his memory and turning him in circles out there. It'd been a successful enough tactic for the past couple days, but she couldn't be glued to that damn contraption forever; she had other things to do, other things to prepare for. Like the turn of seasons.

Finally, however, after several hours of going nowhere, the lizard climbed into a tree and tied himself to its trunk. That was her sign that he was about to sleep. Only when he was fully secured did she feel it was safe to withdraw her magic from the contraption and sit back in her seat. What a hassle. She could've cursed Klassech to the Iswold and back for suggesting this idea—but then, Clara was the fool that took her up on it. If he didn't let up, then Klassech's warnings be damned, Clara would simply have to take him over completely and pilot him like the puppet he was.

Careful of her stitches, Clara pressed her hands to her face. The stiffness in her joints told her that before she did any other work that night, she'd need to find something to eat. With her soul squeezing in her head, the frustration nearly crushing it, she managed to drag herself up and make her way slowly, carefully, towards the castle kitchen.

Stupid lizard. Based on what she'd observed so far, she had a good few hours before he woke up and caused her grief again. *Gods-forsaken thing.*

RISTEF SHUFFLED AROUND THE SIDE OF THE manor and kicked at the ground. If he were any good at his job, he would've been right there with the rest of the guards, squawking over who would carry which trunk of clothes and other nonsense into the carriages for another round of travel. But he wasn't good at his job, not at all, and so he stood there by a dead bush that still had a single brown leaf on its bare sticks.

On any other day, he might've thought about that leaf: how it managed to stick to this bush for a century, what gust of wind would be enough to shake it off. But none of that even registered to him then. All he could do was think about the wings. Even what veins remained in that decrepit frozen leaf reminded him of the veins in those two silvery pale wings on the back of what he was so sure was Cervora's icon. But what doe had the wings of a dragon on its back?

He knows.

Those two raspy words haunted him for the better part of the week. If the King really did know about her, then he probably knew about that half-fox, too, and that only made all of this worse. The King knew there were mixed-bloods afoot, and he knew Aveline wasn't who she said she was, too. And yet—well, if he knew, and he still found her worthy of calling both Queen and Mother, then *wasn't* she those things after all? Wasn't she, wings or no wings, Summer blood or Winter ice, the goddess his people had been looking for all this time? Her dragon breath was made of frost and could cure any damage one of her fire-born kin could cause. And her blood was so potent that it fed an Ismar forever. Wasn't that nothing short of a miracle?

And yet, and yet, and *yet.* For days, these things twisted in Ristef's mind and tormented him, whether he patrolled the streets, stood outside Aula's studio door, or sat alone in the guard barracks, too distracted to hold any conversation past a few words. Maybe he should've been more social with the others. He knew how they whispered whenever he left the room; he saw their hazy orange suspicion whenever he entered it. But there was nothing he could do to free himself from this circle of thoughts—and nothing he could do to remedy things, either. Aveline refused to so much as look at him and hid in her room whenever she was done plastering that tight smile on her face each day.

And Aula—what a look Aula gave him when they'd come back to town. What a wretched look. She, too, hadn't given Ristef any more than a venomous stare every time she saw him, and he didn't dare ask her to join him for a round of cards or a bit of idle chatter during their breaks from duty.

Have I sinned? If so, there was no one he could ask for forgiveness save Aveline herself. But how did one beg forgiveness from a goddess that refused to even look their way?

"Gürrensig!"

The sharp snap of another guard's voice yanked Ristef's attention off the one dead leaf. He whipped around to see Gunther standing there, arms crossed. One sharp nod of his head was all Ristef needed to know there wouldn't be another chance to get moving, so he found himself trotting over, kicking up a good deal of snow off the stone pathway. All the while, Ristef avoided Gunther's stare. Ever since they'd come back with Lady Ronterweis, it'd been impossible to look Gunther in the eye—even after the allegations against Ristef for treason were dismissed. At that point, though, it was hard precisely because everything Ristef fought to defend his goddess against turned out to be true.

"Here," Gunther grunted once Ristef came by his side. He kicked a chest, and something in it—many things, actually—rattled around inside. "Take this—"

"Don't you kick that, you big oaf!"

Both Gunther and Ristef couldn't help but blink at a voice that sounded sharp as their swords. Before they could turn to see the owner of the trunk, she appeared between them in a blur of simple grey linens and a deep blue seamstress apron, with a blue handkerchief on her head doing nothing to keep her silver hair from flying in a thousand directions. The bright red halo of her alarm only made her look more like some vengeful spirit out to crush them all. Aula snatched one side of her trunk's handles and, with her back bent with the effort of picking it up, she managed to shoot a nasty look at Gunther and Ristef.

"This has *delicate* equipment in—!"

When she saw Ristef, though, the scowl dropped right off her face—only to be replaced a moment later with a frown so deep, a furrow in her brow so sharp, that her face pooled with shadows, and that bright red halo became a cloud of angry, murderous maroon. Such a dark look took Ristef aback. Then, without a word, Aula went tugging that box across the walkway, each step an obvious labor for her with whatever she'd stuffed in this chest.

Gunther raised a brow at Ristef and walked away, leaving Ristef to watch Aula make agonizingly slow progress towards the carriage at the end of the mayor's walkway. With a click of his tongue against his teeth, he marched over to her and took the other side's handle, lifting it easily. It wasn't that heavy, not to him, but then, he was carved bigger and sturdier; heavier things didn't feel so hard on him like it must've on someone so small.

"I can get it myself, Ristef," Aula muttered.

"With magic, maybe, but you're not using magic for some reason."

"Don't need to use magic when hands will do."

"Don't need to conserve magic when you've been given an infinite amount of it."

She lifted her head and snapped, "And who gave us that, Ristef? Who let us have that?"

Past her, in the doorway, a couple guards glanced over at the sudden noise. They saw Ristef and whispered amongst themselves, then left. They didn't know, though; they didn't know what Ristef knew about Aveline. They only knew that he was a favorite of their Queen—at least until recently. But it just didn't make sense, how they could act this way over him *defending* the goddess they didn't even know was—

"Aula," Ristef started, "can we talk? Please?"

When she tugged the chest, she tugged Ristef along with it and nearly made him stumble. "I've got nothing to say to you."

"Well, maybe if you'd said something to me earlier, I could've avoided all that mess we made in the forest," he hissed. Only then did Aula pause. "Please. Let's talk when we get this to the carriage—"

"This has nothing to do with the forest, Ristef. You—I can't believe you." She stopped hard, sending more things sliding in that chest, and she set it down so gently before marching up to Ristef and shoving a finger in his face. "I can't *believe* you would put Aveline through all that. And act the way you did when it was *you* that put her in that position."

"Hey," Ristef could at least feel better about the fact that the guards and other servants had mostly cleared away by then, "not so loud—"

"She nearly died, Ristef. And had we not found her, she *would've.* She would've died, and then we'd be left here with nothing—no Queen, no goddess—"

"And no more secrets like the ones you were all keeping from me," Ristef bit out. His words were so sharp that his teeth and tongue snapped against his lips, and his face was so close to Aula's that their noses nearly touched. "Had I known she wasn't what I thought she was—"

"Then what, you'd have spit her blood back out?"

"*I'd have never insisted she do this for us,* you mouse." Ristef ran a hand through his hair, and as his frustration fumed from his soul, it sent a rush of hotheaded words hissing from his mouth. "How was I supposed to know a *god* could die of blood loss? I didn't know that about normal fleshlings. And it seems our 'goddess' is exactly that, isn't she? A fleshling. A *mutt.*"

His face suddenly flared with pain, and he felt a crack in his jaw line. Magic was already seeping into it and looking for snow to seal the cracks again, but that didn't make the injury shoot any fewer spears into his soul. The snap of Aula's hand against his face was a thunderclap, the sound echoing across the air and out into the town.

"She is our Mother," Aula muttered. Her eyes gleamed with magic, as if there was a whole sky's worth of stars coming to life in those pieces of onyx. "It doesn't matter where she's from, what she looks like, who she was before all this. Now, she is our *Mother,* and she is helping us heal this country and its people. Even at the expense of herself. What about that isn't good enough for you?" Aula picked up the trunk handle again. She paused and stayed silent for a long time before her hard voice became little more than a whisper of Winter wind: "Do you want her to be fully devoured a second time to prove herself?"

Ristef froze with his fingers still at the fault lines in his jaw. While he stood there, staring at her like an idiot, she took up his advice and let her magic flow freely from her palms. A thick cloud of it wrapped around the trunk and lifted it up, and as it floated over Aula's head, which flashed with maroon so deep it was almost black, she pinned Ristef with a crushing stare. Then she turned on her heel and left for her carriage, all while her words made Ristef's chest feel like it was about to cave in.

Because he already had let Aveline, *Cervora,* be devoured a second time. In fact, he got his own King to command it, there in front of those Bishops. And if any crime in this world could make him a sinner wholly unworthy of forgiveness, it was that.

It was still dark when Aveline crept back into bed—though she knew that didn't mean anything. The Winter mornings were always dark and cold, whether because the curtains of a room were drawn or because the moon had disappeared behind the clouds. On this night, it was because of the latter. However, she knew when she returned to the mayor's house that the stars were still high in the sky, and so she knew she still had at least a couple of hours to sleep. So she slipped into the still-empty bed, and when she was somewhere between sleeping and waking, she eventually felt the bed dip beside her—felt the cold radiate off her husband's body.

Did he feel it? Aveline curled into herself and clenched her twitching hands into fists. *Did he feel the contract dissolve?*

Her hands continued twitching, as if they were reaching for Jädrich on their own. After some time, they went stiff, and her joints ached with how hard her fingers strained into the shape of claws. Something in her bones was urging her hands forward, urging her arms to slip across the sheets, begging to grip the man lying beside her and squeeze until fault lines appeared in his ice. Until the ice shattered enough to take the arm clean off. She knew what that something was. Didn't have to close her eyes to come face to face with it anymore. No, since returning, that doe-wraith had come to root in her very ribs, like some thick and thorny vine. It didn't need to speak to tell her what it wanted her to do. It didn't need to tell her anything at all, in fact, because it was beginning to try, with all its might, to take her hands and do it on its own.

All things. Let all things die. Justice.

So it whispered in her dreams. And clearly, it wanted to start here—with the son of Orr's sons. It would start here—it showed her, in those dreams—and then it would continue, cracking the people down bit by bit, blowing cold so deep even the Winter plants and animals would soon crumble under its chill, and then blanketing all the Ringlands in a frost so deep it could only be called Death. That's what it wanted, and even if it agreed to get them both to safety first, it seemed

it wanted to get a head start on the work it promised
Aveline it would one day do.

What a bratty thing you are, Aveline whispered to her
own blood and bones as her fingers twitched. It was still
too much to name this thing or address it too directly;
she didn't want to admit what force had tangled itself in
her bones—what thing shared her body. *What a miserable
child, wanting all to suffer as you've suffered.*

Her heart squeezed so tight that she couldn't breathe
in. The pain flooded her chest as if an arrow had
pierced her clean through. When she curled tighter into
herself and balled her fists against her chest, it eased
a little, but it still hurt—and when she squeezed her
eyes shut to try and force the pain away, she saw in her
mind's eye something pale blue. As blue as Jädrich's
eyes. Except it wasn't just a polished stone—it was a
dragon's eye, its pupil like that of a cat's.

Give me, that eye seemed to say. *Give me, give me, give
me. Give me this.*

But what was "this"? Aveline didn't know. The vision
of that blue dragon eye disappeared as soon as it came,
and Aveline's body soon went limp, the doe-wraith gone
to sulk somewhere deep in her marrow. Only then did
Aveline manage to relax—but it took a while longer for
her to trust her body enough to let herself sleep.

When she woke some few hours later, she stared at an
empty space beside her in the bed. More, she stared at
it with light pouring in from behind her—sunlight. The
diffused, weak sunlight of yet another cloudy morning. Aveline blinked the bleariness from her eyes and
looked around, confused. This was late in the morning,
for the sun to be up already. She sat up, and only then
did she see the straight shoulders, the ice crown, of her
husband.

He sat at the edge of the bed and faced the door. Sat
so still that she thought maybe his soul finally left his

head and let his body become a true ice doll. His hair draped down his back, shiny and soft, and the silver tassels hanging from his shoulders were so still that it was uncanny. With no breath to make Jädrich's chest rise and fall, of course, there was no reason for a single piece of him to move.

Even when he spoke, he kept still as stone. "Where were you last night?"

Aveline stilled. Of course he'd noticed her absence, of *course*. Even if she hadn't spotted a single guard out on those streets, no doubt someone saw her and reported to Jädrich—or perhaps they'd even reported her *Unseelechs*. They had been making quite some noise as she left. Maybe he'd come by to check on her, only to open the bedroom door and find her gone. But then, why hadn't he come out to find her?

Trap. The thorns in her ribs began twining around her heart. *Trap.*

Yes, that was it—a trap. But what did Jädrich want to accomplish with a trap like this? Maybe he did feel it, after all: the snap of the string that bound their magical marriage. Could he have been upset about that? He certainly didn't have the right to be—not with what he'd tried to make of it, being so one sided and *false*.

The more Aveline thought about it, the more her throat filled with bile and tainted her tongue with its bitterness. There were a thousand nasty things she could've said. Would it not have been dangerous to Ristef, she might've even said she was out in the woods with him, just to make Jädrich look at her again the way he had in the bridal competition: with that anger in his face, that jealousy she didn't think ice people could feel. But the cold that radiated off that man, the stiffness of him—no. Aveline knew anything she said would be used against her.

Follow me, she whispered to her blood and her bones. *Hunt with me.*

A wash of prickles ran over her scalp. Her fingers once again crooked into claws. The doe-wraith's excitement made her breath shallow.

Not like that, she added, and she leaned forward until she was on all fours. She crawled to the edge of the bed and sat behind Jädrich. *Watch. Follow me. Learn.*

Aveline relaxed her stiff fingers and took a gentle hold of his hair. It *was* soft, even if it wasn't real hair like hers; it was smooth, silky, like living water. She kissed it, then moved it aside so she could kiss his neck, and she whispered, "I couldn't sleep, so I watched the stars."

"Where?" Jädrich stayed stiff under her fingers. "With who?"

"In the town square. By myself."

Only then did Jädrich move. He turned his head until his nose nearly knocked into hers, and those blue diamonds bore into her. As Aveline studied them, though, she could only remember that dragon's pupil, black and carved like a talon mark into the blue stone's middle.

"Did you have any guards with you?"

Was there some jealousy left in him? Aveline could only guess. She rested her chin on his shoulder and said, "No. But I hid my hair and antlers and such, at least."

A crackle of magic crossed his eyes. "You could've been in danger. You can't just go somewhere alone. It isn't what our people need of their Queen and Mother: a woman who has no regard for her own safety."

That language—he was trying to trip the contract. Maybe he hadn't felt the end of their bond, then. Aveline waited, but sure enough, the bitter, killing cold never entered her heart. In fact, the thickening thorns in her chest made Aveline think nothing would ever encroach on her heart again. Nothing like the cold of a magical contract—and perhaps nothing like what she once mistook for *love*, either. That thrill, that madness, that inexplicable force drawing her near—was it ever for the man himself? Or just for the danger of taunting so wicked a predator?

It doesn't matter now. That's what the doe-wraith said as it curled Aveline's lips into a satisfied smile, and Aveline had to agree. In fact, she had to let Jädrich know, too.

"Our people will get what they get from their *Queen* and *Mother*," she whispered. Her hand found its way under Jädrich's chin, and filled with madness once more, she brushed a kiss over his frozen lips. He didn't respond to her kiss, but she didn't need him to. As she drew away, she slipped off the bed and stripped her nightgown off, letting it crumple to the floor. "They will get what I give them. They will get what they deserve." Then she looked over her shoulder at Jädrich, whose eyes were so alight with magic that she couldn't see their blue tint anymore. "Do you understand, King?"

He shot to his feet so fast that Aveline flinched and cursed her body. Still, she kept her smile pinned on as he stalked closer. The magic slowly dissipated from his eyes, but they stayed trained on her like that of a stalking wolf's eyes on a doe.

Is that what you still think you are? Aveline's smile stretched wider. *My predator? Mine?*

The thorns thickened further, until they became like wicked armor around her heart.

"You have no reason to punish your people," he muttered. He stood over her and looked at her as if his gaze alone could flatten her into the ground.

Tell him. Her lips quivered in their smile as if begging to make words; her nose twitched in a rage that didn't live in her own heart; her fingers, again crooked into claws. All of her body demanded of her: *Tell. Him.*

Easy, now. We're hunting.

Because it seemed she hadn't made as much of a hangman of this King as she'd have liked. No, she knew she wasn't like her mother or the other women of the brothel; she tried, and did decently, but between the way Ristef looked at her once he realized what she was, and the way Jädrich tried, that bastard, to trap her in a lopsided contract under a pretense of love—no. No, no, no, she was no good at hanging, clearly. Not the right kind of clever for it.

But hunting—that didn't take the same tricks. That didn't take the same kind of cleverness as the brothel demanded.

Aveline put a hand to his chest and pushed him back, and to her surprise, he let her. The smile on her lips grew into a grin, and with every step, she let her feet crack and fuse into hooves—let her antlers pierce the skin of her scalp and rise up to match his crown. By time Jädrich hit the edge of the bed, they were eye to eye once more.

"I've seen," she whispered, and she raised her hand from his chest to his jaw, cupping it gently. "I've heard. I've witnessed what's become of my people and their King—for well over a month now, since I crossed your foolish Wall."

Hunting.

Jädrich stared at her, his magic crackling only here and there across his eyes—quick flashes, as if he were nervous. They gave color to his otherwise lifeless, blank face. Like a mountain lion herself, Aveline had gone unseen by her mark. She'd collected all she needed to know exactly where and when she could sink her teeth into him. If this was the same King that could hunch over in shame in the bowels of the castle, who could whine to her about his failures over those melted sacks he called women, then she had full view of his softest spot.

Aveline shook her head and let her grin fade. "How could you do this to your people?"

Killing.

There was more Aveline could've said, but that one sentence seemed to smash Jädrich's mask clean open. His face crumpled into a deep frown, into the wide eyes and furrowed brows of a man who'd been told a tragedy. It only lasted a moment before the mask went back up, but Aveline knew that she'd struck him deeply. He tilted his head down, like a mountain goat about to challenge another in its territory, and in fact, his crown almost knocked against her antlers. But his silence said everything, told her *everything.*

Rip him open.

Who taught the doe-wraith to be so vicious? The wolves she was so scared of in her early years? Or the children that betrayed her? Aveline didn't know, nor did she need to know. She only knew that, at last, she and that doe-wraith agreed on what needed to be done—at least in this case, with this one Ismar.

"And then you thought," she whispered, and a huff of her own laughter interrupted her, "that you could twine up your own god in your worthless contract." Her hand went from cupping his face to gripping his jaw, her nails scraping into his ice as she squeezed him. She leaned in until their noses were almost touching, and she hissed, "You really thought you could trap me in the magic *my flesh and blood gave you?*"

Was it her who spoke or the doe-wraith? Perhaps it was Aveline speaking for that vengeful thing. As Aveline stared into the same pale blue that once colored the hatred the doe-wraith once hurled from the heavens, she found that the rage of her heart and the rage of her body were becoming one bright, burning flame within her. But before she could say anything else, though, Jädrich's voice cut her off. His jaw didn't move, but his words echoed, softly, from deep within his head.

"Why do you still pretend to be Cervora?"

Pretend!

Shattered. All their play, all their games, that question shattered it. He knew. And while her body begged her— *tell him, tell him, tell him!*—she could not bring herself to admit what so deeply terrified her, even if she knew full well by that point that her body was not only hers. So she licked her lips and closed the distance between them, until her naked flesh body pressed and fitted itself to his carved ice body. Then she dug one hand into his hair and pressed her lips to his neck again, just where it met his shoulder. And she bit, with all the force she could, until ice gave way under her teeth. It crunched into pieces just as she always imagined it would, that killer's bite—and funnily enough, it tasted sweet. Like frozen syrup water.

Jädrich jolted and thumped his hand into her shoulders, pushing her away. He hissed some word she didn't understand, and the next moment, Aveline found herself on her knees, her arms pulled back behind her and bound to the floor by some magical restraint. Another *helzuring* spell, no doubt—like the one that bound her to the tree during the bridal competition.

"The same reason you pretend you love me," she said, and she crunched what ice she'd taken from him between her teeth. He watched her eat him up with a hand pressed to his broken throat; his ice cracked and squeaked so loudly in her mouth that she thought the entire town might hear it.

Kill him.

It was a demand so sharp that it cut clean through Jädrich's restraints, just as it had through the magic of their contract. Aveline could almost see the sharp talon of the doe-wraith when she blinked—and what glory, *glory*, when she stood up again and witnessed Jädrich flinch at the sound of her hooves on the stone.

But she wouldn't kill his body. No. Not when he had the good sense to stare at her in that beautiful, wide-eyed disbelief. There was a better prize than his body, and it was that odd orb floating in his head—the same kind she'd seen, in her borrowed memories, floating in one cave on the very edge of the world. She once again approached Jädrich, and she smiled when he leaned away from her.

"Am I pretending, though?"

Her hand reached for him, though she stopped herself from touching him when those fingers once again crooked and tightened, ready to grab his throat and finish disconnecting his head from his body.

No, no. Behave.

Aveline stayed still and cocked her head. "Am I really false—like you were?"

The thrill, it was back—and it was the way Jädrich recoiled from her that revived it. This was better than a quick kill, and she hoped that doe-wraith felt what she felt: the sheer satisfaction of stepping away from so powerful a predator, knowing it cowered underneath her. Maybe it did, because she went slack, *truly* slack, for the first time in what felt like years. It was as if the doe-wraith were finally giving back the reins of Aveline's own body. Her head tipped up, and she grinned as she stared down her nose at that King, whose face was the perfect picture of those mountain lions she used to lure close and kill on Kha-Bawaj: eyes wide, body rigid and leaning away in shock.

"We're going to Taubech today, yes?" Aveline clopped to her trunk of dresses and went rooting through them for something comfortable to wear for another long and bumpy carriage ride south. When Jädrich didn't respond, Aveline stood up and stared at him. "Yes?"

He blinked. "Yes."

Aveline nodded and went digging through the mess of fabric again. "Good. Get out, then. I'll meet you when I've dressed." She paused to look up, then tapped her lips as if in thought. "Rabbit," she finally said. "I could do with rabbit for today's meal. Get that sorted, will you?"

Jädrich stood there a moment longer. Aveline braced for an argument, or for some backlash; her body once again tensed, but this time it was because of her nerves, not the interference of the thing that lived in her bones with her. However, soon enough, all Aveline heard was the thump of Jädrich's boots as he walked away, and then the creaking of the door as it opened and shut. Aveline paused her dress searching and squeezed a handful of purple velvet to keep from laughing.

This was what she wanted. *This* was what she'd imagined, when she understood herself to be not Jädrich's Queen, but Winter's god: the means to bark orders at that fearsome King and have him bend to them like tree branches bent to strong winds. But with Taubech so close, Aveline tasted the bitterness lacing her victory. Of course, she had to win this victory now, at the end of this mess. Of course, she could only savor it for a moment before she had to walk away from it.

But it didn't matter. Aveline found her favorite swath of black wool and tossed it on, the thing hanging heavy, loose, and warm around her as if she were wearing a blanket. No, none of it mattered, because soon enough, she would be freed from this wretched country and its King, and then whatever happened to it would no longer be her concern. Her father's country, it was clear, had nothing for her, nothing—and knowing what she knew of Jädrich, she didn't imagine he'd take her cruelty without trying something to temper it and cage her again. He needed her, and he needed her *predictable,* containable.

Never again.

Aveline let one deep breath fill her lungs, then gushed it out, fully aware of the thorns that filled her ribs and the presence that watched her from among their vines. She shook herself loose and stretched the memory of the morning out of her body, and then she steeled herself for the long carriage ride to her last stop: that fallen port city of Taubech.

Then I'll be free. It made her hold her head high as she left that guest room. *Free.*

It was a silent two days in the carriages after Aveline showed her hand to that King. Silent, yet with such thick air, as if all the things that remained unsaid still had weight to them—still threatened to crush them both. In that time, Aveline noticed that Jädrich had packed snow into where she'd bit, and already, it was like he'd never been injured at all. A shame. Aveline did her best to avoid Jädrich's eye during the whole journey, thinking instead of the moment she would once again find herself on the other side of that great wall in the distance.

It'd only been a little more than a month and a half since Aveline saw the Winter Wall, and yet it felt like it'd been years. She stared at it from the carriage window, where the trees were beginning to thin and give her a better view of the great ice structure. It seemed almost like a sheer cliff of ice. As they came closer still, and the trees faded for good, Aveline saw how the city of Taubech's many towering wood-and-stone houses clustered towards that wall, as if they were just as desperate to escape this country as she was.

That was likely the truth, given this was supposed to be a port city, and there was no port. The huge wall loomed over the town like some great prison warden, making it seem as if they'd reached the very end of the world with no hope of ever seeing anything beyond it. Aveline knew, though, that there was far more to this world than this town—and the people here knew it, too. After all, from what she'd heard about the place, its major exports used to be the certain kind of fish that lived around Winter's territory, fish with glass skin and clear water for blood. But since the High Summer, it'd lost its access to the outside world. Jädrich wanted to make sure no fleshling from the other three seasons of the Ringlands would ever make it inside, and so he sacrificed some few miles of Winter territory, pulling that wall inside so none would ever even be able to enter via the Ringlands' great lake. But what was a port city with no port?

Aveline didn't know, nor could she spend much energy thinking about it. She chafed against the dress she'd chosen for her first day in Taubech, even though it was one of the most comfortable ones she owned—another loose one with the spaces in the back to slide her wings free. The only difference with this one was that it was a faint lilac color, like Spring flowers. However, she may as well have been wearing full armor, with the way she wanted to charge into that city and get all this nonsense over with. Etiquette was dead, decorum slaughtered—and she'd shred that dress clean off her in front of a thousand people if it meant she could shoot for that wall and disappear for good.

Wait for the right time. So Karina told her before they left that last town; she'd caught Aveline in the stairwell of that mayor's house and said it so quick, so fast, that Aveline almost missed it. *We'll leave together. It'll be safer that way.*

Aveline hoped it would be. She certainly would've liked to believe her unlikely ally, that anything from this point on would be safe or assured. But no matter what, she was ready to bolt at a moment's notice if it meant getting away from this King and his false promises, these people and their greedy mouths—perhaps making her a true doe after all.

Her fingers twitched with the thought, and her tightening skin, her tensing shoulders, was the doe-wraith's rebuttal. All that tension said: *I'm no doe anymore.* And again, when Aveline blinked, she caught a glimpse of that blue dragon eye.

Hmm. Aveline blinked the image away and forced her body slack. Ever since that thing cut the contract's cord, it'd been a little easier to manage—and she felt that ease when she slept, felt it in the way the doe-wraith haunted her mind. In her dreams, it looked at her the way a bird might warily look at someone with a heel of bread in their hand—like it trusted her to some extent, like it expected something from her, and like it would happily take what Aveline had if she left it unguarded. There was a sudden patience to the beast that made her bones feel heavy, and a comfort in the thorns and vines it guarded her heart with.

As the carriages rolled through the streets of Taubech, however, Aveline found them suspiciously empty. Silent, too. No one was there to watch the carriages, nor to shout from windows and rooftops or throw little carvings of ice "gems" to bounce off the carriage doors. No, all the ruckus Aveline had seen over her time traveling south didn't appear here in Taubech, and the silence left her uneasy—until they turned towards the city square.

The carriages slowed down as a wall of people all but blocked the roadway off. They began to move aside, and soon the carriages were moving forward again, all while the people peered into the carriage windows. They were still silent, though, all of these people—all of these broken things, some missing noses, some with frail jaws, some with entire hands or even arms missing. These people were hairless, too. Most of them were just as bald as Aveline's *Unseelechs* when she'd first found them. Even if Aveline saw people in poor shape all along the tour, to see them *this* bad was—

"You're watching them, too?" Jädrich's voice shattered the silence.

Aveline glanced at him, then nodded. "Don't make me fix them right away, Jädrich."

His stare needled her. "The longer you wait, the more likely they are to break in ways that'll be very expensive for them to fix."

"Then pay for it with the Crown's money," she muttered. "Not like you ice-folk have any serious need for money in the first place."

Jädrich paused. Maybe he didn't know what she meant: that ice people, who didn't need to buy food and the means of producing food, should have had money to spare on ridiculous things like re-sculpting their bodies. The more she thought about it herself, the more she wondered: what exactly *did* a *Korbeldauer* charge so much for, that any in this country would be unable to properly fix themselves?

This land is cursed.

"You get two days," Jädrich finally said. "I'll arrange for you to have plenty of food to recover with. But the faster you do your duties—"

"The faster we go home, yes, I know."

Jädrich once again fell silent. The carriage came up behind the city center's stage, which sat under yet another statue of Cervora: one where the fallen goddess was holding a net full of fish and had freshwater reeds hanging from her antlers. An odd picture, no doubt, but Aveline understood it to be a nod to the city's past. It only contributed to the strange air that hung around their carriages, and to the silence that threatened to suffocate Aveline as a couple guards eventually came to open the door for her and her husband.

Jädrich climbed out first and offered Aveline his hand. She took it, if only to keep steady as she navigated the carriage's tiny step, and then she snatched it back to look down the line of carriages until she spotted the one she wanted: the one jostling about, with something sharp tapping against the carriage glass. The one with her babies inside.

"Aveline," Jädrich warned.

But she ignored him—even swatted his hand away when he went to grab her wrist. She all but ran for that carriage, and its door came open easily enough with a crack of her magic through its lock. Only with the door open did the commotion inside settle down, and her full-haired babies stared at her with those moon-bright eyes.

"Come along, now," she said, beaming at her *Unseel-echs*. They looked far better off than the people of Tau-bech, what with all that hair, and with their ice bodies a brilliant milky white—so white that even the strands of magic that made their puppet-like pieces fit together couldn't be seen. Whoever put them in that carriage clearly gave them something to chew on for the ride; their mouths were smeared in red, and the carriage floor was a mess of sticky, half-frozen goo. Jädrich told her to leave her babies in the carriages, but how could she, when they'd always been by her side? In quick, quiet Yasilan, she crooned, "Come, babies."

The suddenly fluid, curling words made them perk

up. When she beckoned them, they abandoned the shreds of their meal and came scampering to her. They brushed against the ends of her skirts and smeared a bit of their mess along the silver embroidery at its hem, and she thought that bright flash of red suited the black of her hooves well—the red of a low hanging desert sun.

My babies, she thought as they followed at her heels, croaking and gurgling all the way. Her bones sang to her, and the hairs on her head rustled in such a way that she swore she heard a word spoken in her ear: *Kviraeg.*

When she looked back to the line of carriages, she delighted in the stares of the guards, the tight, hard mask of Jädrich's face, and even the scowl of Erik as he left his own carriage with Karina. They didn't approach her, either—not with her babies clustering around her ankles and scratching at the icy stone beneath their feet. So Aveline, with her head high and a bright smile on her face, let herself be the first one to come up onto the stage with her babies in tow. She wondered, as she moved to the middle of that old wooden thing, what the broken and magicless people thought as her *Unseelechs* and their thick manes of hair followed her.

They aren't worthy. The thought wasn't her own, but the doe-wraith's, and as the others joined her on that stage, she let it curl into her mind like a cat into a cushioned basket. *Unworthy things. Kviraeg—my Kviraeg deserve more.*

"People of Taubech!"

The sudden ring of a woman's booming voice made Aveline blink. As she stood beside Jädrich, no doubt the perfect picture of a royal couple—save for the *Unseelechs* gripping Aveline's ankles and threatening to shred parts of her skirt—the sound of a woman's steps soon punctuated this wicked silence.

Aveline pulled her eyes off the near lifeless crowd and looked at the stage's stairs, where what appeared to be the city's patroness climbed up to join Aveline and her entourage. The lady of Taubech made her status obvious: despite being so small a woman, she wore a grand, deep blue, yet not so puffy dress, with white lace at her low collar and draping long off her sleeves, which only came down to the middle of her forearms. On her head was a deep blue tricorn hat with a huge white feather curling off it, resting atop a head of thick, loosely braided hair, and she wore a great green gem wrapped in an ornate silver frame around her neck. Her lips were painted a bruise-purple color, though her eyes were the same as any other woman's: black and endlessly deep. While the fashion for this place was certainly different from the capital, there was no mistaking the lady of this city: Margravine Isolde Beurvich, a master tradeswoman, merchant, and noblewoman caring for quite a decent stretch of land in the absence of any dukes or duchesses in the area.

Do not trust the Margravine. Karina's words echoed in her head. She'd said these things that day in the forest clearing, as they discussed a possible plan to escape this country. *Keep on your guard.*

But Aveline didn't need to be told something like that. She didn't trust any of these Ismären when she came to this place because she didn't trust those she didn't know. And she didn't trust any Ismären then, either, because she learned not to trust the people she *thought* she knew, too. Sometimes, when she let her thoughts wander too far, she still saw the look on Ristef's face when she'd pulled her wings free in that field.

It felt like it'd been ages since she so much as looked in his direction. She wondered if he realized that—if he felt her absence at his side the same way she did.

The Margravine came before Jädrich and Aveline and bowed deeply; her hat's feather nearly brushed Aveline's arm. She rose soon enough with a smile, though there was a quick crackle of magic across her onyx eyes as her gaze lingered on Aveline and the *Unseelechs*. Then she turned back to her city folk and let her voice carry across the crowd once more.

"We stand here blessed, truly, to be in the presence of not only His Majesty the King, but his beloved bride, the Queen of Winter, the Mother of all Ismären, Cervora reborn."

Aveline braced herself for raucous applause, as she'd received in a few of the more populated towns they'd come across—but it never came. The people stayed silent, save for a few murmurs, and it seemed that all their gazes were focused solely on her. Their faces were flat, their bodies stiff, their stares haunting. Aveline's stomach twisted as her nerves made sharp pinpricks flitter across her jaw.

They want to eat us. She'd seen that look before. Or, rather, her bones had. Her blood had. Her tendons had. *They're hungry again.*

That's what it was in their face, yes. Hunger. These ice-people didn't know that word, and they claimed not to know what it felt like, but all those wide eyes set deep in those broken bodies told Aveline otherwise. But hungry they would stay. Not one more drop of Aveline's blood would leave her veins, nor would one more crackle of frost leave her lips—not for them. Not because she wanted to spite these people. Not because she hated them. Even if her heart felt as if set on fire with the doe-wraith's conviction, Aveline herself didn't feel any ill will for these mangled people. In fact, that was precisely the problem: she didn't feel anything at all in the face of their misery. She was, as her mother's peers called her, a hollow egg.

Oh, Lina-Lina, don't listen to them. How quiet the memory of her mother's voice suddenly seemed in comparison to the messages the doe-wraith wrote with her own flesh. *You're plenty lively. Just in your own way.*

"To celebrate," the Margravine went on, "we'll allow the King and Queen a night of joy in the Beurvich manor, for a grand ball, before they begin their work to restore our beautiful city's people to their rightful status."

Aveline glanced at Jädrich, but if he was surprised by this, he didn't show it. His face stayed as blank and lifeless as ever. So Aveline stayed still, too, as the Margravine waited for applause and once again found herself rewarded with little more than murmurs.

"Tomorrow morning in the cathedral, come all ye faithful, and be healed," the Margravine said with a clap of her hands. "Until then, may your day be bright as the Melded Lake's waters, your fortunes as full as a fisher's nets."

And then she walked off the stage, casting one last, sharp glance at Aveline and Jädrich.

This is a disaster.
Isolde paced her study and tried to ignore the hustle and bustle going on down the hall, in the manor foyer. She did her best to prepare, but all her best couldn't change the simple fact that it was too early for the King to be on her doorstep. *Far* too early. Isolde heard far too late down the line of rumors that the King and Queen were nearing Taubech, and so she had to throw every resource she had into preparing the trap she and her compatriots devised for that Queen: a ball, a great and raucous occasion, where the Queen would easily be snatched in the chaos and the King would be outnumbered in trying to reclaim her. Where he would be de-crowned, de-throned, and done away with for good.

But where is Ti-Vaour? She'd cut that communication line the moment she realized Efir came in contact with a *lady*, which could've only been the King's advisor, but that still might've been too late. Far too late. Who knew what that brute of a woman might've planted on that dragon? What things she might've had recording his every step, word, every *breath?* She'd heard enough about Clara Ronterweis to know just what horrors a little thing could do with enough tools and time. All there was left to do was bolster security in the manor and hope to any god that would still listen that her plans would play out without incident. *Where is he?*

A knock at the door startled Isolde out of her thoughts. She hurried for it and turned the handle, though she barely had time to get out of the way before yet *another* irritation came slipping through the door. Erik—gods, Erik. He carefully shut the door behind him and bore down on Isolde with his stare, magic crackling across the dark blue and gold of his eyes.

"Isolde," he muttered through clenched teeth, "what do you mean, the ball is *tonight?* How was I or anyone else supposed to be prepared for—?"

"The same way I was supposed to be prepared for you all to come here *two weeks early,* you—you—!"

Words failed her. She clutched at the empty air and turned away from him, hoping to regain a scrap of composure. All she could do, though, was lean a hand on her desk and rub her temple's velvet. Her study, a quiet, small place stuffed with books and papers and with a desk only marginally bigger than a student's, was supposed to be her refuge. Her place to think. The place she'd concocted many a scheme, many a lie, over the past few decades. And yet those deep blue walls with the little fish painted on them, the beams of dark brown wood, the familiar, weathered tomes that lined her bookshelves—they brought her no peace then. Not with Erik's stare needling into her back.

His voice, similarly, did nothing for her nerves. "I know. I'm sorry. I had no chance to get a message to you, not with the King always nearby or with his men all around us. But—"

"No *buts,* Erik." Isolde whipped around and pressed her hands together as if about to pray. She tapped her fingers to her lips as she stared that whelp of a viscount down, and then she muttered, "We are out of time. I cannot have that tyrant wandering around this city with his bride, doing whatever nonsense I've been told she's doing. What is this now, about blood? About permanent magic?"

Erik hunched towards her and hissed, as if the walls themselves might be listening, "It's for the *ransom*! It's a good thing—"

Isolde held a hand to him and snapped, "No. It's a stick in the spoke of the wheel we've been turning, Erik. Decades' worth of groundwork is in this city. *Decades.* You've played your hand too far. You'll make that King a hero, with his bride fixing everything we've done."

And that's what you want, isn't it? The thought crossed her mind just as that last sentence left her mouth. She pressed her lips into a tight line. *That's what you want, you back-stabber.*

As if Erik could read her thoughts, he shook his head. "It'll be fine. It'll be fine, Isolde, I swear, but you risk making the King suspicious, hosting a ball on such short notice."

"What, is it strange to welcome a King with a grand celebration?" Isolde's mouth twitched into a stiff smile. "We'll be fine. *You,* however, should be careful. And be *ready,*" she came closer to him, close enough that she all but tucked herself under his gaze, "to execute the plan *you* pitched to me. Do you understand?"

She wouldn't tell him about the Sekhran's son skulking around. Didn't need to. With luck, this would all be handled in one fell swoop, and she could act on the plan she and the other lords developed without this runt: the plan to cast him into the pit with that King, as a traitor and a royalist, a lapdog of the King who installed his cousin for political power against the better interests of the people of Winter.

Erik squeezed his lips together so tight that they squeaked. His eyes glittered with magic, with his uncontrolled rage. Then he nodded and muttered, "Fine. I'll do my best. May all go off without a hitch, hmm?"

Isolde didn't respond. She only tipped her chin up and waited for him to leave—and he did. He turned and left without another word, and this time, he let the study door slam shut behind him.

"I can't believe this," Aula muttered as she fluttered around Aveline with pins between her teeth. She was pulling in bits and pieces of Aveline's new dress so quickly that she almost believed she *could* make it perfect by nightfall. "Who decides to host a ball like that with no warning? As a welcome party? Don't these nobles know things like this take *time* to prepare?"

A huff left Aveline, and Aula paused. She glanced up at the mirror, expecting some kind of reprimand, but then, what was she thinking? Aveline herself was nothing close to nobility until only very recently, and that little smile on her face reminded Aula of that. As she stood on top of the little stool they'd dragged from the corner of this huge guest room, Aveline stayed silent, but Aula noticed how quickly her gaze returned to the dress she was to debut at the ball.

This dress was one Aula hoped would signal *Summer,*

even if only a little bit. She didn't really remember
what Summer fashion looked like; her only record
of any such clothes was a century-old magazine she
managed to hide in her house, miles and miles away.
But she remembered something about long chiffon
sashes with fine lace on their edges, ones that draped
over tight beaded sleeves with long, loose, near flag-
like ends. She remembered dresses with loose ribbons
of chiffon on an otherwise open back to allude to a
dragon's wings, too, and ones with long, intricately
beaded and embroidered skirts that gently belled off
the body—nothing like the poofy things the capital's
ladies commissioned Aula for. So she'd made one of
these in black and gold: a fitted thing, a dazzlingly bold
and glittering thing, one Aula felt was fit for a Queen.

Once all the pins were in place, Aula called up her
magic and sent needles zipping through the air, twining
up all those pinned spots in black thread. It felt strange
to use so much magic for her projects, but because of
Aveline, she didn't have to worry about conserving it
anymore. Because she'd drank from that communion
cup, she could finish even the most intricate projects in
little more than a night. The work she'd be able to do
when she got home would put her best months in her
trade to shame.

"There," Aula said as the last thread knotted and severed itself. She stood back to take a look at Aveline, then
squeaked when she realized she forgot the sash. After a
moment of digging through her basket full of tools and
threads and fabric scraps, Aula found it, then went and
tossed it over Aveline's shoulder. Once adjusted, Aula
stood back again. "Okay, *now* it's done. What do you
think? Is this close enough to what you had in mind?"

"It's," Aveline looked at herself a little longer, her
brows pinching despite her smile, "it's something a
Sekhvaah would wear."

Aula blinked. "A what?"

"A Council Member," came another voice, "a Sekhran's wife."

Only then did Aula have the misfortune of remembering who'd been assigned to watch over them in that guest room. Aula rolled her eyes and looked over her shoulder to Ristef, who sat in one of the two cushioned armchairs towards the guest room's long dead fireplace.

He stared at Aveline with a hard-set brow, lips pressed tight, and then he muttered, "That'll turn heads, alright. If anyone has the magic to turn them."

"As it should! She looks beautiful in—!"

"Aula." Ristef's blunt tone made Aula frown, and she knew he could see the irritation bubbling in her soul—which made it all the worse that he kept talking. "You know we're trying to *hide* her other half, don't you? This'll make people talk even—"

A rustle of leather and a crunch of bone made both Ristef and Aveline flinch. Aula barely moved out of the way in time to not get slapped by a stray wing as it peeled off Aveline's back and stretched up high. The open back of her dress let Aula see exactly where they connected to her shoulder blades, and the little dangling bits of chiffon gathered right along her spine between them. It was a perfect fit.

"I'm not interested in hiding anymore," Aveline whispered. Her gaze stayed on her reflection a moment longer. "I'm tired."

A moment passed before Ristef's boots thumped across the room's old floorboards. Only the bearskin rug softened the tap of his steps. "You don't mean to tell me you'll let these go during the ball, do you?"

"Of course not," Aula snapped. She thumped his side and muttered, "She's not stupid."

When Aula went to face Aveline, she found those deep blue eyes boring down on her hard enough to make Aula feel small as a mouse. Aveline looked between her and Ristef, a ghost of a smile on her lips, and then she rolled her shoulders back and flexed her shoulder blades. Her wings folded up tight and disappeared against the skin of her back, melting together as if the thin wings' membrane were made of quickly melting snow. But she didn't make any remarks to either Aula or Ristef. She only looked at herself one more time, then nodded.

"This is fine work, Aula." Then she turned that stare back on the seamstress. "What are you wearing?"

"What—me?" Aula blinked. "I'm not going. Why would I be invited—?"

"Of course you're going. I want you there." Aveline crouched down to Aula's height and smiled. "You've been good to me. More than good. I want you to enjoy yourself tonight, too."

Is this the same Aveline I met weeks ago? There was still that sharpness to her features, that wildness lurking under the surface of her gaze, but Aula couldn't help but feel that there was something else in her, too. Something old, something tired. No doubt after a few weeks of this tour, she had every right to have such a weight to her gaze, but it was still strange—both the weight in her, and the softness in her words that seemed to balance that weight.

"Well, if you insist," Aula muttered, suddenly bashful, "then I suppose... I suppose I could change into one of my better things."

"Good." Her smile grew, and then she looked at Ristef. "And you? Will you be nearby for this ball?"

Ristef shook his head, crossed his arms. "I'm on manor security with the rest of Beurvich's men for the night. You'll have others with you, though."

Aula frowned. It seemed her last slap hadn't taken any of the coldness out of him. He hadn't even had the sense to repent the last awful words he'd said to Aula before, and she hoped that Aveline didn't somehow know what he'd said. But then, if she were a goddess, she *would* know, wouldn't she? And she didn't smite or disown the guard, so maybe he *had* repented, and Aula just didn't know. Either way, just thinking of what Ristef said before, and how he'd acted when he found out Aveline was half-Yasilan, made her soul squeeze with rage—and by the way he glanced at her, he could see that. Aula let him see it, too, just as she had the entire silent carriage ride to Taubech.

Heathen. She hoped that thought would drill its way out of her head and into his. *Ungrateful heretic.*

"You should get dressed, Aula," Aveline said, and her hand landed gently on Aula's shoulder.

Then Aveline slipped towards Ristef, and even he blinked as she put her hands on his arms. She tugged at them until they came loose, and then she held one of Ristef's hands—even pressed a kiss to it. Aula stared, dumbfounded, as Aveline held Ristef's hand tight and hovered her face so close to his.

What in the world—?

"You were the only thing that got me through that bridal competition," Aveline whispered. "The whole time, you were the only thing that kept me sane." Then she stepped away and went back to looking at her dress in the mirror. "Both of you can go. Aula, I'll see you tonight."

Aula didn't know what to say, so she simply tipped her head, took her basket, and left, with Ristef walking behind her. The whole time out the door, though, all Aula could think about was how Aveline kissed his hand like that. And what she said—what did that mean?

Was she catching that guard's love, too? The thought made Aula's soul sharp with something she didn't understand. *What did she need him for? What about him kept her sane?*

When she glanced behind her, towards Aveline's door, she ended up catching Ristef's eye instead. He quirked a brow at her, no doubt seeing whatever it was Aula was feeling, and she forced all her thoughts away before storming off to her own modest quarters without another word.

There was no time to think about whatever Aveline and Ristef were doing before she became Queen. It wasn't her business. All she knew was that she suddenly had a ball to dress for, and only one halfway decent dress to wear to it. A few alterations wouldn't hurt, and she occupied her mind with those alterations, all while Ristef's footsteps tapped behind her. Only when she reached her room, and Ristef's footsteps trailed off, did she let her mind wander again.

Did she love Ristef, too? That bastard. He had no business stealing Aveline's eye. *Did he love her back? Could they even love each other in only a few weeks' time?*

Aula shook her head as if she could rattle the thoughts free and throw them away. Stupid thoughts, pointless thoughts—and yet they brought back that strange, sharp feeling in her skull. She didn't dare think of the last time she might've felt something like that. No, Aula simply went for her trunks and took up her tools again, letting her work numb her mind of all such foolishness for at least another hour or so.

What did she do to me? What did she do, that bitch?

Efir staggered through the outskirts of the city, where the last few trees marked the end of the forest. The glow of Taubech caught his eye a long time ago, and he'd been hurrying for it ever since. However, between the stinging cold air and the sharp pain ricocheting across his skull, he could hardly keep his eyes open. All he knew was that he was to keep going south. That the Winter Lord was south. That the traitorous witch-woman was south.

That his home was *south.*

There was nothing he could do except keep trudging through knee-high snow, out there on what seemed like the edge of the world. There was a road not a few feet away, clear and open and easy to walk, but Efir had to keep to the thickly wooded outskirts, lest he be spotted by travelers or stumble upon one of the many slums that made up the edge of the port town. What a mess, that he'd ended up coming straight back down the path he'd gone up in the first place, trailing after that damned mixed-blood and her Winter Lord; his mother would've lashed the skin straight off his back for such a failure to track efficiently. But at least he was already back there, even with the handicap that the castle's ice-woman gave him—whatever it was.

It didn't take long to reach the edge of the city and the first few buildings of its outskirts. Normally, he might've crept closer to listen in and see what he could learn, but in this condition, doing any such thing would be a liability. It would only take one slip on the ice—one stumble, one cough, one single mistake—to bring his entire cover down and alert every guard, every Ismar, to the "fleshling" prowling around their ice-city full of little ice-children. The thought made his stomach turn; his throat clicked and burned with acid. Wretches, all of them. It would've been a blessing of Drakash to be able to come back to this country at the side of the Sekhran's militia and watch the whole Ismar world be melted into a great sea. Such a sea would start with that damn wall that loomed over the city. Efir could see it even over the first buildings of Taubech: a huge swath of hard, white nothingness, so tall it grazed the very stars.

A flash of pain lanced across Efir's temple and drove him to his knees in the snow. He clutched his head and bit his lip until it bled just to keep from making any sound. As much as he wanted to scream and dig his fingers into his skull until he found the source of this pain, there was no chancing anything. His mother taught him how to survive the worst pain without so much as a grimace; this would be, *could* be, no different.

What did she do? It was the only thing he could properly think in his head. The pressure he'd felt before, the curiosity and mild concern it'd spawned, it was nothing compared to the heart-thudding panic, the cold sweat *What did she do to me? The small woman?*

At this point, the only one that could've helped him in any sense was one of his father's wives. The one that unnerved him as a child, that Raliyah, the Head of Medicine. As uncanny as she was, with how she would stare out of her medicine rooms late at night, and as eerily quiet and still her children were, who never spoke unless they needed something from someone, they had the knowledge that kept the country from dying of every wayward disease that might've floated in on still waters or in spoiled meats or some such.

But he'd given up on that stone the Margravine gave him. There would be no one answering his calls anyway. All he could do was continue, and so he did. He went ignoring that pain in his temple and skulked through the city streets, winding through alleyways where those eerie blue lights didn't reach so far. And just like the first time he got through this city, he found the streets so terribly, deathly quiet. So absolutely devoid of life, of people—save for the odd ghoul that went creaking and crumbling with every jagged step. These people, these dolls—they were unwell. Beyond unwell.

Efir had no pity to spare for them, though. Even as he slipped past one especially cracked man, who was missing an arm and his entire jaw, and who stumbled along like little more than some soulless undead from the worst of Summer ghost stories, all Efir could feel for them was annoyance when they slowed him down. The pain still throbbed in his head, but it was getting easier to ignore. Even when he blinked, and his vision smeared and threatened to disorient him, he kept a much better track of landmarks here in the city. The forest was easy to get lost in, what with how everything looked the same, and that was why he waited for his mind to clear in that tree before taking the incredibly risky move of flying in the sky a few nights ago. Luckily, the build of a Swamplands dragon wasn't as bulky as that of a desert dragon. If anyone saw him, perhaps they only assumed he was a large bird. Without doing that, though, he never would've found his path to Taubech.

Eventually, the buildings emptied out into the city square, and Efir had little other choice: he had to climb the buildings and get onto their roof. With the occasional broken part of a wall or window ledge to get his footing on, and with his nails lengthening into the beginning of his talons, he soon found himself overlooking the entire city and spotting the Margravine's manor in the distance. The whole city was lit, yes, but that manor there—it was *alive* with that ghoulish glow. Shining like a Winter night star. Efir didn't need to be so close to know that it was full of activity, that something big was happening there.

Some thought tickled across his mind—something that was his voice, but that did not feel like his words.

Kill the mixed-blood.

He kept himself tucked in the shadows, his legs burning from how low he crouched to keep towards the walls of each building.

Kill her.

Soon, he'd have that mixed-blood in his possession. Whatever menace she was to the rest of Winter and that woman from the castle was no concern of his; he'd drag the beast across the wall to let his father judge—

Kill.

He would kill the mixed-blood with his own hands, of course; he would execute judgement on his father's behalf, as was his right as a Sekhran's heir. And the thought of her gasping for breath, her throat crushed between his hands, filled his mind. He trudged even faster, ignored how his heart felt like it would burst.

I'll kill her. I'll put this disgrace behind us all—behind Winter and Summer alike.

But not without getting justice for himself, too.

ERIK'S LEG BOUNCED AS HE CHECKED his pocket watch. It was nearing the start of the ball, yet there was no activity in the Beurvich house that he could see as a sign that any of his plans with Isolde were in effect whatsoever.

Isolde told him she'd take him as her partner for the ball that night, making it seem as if he were bringing a powerful woman like Taubech's noble into the fold of the Rachfemd family. Such a thing made sense to him, and it would hopefully make it seem as if Taubech was a city eager for the Crown's help rather than one plotting against it. Until Isolde came to retrieve him, however, there was nothing for him to do except wait.

He found himself staring at words in a book without registering them and wondering what would happen once the plan was finally set in motion. In Beurvich's tiny library, which was really just a room with a couple loveseats, a few bookshelves crammed with old tomes, and a long dead fireplace, Erik was in a perfect spot to keep tabs on things. He was close enough to the ballroom that he could hear the noise of the guests that had already streamed past the foyer below, yet he was far away enough, hidden enough, that no one would find him if they didn't know where to look. It was the one good thing about lords and ladies with high titles: their houses were always too large for their own good, mazes where secrets could gather in the shadowy corners and plots were easier to make look like accidents.

With a shake of his head, Erik dropped the book into his lap. He could only hope that whichever lord would be the one to poison the food they would serve Aveline wouldn't put enough to kill her. It worried him, the way the townspeople stared at her so coldly and quietly. Moreover, the higher members of society that were invited to a ball were the ones peddling all manners of rumors to begin with, filling those already downtrodden people with such terrible ideas about what was supposed to be a goddess. But then, it wasn't entirely their fault; Aveline herself hadn't made it very hard to spread wicked gossip. Even nearly a month later, that harrowing stunt she pulled over Cervora's skull would appear in Erik's memories and make him wince. *Wraith Queen* indeed, with how she screamed herself hoarse.

But once Aveline was properly poisoned enough to lead away into the dark, the rest of this plot was simple: take Aveline, threaten to kill her if the King didn't step down from his throne, and wait for his answer. Once he accepted their terms, the rest was out of Erik's hands; whatever they did to Aveline was of no consequence to him. He imagined, though, that someone with gifts like hers would be kept alive a while longer for the sake of healing the odd melted one or blessing people with permanent magic or whatever else that mutt could somehow do.

As he sat there waiting, he couldn't help but wonder if this was how *all* crossbreeds between Summer and Winter would be, and if it wasn't possible to make more of these doe-people to freeze Winterfolk with. Would their blood run silver, too? Would they also feed the people for the rest of their lives? Maybe once the seasons moved again, they could test that theory.

A knock at the door made Erik blink. *Finally,* he thought as he tossed his book on the coffee table. He didn't even know what it was about; he hadn't read more than two words in the past hour. As Erik got up, he wished this were any other circumstance, so that he might scold Isolde for taking so long to get to this part of the plan. *It's about time.*

As Erik went to open the door, he thought again of what he might talk to the King about later, in an effort to get his eye off Aveline long enough for her to be stolen away. What *was* there to say to him? He'd spent a good hour thinking of reasons to talk to the King, and so far, the only one that made sense was to ask after the state of his "cousin." The woman looked haggard lately, ashy and drained, and if Erik didn't know better, he would've said the King was trying to overharvest the frail thing. That wouldn't have been very good for the country, to have their goddess only live a few short weeks before shriveling up and dying.

Or maybe she's just not taking care of herself right. He turned the doorknob and swung the door open. *Maybe she's—*

Pain.

Blinding pain. Something shattered, but it sounded like it was far away—and muffled. He couldn't see, either, as that pain engulfed his very soul; he only knew that he suddenly felt lighter, smaller, and that there was something in front of him that didn't at all look like an Ismar, or any kind of person, for that matter. What he saw was a world that had become a smear of oily paints, all different colors taking vague shapes of things like console tables or doors or the like. Before him was some kind of lizard. A black and green lizard, one that moved in such a strange way. Even though Erik could no longer blink his eyes for some reason, he found the lizard moving bit by bit, as if it could disappear and reappear every second.

Erik looked down. There was something on the floor: a mess of deep blue, and scattered pieces of silver. It looked like someone had shattered a porcelain doll. Right where he was standing, someone had shattered a porcelain doll—

Come home.

Something called him, though he didn't know what. He only knew that he didn't want to look at that smashed up doll, and that there was somewhere better waiting for him. Somewhere far, far north, somewhere dark and cold and safe.

Come home. Come back. Come to us.

And he did. Smaller and lighter, he easily fit up that dead fireplace chute, easily squeezed out of its top, and shot across the sky like a star towards that voice. He was free, at peace, and ready to hide away and rest, ready to forget everything. As it was, he already forgot a few key things: about the plan, about Autumn.

Who am I? The scenery blurred beneath him as he flew. *What's my name?*

Whatever it was, it couldn't have been that important.

Aveline could've gone her whole life without hearing those gods-forsaken violins again. They screeched and wailed on the right side of the ballroom, where a few nobles clustered at empty tables. The rest of the guests were swirling round and round on the parquet, their long lacy sleeves hanging low enough to nearly cover the rest of their otherwise open forearms, and their dresses cut so low that Aveline wondered why they bothered with a bodice at all. And what women still did have enough hair piled it into some monstrosity on top of their heads that looked like a melting lump of snow.

She stood just outside the ballroom door, as much out of sight as she could be. Luckily for her, the ballroom entrance was on a steep flight of stairs that kept her hidden. The two Taubech guards stationed on either side of the door didn't say anything to her; in fact, they didn't even look at her. What a shame. She wondered if she might've gotten an early glimpse of what her dress would do to the crowd based on their reactions, but it seemed she had no choice but to simply walk in. However people would think of her clearly Summer-inspired dress would have to be a surprise. With a deep breath, she steadied herself, and just as whatever squealing sound died down on the violins, she let the sharp clack of her hooves announce her presence.

The blue starlights washed over her, and as she stood at the top of the stairs, she felt as if she were watching a great herd of goats from the top of Kha-Bawaj—especially with how, as people noticed her, they shrank together and whispered to one another. There was something thrilling about the way dozens of heads turned and dozens of eyes landed on her. Something satisfying about the way the room fell into a deep hush. The deep, expectant silence that filled the room—that was sweeter than music, sweet enough that Aveline didn't want to spoil it.

Someone else spoiled it for her, though. From the clump of dresses and fine hats and frilly lace came a much starker figure: Jädrich, his crown sparkling in the starlight, his fine white suit all glittering with its silver buttons and detailed embroidery. He wore a sword of black ice at his hip—for what, Aveline didn't know, because his magic alone was enough to erase the world two times over.

And I've given him an endless reservoir of it.

"My people," he said as he came to the base of the stairs, "welcome your Queen and Mother."

Aveline took that as her cue to continue down the stairs. She clopped down each step until her hand could reach out and find Jädrich's. When they stood together, they were shoulder to shoulder—and her antlers, she dared to believe, outmatched the height of his crown. He squeezed her hand tight enough to make her bones uncomfortable, but she smiled anyway as the people bowed low, men tucking a hand behind their back, women picking up the skirts of their dresses. They stayed that way for some time, until Aveline realized it was up to her to release them.

"Rise," she called.

Her voice carried over the people; it seemed to reach every corner of the room and echo back. As the people stood and stared at her—or, rather, her dress, given how the eyes of the men tracked all over her—she let her lips curl back into a wicked smile. Suddenly, that dress was no longer a thing made of satin and chiffon and beads and thread, but a covering of black and gold scales, an armor that put stiffness in her back and set her shoulders straight.

Yes, good.

"Glory to you, Ismären." She lifted her hands, the loose ends of her sleeves falling away and revealing her bandaged arms. "Your god stands before you, grateful for such a celebration. May healing find you all," her lips became a grin, her teeth caging a laugh she couldn't release, "and may you never thirst again, once I've left this place."

Empty blessings from an empty heart. As the people clacked their hands together in polite applause, Aveline dropped her arms and looked around. Jädrich raised a brow at her, and she answered his silent question with a smile.

Once they'd locked arms and gone to the parquet, Aveline muttered, "Where's the lady of the house?"

"Apparently the Margravine has some security matters to attend to." Jädrich steered her off the parquet, towards one section of tables where a familiar face sat: the Baron of Trevannt. "She'll be here soon, no doubt."

"Ah, Your Majesties!" The Baron's voice boomed over them both, and that round little man came to Jädrich and Aveline. "Good to see you again so soon! And you, dear Mother," the Baron tipped his head, "you must give my compliments to your seamstress. This dress is truly unique, truly!"

Aveline smiled, then looked around. "You may very well be able to give her your compliments yourself. Oh," Aveline spotted Aula some ways away, tucked at a table by herself and all but staring holes into Aveline's head, "there she is."

It only took a wave of Aveline's hand for Aula to get up and come hurrying over. Her dress was, as expected, a beautiful one—a deep blue thing that reached her mid-calf, lengthened by a petticoat of lace that brushed the floor. It had a high neckline of blue chiffon, ending in a heart-shaped bodice of shining blue satin, and it was crusted with white and silver beads that looked like little sparkles of ice along her breasts. A silver belt with a snowflake buckle held her waist in. It certainly wasn't a court dress, or the typical formalwear—not nearly so flashy as the other noblewomen's dresses—but it matched Aula's sweet face and the soft waves of her hair, which Aveline only then realized she hardly ever saw fully down.

"Your Majesties," Aula said as she came close enough. She curtsied and smiled, though she didn't say anything afterwards. By the way she stood so stiff and held her own hands so tightly together, though, Aveline could tell where her nerves were.

Aveline put a friendly hand on Aula's shoulder and said, "This is Aula Verrinson, my seamstress. She's made all my dresses; she knows exactly what I like."

"I see," the Baron said. He smiled, his mustache moving with his lips, and he offered Aula his hand. When she took it, he raised her hand to his lips for a brief kiss, then said, "I should ask you to make dresses for my wife. She adores a unique piece like this one you've made for our Queen tonight."

"Oh, well," Aula smiled and pulled back into herself, "I—if Her Majesty thinks that's fine, then I suppose—"

Aveline slipped off Jädrich's arm and sidled closer to Aula until the little thing fit under the crook of her arm. "Of course," she said as she gave Aula a light squeeze. "You make dresses for whoever you'd like. Don't feel constrained to me.

Especially since Aula didn't realize she'd made the last dress she ever would for Aveline already.

Aula smiled at Aveline. Her attention snapped back to the men, however, as Jädrich's voice rumbled over them all.

"How did you come to Taubech so quickly, Lord Fervall?" Jädrich's face stayed flat as ever. "Did you know of this ball beforehand?"

Baron Fervall gave a tight smile and said, "Ah, well, of course. It was meant to be a surprise for you both; our Margravine does love a good surprise. Speaking of which," he turned to Aveline, "we have a mighty surprise for you, as well. A proper meal, a *feast,* in fact."

"A feast?" Aveline chuckled. "For but one woman? I'm afraid much of it may go to waste."

"Oh," the Baron waved a hand, chuckling along with her, "you'll have all night to eat it, no doubt. In fact, just say the word, and we'll bring it out for you right now. Are you hungry?" Baron Fervall said that last line as if it were a foreign phrase he'd just learned. "Should we—?"

"No, no." Aveline waved a hand. "I'm not particularly hungry now. I'll let someone know when I am."

The last thing she wanted to do was fly on a full stomach. She'd done so before, and the pain of her overstretched stomach made her time in the air unbearable. But the Baron's face fell a bit, as if he were disappointed. Just as he was about to say something else, however, the violins squealed again, and Aveline couldn't stop her smile from twitching into something more of a grimace. If she were true Queen and tyrant, she'd demand every violin in this country be burned.

"Ah, this is a lovely song!" The Baron clapped his hands; his eyes sparkled with his apparent glee, and he said, "Let us enjoy it, Your Majesties. My lady," he turned to Aula, "might I have this dance?"

Once again, Aula glanced at Aveline as if asking permission, and Aveline nodded with a smile. Sweet thing. As the Baron took Aula away to the parquet, already chatting with her and earning a laugh from her with whatever he said, Aveline couldn't help but feel as if stones were dropping in her heart. She would miss that punchy little creature. Her and even Ristef, who, despite how rigid he'd been, seemed to be gravitating towards Aula the way he once did with her. There was no way she could miss it as Aula fixed her dress earlier that day: how his gaze tracked Aula's every move, how his lips twitched into the tiniest smile when she'd used her magic to so masterfully complete Aveline's dress in one fell swoop.

Have I really lost my hangman? Her heart twinged at the thought. *My dear friend?*

"Come," Jädrich said. He gently tugged her towards the other tables. "We have more pleasantries to make."

"You don't want to dance first?"

"We'll have all night to dance. First, there's faces to be reacquainted with." Jädrich scanned the room like a falcon scanned the skies. "I've been away from the border for far too long, it seems."

Aveline blinked, but she didn't say anything else. She simply followed Jädrich to the various faces that apparently concerned him: those of some Duchess from an eastern hold, from some Count and Viscountess—all of which stared at Aveline as if she were some uncanny, unfathomable creature. For all their smiles and pleasantries, all their polite, if strained conversation about finances and the health of their people, they couldn't hide what Aveline picked up on from their stares: their malice.

They did not like Aveline. Their wide-eyed, lingering stares, the occasional twitches in their pinned up smiles, the way they leaned ever so slightly away from her—they were all the little things that made up the picture of their ire. Aveline knew it in her bones: they did not accept her, even if they made a show of fawning over her and listening to the few words she spoke to them about her "miracles." Body language as subtle as that was necessary to gauge if a goat she'd been tracking was actually unaware of her, or if it was waiting for her to move so it could bolt. Or if a mountain lion intended to call her bluff and charge her. Little things, such silly little things—they were all that stood guarding the bridge between life and death.

After some time of going around the tables, the violins swelled into yet another song, and Jädrich finally turned his face towards the parquet. He looked at her and said, "Now's a fine time to dance."

Is it? Aveline didn't find this song any more pleasant

than any other. But she kept her façade up; she smiled and nodded and let her ice-doll of a husband lead her to the growing crowd of dancers. It'd been a long time since she did this funny little twirling dance, but Jädrich reminded her of where to put her hands and where to keep her feet.

"One foot on mine," he said. "I'll guide you."

"You don't think I can manage myself?"

"No. You haven't had any practice since you first learned it."

Blunt, rude thing. Aveline sucked her teeth and put her hoof over his. There was something about that bluntness she would miss. Especially after watching so many nobles put on pretenses of politeness with her and their King. It was a cutting honesty that came off Jädrich's tongue—at least, until it came to that contract. The thought of their marriage contract soured her, but she did her best to keep her face as blank and unreadable as Jädrich's.

"This dress," Jädrich muttered as they spun in circles over the wooden floor, "it's a Summer dress."

"I did ask for it to look like one, yes."

"Your seamstress should've denied your request."

"And how could she ever deny her Queen?" Aveline felt the rueful smile growing on her lips and did nothing to stop it. "What I want, I get. Is that not the power of a crown?"

His face stayed blank, but a single shimmer of silver cracked across his left eye like a lightning bolt. "You wear no crown."

"You're right. I wear something better." She glanced over Jädrich's shoulder, to all the other people swirling around them. "I have antlers and hooves. Two miracles to share. Even the confirmation of the Bishops themselves. My word," her smile became a grin as his eyes flashed again with magic, "my word is true Law now.

And you know it. You know your contract with me is dissolved. You know I hold your country in my hands."

"One glimpse of your wings, and the name you've built for yourself falls apart," Jädrich said. The way he said it, so blunt and matter-of-fact, almost made Aveline believe him. "You test your luck with a dress like this. The people here don't believe you to be Cervora. They believe the rumors—that you're a mutt, a bastard child. I've done all I can to overturn such rumors, as has your cousin. Even he has been speaking your praises all this time, as much as possible. Yet you'd throw all that away for a feeling of power and pride."

Aveline barked a laugh. It was one thing to lie about how he wanted to protect her so badly, but Erik, too? No. Both of them, she knew then, cared for her as much as the brutal nightkeepers of Summer cared for the women they stole from warm homes and sold for high prices in alleyways and underpasses—in places where the disturbing things their clientele wanted wouldn't have them turned away, as such men were from the more respectable brothels like her mother's. Moreover, to talk of *power and pride*—what nonsense. Those were the treasures of fools. All Aveline wanted was safety. All she wanted was a bed to sleep in and food in her belly. And all the doe-wraith wanted was something much more pointed, much more direct, than all that nonsense: *justice.*

"Oh, Jädrich," she crooned as the last of her laughter faded. "You're funny."

His grip on her tightened. He squeezed her waist, nearly crushed her hand, and he said, "You're planning something. With that Sekhran."

"With—?" Aveline was almost too stunned to laugh, but her mouth fell open, and her hiccups of laughter peeled out. She slapped his shoulder as he guided her to step back, and she said, "Now you're just being ridiculous." Then, as she stepped forward, she leaned her face in closer and whispered, so quiet that the violins almost stole her voice away, "I think that Sekhran would burn me alive if I ever stepped foot in Summer again. Why else would I have come here instead of stay home? Why would I have become your bride, rather than his?"

Aveline pulled away and smiled, and only then did Jädrich's mask break. He stared at her with brows pinched tight, with eyes alight with magic, and with his mouth open as if he wanted to speak—wanted to accuse her, question her—yet he stayed silent. So silent. She'd apparently stolen the words right from his mouth with that vague confession, and she delighted in that fact.

Just as the song died down, however, Aveline caught a flash from the top of the stairs. With Jädrich's back to those stairs, Aveline could only afford a quick glance and hope that he didn't turn around to see it: a mirror, flashing the starlights down at her. It was a small mirror resting in the hand of a bandaged woman in shapeless, thick robes—Karina, giving her the signal that it was time to leave. As soon as Aveline's eyes met Karina's one onyx sphere, the snow fox tucked her mirror away and hurried out of the ballroom, no doubt to Karina's guest quarters. That room had a window facing the side of the city, towards a sloping, snowy hill above the houses, one with a much more direct path to the Winter Wall than Aveline's quarters.

With a smile, Aveline disentangled herself from Jädrich's grip and said, "I need some space. I'll be back in a few minutes. Go find some other lady to dance with in the meantime; I think that Duchess could do with a bit more interrogating."

Then she slipped past him, even sidestepped him when he tried to block her path; she was too quick for him to snatch her, too.

"Aveline," he called, quietly enough so as not to cause a scene.

But she didn't listen. She gathered her skirts and hurried up those stairs, hoping Karina wouldn't fuss too much about how long it took her to get out of the ballroom. There wasn't much else she could do to go any faster, but that woman, she seemed to be a nitpicky one. Aveline marched on anyway, hurried out of sight of the people, and even though the lightness in her chest from her laughter was beginning to fill with weight—as if someone were pouring freezing water into her heart—she did not dare look back. Not once.

Failure.

Every step she took filled her a little more with that freezing weight. It was as if her heart were little more than a stretched waterskin.

I failed.

No hangman guard, no hangman King—all those weeks, all that effort, and it ended in her fleeing like a rat. What did she expect, though? She knew as much weeks ago: she was no Ismar, clearly, even if people looked at her with a grain more wonder than disapproval. And she was no dragon, either; wings alone did not make a dragon. All the talents her mother and the others of the brothel tried to teach her, all the webs she watched them weave time and time again, all the golden glory that poured from their dragon mouths—she had none of that. As the weight filled Aveline to the point of threatening to slow her steps and drag her down, she could do little more than huff something between a laugh and a cough.

I'm a fool.

Maybe Jädrich was right. As Aveline turned the corner, and the light of the stars poured through the open manor windows, she thought that perhaps there was a little pride to her antics—a little desire to prove herself worthy of her mother's memory. But she'd failed once already to kill the King for that great Yasilanah, and she failed again to ensnare him, it seemed. She was the only one to get entangled, and not even in love—no, not even in love. She could not call the thrill of provoking Jädrich love.

I'm sorr—

A hand closed on her wrist and yanked her back, then tossed her against a window. Her back and antlers hit the ice-glass hard enough to make it squeak; the impact knocked the breath clean out of her. Aveline's heart shrugged off all that weight as she found herself pinned to that window by her hips and caged with an ice hand on either side of her. No, there was no time to feel any such heaviness then—and so her heart launched itself into her mouth as she stared into the silver-bright eyes of the Winter King.

"Where are you going?" The softness of his voice didn't match the thunder in his face. "Running to our quarters already?

"Am I not able to take a break from the ball?"

He knocked her question out of the air with another one of his own. "What would you need a break for? Unless you're meeting someone." Before Aveline's nerves could scramble, his eyes narrowed. "Gürrensig?"

Oh, why do you always assume—? Aveline tried to slip out from under him, but he only pressed tighter into her, until he was practically crushing her bones with his ice. She had no choice but to answer him.

"No—but even if I were, what would it matter?" Aveline leaned up and put her face close to his, close enough that he no doubt felt her breath on his lips. "You don't love me. You don't know what love is, I don't think. So you don't have the privilege of pretending—"

His lips met hers. Then, so did his teeth. Aveline yelped into his mouth as his teeth bit down on her lip,

and then her tongue ended up slipping against his—
flesh against ice. His crown knocked against her antlers;
his hands found their way into her hair and under her
jaw, cradling her in a way that she couldn't even turn
away. All she could do was push on his chest, rake her
fingers over the buttons of his coat—and so he covered
her completely, until they were chest to chest, and her
arms could do nothing.

So she stomped as hard as she could on his boot. Its
crunch echoed through the hall. Only then did he pull
his face away enough to let her draw breath in desperate
gasps. Jädrich paused to look at his boot, and then he
put his lips by her ear.

"You are mine," he said. "You will always be mine.
That I know."

Aveline shuddered under him. The certainty in his
voice made her quake—and it made the doe-wraith
fill her veins with burning venom. She muttered, "The
contract is severed."

"Damn the contract." He gripped her chin and tilted
her head back until her neck was exposed. Then he
kissed under the base of her jaw, as he had in that first
week after they signed that worthless marriage paper—
kissed her, skated his teeth over her in a way that made
her shiver, and trailed a gentle hand along her hips and
waist. "It changes nothing. Or are your fleshling bonds
only worth something on paper?"

Aveline blinked. She pushed him back, this time with
magic bursting from her palms—enough that he had no
choice but to back up or have a dent made in his chest.
Staring into his eyes gave her no answers; they were as
bright and resolute, as alive with magic, as they'd been.

"You ask yourself that," she muttered. "You bound me
up in that damn paper. Do you think I don't see what
you've been aiming for? Running me ragged, bleeding me dry?" Before he could say anything to that, she

thumped her hand against his chest and hissed, "Do you think a bond can be made between a man and a doe he's aiming an arrow at? Don't lie to me, Jädrich."

He stared at her for a long time after that. All the while, the sparkle slowly faded from his eyes. His face once again settled into that cold, blank mask, and as he pulled away from her, his arm stretched out. His hand took a gentle hold of her throat. She grabbed his hands, but they weren't flesh like hers; they couldn't be bent or coaxed away. Her body went alight with prickles of panic; she knew, from the front of her mind to the marrow of her bones, that he could squeeze the life out of her, and she'd have to lose all sense of reason to escape it. She'd have to let the doe-wraith out and let her have her first taste of that *justice* she wanted so badly.

Whether she would gain control of herself again after, however, was a question Aveline didn't have an answer to, and that made her shake more than Jädrich's hand at her throat did.

Just as he opened his mouth to say something, however, a burst of strange sounds echoed from the ballroom, as if bags of sand and glass had burst open. A mere moment later, all that was followed by the shouts, the screams, of the guests—and then came the thumping of footsteps, the crunch and shattering of ice.

Jädrich's grip loosened on Aveline's throat just enough that when she put all her might behind a burst of magic, he stumbled back a few paces. It was the space she needed to finally *bolt*—not walk, not even hurry, but bolt, with all the strength her legs could muster. And she did so without thinking, without looking back. Without feeling, without slowing down. Without wondering, and with only the image of Karina staying fast in her mind. Only one instinct drove her on, past her screaming muscles and her aching lungs, and it was the desperate animal urge to *escape.* To survive.

Damn Winter. Her life came first. Hers. No one else's. *Damn it all to melt.*

The whole world, came the answer from her bones, as if to remind her. *Let all things die.*

All things except her.

"**D**O WE KNOW WHERE THE MARGRAVINE'S study is?" Barlan looked up and down the silent manor hall, at the several open rooms they'd already looked around in. Most were sitting rooms or tea rooms, all of which might've fallen under the definition of a *study* for a little woman like that Margravine. "Are you sure this is the right—?"

"I'm sure," Jolenn called from down the hall.

When Barlan glanced at his peer, he found Jolenn staring into one of the rooms. Barlan jogged over and muttered, "What'd you—?

Scraps of velvet were scattered around a tiny desk, along with thick chunks of ice. They lay draped and dumped over a woman's open hands, but on her shoulders was no head—only a stump of a neck and a few jagged pieces of cranium that barely stayed intact. By the lace at her short sleeves, and the tricorn hat that laid turned over on the floor, Barlan guessed it was the

Margravine. He saw her only once, and those were the two things he remembered about her.

"Cervora's velvet," Jolenn muttered. When Barlan went to inspect the headless doll that was the Margravine's body, Jolenn yanked him back by the arm and snapped, "Move! Find the King. There's obviously an intr—"

The ground rumbled beneath them, enough that the two guards held onto each other and the doorframe to steady themselves. Barlan worried the whole floor would drop out beneath them, but as they peered out to the foyer, it seemed *that* would drop out before anything else, what with how the floor tiles cracked.

"Come on!"

Jolenn dragged Barlan along even as the ground still trembled with aftershocks. They ran as fast as they could and turned the corner towards the ballroom, where the King was—only to find the halls flooding with guests that were gunning straight for that unstable foyer.

A nasty curse flew out of Jolenn's mouth, and he went to scribble runes in the air along the railing and in front of the stairwell leading down. A massive sheet of ice came up, and he traced another rune on his lips to amplify his voice as the guests rushed on with dismay carved into their faces.

"Not here!" Jolenn backed up and motioned the guests towards him. "This way! The floor below is unstable; follow me!" Then he looked at Barlan as the people swarmed towards him. "Get to the King! Find him!"

Barlan didn't need to be told twice. What he *did* need was for these damned people to get out of his way. After a moment of struggling against the people like a Winter fish up a frozen stream, he drew his own rune for a makeshift shield and pushed through. The pointed front of that shield meant people slipped off it and fell around him rather than him having to actually push anyone back; it was the best he could do to keep them moving away from danger and him moving towards it.

What is all this? He was assured this tour would be an easy job, suitable for newer recruits like him and Jolenn, yet this seemed more like something out of the battle trainings he'd done in military academy. Once past the people, he sprinted around the corner and nearly skidded into the wall. *What—who is—?*

Barlan stopped short when he saw one figure in the middle of the hall. It was a slim, but oddly shaped thing—something tall and yet bulky around the middle, a man with black hair and a scarf tied tight around his face. A long pickaxe-like thing hung at his waist. And his eyes—that was the strangest of all. Even in the light of stars and moon, Barlan could make out the glint of green eyes under all that dark hair, and the thick hat he wore on top of it.

What—? Barlan drew his sword. This was no Ismar; that much was obvious. *What in the world is that?*

Something glimmered in the moonlight. That man held something dark, a dagger made out of some black, glassy stuff. It looked like onyx, but that couldn't have been right; who made a dagger out of onyx? What for? Even fleshlings, as far as he knew, didn't do that.

"Stay where you are," Barlan barked. He held his sword defensively, which felt silly, given the intruder had just a dagger. But something about it made his soul shiver. "Drop your wea—"

Those green eyes were up close to Barlan's face before he even knew what happened. Without thinking, Barlan brought his blade up to his face, the edge flat across his nose, and he pushed up until he felt it thump against that intruder's bulky clothes. The scrape of his dagger against Barlan's sword rang in his ear, and then came that clicking sound he'd come to know all too well ever since the Queen began dousing the people in her healing frost.

That's not—

Intuition was the only thing driving Barlan's movements. He rolled forward, just enough to miss getting hit with a spray of some greenish-black fumes. Barlan didn't have time to look behind him, though, because that intruder was on top of him again, plunging that dagger straight down towards Barlan's head. Barlan rolled back just in time to stick his foot up, and he caught the creature in his stomach just before that dagger could connect. The lizard coughed, and a fleck of that greenish-black stuff dropped from his mouth onto Barlan's armor—and sizzled.

Venom. This was a Yasilan. Of the Swamplands. He'd never seen one before, but he'd heard about them, and this one—this one was in Winter. Beyond the wall. Attacking the manor and the people in it.

Gods.

Barlan kicked the intruder off him and scrambled to his feet, but he was much heavier, much slower, than that damn lizard. He could hardly orient himself before the lizard's blade swiped at his face again, and it only missed Barlan because he'd jerked back in time. Still, it missed him by a hair; Barlan felt the wind of the swipe over his cheeks. And the assault didn't let up, not one bit; Barlan was pushed back, left with little to do but dodge the madman's attacks. He had to do something, had to trip the man up or find a way to attack back, but there was no opening. Swing after swing came down, came up, came from the sides—so many ways to move with so little a blade, so many options a sword didn't give—and it didn't even give Barlan enough time to use his magic. He couldn't have dragged it through his ice fast enough to deflect this flurry. If only he had one more guard with him—Jolenn, anyone—

The lizard hissed with the effort of one more swipe, and Barlan stumbled as he tried to block it. His sword wouldn't connect with that strike; the blade was headed straight for his eye—

An arrow of silver light caught the lizard in his shoulder, and a hand pushed Barlan down, sending him sprawling against the carpet. Barlan rolled once and steadied himself, but by then, he couldn't do anything to stop what he saw: the King, his own sword drawn, with dozens of crystal lights hanging near him and ready to shoot, all while that lizard was already at the King's throat with that black knife.

Ash and coal! Barlan scrambled to his feet, but it was too late. The King was fast, but not fast enough; the lizard plunged that blade straight for his face, dead center, all while the spears of raw magic formed and fell apart; they couldn't hit this lizard without hitting the King, too.

Yet the King was a better swordsman than Barlan, clearly, because he still somehow managed to slide that blade up between him and the lizard. But—*wait*—he shouldn't have been able to, no; the beast was too fast. For some reason, the lizard's feet hit the King's chest before the blade did, as if some invisible string were pulling it back, and at the last moment, the lizard changed trajectory, shooting his arm out to swipe the King's shoulder with the smallest, most useless cut from that knife. It barely split the King's coat, and Barlan wasn't sure it touched his ice at all. And the King certainly didn't waste such an opportunity. Even if all he returned was a slice, he moved his sword, shining with wicked, flesh-eating frost, and slid it across that creature's arm.

A flash of red gushed through on sallow skin and made the cloth shine as that *blood* soaked into the dark fabric. The lizard bounced off the wall and hissed, the frost no doubt already seeping into his flesh, but he still stood tall with that knife in his hand. It was nicked, though, as if a piece came off somewhere. King Jädrich advanced on him, and Barlan moved to join him, but it was too late. With a movement so quick that Barlan hardly registered it, the lizard took something from the pack on his hip and tossed it down. Black smoke exploded in the hall. The King conjured and shot a flurry of silver spears through the cloud, but by time the smoke settled, it was anyone's guess as to where the lizard was, or whether those spears even hit.

A beat passed before King Jädrich turned to Barlan and snapped, "Come with me."

I should've known better.

Aveline's chest stretched against her dress as she gulped every breath down. Her *Unseelechs* squealed and crooned as they rubbed their heads against her legs; the only thing she'd managed to do in her frenzy was recognize her guest room door as she flew past it and rip it open with a crack of her magic. Then, funnily enough, the sound of their talons clicking across the stone as they scampered after her only made it easier to keep running. She'd barely waited for them to get into Karina's quarters after her before slamming the door shut and locking it.

The windows that led to the snowy hill behind the manor unlatched, and a small hook of wind pulled them open. A moment later, a white fox pulled itself up and sat in the windowsill, staring with one golden eye. It didn't need to ask the question that sparkled in that eye; Aveline knew what it wanted to know.

Are you ready to leave?

With a sigh, Aveline pulled herself up from the bed. She had no bag packed. No clothes except the dress she already had on. No possessions, no treasures, no trophies—not even the obsidian Sekhran Ganaresh bothered to send her. No, Aveline had nothing but herself and her magic, and that was all she needed to start all over again, just as it had been when she first came to this place. She pulled her wings up and out of that open-backed dress, and her *Unseelechs* gurgled around her, spreading their own wings to join her.

You can't come. The thought shattered her in a way all her past thoughts—about Ristef, Aula, Jädrich, even her mother—hadn't. Her babies, her sweet babies—they stared at her so expectantly, ready to follow her to the ends of the earth. They didn't know she'd be saying goodbye. *You have to stay here. In Winter.*

Karina stood up in the windowsill. Her paws were perfectly balanced on that thin ledge of stone; it made her look more like a cat than anything else. Her big, bushy white tail flicked, and her eye glittered as if to say, *are you done fooling around?* It was almost funny, how even dressed as an animal, Karina could still manage to be so sharp and impatient. Aveline stretched her wings, and then she finally unstuck her feet from the ground and went to join Karina at the window.

Then there was some loud sound from what seemed like the other side of the manor. Aveline paused. So far away, she couldn't quite make it out, but it seemed like the splintering of wood, the dull thumps of something being embedded in the walls. Her spine lit up with prickles. Karina said they'd leave the night they planned to take her from Jädrich, double-crossing the King and her cousin, but why did it sound like someone was breaking the manor to pieces—?

A fox's yip came from the window at the same time as something else came thundering down the hall, towards her room. In a fit of panic, Aveline shot an unfocused spray of her magic at the door, solidifying it into a sheet of ice that would've maybe kept it sealed. From what, though, she had no idea. Erik's other allies coming to collect her? But would that mean Karina betrayed her after all, for them to be coming this way while Karina blocked her only exit?

That thought died as soon as she turned around, however. Aveline looked out that window, only to find it empty. Karina was gone. And that, in and of itself, was an altogether different kind of betrayal—especially as the frantic, thunderous steps shot down the hall and came right upon her door, beating against the ice-coated wood with a fury.

Thump. Thump. Thump. Each beat on the door had the ice cracking, squeaking. Aveline pooled her magic until it solidified into two silver blades. The magic wrapped around her hands, too, fixing the blades to her so that she'd never let go. It'd been a long time, a *long* time, since she had to fight something head on—the scars on her legs were her trophy for the last thing she'd killed like this, so long ago—and her heart beat as fast as a rabbit's, her sight narrowed on that door. Even the sound of whatever was beating on it became muffled in her focus. *Thump. Thump. Thump.*

And then, the door began to melt. Not the ice on the door. The door itself.

It started from the top. As the wood melted, it foamed with something greenish-black, and fumes rose off it that made the ceiling's wood bubble and blister. Aveline backed up to the window. She knew that vapor. That color, that venom. But she was so stunned by the implication of it all that she couldn't get her thoughts in order—couldn't get her leg up on that windowsill and get herself out of that room.

In Winter? How? How is one of these in Winter?

There were too many questions in her head. A thousand of them barraged her at once and made her head feel as though it would split open. All she could do was keep shuffling back and clutch those silver knives tighter, make them sharper, until the back of her legs hit the windowsill. Her whole body was one tight bundle of racing, prickling nerves as the door melted down to nothing, and the ice along with it.

Through the fumes, Aveline made out the shape of a man. It was a dark shape, one wrapped in thick black clothes and with a black scarf over its face, black hair peering through an oiled leather cap. Even through the fumes, and even with all the shadows around that man's face, though, Aveline swore she could see it: the glowing green eyes of a Swampland Yasilan.

He entered the room, his steps soft and nearly silent. He was completely undisturbed by the wisps of blistering vapor that still hung in the air, and in his hand was an obsidian blade. It seemed like it'd been nicked at the tip, though. He'd used it somewhere, on something—or someone.

"Look at you," the man drawled in Yasilan—but with the accent of Sekhbal, not the Swamplands. "All the trouble you cause, and you still want to fight?"

Aveline said nothing. She knew better than to play with these types. Her mother, and Ayema, too, always told her: Swampland folks with knives like that had already decided what to do with the ones they stalked, and no talking would change it, no matter how much *they* chattered to loosen their mark's nerves. Things of poison and shadow, the Swampland people—things of death looming in the dark. But his arm—Aveline noticed then, on his arm. A cut. A cut that made his black clothes sticky around the fabric. He'd been injured.

Who? By Who?

"My father's been missing a bride for some time. Seems she's run off to go and play with her prey rather than kill it."

The man's eyes caught the moonlight and glinted with such a venomous sheen that Aveline shrank. Her *Unseelechs* growled at her feet, but they, too, were bunched up and afraid; they wouldn't move recklessly any more than Aveline would. His words registered a moment later, and she squeezed her teeth together to keep from gaping like a fool.

Those green eyes practically glowed. "Time to come home now, pet."

Even though her heart fluttered, Aveline fixed her stance and held her knives up. This was one of Ganaresh's brood. Likely with the Head of Surveillance. Those spies she raised were wicked beyond sense. Aveline's hands shook, as no doubt a palace-sent assassin would be a touch more difficult than the three mountain lions that ambushed her some many years ago, but what else was there to do? She watched him, dressed in those thick, over-padded leathers—watched the way one of his feet didn't quite pick itself up the same way as the other—and she wondered. She stood frozen between two choices: fly and hope he was too injured to chase her, or fight and hope that little limp was him covering up a more brutal wound.

In the moment she took to make that decision, however, he suddenly moved so fast that she couldn't make sense of the dark blur racing towards her. Her throat snapped on impulse and flooded her mouth with frost, sending a wave of it billowing out as she leapt onto that windowsill. As she moved, her *Unseelechs* growled and snarled like fighting cats; they clawed at something, and then something shattered. Aveline couldn't think on it, though, not when one obsidian blade swiped through her cloud of frost and narrowly missed her neck. Had she been a moment too late to move, her throat would've been split like the skin of a grape.

Still, he hissed as the frost sank into his skin, and with

one silver knife slammed into the walls for support, she raised her other knife and cut at the obsidian blade until hers embedded into its edge. Then she willed her frost into it until a coating of glassy ice covered it and rendered it little more than a child's blunt toy. One of her hooves shot out and connected with his chest; a sickening crack echoed through the room as the assassin crumpled and fell back. Even if he had leathers on his chest to guard against a blade at his critical points, they wouldn't do much against blunt force like that. But these types of Yasilanri didn't stay down for long. By the time the cloud of frost dissipated, and by the time Aveline got her suddenly sluggish body to move from that windowsill, a *second* obsidian blade was shearing down towards her. She only barely caught it with her antler, and she was thankful her antlers weren't shedding.

However, before she could swing one of her own blades into that man's stomach, something dropped on her—something wet and sticky. For just a moment, Aveline braced herself for the sting of venom on her skin; whatever could melt wood like nothing would no doubt have destroyed her arm down to the bone. Yet the sticky stuff landed on her, warm and thick, and she found it didn't hurt at all. When she focused, she found that suddenly, he was quite still—and that the thick shirt he wore under his leathers was shining. The stuff that dripped from him, too, was red. Deep red. And his eyes, once so sharp, so full of that venomous shine, were suddenly dull—that bright green faded like moss in the shadows.

Something pulled him off Aveline, and the body slumped over, with another two sharp iron knives sticking out from the few awkward parts of his torso that his leathers didn't cover. One stabbed upward into the ribcage, one stabbed by the hips. Behind him was Karina, whose white robes were completely spotless, free of blood. She even held a third knife gingerly, as if the thought of getting any of that Yasilan's blood on her made her nauseous. She huffed and stared at the man with an expression Aveline never saw before on that half-Akerijin: one with her one golden eye wide open, her brows slanted in silent fury, her lips curled and nose crinkled like a fox ready to growl.

"Out the window," Karina muttered. "Now."

"Wait, take him, too!" Aveline grabbed the Yasilan's coat and tried to pull him up, but lithe as he looked, the man was still heavy with muscle and bone, if not blood. Her mind whirred to the point that she thought she'd be dizzy, but her panic still drove her to tug at the man and wheeze with effort. "He can't be seen. The mess it'll cause if they find a Yasilan here—"

"He—Aveline," with a huff, Karina pulled the man onto his back and pointed to the big, damp spot on his arm. "He's been injured. Someone saw him already. It's already too late."

"But—"

"You think that wound on his arm came from an accident? You think no one heard this fool crashing down the hall? No. So let's—"

"Aveline."

Both the half-dragon and the half-fox flinched to hear a voice so low and smooth and *cold*. It was as if the very Winter air had come to steal the breath from their lungs and bite their cheeks. Despite the wave of hot gooseflesh that washed Aveline from her scalp to the base of her spine, she met Karina's glance—and goodness, was her face a mirror, because she wore the exact wide-eyed horror Aveline felt. Aveline didn't want to look at the doorway, and she avoided it for a moment—but the sights she did see, one *Unseelech* shattered from the head to the collarbone, the other crumpled in the corner and immobile, was worse. So much worse.

What—my—

Her head jerked up as if forcing her to look away. All there was to see instead was the path in front of her. Filling that melted, warped doorway was, of course, Jädrich. No doubt he'd silenced his steps; neither Karina nor Aveline ever heard him coming. But he stood there, the fur of his coat's lining matted red with blood, and a small whitish cut at his shoulder that split his coat open. Something black glittered in the cut, like shards of the night sky. Aveline blew out a breath and let go of the Yasilan. His foot dropped from her hand with a *thud.*

In the moment that passed, several guards filled the doorway with him, their shoes just as silent despite how frantically they rushed to the side of their King. They stopped short and stared at the awkward picture before them: two half-beasts, one with white wings, one with a white tail and hairless, pointy ears, and a dead dragon at their feet. He was even starting to foam and smoke, as dragons did when they died; his skin was giving way to black scales, his hood pierced and soon shredded by greenish-black horns that lengthened from the man's shifting scalp. Yasilanri, when they died, lost the illusions that kept their dragon forms hidden; they lost the blessing of the Sun that gave them glory and the blessing of the Moon that gave them honor.

But there wasn't much time to watch that Yasilan go from man to drake. The silence was growing too tense, too strained; it already clawed at Aveline's skin while the stares of those guards nearly made ribbons of her wings. She flared them, and the guards gripped their weapons tighter—though, to their credit, they kept their mouths shut. If there was anyone that was going to say anything, they and Aveline both knew it would be Jädrich, who finally dragged his eyes from the dead Yasilan to dragon-winged doe.

"Aveline," he muttered, and he extended a hand, "come. You must be shaken."

Her very bones had her leaning towards Karina, and it wasn't until Karina's hair brushed Aveline's shoulder that she realized something dragged the half-fox to her, too. They both stood up straight and watched that King, and right there, Aveline shook her head.

Jädrich blinked, then dropped his hand. "My shoulder," he said, with an edge to it that was about as sharp as those obsidian blades, "it needs your attention. That material melts us—"

"I know."

That made him pause. His brows twitched as if they wanted to pinch together; his lips twitched as if he wanted to frown. A moment later, though, his face was perfectly smooth and blank, unreadable.

"I have my own tools made of that glass," Aveline found herself saying.

And she was a fool. She knew that then. Because as she looked at that dead dragon at her feet, and at that King she should've had the sense to plunge those two obsidian eyes into weeks earlier, she knew she'd made a mess bigger than she knew how to clean up. So she decided to make it worse instead—because what did she have to lose anymore? Nothing.

Maybe he'll realize now that I was never his.

"I was supposed to kill you with them," she whispered. "The Sekhran sent them to me. Two obsidian spikes that looked like eyes. To plunge into your empty sockets while you slept."

And that was the truth, the whole truth, the last bit of truth she'd been keeping from that empty doll of a King. The one breath she drew in then seemed to last forever, as did the exhale that let all the tension out of her body. Jädrich, the guards, Karina, her own self, even *time,* all of it was frozen as if no one could move until that breath was finished. The silence was so deep that it rang in her ears, and it was as if the whole world were exhaling with her, delaying the inevitable next second that would have to come to pass. However, it wasn't an exhale that broke the spell of silence right then, nor was it an inhale that started time again.

It was the way Jädrich's blank mask of a face broke. How, for a sliver of a moment, his eyes were wide and bright as the full moon, his face creased with the furrow of his brow, his teeth bared like a wolf's.

That was the last thing Aveline saw before something struck the ground and a curtain of smoke hid that wretched face away. Then Aveline found herself being ripped towards the window. Karina all but pulled her arm out of her socket and tossed her out, following close behind and wrapping her arms around Aveline to keep her from flying right away. The little half-fox's arms crushed her wings to the point that the joints twinged.

Aveline didn't have time to speak, or even yelp. She certainly didn't have time to try and free herself or fly away, so that maybe she wouldn't smack directly into the ground. She could only blink—and then watch as the window, and the surrounding wall, were suddenly blown to pieces by a huge spear of ice. It shot through the wall with such speed that Aveline didn't understand what happened, and she wouldn't have unless she and Karina both landed on a cloud that moment and shot away towards the border wall. That was when Aveline saw the spear as it disappeared over the horizon, and saw the bricks falling out of the wall. A cloud of dust, snow, and other debris rose from the bottom of the manor.

Whatever wind Karina conjured for them to ride was faster than Aveline could've ever flown, though—and perhaps safer, too, because whatever magic the Akerijin used made it so that Aveline hardly even felt the wind whipping past, even as the manor grew so small, so fast. It was hardly more different than sitting on a chair on stable ground. Aveline could do nothing but stare, however. Karina, too, stared—but she kept her gaze on the rapidly approaching border wall.

And that's the end of it.

"What were you thinking, provoking him like that?" Karina's growl nearly got snatched up by the sound of the wind whistling around them. "Telling him that? Gods, Aveline, what were you *thinking?*"

That's the end of my time as an Ismarrin.

Aveline hugged her knees to her chest and stayed silent. She didn't want to think at all, was the problem. She was done thinking. Done scheming, done living in wait for the day the knife would eventually fall on her neck and end her ruse. In fact, she was sure the ruse had ended a long time ago, when the first whispers of her parentage and her mixed blood started circulating. A god in a body these people couldn't stomach—that was what their vague, nonsensical *prophecies* said she was. And it seemed not even all her miracles and gifts and healing and good words could make her any more palatable to a race of ice-folk, looking for a purely doe-god.

She buried her face in her knees. A century on Kha-Bawaj felt like nothing compared to those last few weeks of hiding in plain sight around those god-killers. But she was free. Finally, she was free. The bramble kept wrapping its thorny branches around her heart, enough to make her sick—and in the darkness behind her eyelids was the slight glow of something white. Bone. Specifically, teeth. The doe-wraith had a jaw all of a sudden.

And it was grinning.

RISTEF FELT LIKE HIS THOUGHTS WOULD never reorganize. His head ached as if someone had tried to siphon his soul straight out of the ice, but as he patted himself, he found his head unbroken. It wasn't even scratched, actually, which was lucky enough. But as the fading rumbles of footsteps and screams echoed far, far away, he had a feeling that his sense of luck wouldn't last. That feeling was confirmed when he finally gathered himself enough to open his eyes and look around.

There was nothing but darkness. His arms were pinned, too, and something was dripping on his face. Without thinking, he grabbed for his magic and pooled it into a single starlight, just so he could see where he was and what he was stuck under.

When the light bloomed, he found himself face to face with the half-shattered head of one of his fellow guards.

With a yelp, Ristef pushed a sheet of raw magic from his hands, enough to lift that body and anything else off him. That man and two other dead, battered bodies slumped off him and onto the floor. Ristef scrambled away. His soul needled him in his panic, and he soon found his back against the wall. The soul of that half-shattered guard was gone, no doubt about it, but Ristef couldn't, for the life of him, figure out how it was already starting to melt. Bodies didn't melt that fast. Moreover, what could've shattered him like that in the first place? Only one peridot eye stared at him, the pale yellowish-green unfocused and dead of all shine.

Then he looked up at the rest of the guards' barracks and found it similarly in shambles. Two guards were slumped over tables, another two guards were draped on the bar counter, and then another two guards laid on the floor like broken dolls. From a quick look, however, it seemed only two of them were from the castle; the rest were Margravine Beurvich's men. In between them all were pieces of what looked like dark glass. Some still stuck into the guards' backs and faces, and it was from those places that Ristef could see little beads of water just starting to come from the ice. That was when the last bit of haze lifted from Ristef's mind, and he re-membered.

The door opening. Some kind of cannisters rattling on the ground. The stench of sulfur, the sudden explo-sion of wood and stone and glass. Had Ristef not been behind a group of guards at that table, just playing cards, then that heat and gas and glass might've—

He leapt over the bodies and sprinted out the still-open door. The other guards, out there overseeing the ballroom, likely weren't aware of the situation: that there was someone dangerous in the manor, who was equipped with things full of Ismar-melting shrapnel. Ristef nearly crashed into the wall with how fast he shot from the barracks, but soon enough, he found his footing and bolted to whatever route would take him to-wards the ballroom. All he knew was that the ballroom was on the far end of the manor, a floor up from the basement barracks. A quick whisper and a bit of magic activated the speed-runes in his boots, so he could race up the manor stairs twice as fast as he would've been able to otherwise. His only priority was making sure that Aveline—and Aula, who was also attending the ball as Aveline's honored guest—were safe.

Aula likely still won't want to see me.

But Ristef did not care.

All the starlight sconces, all the paintings of Margra-vine Beurvich and her family, all the wall-embedded aquariums full of cold-water fish and the many lakeside plants from well before the Wall went up—it was all just a smear of colors to Ristef as he kept running. The only thing he cared about was finding Aveline, Aula, and the others, and the only thing that kept him from kicking every door in to check for them was the fact that no colors sparkled from any of these guest bedrooms. No black fear, no red anger, no nothing—not until a spark of deepest, darkest blue grief beckoned him around the corner.

Ristef cut the magic to the runes on his shoes and all but stumbled to a stop as he rounded the corner. Then he blinked, unsure of what, exactly, he was looking at. This was where Lady Beurvich's library was, and the door was open, and Aula was on her knees at that door-way, staring in silence at a man's legs. The blue grief hovered over her like a stray ray of moonlight; it made a halo that reminded him of the gauzy veils women sometimes wore to church services. One of her hands was on the man's glossy leather boots.

"Aula," Ristef rushed to her side, "are you alright? What happ—?"

She grabbed his face without even looking at him and turned his head until he looked into the library. There was what Ristef recognized as Lord Rachfemd's body, but past that was nothing but a spray of ice shards scattered all over the carpet. Where there should've been a head was only stray strands of silver hair. Lord Rachfemd's neck was a shattered stump. And Ristef realized then that he was glassy, too, his hands and neck; the magic was long gone from him.

"What," Ristef blinked as if he would get lucky and open his eyes to a perfectly in-tact, perfectly alive Lord Rachfemd, "who did this?"

Aula only shrugged, and Ristef's own deep, shadowy fear nearly swallowed his soul and cast it into the void.

"Where's Aveline?"

Again, she shrugged.

"Aula!" Ristef grabbed her shoulders and pulled her away from Lord Rachfemd's body, until she had no choice but to look at him with those giant onyx eyes. "Aveline! Where is she? Where is anyone?" He looked around at the empty hallways. "Are they all gone? Did they evacuate? Or—?"

She peeled his hands off her shoulders and dragged herself to her feet. "I don't know, Ristef," she said, with gravel in her voice. Her eyes were empty and dead of shine. "I don't—this wasn't supposed to—"

And then Aula's face crumpled, and a low whine echoed from her very soul. She fell against Ristef's chest and buried her face in his chest plate, then beat her fist against it over and over. Each time, her hand made a *clack* muffled only by the velvet that wrapped her ice.

As much as Ristef wanted to hold and comfort her until that terrible blue veil faded from her, there wasn't time to waste. He squeezed her shoulders, then pulled away and grabbed her wrist with the hand that still had all its fingers; he'd drag her with him if he had to, and he'd protect her from anything that jumped out at them, too.

"Save that, Aula. Tell me: do you think Aveline got caught by whatever did," he didn't want to look at the boots poking out from the library as they went further down the hall, "that? Or do you think—?"

Before they could turn the corner, though, Ristef nearly crashed into a wall of furs and silks and shiny silver buttons. He skidded to a stop, Aula nearly crashing into him, and the first thing he noticed was the great splash of red on the furs around the *King's* neck.

King Jädrich stopped. Ristef was so close to the King that he didn't notice the other guards at first, but as they crowded around the King, Ristef could've melted in relief alone. Not everyone went down in that blast, it seemed—

"Gürrensig," King Jädrich muttered. His voice cut Ristef straight through despite there not being a shred of color around his head. It was as if he'd sealed himself off from feeling anything, as the air around his head was *so* colorless that it felt empty of life, like the King didn't even have a soul anymore. "Where were you?"

"The barracks, Your Majesty." Ristef stood at attention, and only then did he notice the tiny scratch on the King's shoulder—and the small, dark shard of glass stuck in it.

No.

"Where are the others?"

"I—dead, Your Majesty." *He's been hit.* "Something exploded in there, and it—many went down from being shattered or hit with some dark glass."

A sparkle of magic crossed King Jädrich's eyes, and then there was nothing. He brushed past both Ristef and Aula as if it were any other day, as if there wasn't a barracks full of dead guards and a room with a dead lord, and as if he didn't have an injury on his body that would soon eat a hole in him. In fact, as King Jädrich kept walking, he hardly spared Lord Rachfemd a glance. Ristef followed after him, half-forgetting he still had Aula in his grip. Outside of her footsteps, though, it was only because she was so quiet that he could forget at all.

"Your Majesty, the Queen!" He rushed after them and smacked whatever hand a guard raised in his way— maybe to hush him, maybe to hit him, either way, it didn't matter. "Where's the Queen? Is she safe—?"

A hideous snap of maroon lanced over the King's head, and then it was gone. He stopped short, forcing all the other guards to stop with him, and he said over his shoulder, "She's gone."

Ristef thought his soul might've fallen out of his head. "Gone—dead?"

"No. Gone."

"Shut up, Gürrensig," one guard hissed.

Ristef didn't even look at him. He was focused solely on the King. *What does that mean, "gone"? Kidnapped?* "So—Your Majesty, should we begin organizing a search squad?"

King Jädrich paused. Seconds passed, precious seconds that they could've been using to find Aveline, seconds that Aveline might've been taken further and further away from her home and her King and her people. And all his King was doing was staring at the wall.

Eventually, Ristef couldn't take the silence anymore. "Your Majesty, please—!"

"No," King Jädrich said. "No search party will be necessary. Instead, pack everything into the carriages. You," he said to the guard closest to him, "find Margravine Beurvich, wherever she is. The rest of you, move." Then he turned and looked Ristef directly in the eye, and Ristef swore on Cervora's two antlers that he'd never seen eyes so bright and brutal in that King's head—not

even during the harshest of sentences he gave to crimi-
nals and traitors. "We return to the capital immediately.
Then, as soon we're prepared, we leave for Autumn."

Ristef blinked. *Autumn? Is that where Aveline is?* But
the King's eyes were too grave, too bright and full of
ice, for Ristef to dare ask another question. No matter
how blank the King kept his face, no matter how hard
he suppressed the glow of his soul, his eyes revealed
every scrap of silent Winter fury—an avalanche waiting
to fall on the first person to say one more word. Instead,
he waited, and sure enough, King Jädrich looked to his
remaining men and let his voice fill that hallway.

"Our Queen and Mother demanded we move the
seasons, and that's exactly what we'll do." He paused,
and he seemed to stare at Ristef directly as he muttered,
"Now move."

Clara gripped the arms of her chair. The aftershocks
of the pain that lanced through her soul were savage, as
if her soul were a soft-bellied animal torn up by some
big beast. If not for her quickly severing the connection
between her little silver contraption and the lizard boy,
she imagined she would've gotten as tangled up and
lost in that pain as he'd been, all stabbed full of holes
and bled between all those thick and clumsy layers he
wore. Yet, at the same time, it was a blessing; the pain
gave her a clarity she simply hadn't had ever since she'd
connected her mind to that fleshling beast. At least she
could finally say she was done with this ridiculous sci-
ence experiment—though with what she'd witnessed using the headmistress's tool, she almost wanted to write a
user experience report for Klassech just on principle.

As Clara clutched at her temples, though, and the
pain began to ebb away, she found those last memories

drifting across her mind. The mutt fought back—interesting. And the mutt did not kill the lizard boy—more interesting still. And while the lizard himself may have caused quite the chaos in that traitorous Margravine's home, thanks to this contraption, he wasn't able to kill the King—though Clara did have to override his senses much more than Klassech advised to stop him. Still, that nasty blow the King gave him in return for trying was likely what made him so easy to destroy for even someone as frail as that spindly half-breed.

I shouldn't have given him those cannisters back.

But it was too late for regrets, far too late. And with the lizard dead, all she knew was that this whole charade was done. Had to be, given the mixed-blood had her wings out like she meant to go somewhere. No doubt the King could see exactly what that mutt was really aiming for, what with the mangled lizard left bleeding out for him to find. Thanks to what Clara heard that lizard say, too, she finally had confirmation: the Sekhran was looking to reclaim his planted "bride" all along.

But once the pain finally faded completely, Clara found herself crossing her arms and slumping under the weight of her thoughts. The lizard was dead. Clara didn't know what became of the mixed-blood. So what then? What would the King—?

On the other side of the desk, one of her communication runestones flashed. Once, twice, three times. A call waited for her, though from who, she couldn't guess. The only way to find out would be to answer. She pooled her magic into the tip of her finger and tapped the stone.

The flurries of magic swirled up like disturbed, soft snow, and they spun up and up into a large, imposing shape. A long coat flared out, long hair drifted down, and the face carved itself sharp and sure—a face Clara would recognize anywhere, anytime. King Jädrich's image soon stared out at nothing, perfectly still and unmoving, and Clara blinked.

"Your Majesty," she murmured, "what—?"

"Are the preparations for the Tour of Seasons complete?"

"Um—"

"The Tour, Clara. Is it prepared?"

His voice was so sharp it could've sliced Clara's nose from her face. It made her shrink for the first time in decades, as if being small would get her out of the line of sight of that fearsome, mighty Ismar and the wrath she knew was brewing underneath that tone. Clara steeled herself and nodded, even though the King couldn't see.

"Yes. The horses are ready; the special forces are assembled." Then Clara probed for an answer, even though she didn't dare ask her King any direct questions. "We're only waiting for you to decide which of the noble houses will join you this year."

"None." King Jädrich's voice flayed Clara's nerves, with the sharp, cold way they crackled across the study. "Expect us within the week. I'll give you the full list of your duties for the time I'm gone."

Clara paused. Not only did she not dare to question her King, but right then, she didn't dare to speak at all. It seemed she didn't need to, either, for suddenly, the King's image fell to silver dust, and the runestone went dark. Clara could do nothing but turn those words over in her head. Her soul squeezed down so small in her head, quivering with terrible anticipation that made her velvet feel tight against her ice. She glanced at the orb full of her memories of the lizard's every move and wondered.

Is this it?

War horses. No nobility.

Is this finally it?

A winged Queen. A dead lizard.

Is this—?

Clara closed her eyes and laid back in her chair. For a moment, she was almost foolish enough to smile. But she kept herself still, kept her mind quiet, and kept her growing anticipation in check. No matter how much she wanted to finish that last question and give form to her desire, she quieted her soul until there was nothing but the eerie whisper of Winter's silence to fill her head. Then she prayed a brief prayer to Cervora—the *real* Cervora.

Lead the line of Orr to completion, Mother. Lead this wretched world to perfection.

A forever frozen, perfectly preserved perfection.

ACKNOWLEDGMENTS

And just like that, the book I've been dreading writing most in 2024 is done.

This book challenged me in ways I didn't think it would. I remember trying, and failing, over and over again, to get things just right in 2021 and 2022, shortly after finishing *The Glass Witch*. Nothing worked, no matter what I did—so I put it away and focused on other projects with wonderful people. And in that time of working our back ends off, I found what I was missing after leaving Emerson's Popular Fiction and Publishing program: the confidence to trust myself and get this book done, without all the "what if"s and doubts and everything else that screwed me over when it was just me writing by myself.

To which I have to say: I genuinely could not have done this without the support of everyone around me. From my mom and dad to my partner Roman to my dear friends Mimi, Hannah, Lina, Fr. Kyle, Edi, and Chris, all of them did their part to keep me sane while I beat my head on this manuscript for nine long months. Edi, you especially. It was your one comment that kept me going even when I was starting to think I wouldn't make it to the (self imposed) deadline for this thing. Thank you for that, seriously.

Along with that, I have to give thanks to the incredible online community I've had the privilege of being a part of, too. You saw it all: my successes, my frustrations, and everything in between, and you showed up with words of encouragement and faith that helped keep the ship sailing.

So here's to another great book, and a wrap on the year's writing endeavors. What a ride it's been!

ABOUT THE AUTHOR

Sara Raztresen is a Slovene-American writer, Christian Witch, educator, and content creator, with an MFA from Emerson College's Popular Fiction and Publishing program.

As the daughter of an immigrant raised with one foot in two worlds, and a person drawn to all things mystical and strange, Sara draws on her cultural heritage and religious experiences, when writing her work. Her writing is an attempt to explain the world she sees, deliver the insight she gathers, and discover how all the world's pieces fit together.

OTHER WORKS BY SARA RAZTRESEN:

The Glass Witch
Where the Gods Left Off
Discovering Christian Witchcraft

FIND SARA ON:

TikTok: @srazzie97
Instagram: @sararaztresen
Bluesky: @srazzie97
YouTube: @srazzie97

www.sararaztresen.com